THE HOUSE OF SUNDERING FLAMES

Also by Aliette de Bodard from Gollancz:

The House of Shattered Wings
The House of Binding Thorns

THE HOUSE OF SUNDERING FLAMES

Aliette de Bodard

GOLLANCZ
LONDON

First published in Great Britain in 2019 by Gollancz
an imprint of The Orion Publishing Group Ltd
Carmelite House, 50 Victoria Embankment
London EC4Y 0DZ

An Hachette UK Company

1 3 5 7 9 10 8 6 4 2

A CIP catalogue record for this book
is available from the British Library.

ISBN (Trade Paperback) 978 1 473 22340 0
ISBN (eBook) 978 1 473 22342 4

Typeset by Deltatype Ltd, Birkenhead, Merseyside

Printed in Great Britain by Clays Ltd, Elcograf S.p.A.

www.aliettedebodard.com
www.orionbooks.co.uk
www.gollancz.co.uk

To my friends, who keep me going

I

The Burning House

Thuan's day had been utterly routine: petitions from House Hawthorn members; unpleasant political maneuvering; a brief, barbed lunch with his husband and co-head of House Asmodeus, in which they compared notes about an upcoming dinner with envoys of other Houses. Nothing surprising or insurmountable.

He was out in the gardens, halfway between his office's open French windows and the river. The lawn, pockmarked with debris and ash, sloped down to what had been the quays by the river Seine and which was now a roiling mass of gray, iridescent water. He'd made the mistake of sitting on the grass, which meant the trousers of his swallowtail suit were completely damp, and with rather interesting oily stains.

His other mistake, of course, had been to use his one hour of leisure in the day to be nice to overwhelmed parents.

"Unka Thuan, Unka Thuan! She's stolen my doll!"

Ai Nhi had drawn herself up to the full and rather limited height of a five-year-old and pointed an accusatory finger at Thuan's niece Camille. Her shape wavered between human and dragon, with the shadow of antlers above her pigtails, outlined in the bluish light of *khi* water.

"Give it back, or I'll tell Auntie Ly!"

Camille's only answer was laughter, waving the doll around in one hand and the moldy blanket she dragged everywhere in the other.

"Now now ..."

Thuan stopped. He stared at the Seine, at the vast expanse of water beneath which hid the troubled dragon kingdom where he'd been born. Something was wrong, but he couldn't put his finger on what. He grabbed the doll from Camille.

"No stealing," he said, firmly.

Camille wailed. He ignored her, and put the doll back in Ai Nhi's hands.

The *khi* currents of water, faint lines of blue light, seemed undisturbed. They curled, lazily, along the wide paths of pockmarked gravel, around the wide trees whose trunks were flecked with fungus, and stopped at the water's edge. Nothing wrong. Still nothing he could put his finger on. And yet ...

"Unka Thuan!"

He forced a smile he didn't feel. "Yes?"

Ai Nhi's aunt, Vinh Ly, was in Thuan's retinue, part of the dragon court who had come with him to Hawthorn. Both of Ai Nhi's parents had died when she was still a baby, and Vinh Ly, often overwhelmed, let Thuan take care of Ai Nhi on her behalf.

Ai Nhi and Camille were both looking at him. In that uncanny way children had, they stood side by side as if nothing had ever been wrong between them.

"What are you looking at?"

Thuan shrugged. "The water. The city."

"The other Houses?" Ai Nhi asked. "Auntie Ly said they were ... ag-gres-sive."

The way she detached the syllables, she clearly didn't know what the word meant.

Thuan sighed. "She means they want to attack us." Before Ai Nhi could look worried, he said, "You don't have to worry about it. Asmodeus and I have the situation well in hand."

Or rather, House Hawthorn was keeping its head down, and hoping the other Houses in Paris would believe them too uninteresting and too uninvolved to bother attacking. A tricky balance to strike: too weak, and other Houses would swoop in like vultures; too strong, and they would ally to take Hawthorn down. And, of course, Hawthorn itself wasn't currently in the best of states. Thuan had only recently started to rule alongside Asmodeus, and the House was still adjusting to the merging of Thuan's dragon magic with the Fallen magic of Asmodeus, which it had always relied upon for its own defense. Dependents were busy rebuilding wards, and the Fallen in the House—the former angels, living sources of magic—were working overtime to repair buildings and cast protective spells. Hawthorn was in no shape to get involved in anything.

Again, that tingling in the air—something wasn't as it should have been, but before Thuan could start weaving *khi* currents, someone spoke.

"My lord. I hadn't expected to find you here."

It was phrased like a reproach. Thuan turned, his heart sinking.

"Iaris."

Iaris smiled. Her face was smooth, ageless—nothing close to her real and considerable age, but then Iaris was one of Asmodeus's favorites, and her closeness to Fallen magic had stretched and slowed down the passing of time for her body. She'd been with Asmodeus from the beginning, in the Court of Birth, before the coup that had made him the head of the House, and was now the chief doctor in Hawthorn's hospital. She was virtually untouchable, at least by Thuan, and they both knew it.

"What do you want?" Thuan asked.

"A word," Iaris said. She didn't sit down on the lawn, forcing Thuan to get up, dirty trousers and all—obviously. "This is unseemly."

Thuan raised an eyebrow. "Unseemly?"

Iaris's face did not move. "You know exactly what I mean."

Thuan snatched Camille up before she could go wandering off near the water, and bobbed her up and down, carrying her on one hip. Ancestors, she was heavy. Ai Nhi had turned into a dragon: a serpentine shape with the antlers of a deer that curled up around Thuan's legs, making a deep rumbling noise of contentment. The cold touch of her scales through the fabric of his trousers was comforting.

"You're his consort," Iaris said, dryly. "Head of the House."

She made it all sound like an insult. She thought Asmodeus had embarrassed himself when he'd married Thuan, and even more when Thuan had started to rule in his own name. Never mind, of course, that Thuan had to seize power from Asmodeus to do it, at a moment when

Asmodeus had been on the brink of death. In Iaris's mind, the perfect House would still be under the sole control of her own master.

"That's an accurate description of my position," Thuan said, deadpan.

Iaris ignored him. "You're not a childminder. The Court of Birth—"

"Isn't these children's family."

Iaris opened her mouth. She was going to ask if Thuan was family, but realized that this would cast aspersions on Asmodeus—who might have been a disaster at childcare but definitely considered Camille his niece.

"Lord Asmodeus—"

"I don't know where he is," Thuan said. "We're not each other's minders, either. The last time I saw him was at lunch."

Iaris exhaled. "You don't understand."

He did. The House was changing, and Iaris didn't like it—she clung to what she'd always known like a lifeline. She wanted a head of House who was dark and frightful, a monster to defend them against the other monsters of Paris: all the things that Asmodeus effortlessly was, but that Thuan would never agree to become.

But understanding didn't mean he had to indulge her.

"Down down, Unka," Camille said.

Thuan reluctantly let go of her, but kept a wary eye on what she was doing. She was crouching on the grass, watching a bit of dark earth with fascination.

He said, to Iaris, "Was that all?"

Her lips thinned. She started to move back towards the House, but turned, slightly, towards him.

"You'll never be accepted if you don't make an effort to fit in."

Ah, the old classics. Thuan exhaled. He let his dragon shape half-shimmer into existence around him: the antlers, the scales on the back of his hands, his fingers thinning and sharpening into claws.

"I take care of this House," he said. "That's all that really matters. You want me to make myself smaller in the vain hope that the dependents will forget who I really am. We both know that's not going to happen."

"Certainly not in these circumstances," Iaris said, coldly. She glanced at the children, and then at the other side of the riverbank, where empty factory buildings stood against the sideline. House Harrier. One of the Houses sharing a border with Hawthorn: the Grenelle bridge, where House dependents stared at each other across the checkpoints.

"Our neighbors have seen us in disarray, my lord. The faster they realize that we're united, the fewer attacks they'll try."

"Harrier isn't attacking us," Thuan said, mildly.

Harrier was classist, separating human and Fallen and insisting on the innate superiority of Fallen. Lord Guy and his wife Andrea had cut Thuan dead at every event they'd attended. If nothing else, it had been entertaining to watch Asmodeus getting increasingly cutting and sarcastic in return.

Iaris's face didn't move. Camille was wandering off again: Thuan raised a barrier of *khi* water across her path and she bumped into it, poked at the blue light with pudgy fingers, curiously.

"Harrier is too busy at the moment," Iaris said. "But

make no mistake—when they see an opportunity they'll take it. And they're not the only ones. House Mansart and Fontenoy are emboldened by Harrier's own internal troubles." She ticked them off on her fingers, items on a list of issues Thuan had no doubt she carefully maintained. "House Lazarus won't act directly but they'll push other Houses to do so. House Shellac have always felt they ought to be larger and more important."

She listed half a dozen other Houses Thuan could barely keep track of. Which was the point, of course: to show him his own ignorance and obliviousness.

Ancestors, he was getting so tired of this. Life was harsh and short in a city still in ruins after the Great Houses War sixty years ago, and even within the relative safety of a House, all they could seem to think of was how to hurt each other, like crabs in a bucket.

"Was that all?" he asked, again. He made his voice much colder.

Iaris grimaced, but said nothing else. She headed back into the House with ill grace, leaving Thuan to disentangle Ai Nhi from his legs.

The little dragon girl stared, thoughtfully, at the retreating figure of Iaris.

"She's not nice," she said, with a gravity that seemed completely out of proportion.

Thuan couldn't help laughing.

"No," he said. "But you still have to be nice to her."

"Unka!" Ai Nhi said, scandalized.

"Do we need to have the talk about politeness again?"

He stopped, then. The odd tension in the air was not only still there, but now unbearably strong. He hadn't noticed because he was too busy trying to assert himself and face Iaris down, but …

The entire world seemed to be drawing a breath. The *khi* water around Ai Nhi and Camille stiffened, and flowed away—and so did every other *khi* element in the air.

"Unka?"

Thuan turned towards the river. He had no choice, because the flow of *khi* elements was drawing him as a fisherman's hook, a ceaseless tug in the hollow of his chest—not straight ahead, towards the muddy mire of the flooded gardens, or the dragon kingdom that had once been his home, but towards the left, past the ruined Eiffel Tower. A plume of flame and smoke rose over the horizon: the flames pink and yellow, darkening into billowing clouds. A dull sound like a gunshot, and then another one—each burst changing the sky, briefly, to a bright green that slowly washed into trembling, dusty light.

Fire. Smoke.

From the heart of House Harrier. Neither wood nor stone burned that way. And the explosions—too far away for now to send shock waves they'd feel, but they would only be the start.

He'd not fought in the Great Houses War. Sixty years ago he'd been young and sheltered, a minor and spoiled prince of the Dragon Kingdom more interested in sleeping with a succession of lovers than in the dreadfully boring business of the court—but he'd heard the stories of the fall of House Hell's Toll, and how the armory's fire had painted the sky green and pink. He was seeing no ordinary fire; and he had perhaps three minutes before the largest and final explosion.

"Unka?"

The windows were too close. The House was too close—everything would become cutting shards and wounding debris when the shock wave hit.

He shifted into his dragon shape, as easily as slipping on the tailored clothes Asmodeus kept pressing on him. He scooped up both children, ignoring their protestations—the wriggling, screaming Camille, Ai Nhi saying she was all grown-up and too old to be carried, trying to grab her doll from Camille on Thuan's other side—and started flying towards his office. The pressure in the air was becoming unbearable; that dreadful, unnerving calm before the storm, slowly spinning itself together. The plume of smoke from the burning House Harrier now cast a long shadow across the lawn, the trembling, billowing finger of some malevolent deity lightly resting on a wound. There was no *khi* water left in the air at all—Thuan felt he was swimming upriver through tar, caught in sticky air that only slowed him down. The river wavered in front of him, patches of oily sheen distorting into vague, unrecognizable shapes. An illusory safety: the dragon kingdom would not help him, would not shelter him, would not save him.

He was perhaps halfway to the closest building when the explosion hit. A booming sound was the only harbinger of what had happened—followed, a fraction of a second later, by a wind that tore the grass from the lawn, as sharp as knives against the skin of his hands. He threw himself to the ground, raising desperate wards to protect the children, just as everything was torn apart in a maelstrom of sounds and flying debris which hit, again and again, the wards he'd raised. Thuan curled over the children, feeling the dull bounce of the broken objects which got through against the scales of his dragon shape, just as the House's sense of danger rose to a screaming crescendo in his mind. He had to do something to protect his people, he had to do it now …

Silence spread over the House. Thuan pulled himself up, cautiously. The large oak tree by the side of the lawn had lost a few branches, but seemed otherwise unharmed. The French windows of his office—which he'd left open—had been torn off their hinges. Every pane of glass on the entire wing had shattered inwards. There was a distant smell of fire—something burning in the kitchens? The air was the purplish hue of recent bruises, and everything smelled too sharp, too crisp. The *khi* currents that normally saturated the House were all but gone.

He caught movement on his right, out of the corner of his eye, on the edges of the riverbank that were perpetually shrouded in mist: small, agile shapes coming to crowd on the lawn, invisible to anyone else but him. The children. Not the ones he was currently minding, but the others, the House in physical shape: skeletal branches of hawthorn shaped into the vague shape of children. His flesh crawled—every time he'd seen the children he or his friends had been in grave danger—but they seemed not to pay him any attention. Their faces were turned, unerringly, to the plume of smoke rising beyond the river.

Harrier. House Harrier. Their closest neighbor, aflame and reeling from the explosion; and they would have it even worse than Hawthorn, since they had been at the center of the blast.

What would happen now?

"Unka?"

Ai Nhi stared, open-mouthed, at the devastation. Even Camille, for once, seemed to be at a loss.

"It'll be fine," he said, with a confidence he didn't feel. He threw another glance at the children of thorns, but they still hadn't moved. That was not good, but he had so many other things to worry about first. "Come on, let's see what's happened."

He flew rather than walked over the lawn, and dived head first into his office. Or rather, what was left of it. His bookshelves had toppled—torn fragments of books lay everywhere—and the papers he'd left on his desk were probably hopelessly mangled by now. The desk itself was more or less where he'd left it, though its leather was scored in multiple places by gashes. Broken glass and splinters of wood and metal covered every surface. If anyone had been by a window when it had shattered …

Asmodeus. Thuan reached out in his mind, where the dependents of the House were arrayed like candle flames—so many of them guttering, on the verge of failing—and a familiar, sarcastic presence, though diminished and far away.

Still alive. Asmodeus was still alive; but of course the House couldn't tell Thuan anything useful, beyond indications of immediate danger—and there were so many ways to die that weren't immediate or merciful.

He—

"Down! Down!" Camille said. Thuan tightened his grip on her.

"There's glass, little fish," he said, firmly.

And, ignoring her disappointed wails, he flew further

into the wing, trying not to dwell on the fear that tightened his insides like a fist of ice.

Inside the House, it was chaos. Stunned dependents wandered, calling for their loved ones; distant clatters of debris as people freed themselves. The smoke he'd smelled earlier was coming from the kitchen, where Koia and a few others were frantically emptying magical artifacts of their stored power to attempt to snuff out the flames that had spilled out from the ovens and hearths. Koia nodded at Thuan as he stood at the door: she had it under control, or hoped to.

"Have you seen Lord Asmodeus?" Thuan asked, as he'd asked every other dependent on his way there.

Koia gave a tight-lipped shake of her head. "Sorry, my lord. He doesn't come into the kitchens that often."

Almost never, unless it was to frighten the kitchen hands. Thuan sighed, and pressed down his nascent worries. There was a lot of business to take care of. Other people whose safety he had to ensure. And Asmodeus would be fine. He was too smart and too resourceful to be otherwise. Thuan tamped down the little voice that kept insisting that smartness and resourcefulness meant little in such situations.

"Find me someone you can spare," he said. "There was a fire across the Seine, and I want to know where it's coming from."

"My lord ..."

Koia gave him an appraising look; but Thuan was in full dragon form, and disinclined to argue with people who still thought Asmodeus was the center of the universe insofar as the House was concerned.

He pressed himself closer to her, so she could see the full

width of his maw, and the glistening fangs of a predator in a mouth large enough to gobble up half of her in one go.

"Now, Koia."

"Of course, my lord."

"Thuan!"

It was Berith, Asmodeus's Fall-sister. She strode through the din as though nothing was wrong: silver-haired and tall, infused with the glow of Fallen magic—though it was flickering and weak—and her eyes circled with deep gray. Berith had taken grave wounds during the Great Houses War sixty years ago, and not even the protection of the House could heal her.

"Mamma!" Camille wriggled out of Thuan's grasp and ran, screaming, towards Berith, hugging the Fallen's legs with a wide smile on her face. "Mamma mamma mamma."

Berith gave Thuan an apologetic smile.

"Come on, child," she said to Ai Nhi in perfect Viet. Ai Nhi shook her head, and continued to cling to Thuan.

"Don't worry," Thuan said.

He shook himself and resumed his human form, which made it easier to fit into the space below the ceiling. Ai Nhi remained on him—no longer riding on his back, but now balanced on his shoulders. He was obscurely glad someone was there to take care of Camille. Ai Nhi was five, old enough to have a modicum of self-preservation, but Camille just barreled through life as though fires and large bodies of water would somehow make way for her imperious will.

"Françoise . . .?"

"She's fine." Berith's face was closed. "She was with the seamstresses, embroidering some tablecloths."

Some undercurrents there: Françoise was Berith's partner, and thus related to the head of the House whether she liked it or not—and both Berith and Asmodeus thought it unseemly for her to concern herself with base servants' work.

A worry for another time.

"Auntie Berith, Auntie Berith, there was a big boom!" Ai Nhi said.

Berith smiled, brightly and with a tension even the little dragon had to see.

"I'm sure there was. It happens sometimes in old Houses, child."

"Mmm." Ai Nhi didn't sound convinced.

In the silence that followed, Thuan said, "No one has seen Asmodeus."

Berith lifted Camille to her face, up and up until the toddler squealed with laughter—with no hint of the strain it must have been to her dying magic. Then she lowered her, and balanced the small body on her hips.

"I haven't, either," she said. "You should go and see Iaris."

Thuan sighed. He'd delayed going to the hospital because he didn't want to know how bad it was. But he was head of the House—one of two people everyone depended on for protection—and he couldn't afford some illusions.

"I will. Do you have any idea what's going on?"

Aside from the obvious fact of an explosion. These had been commonplace during the war, but that was over: though buried spells went off from time to time, nothing should have had that large an impact.

Berith shook her head.

"Doesn't matter," Thuan said.

They were going to find out eventually; and he had an inkling they wouldn't like it, not one bit.

They were halfway to the hospital wing when the messenger caught up with them. It was one of Iaris's underlings, out of breath.

"My lord ..."

"Steady," Thuan said.

"You have to come now." The messenger paused. "The cells ... Lord Asmodeus ..."

Thuan's blood went cold.

"Take her," he said to Berith, lowering Ai Nhi down.

"Unka!"

But Thuan was already up and running—rising, shedding his human form and flying above his startled dependents. He flowed through the labyrinth of the West Wing, corridors of cracked wainscoting streaming past, adroitly ducking so that his antlers didn't get tangled in broken chandeliers, deftly avoiding the crossroads leading to the rooms of the various leaders of Hawthorn's Courts, into another, even narrower complex of guardrooms and servants' quarters, where his body twisted to weave around the crowd of people rushing towards the exit.

When he reached the entrance to the cells, he found a pile of rubble blocking the staircase; and Madeleine, the House's alchemist, drawing a circle on the floor, pausing from time to time to shake an errant strand of graying hair from her eyes. Thuan landed among startled dependents, and—with difficulty—kept his mouth shut while Madeleine finished drawing her spell.

Fallen magic still wasn't his specialty: all he could judge was the size and complexity of the spell. As he watched, Madeleine emptied another artifact of its stored magic, and it joined the piles of discarded ones on the floor. They didn't have that many left, and they'd gone through a great number of them already—Thuan bit back the thought, which was useless. They needed to get to Asmodeus. The cells. Obviously. Asmodeus had never been part of the Court of Persuasion, but he still haunted the cells as if they were his second home—satisfying his cravings for others' pain by interrogating the dissidents imprisoned within the House.

"It's just rubble," one of the dependents said to Thuan—Mia, a no-nonsense Fallen with long flowing hair and a swallowtail jacket speckled with shining silver threads. "The cells should be intact, my lord."

Should be. Might be. Thuan knew better than to put faith in such statements.

Ancestors, keep him safe.

A scratching sound.

Thuan's head snapped up; so did Madeleine's. The pile of debris that blocked the entrance to the cells was moving—shifting upwards, as if something buried within was ponderously lifting itself free. It stopped for a moment, fell back down, and then slowly pushed itself up again. Thuan's throat felt constricted. He hadn't even been aware he was holding his breath.

The pile of rubble spun—became, for a brief moment, a pillar of metal and wooden shards—and then burst apart, showering everyone with debris. Mia and Madeleine threw themselves to the floor. Thuan shielded his eyes. The debris fell well away from him, as if an invisible hand was holding it off.

When the cloud of dust dispersed, Asmodeus stood on what had been the first steps of the stairs. He wore his usual gray-and-silver swallowtail jacket, except that it was covered with dust. He had a body slung across his shoulder: someone with long hair Thuan couldn't recognize, whose head and back hung limply on Asmodeus's broad chest. Blood stained his white gloves, and he had multiple wounds on both cheeks. He stood, unblinking, unmoving, watching them all through horn-rimmed glasses, gray-green eyes the color of a stormy sea.

Thuan took one, two steps forwards. "Asmodeus ..."

He didn't move. He just stood, staring at Thuan. The smell of bergamot and citrus hung in the air: a threat, a promise. At length he shook himself; moved away from the staircase in long, graceful steps, his face still frozen in that odd expression.

"Here," he said, laying the body down on the edge of Madeleine's circle: an Annamite woman whose bare arms had been sliced open, blood staining her tunic until it had turned the color of rust. "Get her to hospital."

"Asmodeus!"

But Asmodeus was already swaying. Thuan flowed upwards, catching him on the back of his dragon shape before he could hit the floor.

"Stubborn fool," he said, not bothering to hide his worry, his anger—not to mention utter exhaustion from switching shapes three times in the same day. "Let's get *you* to hospital first."

*

In Emmanuelle's dreams, the world was fire. Angels rose on wings of flame towards a distant, unattainable City: a concoction of mother-of-pearl buildings, enameled domes and white, eye-searing streets in which featureless shapes flowed past each other. At the top of the highest tower was the light of a burning sun—it couldn't be watched, couldn't be held within her field of vision without hurting her eyes or burning her face. She reached out towards it—towards Him—and everything fell apart, the flames becoming the jagged shards of a vast, unknowable puzzle raining down on her.

She woke up, and everything hurt. She lay on her back for a while, staring at a sky that wasn't gray—that wasn't even the cornflower blue of Lucifer Morningstar's eyes, or of the heavens as they had been, before the war, before the pall of pollution. It was an odd shade of purple, shading into indigo. As she watched, sounds intruded: distant clatters, and a rumble, like stones collapsing atop each other. It was hot—too hot.

She needed to get up.

She was lying on gravel in the ruins of a garden: the center of a classic little square with wrought-iron railings and impeccable rows of trees that still peppered the south of Paris. Except that the railings that separated the garden from the surrounding streets were bent, and the trees charred, leafless stumps, and she lay in the middle of a flat nothingness of churned earth and fragments of stone. The doors and windows of all the buildings around the square had caved in. It was not the usual gentle decay she was used to seeing in post-war Paris, more like the result of an explosion.

What had happened?

Emmanuelle managed to pull herself upright on trembling legs. Just as she did, a wave of nausea racked her from head to toe, and she was on her knees again, vomiting on to the cobblestones, and heaving again and again and bringing up nothing but nauseating bile, her entire being wrung as if by a careless giant.

Where was she?

She didn't remember coming here, or …

Harrier.

House Harrier. She was in House Harrier, as an official envoy of House Silverspires. She … Presentation. She and Morningstar had been attending the First Presentation of the child-magicians—the first one Guy had hosted since his accession as head of the House. A historic occurrence, Emmanuelle's partner Selene had said, in a tone that suggested she didn't trust Guy one bit. Then again, with Silverspires diminished and struggling to survive, they couldn't really afford to get into an internecine fight with Harrier. Selene was head of the House, and Emmanuelle was all too aware of the political currents.

She …

Emmanuelle pulled herself upright—she was shaking, shivering, and …

Something was wrong. She raised a hand to her forehead—an absurd idea, she couldn't take her own temperature. Her hand spasmed—she tried to hold it still, but it seized up on its own.

Morningstar.

Where was he? They were supposed to look out for each other. He'd promised her …

From far away, other familiar sounds: people fighting—and getting closer and closer to her.

Away. She needed to get away. Working everything else out could happen later.

She stumbled away, and all but tripped over a corpse. Someone she didn't know, in House Harrier's blue and black uniform, eyes staring upwards at that odd, bruised-purple sky. They looked odd, but she couldn't place how or why. Didn't matter. She couldn't afford to tarry.

The earth under her shook: she almost fell, caught herself in time. Everything seemed like it was happening in slow motion. She walked towards the ruined railings, towards the nearest street, or what remained of it.

The sound of fighting was getting closer—a growing thunder, the sound of metal on metal, the sharp crack of rifles, screams, words all jumbling together into meaninglessness.

Why? What had happened? They ... weren't at war anymore. Peace had been gained at such a cost; and they'd enjoyed it for decades. It made no sense.

Onwards. She had to hide.

She reached the street, and looked left and right. The buildings gaped at her like the maws of Hell, all similarly empty husks filled with ruined darkness. No shelter. And further on were only more buildings with burned, shattered facades, and further still the unbroken dome of the Great Interior, the secluded area where Guy kept the most powerful of his trained magicians—a panicked thought in her mind, a memory of beating wings in a darkened corridor. No shelter there, either, she knew it with absolute certainty. The battle was getting closer. She couldn't hide. She had to run.

She did, past the ghosts of buildings in the devastated streets. Her hands seized—and her legs, too, at odd moments, sending her sprawling to the ground. She'd pick herself up, breathing heavily and fighting the blurring vision that threatened to take over her entire world. The sounds came closer and closer, resolved into voices—into grunts and threats and prayers as people hacked and shot at each other.

"You'll pay for this!"

"You can't win!"

She couldn't run anymore. There was nowhere to hide, but she had to.

She was in another ruined garden, her feet on cold churned earth. Ahead of her was a building: something in a pseudo-Greek or Roman style, except that it had one good wall and three ruined ones, and half a floor, and the railings of its little garden had bent inwards, the tree by its front porch burned and shriveled. Emmanuelle reached what was left of the door, peered inside. Bodies, with blood streaming out of their eyes, limbs hanging at loose angles.

Beggars couldn't be choosers.

She sat against the one wall that still held—praying that it would hold, that the world would stop shaking. And, belatedly, she saw what was wrong: the light. Shadows had played across the corpses on the elaborate tiling of the floor, as she'd looked in. A soft, sloshing light had danced over the ruined walls, moving as she'd moved her head.

It was her.

She was emitting the light. She raised a hand, stared

at it. Her arms and legs were covered in wounds: the debris must have shredded her when the explosion had happened, but that was normal. What wasn't normal was that her dark skin was translucent, its color still true, but she could see muscles shifting, contracting uncontrollably, sending her arm down again in a spasm. She wasn't simply burning with fever; she was burning, full stop, her body eating itself like a candle.

Ablaze, in the middle of what looked like a pitched fight, in a House that was her enemy and with no idea of what had happened.

She needed to hide her radiance: her clothes were keeping most of it contained, but her face, her hands and every patch of exposed skin shone like a torch set ablaze. The walls weren't going to keep that contained, so she needed to cover those parts as well. If there'd been a tarpaulin or a sheet she could crawl under—no, nothing like that left in the rubble.

But she had cloth on her.

Emmanuelle looked down. She was wearing an elaborate silk dress embroidered with flowers and trees, and a discreet patch with House Silverspires' insignia, Morningstar's sword against the towers of Notre-Dame. Ceremonial clothes. Petticoats. Layers and layers of thick cloth she could unwrap to hide under.

It took her three tries to undress. Her fingers had become fat, listless sticks, and the spasms that racked her didn't help.

Screams, much closer this time. The battle was so close—on the other side of the wall—and she couldn't afford to look if she wanted to remain unseen.

She tore her petticoats, and wrapped her hands, face and chest in them. They were a thick opaque cotton—hopefully enough to mask the light she was shedding. Then she leaned back against the wall, the words of a prayer running over and over in her head.

Our Father, who art in Heaven, Hallowed be Thy Name, Thy Kingdom come …

Selene would say He wasn't there—that He'd never been there, that this was where they were all damned. Father Javier would smile, a little sadly, trying to hide that he'd lost his faith a long time ago. Emmanuelle knew it was all untrue; that God was everywhere and in everything, and—in spite of everything, in spite of her Fall—was still listening to His wayward children.

Our Father …

Metal on metal and a confusion of footsteps—a din that hurt her ears, too close to be processed. They had to be just outside the walls. She had to be silent. She had to be unseen.

Our Father …

Silence, outside. A dying man, begging for mercy, and a gurgling, choking sound that was all too obvious. Emmanuelle's hands tightened on her torn petticoats. Her leg spasmed across the tiled floor, sending a small pile of broken wood from the shutters clattering to the ground.

No no no.

"Should we look for survivors?" A sharp, no-nonsense female voice.

Another silence. Emmanuelle held her breath, willing her limbs still.

"There are none."

"They're just buried under debris."

"Not if they were inside. They'll have died. Shock wave shaking their brains inside the head cavity. Or flung against walls. Take your pick."

"I thought I heard a noise."

Please please please.

Emmanuelle gave up on subtlety, and threw herself to the ground, drawing her petticoats over her like a shroud.

Footsteps: a vague shadow, blurred through the cotton cloth.

Please please let them pass me by. Let them turn away.

"You're right. It's just corpses." A sigh of disgust. "Let's go before they come back."

Silence, again. Emmanuelle didn't dare move, not until she was sure they'd well and truly gone. It was almost restful, lying on the cool floor.

Her mind wandered, the prayer no longer first and foremost in her thoughts. How had she come there? Morningstar. She'd come with Morningstar, at Selene's behest. They'd gone to their rooms, and then—

And then there was nothing. Time skipped and blurred. Morningstar at her door, cocking his head the way he did when he was about to ask an embarrassing question. He had a burning sword in his hands, and Darrias, House Hawthorn's envoy, was behind him.

"Emmanuelle, what's wrong?"

There was a sound in the background, a hiss that gradually grew, as if hundreds of strips of cloth were fluttering in the wind at the same time—except it made Emmanuelle's heart freeze, and fear tighten around her guts. She had to run, she needed to run now.

No.

None of that was possible. It wasn't real. The sword—the two-handed monstrosity that had been Morningstar's weapon of predilection—had been lost for twenty years. And the face of Darrias, standing behind Morningstar, kept changing, becoming that of a Harrier menial, that of a Hawthorn dragon, that of the Houseless boy with the broken arm Emmanuelle had helped home a week ago, when she'd met him on her usual runs through the city.

Her mind kept shying away from the immediate past—scrabbling, trying to fill the gap with random, incoherent images. She closed her eyes, took a deep breath. It didn't really make anything better. The images went away, but the sound didn't—merging with that of her madly beating heart, that she couldn't calm no matter how she tried.

Calm down. Calm down.

She could do this.

At length she pulled herself up once again. The sound of battle was distant again, and the rumbles of collapsing buildings had stopped. Safety. She had to get to safety—wherever that was. Out of the House, if she could; though she couldn't see the great wrought-iron gates she'd entered through, and if it had reached the stage of pitched battles in the House the gates would be one of the worst places to be.

She clung, for a moment, to the threshold of the ruined building, staring at the shape of devastation all around her. The landscape bent and blurred—nightmarish shapes, created by the light that was burning her up.

What had happened, and how was she going to deal with any of the fallout?

2

Sweeping the Tombs

Philippe was at Grandmother Olympe's, with the other aunts and the children. It was almost the Mid-Autumn festival, and he'd been roped into helping Colette build a lantern. Aunt Ha's daughter was three, and didn't have the fine motor control necessary to put it together without crushing the delicate wooden ribs. He'd cheated, and used a hint of *khi* fire and *khi* water to create an *am duong* pattern in the air. Each teardrop half of the circular sign hung wreathed in colored light, and it was slowly rotating, much to Colette's entrancement.

He'd wanted to use the *khi* elements to put the lantern together, too, but Grandmother Olympe had put her foot down, darkly muttering something about proper striving. Slowly, carefully, he threaded the silk paper over the last of the ribs. He'd chosen the classic five-star shape, but hadn't realized how complicated it was. But he wasn't about to lose face in front of Grandmother Olympe—who'd make some low-voiced and pointed comments about Immortals not knowing everything, hoping to draw him into an argument about their respective ages. She'd never quite forgiven him for continuing to call her "Grandmother" when he was, in fact, much older than her; over a thousand years old and ageless, by virtue of the ascension that had brought him into the court of the Jade Emperor. She'd chosen to ignore that he'd later been thrown out of it—though at least she wasn't worshipping him. He had a *temple* in those days, a small room in a basement with an altar and people leaving offerings. "Awkward" didn't even begin to cover how he felt about it.

His fingers slipped, sending a small wooden dowel clattering to the floor, and he picked it up with hands that seemed to be on fire. Demons take him, it was a children's lantern—it shouldn't be that complicated . . .

A distant noise like thunder. Philippe looked up, startled, a split second before the floor shook and cracks spread through the walls of the apartment.

"Colette . . ."

Aunt Ha was already there, picking up her daughter before Philippe could even think of moving. She gave him a dark look, as if he was somehow responsible for whatever was happening, but Aunt Thuy was already bending at the window, followed by most of the others.

"There's smoke in the sky," Aunt Thuy said.

A faint, sickly smell in the air—a familiar one, wasn't it? Not fire, which happened now and again in devastated Paris; not the smoke of the pyres on which House Hawthorn burned the Houseless they slayed, calling it justice. But something older and much more dangerous . . . Abruptly, he was back sixty years ago, his hands splintered with the wood of his spear, pushing forward as the company he was part of entered the kitchens of House Draken, moments before it fell and the shock of its extinction sent them all reeling . . .

"Philippe? Philippe!"

Grandmother Olympe was shaking him, her hands smearing grit-speckled mooncake dough on his face, a cold and startling touch, like that of a drowning man.

"I'm fine," he said, but he couldn't quite keep his voice from shaking. "What's happening?"

"I don't know." Olympe's dark, wrinkled face was emotionless.

Philippe walked to the window—it was open in the warm weather, which meant he could see through it instead of squinting through cracked, opaque glass patched in multiple places. A plume of smoke rose from beyond the roofs of la Goutte d'Or neighborhood, its billowing darkness shot through with colored lights as if from fractured jewels. The air was saturated with that sweet, sickly smell—that of battle spells he hadn't witnessed cast in more than sixty years, since the war had ended.

"Look look, Lippe, lightie lightie," Colette said, trying to bend over the windowsill to catch the smoke, but Aunt Ha held her fast.

"Something is burning," Aunt Ha said. "Something big."

"House fights," Philippe said, with a lightness he didn't feel. "None of our business."

He looked at the *khi* currents in the small, crowded kitchen space. They were bent out of shape, slowly draining towards the source of the smoke. Not just any House fight, but a spectacular one. What was in that direction? Hell's Toll, Solférino, Harrier? Not that it mattered.

Grandmother Olympe was silent for a while; he could see her weighing possible consequences for the little Annamite community she was all but queen of.

"You can't fight them," Philippe said.

Ancestors knew he wanted to; but it was a doomed, impossible struggle.

"No," Grandmother Olympe said, at length. "You're right. It's none of our business. And it's not like knowing would change anything for us." She brought both hands together. "Come on, everyone. We have lanterns and mooncakes to finish for tomorrow."

The aunts came back from the window, and Philippe went back to his discarded lantern. But he could still feel the tension and worry in the air—the way the conversations were now terse and taut, that Aunt Ha kept glancing at Colette, wondering how much of that she'd understood. And, when he walked out of the apartment after his lantern was finished, the smoke was still rising above the buildings, now purple rather than black, the sky around it puckered and bruised, and the *khi* currents all bent out of shape, slowly gathering in a huge maelstrom that spun in the sky like a huge, ponderous serpent.

Sixty years. It had been sixty years since the Great Houses War. He hadn't been there at the start, obviously—only brought in, like the aunts' ancestors, when it had been going badly, when they had needed to drain their colonies of blood and silver in order to survive. But—he glanced, again, at the plume of smoke, stubbornly refusing to go away—he imagined it would have started much like this, once upon a time.

*

Philippe's apartment was in a communal building: one of the last ones to be built before the war, its entire ground floor added after the Boulevard Barbès had been leveled downwards, the former hilly street replaced by a straight avenue, the kind that had once been marked by a row of chestnut trees on either side, a testament to Paris's wealth and power. Now all that was left were the circles where the trees had once been—the ground blackened and filled with so much chemical residue that nothing would grow there. Philippe's room-mate Isabelle would attempt, stubbornly, to get tomato plants to flower, but they would shrivel, barely past sapling stage. He doubted they'd be edible—poisoned, like the ground. Like the city.

No patients waited for him on the rickety stairs. In the small apartment, Isabelle was waiting for him, carefully drawing on a scrap of paper with charcoal. Behind her, the one wall giving out on the boulevard was broken, the hole taped over with oiled paper by the dockers and bakers in the Annamite community when they'd moved into their new flat. Few homes in the Houseless areas of Paris were whole—that this one had four walls and three of them were intact made it of great value.

"Philippe!"

He glanced at her drawings. "You've been practicing again."

"I'm getting better." She gestured towards the stove behind her. "I made buns. They're almost pretty."

She smiled, then, and it illuminated her entire face. Once—in another lifetime, when she'd been a member of House Silverspires, before she died because of him, before he found the spell that brought her back to life, not as the

Fallen she'd been, but as a mortal—they'd learned to bake together. He'd shown her how to handle dough, holding it to the light until it was almost translucent, shown her how to fold it into banetons, waiting for it to rise until the cream-white, perfect dough looked as though it was about to burst. These days the dough was gray, flecked with dirt and grit and Ancestors knew what else; she made buns rather than bread, and they danced around the subject of Silverspires as one would dance around barbed bonfires of thorns.

"I'm sure they're perfect."

He glanced at her drawings. The same abstract shapes—sweeping, phantasmagorical clouds that seemed to stretch and waver as he stared at them. Other Annamites bought them as charms. Philippe was secretly glad to have them out of the flat; he was a former Immortal, and not particularly superstitious anymore, but these gave him the creeps. The one he was staring at was shaped like a bird, but as he watched it seemed to stretch and change, until it seemed a blackened plume of smoke.

"You should probably stay inside for a while," he said.

Isabelle's thin, black eyebrows arched. "Why?"

He was about to say, "It's dangerous", when he noticed the petals on the table. They were small, perfectly heart-shaped, scattered around her drawings like decorations, their color all but drained away to the grayish-white of dirty snow, their ribs traced delicately in bluish mold.

Hoang mai. Mai vang. The flower of New Year's Eve in Cochin China. It only grew in the South of Indochina, and there was no way anyone here could have got hold of one.

"Isabelle, where did these come from?"

"These?" Isabelle stared at the petals. "I hadn't even noticed they were here ..."

A cold wind rose through the window, seeping in through the edges of the oiled paper, picking up the petals until they seemed to dance in the breaths of air. They swirled past Isabelle and Philippe, spun, for a split second, around the battered bamboo steamers on the stove, and then came back towards the floor, between the cracked slats of the parquet. They didn't rest on it; they still whirled in the air, turning and twisting and rising, more and more of them, with a faint, almost transparent sheet of air wrapping itself around them, like a net curtain caught in a storm. It was almost the shape of a person now—a faint, threatening suggestion of arms and legs in a figure that only barely resembled one, a flower petal face with only depressions for the eyes, and arms that whipped and stretched in the rising wind.

"Philippe ..." Isabelle said.

Her hands clenched, her brow furrowed—as if she could still access the magic that had been her birthright as a Fallen.

He laid a hand on her wrist to steady her.

"Don't," he said.

The air was saturated with the smell of *hoang mai*, a soft, fruity breeze that would have been a reminder of New Year's Eve in his home—except that he could taste the rot underneath, the earthy, moldy smell that clung to everything in Paris. A reminder that he was there, that the city was dying, and that he was part of it, trapped in it because no boats would take a Houseless back to the country of his birth.

The face sharpened; the petals faded; and a woman stood before them.

She had dark skin, with a tinge of mingled yellow and blue, and the contours of heart-shaped petals were still visible on her cheeks. Her hair was piled in two elaborate braids that formed large arches above her head. Her sleeves billowed in the wind, but so did her arms and hands, as if she couldn't quite tell where the wind ended and where she started.

"Pham Van Minh Kiet," she said in a voice that was the whisper of flowers shaken by the storm, the sound of petals falling over the wet earth. And then another, older name: the one he had taken as an Immortal, in the Court of the Jade Emperor.

His body was bowing—betraying him, finding again the old obeisances of the Court. He stopped it with an effort; bowed simply, without abasing the upper part of his body to the floor.

"Lady," he said.

Isabelle was watching her warily. He'd withdrawn his hand from her wrist, but he could still feel her—could still feel her frustration, her need for immediate information.

"You're a hard man to find," the woman said, gracefully. She moved. Her sleeves moved with her, disintegrating into petals as she did so. "My name is Hoa Phong. I am the Censor Who Reveals the Purity of Heaven." She held out a scroll.

It was thin, translucent paper backed on yellow silk with the entwined shapes of dragons—faint, faded tracings and frayed threads, something carefully and lovingly preserved. The message was in sharp and neat characters—Southern characters, not the Classical Chinese the court had once used. The text itself was short and terse, dwarfed by the familiar vermilion of the imperial seal at the bottom. When he rubbed his hand over it, a tingle of magic crept up his arm—a tight knot of all *khi* elements in perfect balance, a pointed and wounding reminder of what it had felt like to belong. And at the bottom …

"I thought it lost," Philippe said, before he could think.

The imperial seal, the one once given by the Chinese to the Jade Emperor in Annam, had been destroyed by the Fallen at the outset of French colonization.

"Some things endure." Hoa Phong's smile was dazzling.

The text said:

It is a time when the mulberry fields become open sea, and the sea mulberry fields. Foreigners hold our treasures and our subjects' submission. For this reason we have sent Hoa Phong, the Censor Who Reveals the Purity of Heaven, bearing the word, so that we may be saved, and we order anyone who reads this to render her whatever help may be necessary in the accomplishment of her tasks.

Be saved. Philippe breathed in a distant smell of sandalwood and lemongrass, remembered a palace of wide, impossible rooms, of lacquered chairs and silver chopsticks.

"You're from the court."

There was no need to specify which one.

A smile, that would have been dazzling if he hadn't seen the flower stamen in her mouth.

"With a need."

He didn't remember her. He didn't remember most of

them—when he'd been thrown out of the court, lifetimes ago, the various immortals in the various ministries had cut all ties with him. It was the way it had always been. The court didn't waste time mourning, or render pity to those out of favor.

"For a disgraced ex-Immortal?"

"You're still Immortal," Hoa Phong said. "You don't age, you don't get sick. Whereas people like her—"

"I'm here," Isabelle said, loudly, though her Viet was nowhere near fluent enough to follow a conversation this complex, spoken in the archaic language of the court.

And, once, she had not aged either. But no, he wasn't ready to consider the implications of that here. Hoa Phong was his immediate concern.

"I don't understand what you want."

Hoa Phong's face didn't move.

"Help."

Philippe gestured to the oiled paper at the window, the battered table, the chairs with the broken backs—the room that was too clean, too sharply tidied up, to hide what they didn't have.

"What makes you think we can?"

"Not 'we'. 'You'."

Hoa Phong used the singular, and an honorific he'd seldom heard—only in workers' prayers, the ones he walked away from knowing he couldn't satisfy them.

Foreigners hold our treasures and our subjects' submission.

It couldn't be the subjects—well, at least he hoped it wasn't, because he could imagine Grandmother Olympe's face if Hoa Phong walked in and attempted to convince her of the Jade Emperor's supremacy.

"Treasure," he said, flatly, since Hoa Phong didn't seem about to explain herself. He would guess, the court hadn't picked her for her diplomatic skills.

"They took something."

"They took many things," Philippe said.

Behind him, Isabelle pulled out a chair, and sat in it—frowning and trying to follow the conversation, but smart enough not to intervene. Good, because the currents in this were past her. He didn't know Hoa Phong or what power she wielded, but the fact she could just fly into their flat and coalesce from flowers suggested the main reason the court had selected her was sheer strength and endurance—and that he might not be able to match either.

"Why is this one important enough to send someone?"

Hoa Phong pursed her lips. "I'm not allowed to say."

Philippe shrugged. "Perhaps I don't care, then?"

"Don't you?" Hoa Phong asked. "I saw your face, when you touched the seal."

"I was expelled from the court." Philippe's offense had been minor—a celadon cup, broken at a banquet—but enough of a loss of face for the Jade Emperor to cast him out. To make it clear to his guests that no imperfection would be tolerated. "More than a hundred years ago."

He'd wandered the land, then, treading, lightly, on the bones of everyone he'd ever known, finding mausoleums of his own descendants—not even Hoa or Kim Cuc, because his own children had become vague myths in a golden age of inexhaustible rice and rivers bursting with fish. He'd watched the French go from merchants and missionaries and explorers to soldiers and conquerors, and the officials of the mortal court in Huê fight each other for scraps rather than unite against the threat. He'd watched spirits chained; dragons mortally wounded; mountain spirits retreating to their fastnesses. And, finally, the court that had once cast him out had closed itself off, desperate for respite from ceaseless Fallen attacks.

He ought to have been glad, but all he'd felt—all he still felt—was a bleak despair.

Hoa Phong watched him, for a while. Then she moved, fluid and inhuman, to stand by his side—the sweet smell of flowers, the trembling reminder of his past—and made a gesture with her hands. The dress shifted, uncovering the lower part of her torso, just above the hips.

"You're still a doctor," she said. "Tell me. Help me."

The wounds looked like claw marks, their edges jagged and blackened. Within were specks of mold, with that peculiar blue-gray he'd already seen on the petals. Philippe sucked in a deep breath.

"How . . .?"

"Fallen." Hoa Phong shrugged. "They're fast, and they're everywhere. And if not them—their agents are."

Isabelle had risen, come to stand near Hoa Phong. She looked at the wounds, and then back at Hoa Phong.

"You smell of death," she said, finally. "Of . . . *wrongness*. You shouldn't have been touched by it."

Hoa Phong stared at her for a while, and then at Philippe.

"Who is she?"

"A friend," Philippe said, stubbornly.

He could tell Hoa Phong wasn't happy—that she was going to come back to this. But not right now, which was something. He knelt and looked at the wounds. They'd sunk deep into flesh—the only thing preventing the infection from being carried further into the body was Hoa Phong's immortality—and even then, he could see the meridians, and how they were choked off by the rot.

"You're sick."

"Wounded," Hoa Phong said. "It'll heal."

Philippe didn't agree.

"It's a hard land," Hoa Phong said, finally. She wasn't looking at him. Her face was petals again, cheeks breaking off in chunks of whitish-yellow, hair streaming away into smoke and wind. "People ignore me, or try to kill me. Or both. I can't retrieve the object the Court sent me for alone."

Philippe took a deep, shaking breath. He'd walked away from the intrigues of the court. He owed them nothing; and they were offering him nothing.

"It's important," Hoa Phong said. Another hesitation. "In Annam ..." All of a sudden she wasn't a powerful flower spirit any longer, but a young, frightened girl with no future ahead of her. "They're at the gates now. The Fallen. Walking in the gardens, where the grass shrivels where they step, and the longevity tiles split in halves in their wake. They ..." She took a deep, deep breath. "They've killed the star maidens and driven the Weaver and the Cowherd from their domains, and uprooted the sacred banyan in the moon."

It was bad then. No, not bad. Worse than that: it was almost over.

"This thing you seek—"

"Yes."

"Will it help?"

She wasn't looking at him. Because she thought herself his inferior? The possibility hadn't even occurred to him: it was deeply disturbing.

"It's power," she said, finally. "Raw, naked magic. If it doesn't help …"

She didn't need to say it.

"Who has it? A House?"

"I don't know."

Which probably meant it was. Anything that powerful would have been claimed by a House; because that was all they did—suck others dry to maintain themselves. Parasites. But he'd made his peace with that. He wouldn't play their games. He wouldn't get involved with them. He would remain within his small community, helping it survive.

But it was his country, his countrymen, the spirits of his homeland. And if he stood by while they made their last stand, then how could he live with himself?

"I can't promise anything," he said, finally. "But I can try."

Thuan cleaned up his office, slowly and carefully. Most of the debris had been swept up by dependents. He'd insisted on it, knowing all too well the value of appearing strong at times like this, and to assert his authority as, with Asmodeus in hospital, he was nominally in charge of a House that had never really accepted him.

He'd returned Ai Nhi to her aunt Vinh Ly. The child had protested, and Vinh Ly had given her a stern talk about the importance of propriety and what an honor she'd been given—all of which had no doubt washed straight over Ai

Nhi, who considered Thuan a combination of doting uncle and surrogate father.

About forty people had been injured when the shock wave hit Hawthorn. No serious wounds. Thuan had ordered every wounded person moved to hospital, though arguably the most injured was Asmodeus, who was still in the doctors' care, but not in immediate danger. The House in Thuan's mind was quiescent again, the sense of danger to its dependents having passed.

Which meant it was time to regroup, and think things through, and plan.

Thuan penned a small, curt missive to his relatives in the dragon kingdom of the Seine. The kingdom was drained of blood and resources following an unsuccessful rebellion, and had made it abundantly clear they wouldn't intervene in the affairs of the city. Still, Thuan's Second Aunt would expect regular updates on his life, and mercilessly remind him how unfilial he was when he forgot them.

He looked outside, towards the river. The plume of smoke was still rising from Harrier, but the children of thorns were no longer watching it. He thought for a while, then he threw open the broken French windows and walked out, to stand in the middle of the ruined lawn.

He waited. The air was saturated with *khi* water again, but beneath it was the faintest tinge of fire and burned wood. There was no summoning the children. They only showed themselves to the heads of the House—and then only when they chose.

"You were on the riverbank," Thuan said, slowly. "Watching House Harrier burn."

A sigh like the wind in the branches. A sharp noise like dozens of flowers budding at once.

They came silent and invisible. One moment they weren't there, and the next they stood in front of him: children that would have seemed human, if they hadn't been woven of thorns. Three-fingered, skeletal hands, arms of branches and twigs, and bodies that were merely frames on which hung flowers the color of rot. In the hollows of their eye sockets was only darkness—the hungry, watchful kind, the devouring night only held at bay with fire and the ancestors' blessings.

"Thuan," they said. Their mouths opened in unison, but not a muscle of their faces moved. "What do you want?"

"Answers."

Laughter creaking like old wood. Like the buildings of the House. They weren't human. They'd never been: just a mask the House chose to wear when it judged suitable.

"You don't come out for trivialities," Thuan said, stubbornly. "And I don't have time to waste."

A silence.

Then, "Things are changing," one of the children said.

It stared at Thuan, but didn't blink.

"Because of a House on fire?"

The child turned, briefly, to look at the plume of smoke. Its face was almost thoughtful.

"There hasn't been war in such a long time."

"We're not at war!"

The child shrugged. "Perhaps. Perhaps not." It inclined its head, considering Thuan. "Perhaps the House is weak, and has need."

Behind the mist, on the riverbank, was a place only

the heads of House could reach: a grove of hawthorn trees garlanded with bodies. A place where the heads of the House went, hanging on hawthorn branches, their blood and magic forever feeding the wards that kept the House safe. Some dependents, too, once; but Asmodeus had changed that. The House took in outsiders, and asked sacrifices of its leaders, but not of its own.

Thuan didn't flinch. He didn't fear death. He never had. Much like Asmodeus, the only thing he feared was loss.

"Take me, then, if you think it necessary."

They'd formed in a loose circle around him. They left no tracks upon the damp grass, and anyone who saw him would assume he was talking to himself. He stared at them, levelly—at hands with long, pointed fingers, at the hawthorn flowers threaded around the hollowness of ribs.

They were the ones who looked away, eventually.

"Not yet," the child said, shaking its head. "One day."

Thuan shrugged. He kept his shoulders loose, relaxed. "We all die."

That was a worry for another time; Ancestors knew he already had enough of them.

He must have blinked, because they were gone, as if sunk back into the earth, and he was genuinely alone on the lawn. He walked back, chilled, to his office. War. Changes. He'd a lifetime's worth of changes already, all compressed into a few months—rising from being an obscure and unimportant prince of the dragon kingdom of the Seine to co-head of one of the most powerful Houses in Paris. He'd wanted time to enjoy it; or at least to make the most of it, to reform the House into a place where dragons and mortals, Fallen and natives could live together as equals.

War.

They wouldn't survive another one.

He was looking for clean paper and reports in the drawers of his battered desk when Iaris walked in.

"My lord?"

"Other people knock," Thuan said, mildly.

"Do they." Iaris smiled.

She had two underlings with her, like an honor guard—one of her nurses, Ahmed, and Mia, the Fallen with a taste for flamboyant clothes whom Thuan had seen at the entrance to the cells. The last person, who entered the room at the back of everyone else, was Phyranthe, the leader of the Court of Persuasion and, as such, Vinh Ly's hierarchical superior. She wore her fair hair cut short, and was clothed in a long flowing red dress, her usual garb when outside the cells—though the hems of its sleeves smelled faintly of encrusted blood.

That ... was not good news, whatever it was. Phyranthe was like Iaris: old guard. A Fallen who'd met Asmodeus back when he'd been head of the Court of Birth, befriended him in the Court of Persuasion, and had risen to become its leader after Asmodeus became head of the House. A stickler for rules who worshipped the ground Asmodeus trod on, and resented Thuan and the other dragons for disturbing her routine. And particularly Thuan, for convincing Asmodeus that everyone was due a fair trial before being sent to the cells.

He'd prepared poorly. Thuan should have had dragons with him: his own, loyal followers brought in from the kingdom and dispatched to every court that made up the House. He could have asked Iaris what she and Phyranthe wanted, but that would give them the upper hand, which was little better than waiting for them to speak. Instead, he pulled up the chair behind his desk, and sat down.

"Tell me what we know," he said.

Iaris grimaced. Good, bad. Good because she didn't know, and wasn't going to get the upper hand on him. Bad, because it left them in the dark. Ancestors, how much he hated playing those games, but it was the price of power. The price of having a home where he belonged, where he mattered.

"Lord Asmodeus is sleeping," she said.

Something in her voice suggested barely hidden panic, to see her idol weak.

"He needed the rest." Thuan was deadpan. "He expanded a lot of magic breaking out of the cells."

"No one else had the power to do this," Iaris said, with absolute certainty.

Sometimes he wished he shared her faith in her master—instead of seeing Asmodeus as merely … no, human was the wrong word, obviously. As a person with their own failings and strengths.

Phyranthe stirred from her chair.

"Speaking about the cells," she said.

Her voice was mild, her blue gaze expressionless, but that didn't mean anything. She'd grown up in the House under Lord Uphir, Asmodeus's predecessor, where to show the depths of her friendship with Asmodeus would have had her killed. She was used to remaining impassive.

"Yes?"

Thuan turned to her and waited. Iaris was smiling. Not good.

"I understand you made a decision to move prisoners in the cells to hospital."

Thuan stared at her. Of all the things he'd thought she might complain about ... But of course, he'd forgotten that the House still ran on fear and punishments—no matter how much he might wish otherwise.

"Hospitals is where you move gravely wounded people," he said, mildly. "No matter where they are in the House."

Phyranthe said, levelly, "They're traitors and in my care. They get to see a doctor only if I deem it appropriate."

Thuan massaged his temples. "You realize," he said, finally, "that the cells are still half-blocked off by a pile of rubble, and that several of them have collapsed walls. One of your prisoners had shattered ribs." One of the other ones—the woman with Asmodeus—had lost so much blood it was a miracle she was still upright. "Lord Asmodeus said to get them to hospital."

Mia stirred, behind Iaris. "I heard him. He said to get the woman he was holding to hospital. Not any of the other prisoners."

"I assumed ..." Thuan started, and then stopped.

He'd wanted to say he'd assumed Asmodeus's order applied to everyone in the cells, but it was the wrong tack, because he might as well be driving the knife into his own chest.

Too late: Iaris had heard him. Her smile was malicious.

"You assumed you knew the way the House worked. An easy mistake to make, when you haven't been in it long enough."

He hadn't been there twenty years ago, when Asmodeus's coup had deposed Uphir—when the old, old guard had formed, the ones who now undercut him at every turn. Because he was dragon; because he was other, but mostly because he was too newly come.

"I'm head of the House," Thuan said, mildly.

"Yes." Phyranthe's gaze held him—weighing him, seeking the exact place to insert the knife and slowly draw it, watching blood bead and muscles clench in pain. "There is that." The way she said it, it was nowhere near enough. "I'm sure you'll figure out how we work, eventually. There's a place for everything and everyone. The Court of Persuasion is where we make examples of the disloyal." She snorted. "Shattered ribs is nothing more than they deserve."

Thuan watched Iaris. She'd said nothing when he'd triaged the wounded into hospital. She'd known exactly what would happen; probably had sent one of her own subordinates straight to Phyranthe to make sure she found out, and then "helpfully" accompanied her into Thuan's office.

Ancestors, he was so tired of this. He was used to court intrigue—but at court he had allies, and here all he had were the other dragons, whose position was as beleaguered as his own.

He weighed his options. They'd come to him with the complaint rather than to Asmodeus, or to another official of the House. Which meant that, as much as Iaris was enjoying him squirm, she wasn't sure enough of her hand. He was meant to look for a way to placate her.

"I'm sure you could get the prisoners out of the hospital, and back where they belong."

Iaris was looking at him with that same smug smile. Something obvious he'd missed.

"I don't release those under my care, as Lord Asmodeus knows very well," she said. A slap in the face that wasn't even subtle. "I heal people. I don't patch them together so they can be tortured again. The Court of Persuasion has its own doctors."

Which he should have known, or remembered. Thuan stifled a curse, and gave up on subtlety. Cards on table.

"So an impasse," he said, flatly. "And don't tell me you'll tell Lord Asmodeus, because we both know you're waiting for a failing larger than this."

"Oh, but I will tell him." Iaris smiled. "I don't need a large failing. A host of little ones will do just as well, don't you think? A … realization of how utterly unsuited to the House you and yours are. It's not like he didn't have his doubts already."

"He won't discard me," Thuan said, with more confidence than he felt.

Asmodeus couldn't cut him out of being head of the House—the spell that Thuan had cast, the one that had wrested supremacy of it from Asmodeus, was one that Asmodeus had no way to undo. But being head of the House was in many ways just a title. Asmodeus could most certainly make sure Thuan didn't have any voice in the running of the House. Or, worse—set him aside as consort.

He thought of Asmodeus's lips on his—of bergamot and citrus, swallowed at the same time as a kiss—of clothes hastily torn off and the bed in Asmodeus's room creaking under him, the way the mattress enfolded them both. To lose this—to lose any of this … He had his doubts, Iaris had said. Why had he never told or shown Thuan any of this?

"You're bluffing," Thuan said.

"She's not, and neither am I," Phyranthe said, again in that same quiet voice, a statement of fact rather than a boast. She pulled on the sleeves of her dress, smiling with sharp, white teeth. "Lord Asmodeus spends enough time with us that I know exactly how he thinks. Did you think he was happy with the way things were going?"

Happy? He hadn't been, not at first. But it was over now, wasn't it? He'd become used to it.

Thuan stamped down the wave of sheer panic that shot through him, and said, "You presume a lot about the way he works."

"I don't presume," Iaris said. "I've known him for long enough. And I'll go to him—if we cannot find … an arrangement."

Of course. He was meant to be scared. To beg. To abase himself in front of both of them, so they could smooth things over—in full view of Mia and Ahmed, who'd no doubt carry the word to the House of what he'd done, on how he'd finally bent his neck and behaved. Submissive, the way natives were supposed to be in Iaris's and Phyranthe's world. Or worse, they would all keep silent, and Iaris would use what he'd done as a weapon, a handy blackmail tool to make him go her way when she needed it.

How dare they? Not in this lifetime.

"An interesting offer," Thuan said, dryly. "But I think I'll pass."

Iaris stared at him. "You'd rather risk your husband's displeasure?"

Thuan snorted. "Try it."

He made it come out as supreme confidence, rather than show them how rattled he was.

"An unwise choice." Phyranthe looked like she'd swallowed something sour, and was searching for someone to vent her temper on. "Very unwise, my lord."

Thuan smiled, letting a fraction of his dragon's maw flicker into existence.

"I'll make sure Lord Asmodeus knows about what happened, though in the light of what happened to the House I imagine he'll have bigger fish to fry."

His version against theirs. How would Asmodeus react? Probably smiling, and not doing anything one way or the other.

Not yet.

"Was there anything else?" Thuan asked Phyranthe.

She shook her head. For a moment he thought she was going to say something about how bad his choices were again, and then the moment passed.

"No, my lord."

One point to him, though he felt about as annoyed as Phyranthe—and he knew it'd come back to bite him, one way or another.

"Then you may leave."

He waited until she and Iaris were almost at the door before saying, "Iaris. Stay a moment, will you? I need to discuss House business with you."

Iaris turned. For a moment he thought he'd gone too far—that she'd snap.

"Iaris." Ahmed's voice was low and urgent.

"My lord."

Her smile was edged and forced as she came back into

the room, and sat again in her chair. Mia and Ahmed visibly hesitated, but Thuan gestured for them to leave as well. He'd had enough of Iaris's supporters and underlings as it was.

He made her wait: he'd earned a little pettiness, a little reminder that he was technically her superior. He rearranged the papers on his desk, carefully and completely unnecessarily.

"I want to talk about the fire," he said. "The one in House Harrier, which set off all of this."

Iaris stared back. "You worry too much, my lord. We can most certainly survive fire. Ice, on the other hand …"

Good to know that she didn't let setback keep her down. The allusion was deliberately nasty: it was ice from a rebel dragon that had almost ended the House, weakening Asmodeus so much he'd had no choice but to accept Thuan's coming, and of course Iaris would throw this into his face.

"Ice isn't going to be a problem," Thuan said, firmly. "Or internal rebellions."

He watched Iaris: she flinched, for the barest of moments. Her only daughter had been cast out for disloyalty, and the only reason she wasn't dead was because Asmodeus valued Iaris too much, and had chosen to exercise mercy.

"This is another threat."

"Do tell me," Iaris's smile was edged.

She'd gotten over her initial panic at seeing Asmodeus weak, but she was still on edge. Not that it stopped her being unpleasant to Thuan.

"I have it on good authority that House Harrier was blown apart," Thuan said. There was nothing written on the papers, but there didn't need to be. The smell of sandalwood wafted up from the incense sticks in his desk drawers; he inhaled, trying to steady himself. "There's nothing more than a field of ruins where it used to stand. I don't know who's survived, or not, and if the House is still in play."

"It takes more than that to kill a House," Iaris said. Her voice was sharp.

Thuan raised an eyebrow, his best imitation of Asmodeus. "We don't exactly know what happened, do we?"

Houses had died during the Great Houses War; but they had been overrun by their enemies, their dependents fled or killed, their heart of power annihilated. Even the explosion of House Hell's Toll's armory had merely been the prelude to all-out assault.

But there was no longer a war, and things were supposed to be more civilized. As if anyone believed that: that the new, polite masks were anything more than an illusory facade; that the war hadn't moved into the salons and reception rooms, its battles fought with loss of face, diplomacy and the careful dance of threats from the more powerful Houses to get their way in all things.

Unfortunately, insofar as Hawthorn went, they weren't strong enough to risk threatening anyone.

"Tell me where we stand," Thuan said, again.

"You know all there is to know about Harrier."

He raised an eyebrow. "I was under the impression you didn't think I knew enough about other Houses."

Iaris flinched. Only a little, and not for long, but Thuan had good eyes.

He said, "They're our southern neighbors. Our unfriendly southern neighbors, because they think we're too nice to mortals. They invited us to the First Presentation, didn't they?"

"Yes." Iaris closed her eyes. "I can find more information, but ..."

"Give me what you have."

"For all their bluster, House Harrier's power relies on its human magicians," she said. "And the strength of their head rests on how many they can call loyal. The Presentation was going to be ... a show of strength. A private Harrier ceremony made public for the first time—when its child-magicians leave the Warded Chambers in the Great Interior and become adults in the eyes of the House."

Thuan could read between the lines.

"So Guy and Andrea were in trouble, and eager to show they weren't afraid by having outsiders come deep into the House. Inner power struggles?"

Iaris hesitated, obviously reluctant to commit herself by speculating.

"All our informants suggest so, my lord."

Thuan thought, for a while. House Hawthorn was still putting itself back together after the cataclysmic events that had brought him to be head of the House, its territory shared between dragon and Fallen magic. And the shock wave of House Harrier's explosion had made enough wounded.

"It sounds like someone tried to depose Guy and got a little overenthusiastic," he said.

"I couldn't say, my lord."

No, obviously she wouldn't: it wasn't her business, but Asmodeus's and the Court of House.

"Keep an eye on it, will you? This has no reason to affect us."

It was too early to say, but he dearly hoped they'd sit this one out. They needed time: the House wasn't strong enough, or whole enough, to involve itself in the chaos that would follow as every House in Paris scrabbled to fill the power void.

They could use the breathing space of not being at the top of everyone's target list.

"I presume we sent a delegation to that First Presentation ceremony." Thuan had no memory of handling this, which probably meant Asmodeus had. "If they're not back today, then find them."

They weren't dead, because he'd know it, but the sense of the dependents he had in his mind didn't extend to their precise location, unless they had tracking disks with them.

Iaris's face was a careful blank.

"Find out who went," Thuan ordered.

"My lord."

Iaris bowed, not deep or long enough.

Thuan watched her leave. She was … he wouldn't say cowed, exactly. Merely inconvenienced—and he heard that last word the way Asmodeus would say it, smiling sharply when describing someone's mortal wound. Thuan had called her and Physanthe's plot for what it was: a play on weak foundations. But they would try again.

They'd stymied him before, but coming at him so brazenly meant they were surer of themselves than they'd been. Something had changed, and he was deathly afraid that what had changed was Asmodeus himself.

He wanted to go out and sit by Asmodeus's bed until

Asmodeus finally woke up—kissing him fiercely and asking him for an honest answer, the kind Asmodeus never gave anyway. But he hadn't lost all common sense yet. Revealing a weakness of that magnitude to Iaris would have consequences for him long before Asmodeus was in any state to deal with anything.

Thuan went back to what he'd been doing, and finally managed to retrieve the reports on the House's budget he'd been forwarded before his office exploded. He didn't usually involve himself in the affairs of the Court of Hearth. Like Asmodeus, he was a member of the Court of House only, dealing with the diplomatic business of managing the other Houses. But, with the shaken dependents and the influx of wounded in the hospital, there was work to do. Like increasing the food supply—the rotten food grown in what was left of the countryside after the war. How he wished that the dragon kingdom hadn't closed itself off to all traffic and commerce. Under the Seine there would be jujubes and mangoes and rambutans—not pure or uncontaminated, but tasting sweet and pleasant, and not like the bland cardboard with a faint aftertaste of mold that seemed to overlay everything in Paris. But the dragon kingdom, convulsing and dying from its internal power struggles, had made it very clear they would have nothing more to do with the city, not even in an emergency.

He was halfway through a particularly difficult calculation involving three different pages of three different reports when someone knocked on the door.

"Yes?"

Not Iaris, which was a relief. Unless she'd learned politeness in the past hours, which he doubted.

It was Sang, one of the dragons who worked in the Court of Strength—the court providing bodyguards, soldiers and security to the House. She was wearing the House's uniform, her hair impeccably tied into a topknot. She had to be one of the only dragons either oblivious or confident enough to wear a halfway shape, which showed the antlers on either side of her head, a scattering of scales on her face, and a faint sheen of rainwater around her as she walked.

"Your Majesty," she said.

Thuan winced. He'd tried to explain he wasn't their king, but the traditionalists among them had just ignored him.

"What's going on?"

Sang was one of the dragons he almost never saw in his office. The Court of Strength was not in Iaris's orbit, but rather attached personally to Asmodeus—and they had effortlessly transferred over that loyalty to Thuan. He got written reports from Sang on other Courts' politics, some funny tidbits about who was sleeping with whom in the Court itself, and that was about all.

"It's … hard to explain." Sang sounded embarrassed, as if bringing something too small to his attention. Except it was Sang, which meant the "something too small" really was an emergency. "I think you should come. I mean, strictly, it's not my business, it's the Court of Persuasion's …"

The Court of Persuasion. Phyranthe. Iaris. Thuan was on his feet and at the door in a heartbeat, grabbing Sang as he passed.

"Let's go."

3
Ruins of the House

Emmanuelle wandered the ruins of House Harrier in a daze.

She'd left the distant shadow of the Great Interior behind her, trying to move away from people, from the sound of fighting, from all of it. She'd walked north, or what she thought or hoped was north, along small streets until she stumbled along a larger one—Boulevard de Grenelle? It was hard to tell anymore. The verdant trees were blackened and burned, and all the windows were smashed. No people, either; just bodies poking out from the debris, and an unbroken silence spreading around her like that of the grave.

She turned east, because why not.

The sky was the color of the storm, and as she walked on it darkened, until she seemed to be the only source of light. She wasn't burning as brightly, was she? She didn't feel warm anymore, and the patch of light she'd thrown across the ground seemed smaller now. Was she back to the small, barely visible light all Fallen naturally emitted?

She'd wrapped her torn petticoats tightly around her. Dried blood still caked her arms and legs. She couldn't stop shivering, and from time to time the cobblestones seemed to buckle underfoot, and send her sprawling to the ground—or had she missed a step? It didn't seem possible to forget something as simple as walking, but nothing seemed to fit anymore.

At length she reached a place where there were no trees anymore, just smithereens of blasted wood, and ashes and dust. Above her and in front of her was smoke, a cloud dense enough to engulf the entire world.

No exit that way. She wouldn't even be able to *breathe* in there.

Whatever had propelled Emmanuelle this far gave out. She sat down like a puppet with cut strings, staring at the smoke. Something was burning. Something had shaken the House to its foundation. Morningstar. She needed to find Morningstar—how had they been separated?

She must have fallen asleep again, because suddenly there were footsteps, getting nearer. She tried to rise and run, but she didn't have anything left in her.

A silhouette, getting nearer and nearer. A fuzzy shape against the darkness around her, with the faint light of Fallen magic wrapped around them. A small, whipcord body, with short hair—no, not short hair. No hair at all: merely elaborate henna markings on a shaved head, not in one of the bridal styles used by mortals, but traceries of brushed letters, like the obsolete alphabets in books of magic.

Darrias.

House Hawthorn's envoy. Her … friend, she guessed? She was never sure where she stood with Darrias. They had so much in common, but belonged to different

Houses. Especially Hawthorn, with whom Silverspires had a barbed, quiescent sort of peace: friendship almost seemed possible, in those circumstances.

"Emmanuelle? What are you doing here?"

She still wore the swallowtail coat and trousers of Hawthorn, in silver and gray that outlined the perfect shape of her body. But the swallowtail was cut in multiple places, and one leg of the trousers ended above her knee.

"I don't know," Emmanuelle said, honestly. Running away, as far as she could; trying to avoid unknown territory and making things worse with every step. "I don't understand—"

"How I found you? You've been shining like a beacon from three streets away. It's a wonder I'm the first. What's wrong with you?"

"I don't know."

It felt absurd to admit her ignorance, especially to an envoy of another House. Emmanuelle tried to get up, but the world spun and spun, and the cobblestones rushed up to meet her.

Darrias knelt by her side.

"Never mind. You're not well."

"You don't have to help," Emmanuelle said.

Darrias rolled her eyes. "Yes, I'm sure I could leave you here to die."

"I don't belong to—"

"Hawthorn?" Darrias laughed. "In the current circumstances, we envoys need to stick together. Arguably"—she smiled, and it was grim and unamused—"I owe you a debt, anyway."

"You don't," Emmanuelle said. "Anyone would have done the same."

Darrias had formerly been House Harrier's hound—sent by Guy to enforce his will in the world outside. She'd defected from Harrier to Hawthorn when her sympathies for mortals and the Houseless had earned her Lord Guy's enmity, and Emmanuelle had happened to be in the right time at the right place. Yes, she could have stopped Darrias, but that would have meant handing her back to Guy and his twisted ideas of punishment. It hadn't been a choice.

"I don't think so," Darrias said, in a way that shut the conversation down. "Come on. We have to get you to hospital—there's a school on rue Fondary. Their infirmary might have first aid supplies . . ."

Of course, this area had once been Darrias's home. She would be intimately familiar with the streets, although some things were bound to have changed. Emmanuelle bit back bitter laughter. Obviously *everything* had changed.

"Not in Harrier," Emmanuelle said. "I need to get out—back to Silverspires. I—"

"There's no exit here." Darrias pulled Emmanuelle up—businesslike and with no particular gentleness. "The Seine bridges, maybe, but you won't want to get into Hawthorn territory. Hospital, Emmanuelle."

They walked in awkward silence, Darrias supporting Emmanuelle with one shoulder—stopping, without a word, when Emmanuelle's legs spasmed.

They left the smoke behind. Emmanuelle didn't realize how much it had affected her until she took a deep breath and it didn't hurt. As they walked, their surroundings became buildings rather than smoke and vaporized stone. Debris cluttered the streets. There was a faint smell of smoke in the air, coming from minor fires. It wafted through the broken windows of the buildings' ground floors, clinging to the limestone, and to the small garden courtyards they saw through bent and torn-off wrought-iron gates. Darrias sniffed.

"Private hearths," she said. "The embers will have scattered outside the chimneys, and the floorboards just caught fire."

The people they saw had to belong to Harrier, but the colors were torn, covered by blood and ash and smoke. They looked at Darrias and Emmanuelle with curiosity, and then moved on, calling for their relatives and friends. They weren't interested in outsiders: merely in finding their own.

"I don't understand what happened," Emmanuelle said, slowly.

It seemed safer than any other subject of conversation, right now. She was missing part of the previous night, and the morning which she'd spent unconscious: it was now early afternoon.

Darrias grunted as Emmanuelle shifted position on her shoulder. She moved forward, one booted foot striking flakes of limestone from the ground. Beside her lay a middle-aged man with open eyes, chest broken and limbs splayed out. His jacket still hung from the lamppost above him—he must have been flung into the air and then back on to the killing ground.

"Something exploded." She shrugged—a movement that didn't even seem to faze her and lifted Emmanuelle off the ground for a brief moment. "That cloud of smoke? Dupleix has the armory."

Something swam up the morass of Emmanuelle's memories.

"It already blew up. In the eighteenth century. Surely they'd have made sure ..."

Darrias snorted. "It's *ammunition.* There would be wards and safeguards, but it's made to blow up, ultimately."

Emmanuelle tried to remember Selene's briefing.

"Guy was barely holding on to the House."

"Yes." Darrias sounded annoyed.

Ahead of them, the street reached a large crossroads: not the usual square ones of the House, but one with multiple streets at odd angles. Ruined shops, their window displays full of shards and rubble—and people crowding at the entrances, trying to pull others out.

"Here." She turned right, into one of the smaller side streets. "Almost there. How are you?"

She hadn't really answered Emmanuelle's question. Nor was Emmanuelle sure she could answer hers.

"I'm really not sure," she said.

She felt tired, and worn, but surely that was only stress and fatigue? She was not welcome in Harrier, and would never be.

Ahead was a large gate, the classic green-painted carriage entrance. It now lay broken and half-covered in debris. Darrias stepped over the threshold, pausing to help Emmanuelle. Her feet slipped, and she was only saved from falling because Darrias grabbed her. Inside was a small cobbled street with diseased trees. The trees were still there, but the cobblestones had burst upwards like boils. They went slowly, nothing but silence in their wake. No one, either: not even bodies, as if the place had emptied itself early.

"It's a school," Darrias said. "They had the day off for First Presentation."

Emmanuelle bit her lip, thinking of the teachers. Darrias turned right again, into one of the smaller buildings with a courtyard. It was intact: the trees flecked with mold; the iron gates freshly painted; a little path running through the small garden to the front door. The door itself hung askew, the stained glass of its top half yellowed and streaked with magical residue—it left a faint sting on Emmanuelle's hand as she brushed against it.

Inside, it was dark, and cool. Emmanuelle had a brief, confused moment as Darrias steered her through empty rooms filled with rows of pupils' desks, and corridors whose cracked, tiled walls were covered with colorful drawings. Magic still saturated the air—wards that still held, though they had taken a battering. Then she was sitting on a bed, without remembering how she got there, watching Darrias forage through the drawers of a medicine cabinet, muttering to herself angrily as she discarded empty wrapping after empty wrapping. On the walls were posters from before the war: faraway destinations; the Fallen's latest conquests; crinolines and other fashions from the heady, gilded days when Paris was the center of the world; the Universal Exhibition at the Trocadéro and its colonial displays. That last had a reconstruction of an African village in the gardens of the Trocadéro, with what looked like a mix of ethnicities dressed awkwardly in some white person's idea of tribal garb. They were behind bars: on display, like a zoo. Conquests. Emmanuelle's hands clenched. She wasn't from Africa, though her physical manifestation was Black; but for an accident of timing it might well have been her, in the cage.

"Here," Darrias said. She filled a bowl from the water basin, and brought it to the bed. "You can clean your wounds, at least."

She put both hands on either side of the bowl, and squeezed as she said the words of a spell. A faint sheet of invisible fire hovered over the surface of the water for a second and every speck of dust or debris in the bowl burst into flames, in defiance of the liquid they floated in.

"That should be sterile. Careful, it's hot." Her voice was deadpan.

Neither her ash-stained clothes, nor even the petticoats were sterile. Emmanuelle washed her hands, and used the rest of the water to clean her bloodstained arms. Her body was resistant to most infections, and the wounds would heal by themselves, given a chance. In her state of exhaustion, though, it would take a long while. She ran a hand through her hair, which she wore in neat, tight unprocessed curls cut close to the scalp. It felt dry and brittle; the magic that usually kept her body healthy was running low. Not good.

"You really need a doctor," Darrias said. "You do recognize your own symptoms?"

Emmanuelle shook her head, and then memory, inexorable, took over, and provided the answer she'd been dancing around. Vomiting. Fever. Spasms. Irritation and depression. And the hole in her memories: that evening that kept being filled with the oddest excuses. She'd read about this, in the Silverspires library.

"Some kind of brain injury. You know, a doctor would only tell me to rest."

For months; and she didn't have that time.

Darrias echoed her thoughts. "Which you're unlikely to do if you want to survive." She glared at the drawers as if she could conjure bandages and medicine out of them. "Everything of use has been taken. People. The slightest hint of trouble, and they turn feral."

Emmanuelle leaned back against the raised back of the bed.

"That's unfair," she said, exhaling. "They've never endured hardship."

"In Harrier?" Darrias laughed, and it was low, and without joy. "Where the mortals bow and scrape to Fallen for fear they'll be whipped or taken apart? You've seen the flat cages. What Guy does to dissidents."

The flat cages: gratings that looked as though they might lead into the sewers, but which covered exiguous cells, where shackled prisoners sat until their limbs atrophied and they starved to death, or until the guards received orders to pour in quicklime and stand aside as the screams started. Everyone knew what they were, and everyone gave them a wide berth. Darrias had left Harrier before Guy could put her in one, but as she spoke Emmanuelle could see the old tenseness returning to her face.

"You're safe," she said. "You're Hawthorn's. Everyone knows Asmodeus comes after those who harm his own. Guy can't touch you."

Darrias looked as though she was going to say something, but someone spoke first.

"Mistress Darrias?"

A low, puzzled voice from the entrance. An older Maghrebi woman wearing a scarf around her head, in the colors of Harrier, staring from Darrias to Emmanuelle in growing confusion; and a child of perhaps six or seven years old, clinging to her. The old woman's forehead was cut, and blood had crusted over her eyes—she looked as unsteady on her feet as Emmanuelle did, but she still attempted to kneel.

"Mistress, I'm sorry. I hadn't seen you were back."

Darrias's face went very still. "Louiza. I'm not in Harrier anymore. Don't."

"You're Fallen—"

"Don't."

Darrias slammed the drawers closed, and went to the woman. She pulled her up. The child had started kneeling, too: she looked uncertainly from Louiza to Darrias, and finally stood, shaking and tense, protecting herself against the inevitable beating.

Darrias said, again, "Louiza, I'm not your mistress, or anyone else's."

Louiza looked unconvinced. Her eyes moved to Emmanuelle. She couldn't possibly see much, could she, with the blood. Emmanuelle pulled herself up, intending to tear a piece of cloth from her petticoats and give it to Louiza. She wasn't sure exactly what went wrong—something must have spasmed at the wrong time? Some muscles not properly answering?—but she tripped over her own feet, and only a last-minute catch on the edge of the table kept her upright.

"Here," she said, forcing her voice to remain steady. "You can use this to clean your face."

The child walked, slowly to Emmanuelle; stared at her with wide eyes.

"Mamma," she said. "She's Fallen."

And Black, which she probably hadn't expected.

"It's all right," Emmanuelle said.

She didn't feel as angry as Darrias at House Harrier's customs, but only because she was so exhausted.

Darrias said to Louiza, "This is Emmanuelle. Louiza, and her daughter Jamila."

Louiza looked as though she was going to bow down again. She took the petticoats from Jamila, used a strip of them to wipe the blood from her eyes. Her face was wrinkled and exhausted beneath it.

"We're looking for medical supplies," Darrias said. "There's nothing in these drawers."

Looking for medical supplies. And so was Louiza, wasn't she?

Louiza stared from Darrias to the empty drawers. Jamila moved, slowly, cautiously—looking at Emmanuelle and Darrias to see if they'd interrupt her—making a slow and wavering way to the cabinet. She bent down, rifling through the drawers.

"Do you know what happened?" Emmanuelle said.

Louiza looked uncomfortable. It was Jamila—her hands wedged firmly in one of the smallest drawers—who spoke.

"There was a sound," she said. "And all the windows blew in."

"The armory," Darrias said. "It was a challenge."

Louiza grimaced. "I don't do politics, Mistress. Please."

"I told you not to call me 'mistress'!" Darrias raised a hand as though she might strike her, and then caught herself. "I'm sorry, Louiza. Tell me what you know."

The look on their faces broke Emmanuelle's heart—it wasn't that they were hurt. It was *comfort*—because Darrias was finally acting like a Fallen inside the House, ordering them around, threatening them.

"No," she said, before she could think. "You're not playing that game."

Darrias turned to her, the shadow of long, black wings unfolding behind her, hands outstretched with a knife in her right one that looked like an extension of her body.

"Really? This isn't the time for the moral high ground."

They'd had that argument so many times before: Darrias was highly pragmatic and utterly without scruples, and she thought Emmanuelle's desire to do the right thing was just a waste of time. She tolerated it, as much as one might tolerate a puppy play-biting: only so long as it didn't become a bother.

"It's *always* the time," Emmanuelle said.

She wasn't that irritable, as a rule, but she hadn't expected Darrias to bring this up again. After several heated conversations, they'd both reached an accommodation where neither of them brought up the subject anymore, for the sake of friendship: the difference was just too strong and utterly irreconcilable. To have it come up now felt like a slap in the face, and an unwelcome reminder she couldn't count on Darrias all the way.

"The moment you argue that rules need to be relaxed—that it's a matter of life and death and urgency—you're admitting that they're not worth anything."

Darrias tensed, as if to leap or fight, but Jamila spoke first.

"Look, look!" She waved two rolls of bandages at them, and a pill box.

The tension deflated. Darrias shrugged, and the knife was back in its sheath. Emmanuelle didn't even see it vanish.

Jamila handed her finds to Darrias, maintaining a cautious distance from her. Darrias's lips pursed.

"Your mother can use the bandages," she said to Jamila, handing one roll to her. "Here." She threw the other one to Emmanuelle. "The pills are aspirin." She considered. "Too risky, I think. Thinning your blood in these circumstances is probably not a good idea. Fallen can bleed to death."

She sounded like she was speaking from experience. She might be, at that.

Emmanuelle wasn't sure she actually needed the bandages, but she wrapped her lower arms anyway, if only to make it clear to Jamila that her efforts hadn't been wasted. The girl had run back to her mother and clung to her skirts.

"What now?" Emmanuelle asked.

Darrias's smile was the thin edge of a knife.

"We find a way out of the House."

"Morningstar . . ." Emmanuelle said, slowly.

She kept expecting him to turn up. To be by her side as he'd promised, no matter how impossible that seemed. The hole in her memory was still there—whenever she thought of him she'd seen him do improbable, impossible things. Fighting Harrier envoys with his two-handed sword—the one that had been lost long ago—laughing at something Guy said, except whenever had Guy been in Emmanuelle's rooms? Brain injury. Something had carved out pieces of her past, and she couldn't seem to return them no matter how hard she strove.

"I came with him. And a delegation."

"It's each person for themselves now," Darrias said. "I don't know where he is, and you don't either." Her voice was questioning.

"No."

There were tracking disks, and spells—the sort of thing the House would give to dependents before they went into danger. Harrier, for all that it was inimical to Silverspires, shouldn't have been a zone where dependents could go missing.

"We don't have any particular contacts."

"Then he's on his own." Darrias's voice was mildly acid. "I'm sure he could charm the socks off even Guy, if he tried."

Louiza looked horrified.

Emmanuelle said, "Morningstar isn't from the same House as Darrias."

Not quite true: Darrias's opinion of Morningstar was close to Asmodeus's—and Asmodeus hated Morningstar's guts. He thought someone with Morningstar's powers should be much more dedicated to protecting his companions.

Darrias said, to Louiza, "I need to know what's happening in Harrier. Please."

Louiza opened her mouth. "I don't know," she said. And then, slowly, carefully, "Exalted Benedict died last night. I think …" She stopped, again.

Darrias's voice was gentle. "Go on."

"Lord Guy was weak," Louiza's voice was harsh: it was merely a fact of life to her. "Benedict was the last of his children. The most powerful, but even power fails in the end."

Thoughts swam up: a room in Silverspires where Selene and Father Javier briefed Emmanuelle on what to expect about Harrier. The children—the magicians, the backbone of Harrier's power.

All Fallen were sterile: they could take mortal lovers, but neither bear nor father children. They could, however, adopt them. Harrier had raised adoption to—Emmanuelle would have said—an art form ... if the House itself, and all it represented, that thoughtless ideal of Fallen supremacy, hadn't been so abhorrent to her. Harrier's Fallen could take a favorite: a mortal woman with child, whom they would keep by their side throughout her pregnancy and the first years of the child, saturating fetus and then child with their magic as they grew. A Fallen could breed several children in that way, who would owe their loyalty only to them—and Guy had risen to become head of Harrier on the strength of his numerous magician children.

But a head of House no longer had the leisure or inclination to raise children who needed to be by their side at all times. And so, in the end, their power weakened and a Fallen with more children overthrew them, to begin the cycle again.

"Benedict," Emmanuelle said, tasting the word on her tongue. The name made cold sweat break out on her skin. She felt dizzy, her head growing too large, her skin too tight to house her skull—as if there was something she ought to remember but couldn't quite place, something that had once chilled her to the bone. "Guy's son."

"He took too many wounds in a skirmish. House Silverspires killed him."

Mild resentment in Louiza's voice, that Emmanuelle would be from Silverspires and not know that.

Emmanuelle ignored it. She didn't keep close track of every time the House fought other Houses.

"So Guy's foremost supporter dies. He clings to power, and someone blows up the armory to overthrow him?"

"I don't know," Louiza said. "Lord Guy has shut himself in the Great Interior with the magicians. He's besieged."

The other ones, the children of the other Fallen in the House—who would they be loyal to?

"Who's besieging him?"

"It was Ichestra," Louiza said. The name was vaguely familiar to Emmanuelle: one of Guy's best acolytes and mother of five magicians. "But she was wounded, too. So Niraphanes took her place." That name was unfamiliar.

"No," Darrias said.

Louiza's face froze in fear. "I'm sorry, Mistress."

Darrias shook her head. "Don't be. Who else?"

"Minor factions." Louiza cited half a dozen names that were utterly unfamiliar to Emmanuelle. "They'll have exhausted themselves, or been absorbed by Niraphanes before anything could happen."

"All right," Emmanuelle said, cautiously. "I'm not too sure how relevant that is to finding our way out." Other than, obviously, finding out that Niraphanes—whoever she was—and Darrias really didn't get on.

"Because we need someone to escort us out," Darrias said. "The North Gate is cut off by smoke, and there's fighting at the East Gate, and guards. They'll want to make sure that Guy doesn't escape, so they won't allow anyone out. Harrier's succession line works by displaying the body of the previous head, as evidence that they're dead. Well, what's left of the body, anyway."

"As envoys . . ." Emmanuelle started, and then stopped.

"They'll want us to leave? Yes," Darrias said. "If you can prevent soldiers or dependents from stabbing us by mistake." Her face softened. "The stakes are too high. Their first order of business will be making sure Lord Guy and dependents of Harrier and House magicians don't escape. Envoys dying? That'd be inconvenient, but they can always negotiate reparations afterwards. We're not big fish. Well, most of us aren't."

Emmanuelle laughed, shortly. "Selene is pragmatic. She knows Silverspires can't afford a war with anyone."

Darrias looked, for a moment, horrified—and that took some doing.

"You're her partner. Surely . . ."

Surely she'd want to level the House that killed Emmanuelle? She'd want to. But she had the welfare of her own dependents to think of, and eventually Father Javier or another one of her advisers would make her see this.

"I'd rather leave a legacy of Silverspires alive and well," Emmanuelle said, mildly, "than one of scorched earth, and the scant comfort that everyone fought to death to avenge me." It was a kinder, better thought to hold on to, at any rate. She took a deep, trembling breath, and didn't really feel better. "I don't suppose anyone has any food—" she started, and stopped, because Jamila was at her feet, holding out a grimy bar of unidentifiable food like some great treasure.

Darrias looked amused, though her smile had teeth.

"You'll learn anything you say, as one of the Fallen, is treated like a wish to be fulfilled here. Be careful what you say."

Emmanuelle bit back a curse. "I don't—"

"You do need it," Darrias said. "Come on, eat it." She threw something at Emmanuelle. "And take this."

It was a flat, featureless disk with no arms on it, carved from some smooth, translucent opal-like stone. When she took it, she felt no magic on her skin.

"It doesn't look like much."

"You're Fallen," Darrias said. "If it spends enough time on you it'll light up like a bonfire. In the meantime, it'll look like a useless trinket, which has its uses."

"Tracking disk?"

Darrias shook her head. "Beacon. Tracking disks are useless, if both users aren't bound to the same House. This just sends a burst of magic."

"To everyone in the vicinity?"

"That's the drawback. It's not discreet and it's not subtle. But we're past that, aren't we? Eat up. And then we'll figure out what to ..." She bit her lip. "Niraphanes." She sounded annoyed. "I guess we have no choice but to see her."

She clearly didn't like it. What was her relationship with Niraphanes? All bad, it seemed.

Aurore hadn't expected to wake up in a large and well-lit hospital room; or to wake up at all, if she was honest with herself.

Everything hurt. The bandages she could see were encrusted with dried blood—and when she closed her eyes she saw Asmodeus's face, and felt the knife biting, again and again, into the flesh of her arms and chest as she strained at the restraints tying her to the chair.

She'd thought she was going to die; and been surprised, when that thought came, that it didn't scare her anymore. That the only thing that did was a deeper, older memory: a long, seemingly endless evening in Harrier, her and her sister Cassiopée held down and beaten, again and again, until everything fractured and bled, and the world constellated into ten thousand hurts. The only thing that had come to her in the cells of Hawthorn was a dim, distant annoyance that it was her own fault for being this foolhardy and getting caught, so she didn't even have the satisfaction of blaming someone else for her agony.

But here she was. Alive, and healing. Probably just a temporary respite until Asmodeus came back; though why would he bother to heal her first? The orderlies who came to change her sheets were tight-lipped, and the nurses likewise.

She should rest. She should make the most of it; but she was exhausted and drained, and nothing made sense. Cassiopée would be worrying by now, wondering why Aurore hadn't come back; though her sister would know the answer in her heart of hearts. They'd both survived Harrier, and they knew how fickle and bloodthirsty the Houses could be.

In the evening, as the House fell silent—as the hospital darkened and the cracked tiles on the walls turned red in the setting sun—the door of her room opened.

"There you are."

It was *him*. Asmodeus. The Fallen head of House

Hawthorn. For a moment her memory wavered, and he stood at the door to her cell, smiling at her with his sharp, white teeth, the light gleaming on the branches of his horn-rimmed glasses, on the blade of the knife in his hands—everything trembling and unfocused, moments before the pain started.

"I thought it expedient to continue the conversation we were having earlier. Such an enjoyable time. It's a shame it had to end early."

Aurore stared at her hands, and then back at him.

"You're Houseless and you have no business here. Tell me why you thought sneaking into my House was a good idea."

He walked into the room, his pale skin lambent with magic, the smell of bergamot and citrus fruit clinging to his clothes. He was lithe and impossibly graceful: a sated cat. He pulled up the one chair in the room—a large, plump Louis XV armchair with curved legs and blood-red upholstery. He sat in it, watching her as if she were a particularly interesting problem—playing, nonchalantly, with a knife. The same one he'd used down in the cells.

Aurore ought to be scared, but all she felt was anger. His House. His land. His dependents. Owning everything he liked, and bleeding those he didn't exploit in another way for his own pleasure.

She said, slowly, softly—keeping her eyes away from him, as though embarrassed, "They say … They say you have *rong*"—she used the Viet word, and then corrected herself—"dragons in Hawthorn. My child is sick. I thought they could cure her …"

She let the words trail away. Every word was true, but

put together none of it was. Marianne did have a fever that wouldn't break, but Aurore already knew none of the Houses would ever help her, because they were Houseless, because they were poor and insignificant. What she'd wanted from Hawthorn was something different—a pathway to coming into her own power. But he wouldn't react the same way to that truth. A mother trying to heal her child was pathetic and harmless, someone he might spare on a whim, his curiosity sated. A rival for his magic was another matter.

It was foolhardy in the extreme to lie to him, but she had little to lose, anymore. She'd gone through fire and pain once and survived, what more could he do to her?

Still … Still, in that stretched-out moment of silence when he looked at her—when he weighed her words, weighed her worth—she found that she was shaking. Fear, or anticipation? She couldn't tell, not anymore.

A noise, from the chair. She looked up and saw he was laughing. Not maliciously or even indifferently: simply the good-natured laughter of a parent amused by the antics of a child. The knife vanished—as it did, she saw the slight shaking of his hands.

"A desperate mother." Asmodeus took off his glasses, wiped them clean with an embroidered handkerchief in the gray-and-silver of the House. "Mortals can be so … disappointingly surprising, sometimes."

Aurore couldn't help herself. "Because you wouldn't do the same for a dependent? Move Heaven and Earth to help them?"

A sharp, appraising look. "Perhaps I would. You seem very well informed."

A mistake. "You have to be, to survive on the streets."

"Indeed. An unfriendly place."

Mocking her again: his kind had never seen the streets, and never would.

Aurore forced herself to look at her hands. She said, finally, "I don't understand why I'm here."

"Instead of in the cells?" His smile was wide. "There was a little … accident."

"Accident?"

"The building collapsed. A large part of it. You wouldn't remember."

She didn't. Everything had been blood and pain by then, her thoughts clinging to the need to remain silent, not to tell him why she was in his House—because it was her only chance of survival and she clung to it, even when survival had become distant and unattainable.

Then what he'd said hit her. The building collapsed. Houses didn't just *collapse*. They weren't vulnerable. Nor did Fallen shake as though with weakness when putting knives away. She wanted, desperately, to ask what happened, but that was the wrong question. It would be too sharp, too on point—and he was already suspicious.

"Please," she said. "I was reckless. Let me go."

If he freed her, she could try again. She could look for the evidence she wanted—track, again, that legend of an artifact hidden in Hawthorn, one that gave their wielder magic that didn't need to be replenished by the Fallen. Her sister Cassiopée had only given her fragmentary evidence—a building with imprints of deer antlers on the gates, and a path to follow from it—but in her brief time in Hawthorn, she'd found neither building nor path.

That low, amused laughter again. "I think not."

Abruptly, he was standing by the bed, the smell of bergamot and citrus fruit overwhelming. The knife was out again, and magic pinned her where she sat, sharp restraints at wrists and ankles and shoulders.

"I wouldn't move, if I were you," Asmodeus said. "It'd only hurt more, and of course there's the risk I might slip and slash something I hadn't intended to touch. Like an artery."

Please please no.

In spite of everything, she braced herself against the pain to come. Of course he'd never let her go. Of course he'd take what he'd started to his obvious end. His kind always did.

He tilted her head upwards: for a moment she was staring into gray-green eyes, a widening gulf of hunger that couldn't be sated, that would take her and use her and drain her until nothing was left—and then his gaze moved downwards, to the hollow of her collarbone, the knife's blade rising, and nothing she could do to stop him …

It bit, once, twice: a sharp, flaring pain spreading to the upper part of her chest. And then his other hand coming up, flat against the wound he'd opened, and the pain opened like serrated blossoms, sending shoots to every part of her body. She convulsed then, crying out, but he'd already withdrawn, to sit down again in the chair.

"As it happens, I have need of someone expendable, and you're perfect."

He smiled, watching her as he might an insect.

The magic vanished. Aurore looked down, with some difficulty. There was … something in her chest, above her breasts. She couldn't see it clearly. She raised her hand—felt only the harsh smoothness of wood. Engraved wood, with a pattern she couldn't make out; it seemed fused to her skin, moving up and down as she breathed.

"This," Asmodeus said, "is a tracking disk. It has the arms of Hawthorn—you can examine it in a mirror, should you have the leisure."

His tone made it clear she wouldn't. He snapped his fingers, and the disk contracted against her skin. It wasn't painful at first, but then … Then something rose within her, a slow, persistent tug, a burning need to be elsewhere—as if someone had slipped a hook between her ribs and was now reeling her in.

"It'll get worse." His tone was light, conversational, "Every moment when you're not where I expect you to be, the pain will increase."

He was doling out information little by little—keeping her in the dark. Keeping her scared.

Aurore didn't have time for that, anymore.

"Tell me what you want," she said.

A thin smile like a knife's edge between blood-red lips.

"You'll have missed this due to being … indisposed, but House Harrier blew up. I want someone inside the House."

Harrier. No.

"You …" She took a deep breath, trying to steady herself. It felt as though something was lodged between her ribs—as he'd said, not yet painful, but it was already larger than it had been, constricting her. "You must have informants."

"They're out of reach." Again, that smile that was meant

to frighten her. She ached to wipe it from his face. "And I'm not sending dependents into what, by all reports, is a burning war zone. Not until I have a better idea of what's going on. Spend a day and a night in Harrier, and come back to Hawthorn. The disk will lead you. And it'll mark you as mine, should you meet other Hawthorn dependents within the House. You'll help them get out, if you find any."

He seemed so very sure she was going to do as he asked. But of course, he thought he'd broken her, that she'd do anything to be free of pain.

"I could die there," she said, "and then you still wouldn't have your information."

He laughed, and this time the room echoed with it.

"That'd be such a shame, wouldn't it? But mostly for you." He rose, adjusting his swallowtail jacket and his tie. "You're free to go. I'll see to it that the guards let you pass. And I'll be seeing you soon ..." He paused, leaving space for her name.

"Aurore." She spat it through clenched lips.

He was at the door, and didn't even bother to turn.

"Aurore. Good. See to it that you come back."

Harrier. The House that had cast her and her sister Cassiopée out—that had beaten them and left them for dead for the sin of failing a Fallen one time too many. Returning there, feeling again, that bone-clenching fear of putting a foot wrong when she served a Fallen's dinner, standing at the gates, listening to the low moans of those in the flat cages, standing aligned with the other servants in the streets of the House, watching ghostly hawks coalesce from cobblestones and wrought-iron railings ...

hearing Lord Guy's low laughter as they tore disobedient dependents apart.

She couldn't.

4
Past Glories, Past Lies

The Trocadéro palace was one of the great ruins of Paris. Once built for a Universal Exhibition, one of the grandiloquent, self-reassuring displays of wealth and power the Houses had so liked, it was now completely outside House territory, and falling to pieces.

Hoa Phong had still been adamant that they were going there.

They came up from rue Benjamin Franklin. They could have gone up from the Seine quays, but that would have been encroaching on dragon territory. Philippe had seen first-hand how they defended that, rising up dark and fanged, dripping with the oily water of the Seine, to drag pedestrians down from bridges and drown them in the river, regardless of whether they were House or not.

The plaza was deserted, with not even the Houseless scavenging in the ruins of the roundabout. The sky was dark with the smoke, tinged a faint red with the end of the afternoon. Over them loomed what was left of the palace: one of the towers mimicking a minaret had been destroyed, and the other one looted, somehow, its roof scraped of all gilding, bricks along its length gouged out at random intervals. It gave the impression it was going to fall at any moment.

The huge gates were torn, and the vestibule was filled with debris. Beyond the vestibule, the two large, curved wings spread out on either side. In front of them, where the huge festival hall had once been, were rows of skeletons of seats, their fittings long since rotted away. Isabelle paused, for a fraction of a second, as she clambered over broken tiles.

"It's beautiful," she said.

Below, beyond the ruined hall, the view stretched to the broken Eiffel Tower—and the ever present plume of smoke to the right, which Philippe now knew came from House Harrier. The stepped fountain descending into a large basin was still there, but the water was oily and stagnant, a pool of rank, marshy liquid. As Philippe watched, something moved within—a flash of sheening scales, of sharp claws. Dragons? No, it had seemed too short and too small. Some other reptile, a construct or some other remnant from the war. Best be careful: anything that hadn't been taken apart for its magic was likely powerful and not to be trifled with.

Isabelle was still staring at the view of Paris, her eyes wide.

"Philippe?"

He wasn't moved. Everything there—the gardens, the quays, the Tower—had been built by the Houses. Paid for in the blood of people like him—by Ai Linh and Hoang and the members of his former war squad, lying buried and forgotten near the ruins of House Draken.

"Gilded splendor," he said. And, more gently when he

saw her crestfallen face, "It's the kind of beauty people kill for, Isabelle."

Hoa Phong was ahead, her sleeves billowing in the wind that always seemed to follow her around—when she paused, her fingers would turn into thin strings of pale, unnatural *hoang mai* flowers. Philippe thought, again, of the wound he'd felt in her side, the rot glistening at its core.

You smell of death. Of wrongness. You shouldn't be touched by it.

Could Immortals die of something as mundane as infection?

"Come on," Hoa Phong said. Her eyes were two pinpricks of light in the shadow of the stairs.

Isabelle tore her gaze from the wrecked gardens, and followed Hoa Phong into the wing.

It had been a museum, once. Most of it was wrecked: the window displays smashed and long since looted, with only broken, empty pedestals remaining—the whole ones had long since been taken for building materials. They crossed rooms with faded maps and labels, written in ink that had turned a pale sepia, the handwriting of wealthier days almost illegible.

They reached a room, at last, that opened up on emptiness. Something had torn the wing in half, and scattered debris in the hole. The gardens had grown over it: twisted, gnarled trees over fallen column sections, and frontispieces engraved with idealized, plump men and women—and distant, smiling Fallen outlined in lambent stone, with the shadow of dark wings at their backs.

"I don't understand what we're looking for," Isabelle said.

Hoa Phong turned to look at them.

"A box," she said, after a long, sharp look at Philippe. "Wisdom." And two other words in Viet.

Isabelle raised an eyebrow. "Tiger?"

"You're teaching her Viet?" Hoa Phong's face was disapproving.

"She asked," Philippe said, mildly.

"Still here," Isabelle said, stubbornly.

"You're a *foreigner*," Hoa Phong said, using not the word that fell just short of *barbarian*, but the one that meant *colonizer*.

Isabelle stared back. "Yes. But I can still learn Viet."

She glared at Hoa Phong. Philippe suppressed the urge to separate them as he would two squabbling children. Hoa Phong had a point, but this wasn't the place to hash out colonial politics.

"The Burning Tiger," Philippe said, but Hoa Phong shook her head.

"It's ... You know who the tiger is," she said. "The one who comes with the box. He's a spirit. Dân Chay."

An Immortal. A faint memory, from the time he'd been in the court of the Jade Emperor. "I think I remember him. He's one of Heaven's enforcers, isn't it?"

"Dân Chay. Chaos," Hoa Phong said. "The fangs that wait in the darkness. The eternal hunger that doesn't stop, once he has tasted blood."

"And you want this ... Dân Chay to help you?" Isabelle said.

Hoa Phong walked into the garden, keeping a wary eye on the shadows—but there was nothing.

She said, without looking at either of them, "He's our

weapon. Once, man tricked the tiger, and burned him with fire until his golden fur became streaked with black. Ever since, he's wanted his revenge on mankind. He's the Jade Emperor's final arbiter to mortals and other beings, which suits him. He's from a time before justice, before fairness. Before the words of the Sage and the duty laid on us to submit to our superiors."

She was so prim and proper, parroting the words of the Court, that it hurt. Had he ever been this naive, this conceited?

"And you need him."

Hoa Phong said, "He will not stop. He will not relent, once unleashed. But he's been missing for decades, since the box was stolen by Fallen. This is where he is."

"He's just ..." Philippe stopped. "He's one spirit. He's not a miracle. And you'd need to convince him it's his fight. That he still wants to honor the old allegiance to the Emperor."

"Of course. But we're at the stage where anything that looks like hope would help, aren't we?"

His face burned, and he fell silent.

Ahead was the other half of the wing: a room much like the one they'd left, except it seemed full. Hoa Phong stopped, staring at it. So did Philippe; but not Isabelle, who walked straight into it with no notion of danger whatsoever.

"Stop!" Philippe said.

Isabelle stood in the middle of the room. She turned, arms spread out.

"What?"

"The other room has been looted," he said. "This one hasn't. And it's fairly accessible. So ..."

"Someone is guarding it," Hoa Phong said.

Or something.

Isabelle turned around, slowly, carefully.

At length, she said, "There's nothing here." She frowned. "The *khi* currents are weird, though."

Beside Philippe, Hoa Phong stirred. "Where did you find her?"

In his past. He shook his head. It was none of Hoa Phong's business. He could imagine the way she'd look at him, if she learned he'd broken the cycle of death and rebirth for a friend's sake—for a Fallen's sake.

"She's my student," he said.

An impatient, headstrong student who wanted to master everything at the same time. It would pass.

"I see," Hoa Phong said. It was obvious she disapproved. "Shall we?"

Inside, everything lay in shadow. Light played on the intact display cabinets—on the carved statues that must have been hacked from temple ruins, on scattered jade objects that had once been a family's wealth. As they went deeper into the wing, Philippe felt something rise—a tendril of Fallen magic that quested around them, probing insistently for a way in.

"Do you know where your … box is?" Isabelle asked.

She was frowning: she'd sensed what Philippe had. She couldn't quite place it, but it bothered her all the same. Hoa Phong seemed indifferent: he wasn't sure she could see Fallen magic.

There was jade, and porcelain, and statues—carvings of gods and spirits and immortals in every color of stone, bone-white porcelain, and blue flower porcelain, its blue still the sharp tint of the morning sky. Silver chopsticks and jade pendants, and wooden chairs, everything covered in layers of dust. The atmosphere of wrongness got worse and worse the deeper they got: an entire room was dedicated to statues of the Buddha, Bodhisattvas and arhats. They ought to have been comforting, but even the Quan Am statue—with spread arms around her, surrounding her entire torso like a halo—looked out of place, her eyes opened wide in surprise rather than serenity. Nothing was set right: there was an entire piece of temple in a room, an entrance flanked by statues, except that nothing lay beyond. Everything was . . . out of context.

"They stole everything." Hoa Phong's voice was low and angry.

Not even to value it—but merely to pile it here, to flaunt the obscene *excess* of what they had: entire rooms holding broken temples and neglected statues and altars, gathering dust with no offerings. Before, when this had still been in use, he knew, with absolute certainty, that it would only have been crowds of elegantly dressed people, gaping at the wonder of it all—at the *exoticism*, comforting themselves that they weren't so primitive or superstitious.

"I know," he said.

Isabelle's eyes were wide. "I'm sorry."

He opened his mouth to say she wasn't the one who had to apologize, that she hadn't been born—and then closed it. Because she was part of it, wasn't she? Or had been, before she died—a Fallen, a House-bound, gathering such things to her in the name of safety.

"It's not the time," he said, finally.

A glint caught his eye: a room that was much smaller, a

desk of orange-painted wood with butterfly handles on its two drawers. He paused at the threshold, trying to sense something—because this one looked lived in, in a way none of the others had been. A cracked porcelain cup of tea, and a book open on a table. He glanced at it: its text was faded, its paper no longer white or pristine but spotted with mold. Clothes lay discarded on a chair, and so did a small vial of make-up. All suggesting that whoever lived there only occupied this one room. The guardian of the museum? There didn't appear to be anyone here.

He opened the drawer with a creak that must have been heard all the way into Hell. He paused, his heart in his throat, but nothing happened. Reams and reams of paper—and the word *tiger* caught his eye.

"Philippe! Come on!" Isabelle called.

He grabbed the entire sheaf of paper, stuffed it into his tunic, and ran out to join them.

They were at a staircase, where Hoa Phong had paused. The sense of rising magic was worse there. Philippe felt goosebumps on his arms, and Hoa Phong was disintegrating again, turning into hundreds of diseased flower petals.

"Whole," he said, his brain finally catching up with him.

"I'm sorry?" Hoa Phong said, but Isabelle was faster on the uptake.

"Everything in Paris is broken or rotted," she said. "Nothing here is."

That was what wrong with the display: nothing was broken or decayed, or covered in fungus or rot. The air itself was sharp and clean, something Philippe hadn't breathed in *decades*, and it felt profoundly, nauseatingly wrong.

"Of course," a voice said, from above them. "This is a safe place. *I* keep it safe."

She stood on the first landing of the staircase, beside a curled statue of a dragon—a beautiful piece etched in redwood, that looked as though it was going to leap and uncurl in a swirl of waves. She was Fallen, her light almost invisible—but when she moved, thin, luminous threads seemed to connect her to every step of the white marble stairs. Her face was as smooth and as translucent as the porcelain in the cabinets, her eyes a sharp, celestial blue, moving, too sharp and too feverish, to hold each of them in turn.

Her clothes were tatters, the wreck of something that must have once been beautiful: torn lace moved as she did, revealing areas of skin that were too dark and patchy to match that of her face. She had no House insignia or House colors that Philippe could recognize, and nothing in her demeanor suggested she belonged to one. She hadn't challenged them in its name or claimed the Trocadéro as part of a territory.

"My name is Diamaras," she said. "You have no business here."

Philippe raised his hands to ward himself. The *khi* currents had been all but exhausted in the wing: now he could see how they bent around her—and broke, when she moved. She was slicing through them merely by moving.

"We mean no harm."

Diamaras reached the midway point of the stairs, paused. Her gaze raked them all.

"Annamite," she said, revealing sharp, pointed teeth.

"You're mortal and Houseless. Harm requires power. You have none, and neither do your friends."

Hoa Phong disintegrated. One moment she was there, and the next flowers were streaming upwards, their edges sheening like the edge of a blade. They flowed in two sharp streams that surrounded Diamaras. The Fallen leaped back, and she now had two knives, one in each hand. Blood stained the rags she wore. She hissed, a wounded, primal sound.

The cloud of flowers landed on the stairs, became Hoa Phong again. She was breathing hard, one hand holding the side where Philippe had seen her earlier wounds.

So much for no harm. Philippe pulled the *khi* currents to him—it felt like trying to gather blade shards with bare hands. Instead of coming to nest, quiet and comforting, in the palm of his hand, the currents were turbulent, pinpricks of angry magic on his skin.

"Stay out of this," he said to Isabelle.

She was trying to smooth out the *khi* currents to cast one of the spells he'd taught her, but they kept escaping her grasp. He didn't have great hope she'd obey him, which meant this had to end fast, one way or another.

At least he didn't have to worry about Diamaras: Hoa Phong had her attention. He pulled in more currents. His hands were bleeding, and nothing he did smoothed them out. Like handling a swarm of bees, they were short, jagged threads that contorted, trying to escape him, trying to remove themselves from Diamaras's neighborhood.

"You have teeth," Diamaras said to Hoa Phong. "But it won't avail you."

The threads of light Philippe had already seen flared

to painful, eye-searing radiance—and Hoa Phong shimmered, the contours of flowers becoming visible on her face and clothes, as if she were a child's trembling puzzle on the edge of being undone. He pulled at more threads: he had a bare armful, and they were stained red by his blood, quivering and trying to escape. He wasn't going to be able to weave anything.

He walked up the stairs.

"Diamaras!" he called.

She turned, just a fraction. As she did, Hoa Phong shivered, and became flowers again; but the stream that rose to wrap itself around Diamaras was pushed back by the increased radiance around the Fallen.

Close enough.

"What do you want, little man?"

Philippe threw the entire armful of jagged *khi* elements into her face. Diamaras threw her hands up, but too late—the *khi* elements were sliced to pieces as they met the threads of light, but enough of them unfolded in the space between the threads, crowding on Diamaras's face. She howled, clawing at her eyes.

Philippe leaped away. Behind Diamaras, Hoa Phong was reforming again, but her shape kept shifting between flowers and woman. A quick, desperate glance downstairs: Isabelle was still trying to weave a proper, painstaking spell. That was never going to happen, but at least it kept her busy and out of trouble.

Hoa Phong said, "We can keep fighting until we're all exhausted and bloodied, if not dead. Or we could talk."

Small, ghostly flowers came spilling out of her mouth, like breath in winter.

Diamaras looked up, her face a mask of streaming blood from eyes to cheeks. Her hands, when she raised them again, were streaked with red.

"I don't speak with mortals." She made it sound like *insects*.

The threads lit up, sharply. The stairs shook. Philippe stumbled, tried to recover his footing—and then the entire world spun upside down as he fell.

"Philippe!"

Isabelle, pulling him up, her attempt to weave *khi* currents scattering as she reached out to steady him. He breathed hard, to clear the wall of fog across his field of vision. Hoa Phong and Diamaras were fighting again. It was pointless, except …

Where were the threads coming from?

The stairs? No, they went right through the marble and …

The displays. They were coming from the objects in the display. She was drawing her power in a typical Fallen way—by stealing others'.

Symbolic magic. Her way to triumph was through others' submission and humiliation: from the brash display of once-worshipped statues as curiosity pieces in a museum. Smashing the displays would slow her down; destroying the museum would end her. Even at the height of his power as envoy of the Jade Emperor, he couldn't have done any of that.

But two could play the symbolism game.

Philippe grabbed the *khi* elements again, and started putting them together. He didn't attempt to weave, because it was pointless, because they couldn't be put together. Instead, he cobbled them together as though he were putting a broken vessel back together, pouring gold dust and resin to fill the cracks—weaving *khi* metal with *khi* water and *khi* fire, the metal holding the two warring elements close. Water, for old age and memories and all the deep, intimate knowledge of the value of life. Fire, for passion and love, and all the things that were so deeply cherished—a child's favorite rice bowl, an ancestor pausing to listen to a desperate prayer for a husband's health, the vast, encompassing comfort of a pagoda filled with worshippers on the Hungry Ghosts festival, the red and white roses on the monks' chests shining in the twilight…

The light flickered and dimmed. Startled, he looked up, and saw that he was now holding half the threads, except that they pulsed, softly, like a living heart—the red of blood, of New Year's envelopes.

High above, on the steps, Diamaras paused.

"You—"

Hoa Phong leaped on her from behind, and bore her to the ground. The threads folded: *something* unbearably large and heavy pushed against Philippe's hands, sending him kneeling to the ground, gritting his teeth not to be crushed. He pushed upwards, gathering more *khi* elements as he did so—more memories of the profound silence in the ancestral chapel, of the din of firecrackers, of people laughing and reciting drunken poetry during dinners on lacquered chairs. His hands were going to give out, bones snapping like twigs in a storm …

The threads *tore*, with a sound like high-pitched screams—no, the high-pitched screaming was Diamaras, who was on her knees on the stairs, every wound on her face weeping tears of blood. Hoa Phong was standing a few paces from her, holding both the Fallen's knives. She threw them downwards: they hit the tiles with a sound like thunder.

"Talk," she said.

Diamaras was still screaming. Hoa Phong shook her, just as Philippe came up, warily watching the Fallen in case she attempted something else. His hands weren't heavy anymore, but neither were they empty. The light of the threads filled them like liquid fire, sloshing against his skin, a slow, prickling feel that wasn't pain-free or pleasant, but not the agony it had been before.

At length, Diamaras said, "What do you want?"

Her voice was low, and exhausted. Philippe felt not a sliver of pity: as she'd have had none, had she defeated them.

"A box," Hoa Phong said. "Engraved with this."

She made a gesture with her hands, and an archaic character appeared in the air: the one for *knowledge*.

Diamaras smiled. "That's all you want? A wooden box? Not lacquered?"

"Not everything Annamite is lacquered," Hoa Phong said, mildly. She had both hands on the kneeling Diamaras's shoulders.

"It wasn't of value," Diamaras said.

Hoa Phong didn't say anything—Philippe didn't, either. If either of them admitted its true worth, then Diamaras would never let go of it. They'd battled her to a standstill, but how long could Philippe hold the museum's threads in his hands? He glanced at them: they were bleeding now, from a hundred small wounds like pinpricks.

Diamaras closed her eyes. Hoa Phong didn't remove her hands, but didn't move them, either.

"In the primitive section," she said, exhaling slowly, carefully. "It was there."

"Was?" Isabelle asked, sharply, from the ground floor.

Diamaras's smile would have been malicious, had she not looked so drained.

"It was taken during the war. Two Houses came—they said they could use it to make a weapon to bring down their enemies."

"Two Houses."

One of them would still have it—one of them would still be imprisoning Dân Chay, or whatever the tiger spirit called himself now. It was hopeless. A lone envoy and an ex-Immortal, no matter how prepared, did not just sneak into Houses.

Hoa Phong went on, as if none of it mattered. "Who?"

"House Draken."

House Draken was the House that had conscripted Philippe into its ranks during the Great Houses War, its agents the ones that had captured him and other Annamites in Cochin China, and loaded them like cannon fodder on a ship bound for France, where they'd held rifles and knives in shaking hands, and died one after the other in a war that wasn't theirs.

But the House was dead.

It had been defeated during the war, its wards caving in. Philippe could still remember being there: the sounds they'd made as they'd finally given in, as if the universe were tearing itself apart; the panic, as he and other Annamites fled to an illusory safety; their falling, one by one, until only he was left, panting and breathing hard and covered with blood, the *khi* currents bending and twisting, tears sliding down his cheeks, as warm as monsoon rain. He didn't remember the House claiming a tiger spirit as a weapon, but then why would they have bothered to inform their lackeys?

"You said two Houses." Isabelle's voice was flat. "Who is the other?"

A silence.

Then, with an edge that bit deep: "House Silverspires." Diamaras laughed.

Isabelle's mouth was open. Silverspires. The House that had taken her in as a Fallen. The one she couldn't hope to return to, because she was mortal, because she had no value to them—because she'd died and they would take her apart to find how the resurrection spell worked, if she dared to walk back into it.

"That's not possible," Philippe said.

Diamaras's laugh was almost gentle. "I remember. *He* came. His steps made the display cases tremble, and statues of these false idols fall apart into dust. The entire building seemed afire with his light, as radiant and as terrible as dawn over the broken city. When he held it in his hands, he smiled, and everything seemed to make sense, as if you'd had the secrets of the entire universe poured into your ears like molten honey."

He . . .

"Who?" Philippe asked, but he already knew the answer.

"Lucifer Morningstar. First and most powerful of all Fallen." A laugh, that rose and rose until it was teeth biting into his skin, again and again. "Go on, *mortal.* Go and ask him about his *treasure*."

Sang took Thuan, not to the rubble-filled entrance of the cells, but to the offices nearby. As they walked—of course they couldn't run through the House, because it would have looked bad—Thuan was having trouble keeping a handle on his dragon form. Something primal within him was telling him the fastest way would be to soar through the corridors, so much simpler and more efficient.

The House was quiet: shocked, its dependents looking warily at Thuan as he ran by. It was only wounded dependents, but even post-war skirmishes hadn't had that much of an impact.

"Tell me again," he said.

Sang looked embarrassed. "Phyranthe called Vinh Ly into her office about four or five hours ago. When she came back."

Straight after she'd left Thuan's office, angry at his refusal to back down and looking for someone to blame.

"And Vinh Ly has been there ever since."

"Yes." Sang sounded apologetic. "I was minding Ai Nhi for her, and she's not come back."

Thuan frowned. "Where did you leave Ai Nhi, then?"

"Court of Birth," Sang said. She raised a hand. "With Berith. She's playing with Camille."

Thuan breathed more easily. The last thing they needed was Ai Nhi in the power of Iaris or her partisans, especially at a time the entire House was drawing itself together against an emergency, and principles might well go flying by the wayside.

Phyranthe's office had an oak-paneled door: on the lower panel was a faint, almost invisible engraving of a constellation of stars above deer antlers. Two of the stars were breaking off from the group in the sky, entangling themselves in the points of the antlers. The same, more complex, scene was engraved on the doors of Asmodeus's bedroom—Thuan knew it by heart.

Two stars. Two Fall-siblings. Berith. Asmodeus. The old, old crest, Asmodeus's personal one rather than the House one, used when he'd been running the Court of Birth. A message, a vaguely subtle one, as you had to know the crest to be able to recognize it. But, nevertheless …

A faint murmur of voices coming from inside the office—no, just one voice. Phyranthe's, in that silky tone she used when slowly peeling off layers of flesh, literally or metaphorically. Thuan reached out in his mind, heard only silence. Vinh Ly's presence in his mind was still burning: she wasn't in mortal danger then. But, as with Asmodeus earlier, that didn't tell him much.

He hesitated. In theory, nothing was wrong. It was, as Sang had said, Court of Persuasion business. Vinh Ly was Phyranthe's subordinate, and Phyranthe had every reason to call her into her office.

His gut was telling him otherwise. A dressing-down didn't last five hours, and Phyranthe was vicious. A sadist like Asmodeus, she usually kept everything in check, but when annoyed …

It was going to be *such* an ugly diplomatic mess if he intervened. But the alternative was Vinh Ly seriously harmed.

Ah well, nothing for it. He laid a hand on the door handle, and pushed.

It was a huge, cavernous office lined with chests of drawers and bookcases—except that the books on them were labeled with the names of prisoners and dates of interrogations. The room was L-shaped: he couldn't see what lay around the corner, but a faint smell of burning cloth wafted his way. Phyranthe's voice drifted to him—smooth, conversational.

"It's such a shame you're so poorly trained, isn't it? Look at you now—not even capable of performing the most basic of tasks ..."

Thuan moved into dragon form, and leaped between the bookcases, arrowing around the corner and landing straight on the plushness of a Persian carpet, claws digging into the rich embroidered threads.

Phyranthe was sitting behind a marquetry desk with curved legs, facing away from him at the end of the L. On his right side was a chimney and Vinh Ly, kneeling with her face away from her. Her shoulders drooped, and her hands were dug deep into the carpet. The smell of smoke came from a fire in front of her—not in the chimney but on the carpet. Three embers were at the heart of that, some distance from the chimney: there was no way they had rolled out from it. They'd been set deliberately on the carpet. Tight loops of *khi* water and Fallen magic mingled kept the fire contained, so that the entire room didn't turn into a conflagration.

"Ah, my lord." Phyranthe rose. She turned to face Thuan and Sang, leaning against the desk. "What a surprise."

She looked annoyed, so that last part had to be true, at least.

Thuan stretched, sinking back from dragon into human

form, leaving absolutely no trace of the dragon shape to his own, so that all she saw was the swallowtail with the arms of the House. He looked, again, at the embers, at the magic around them.

"What did you think you were doing?"

But he had an inkling already. Control, Phyranthe had said. Five hours. Five hours kneeling on the carpet, keeping the magic wrapped around the embers so that the fire wouldn't expand further, but not pouring so much *khi* water into it that the flames would die altogether. It was the magical equivalent of copying microscopic lines on paper, the kind of exercise one would assign to an apprentice or a child.

And that was, of course, not counting the steady patter of Phyranthe's poison poured into her ears for the entire time.

No wonder Vinh Ly was drained. It was a sheer miracle she was still upright and conscious.

Phyranthe's smile was sharp. "Vinh Ly's work has been … erratic, of late. I thought she could use a reminder that the Court is about precision and utter focus in what we're doing."

Thuan could feel Vinh Ly shaking—trying and failing to disguise extreme weariness. And shame: she was older than Thuan, and that she'd need to be rescued by him stung. What had Phyranthe intended? To keep her there until she collapsed, and then return her unconscious body like a trophy to him?

"I think you've made your point," he said, slowly. He didn't even try to disguise his fury.

Phyranthe smiled. She gestured, and a fist of Fallen

magic wrapped itself around the fire, snuffing it out with the same ease as it'd have crushed a throat. Vinh Ly tried to get up. Words came out of her mouth, so garbled that Thuan couldn't even tell in what language they were—and then she fell full on her face on the blackened embers, drawing into a ball and shivering uncontrollably.

Thuan looked away from her, because he didn't know how much temper he could keep if he kept having to look at Vinh Ly drained and weak. Sang moved in to steady Vinh Ly, with barely a glance at Phyranthe.

"As I said," Phyranthe said, with barely a pause, "not much to commend her."

She'd set Vinh Ly up. She'd tortured her as if she was one of the prisoners, and enjoyed every moment of it. Thuan clamped his lips on the words, because they might relieve his anger, but wouldn't make anything better.

"I see," he said. "If she displeases you so much, I'll be quite happy to send another dragon to your Court, per the agreement I have with Lord Asmodeus to make sure the dragons become part of the House."

He could threaten to withdraw his dragons entirely, but the only way that would work was if she was scared enough of what Asmodeus would say. And there … there he was on shakier grounds, especially with the Harrier situation twisting everything.

Phyranthe cocked her head, staring at him for a while. She hated waste: she wouldn't want to lose time training another interrogator. And she thought she knew Vinh Ly's weaknesses, whereas she'd have to start all over again with another dragon.

"That won't be necessary."

"Are you sure?" Thuan softened his face into mock concern. "I could send you Lan, for instance."

It was a bluff: Lan was a kind and gentle soul who worked in the Court of Gardens, doing her best to coax some flowers out of the shriveled trees on the lawns. The Court of Persuasion would depress her. But it also meant Phyranthe would be short one person, as Lan would be all but useless to her.

"That won't be necessary," Phyranthe said again.

Sang had hauled Vinh Ly on one shoulder, effortlessly. She was making her way out of the office without a backward glance at Thuan.

"Her rooms," Thuan said, sharply, to her.

He wanted to tell her to get Ai Nhi, but he didn't want Phyranthe to remember Vinh Ly had a niece who could also be hurt. Children weren't taken into the cells—disciplining them was the Court of Birth's business—and Iaris wouldn't stoop to hurting one, but Phyranthe … Phyranthe was another matter.

Thuan said, to Phyranthe, "So you're satisfied, then."

Phyranthe cocked her head again. Her blue eyes held Thuan's. She was impassive once again, with not even a hint of anger. He couldn't tell if venting her temper on Vinh Ly had helped her calm down.

"Let's say I am." She smiled. "For the time being."

"Good. Because House Harrier is burning on our doorsteps and we're going to need to prepare."

A raised eyebrow. "Yes. If there's a time for order and impeccable discipline, it's in the midst of chaos."

Thuan clamped down his lips on the first angry words

that came to him. He said, "Also not an ideal time to be turning on our own."

Phyranthe laughed. "You want to tell me how to run my Court, Annamite?"

The way she spat it made it clear it wasn't a neutral description.

"I'm merely looking out for my own," Thuan said. "The well-being of those who belong to me."

"What belongs to you," Phyranthe said, with a bare trace of venom, "is the House. All the dependents of the House. Favoritism is ill-placed."

Thuan raised an eyebrow. "You mean those dependents that won't take an order from me because they think me an arrivistic native, just like you do?"

She flinched at that. "I didn't mean . . ."

No, not in such crude words. His experience was that barbs were acceptable when couched in honeyed terms, far less when people had to face what they'd actually meant.

"Did you, now." Thuan kept his voice soft, the way he'd seen Asmodeus do to those who'd displeased him. And, in a different tone, "You know as well as I do that things have changed here."

"Have they." Phyranthe's face didn't move. "Your pet project of making us a kinder place?" A snort.

"You can't run a House on fear." Thuan had had that argument with Asmodeus so many times before. Fear brewed rebellions—and the House, drained and exhausted, wouldn't survive another one of these. "At least, not only."

Phyranthe's lips curled up, her smile sharp and wounding.

"Idealist," she said, much in the same way she'd said

Annamite. And, in another tone, "Don't make the mistake of thinking this is over."

Of course it wasn't. Thuan exhaled.

"And when will it be?"

A smile. "You know exactly when."

When he was cast out without any influence.

"You mean you want me shut in one of your cells."

He was reasonably confident *that* wouldn't happen. At least in the current configuration of powers in the House.

"Oh, I'll settle for much less."

Phyranthe bent closer to him, so he could breathe in the smell of smoke and blood from her dress's sleeves.

Thuan had misread it. It would, perhaps, have been over, or at any rate less bloody, if he'd not walked in. If he'd let Phyranthe have her way with Vinh Ly. But now she resented him, not only because she was old guard and he wasn't, but also for interfering—twice—in the business of her own Court.

Now it was war.

"I see," he said. "That makes me so fortunate, doesn't it." He turned, following Sang out of Phyranthe's office, and out of the Court of Persuasion. "I'll see you later, then."

He had absolutely no doubt he would; just as he had absolutely no doubt that he was outmatched, and with too few resources of his own to fight her and Iaris. Even Asmodeus's affection for him wouldn't be enough to protect him.

That was, of course, assuming it still held.

Thuan found Vinh Ly's small room overcrowded.

"Unka Thuan, Unka Thuan!"

Ai Nhi was fussing around her aunt. Vinh Ly was sitting on the bed, nursing a cup of tea and refusing steadily to meet Thuan's gaze. Nothing unusual there: Vinh Ly was a traditionalist and thought an inferior shouldn't meet a superior's gaze.

"Auntie Ly is poorly."

"I can see that," Thuan said, wryly.

Ai Nhi's face scrunched up. "Auntie Sang said a bad person"—he could almost hear the quotes around the word—"had hurt her, but she'll be fine."

Vinh Ly shook her head. "I said I had been a negligent person too, child. Not careful enough about who to trust."

Ai Nhi grimaced. Vinh Ly tousled her head. "Don't worry. The bad person can't come here."

Vinh Ly's face was gray, her eyes so deep-set and her dark skin so translucent he could almost see the shape of her skull beneath her skin. She'd heal—she'd gone from unconscious to awake in the brief time Sang had carried her back to her room, and dragons' bodies healed even faster than Fallen ones—but he doubted she was going to forget her ordeal in a hurry.

"Your Majesty," she said.

"How are you?" Thuan asked.

He used the pronoun for *grandmother*, and ignored the weary disapproval from her. Vinh Ly was eldest among the dragons who'd accompanied him. She wore her gray hair in a topknot, entirely too much floral perfume, and had mastered a variety of withering expressions she used on all the other dragons. Including Thuan. She'd given him a memorable speech once on how he was shaming his ancestors by failing to address her as *child*—because, no matter his youth, he was the dragon of highest rank in Hawthorn, the equivalent of their king on land. Thuan had plaintively said she was twice his age, and there was no way his mouth would shape the word *child* to address her. He'd got a withering look that could have split stone.

"Don't worry about me, Your Majesty." Vinh Ly's voice was dismissive. "I'll be fine."

And, if he valued his tranquility, he would never refer to the incident again. Thuan sighed.

"May we talk about the repercussions?"

Sang was leaning against the wall, watching Thuan attentively. Waiting to see how this would all play out? She shrugged when his gaze found hers, pointed to Ai Nhi, who'd given up fussing around Vinh Ly and was now trying to sneak into bed with her. Right. So she thought Vinh Ly was in no state to care for her niece. Good to know he wasn't the only one who'd learn to run rings around the older dragon.

"Talk," Vinh Ly said.

Thuan kept his face impassive. "I don't think it's going to get any better."

Sang snorted.

"That's because you've been lax." Vinh Ly grimaced, her desire to scold Thuan warring with her knowledge one didn't reproach a superior. "Forgive me, Your Majesty."

Thuan shook his head. He didn't have much self-pride to speak of, and was acutely aware of how everything hinged on him. He summarized, quickly, the conversation with Iaris and Phyranthe, and the one with Phyranthe alone.

When he was done, Vinh Ly sipped her tea, for a while.

"You want to yell at me," Thuan said, deadpan. "Feel free. At least you mean well."

Vinh Ly sighed. "You should have left me there. Turned away from the office and pretended you hadn't heard anything."

"I know," Thuan said. "But I can't think that way. And, to be blunt, I don't have a lot of you here and I can't afford to lose any of you. Especially now."

"House Harrier?" Vinh Ly's voice was uncomfortably sharp.

The burning House; their missing delegation; and most of all the ramifications of it all, coming home to roost.

"It's going to become precarious here," Thuan said. And, to Sang, "You'll need to ask the Court of Strength to call up their reservists."

"My lord?"

"We may need to field a show of strength."

Or more, but he hoped it wouldn't come to that. They needed to stay out of Harrier's tangled mess.

"Mmm." Vinh Ly drained the cup of tea, and waved it at Ai Nhi. "Can you pour me more?"

The little dragon positively bounced. Thuan winced.

"Isn't she a little young . . .?"

And watched Ai Nhi weave *khi* water around the teapot on its warmer, until a stream of tea went from the spout to the teacup. The weave was strained: he held his breath. Anything—including Ai Nhi's loss of focus—would make it explode.

"Education," Vinh Ly said, firmly, "starts young."

As long as one didn't mind droplets of hot tea burning

everything in the room. Thuan clamped down on the thought before he could utter it.

"You need to distance yourself from me," he said. "Or to leave the Court of Persuasion. You're going to be a target."

He didn't add that he didn't know how much she could bear.

Vinh Ly's face was hard. "She can't kill me. It would create too many complications."

As if that was reassuring.

"I'd rather it didn't come to testing that," Thuan said, more sharply than he'd meant.

"I'll handle Phyranthe."

Thuan watched *khi* water flicker in her hands, and said, "Let's be clear that 'handle' doesn't involve causing … accidents for her."

They were going to need every available dependent, just in case the Harrier business went pear-shaped.

"Not at all." Vinh Ly was serene. She gestured to Sang. "Play to your own followers."

The Court of Strength, the Court of Gardens. Those who were tired of living in fear. Those who listened to him, or at least indulged him because it amused them.

"Asmodeus," he said, aloud.

Vinh Ly inclined her head. "As soon as you can."

"Before Iaris?"

"You can't," Sang said. "But …"

But he was Asmodeus's husband, and surely it had to count for something. Thuan didn't know anymore.

"I'll see." He pursed his lips. "The business with Harrier might help, too. Force us into unity."

"Hmm." Sang nodded.

"You can't control that, though," Vinh Ly said.

"I can remind Iaris tearing ourselves apart will weaken us all," Thuan said.

She'd been the one to bring up the argument in the first place; perhaps she'd be receptive. He doubted Phyranthe would, but who knew.

Something tightened in the room, seconds before it exploded. A tinkle of glass—Thuan raised wards to protect everyone. Shards and liquid bounced off them, harmlessly. The teapot. Ai Nhi's weave around it had exploded, splattering porcelain and tea all over him. The little dragon stood, desolate, in the middle of a growing puddle.

"Unka Thuan …"

Thuan laughed. "It doesn't matter."

"It does," Vinh Ly said. "She needs to learn control, Your Majesty."

She sounded like Phyranthe, which Thuan found more disquieting than he'd like to admit.

"She's five years old."

"And she'll be judged on far harsher criteria than Fallen or mortals are," Vinh Ly said. "As you well know. Scrutinized for anything and everything that goes wrong, and her shortcomings becoming those of our race."

Thuan stared at her, hard. Vinh Ly's face was creased in worry—and it was amply clear that what she'd said applied, not only to Ai Nhi, but to all of them.

"I've got this," he said, smiling with a lightness he didn't feel. *Asmodeus, you'd better wake up soon.*

5

Dreams of Power, Dreams of Fire

Aurore traveled home through a rising haze of pain.

For every step she took towards la Goutte d'Or—and away from the plume of smoke that marked House Harrier's location—the disk grew hotter against her skin, and the hook in her chest sank deeper, pulling her in the other direction.

It was bearable while she was on the omnibus, letting the vibration of the horses' hooves soothe her into something almost resembling sleep, but when she got down at Château Rouge, where the small, desolate manor loomed over the few pedestrians still out at night, she fell to her knees, breathing hard.

"Younger aunt?" One of the Annamites who'd gotten down at the same stop—Sébastien, one of the dockers who worked at La Villette Basin. "Are you all right?"

Aurore struggled to breathe through gritted teeth.

"I'm . . . fine," she said.

She rose, shaking—felt the tug again, tearing at her gut.

"You're not," Sébastien said. "Come on. I'll help you home."

He supported her on his shoulder along Boulevard

Barbès, and then up the small, narrow street where she and Cassiopée lived. Every step was agony, every breath a constellation of pain in her chest and above her hips. She was torn apart—unmade and remade every time she lifted a leg, burning coals poured into her intestines every time she moved so much as a chest muscle. Her breath came in short, ragged gasps.

"Here," Sébastien said. They were at the door of her flat. She had no memory of getting there, or even of crossing the small, crowded courtyard with charred, half-demolished walls. "I can call a doctor."

Which mostly meant Philippe.

No.

Aurore shook her head. "Cassiopée," she said. The word shivered in her mouth: she tasted blood on her tongue from Asmodeus's spell. "Get me upstairs. She can take care of me."

Sébastien looked at her for what felt like an eternity—a sharp, perceptive look as Aurore stood trembling, struggling not to collapse again, not to run, screaming, towards the distant House that was still filling the sky with smoke.

"All right," he said, finally. "As you wish, aunt."

Aurore pushed open the door, her hand tightening on the knob. Her fingers refused, for a moment, to obey her—as if she'd grasped live flames and they'd opened again in a burst of pain.

For every moment when you're not where I expect you to be, the pain will increase.

Bastard. She wasn't his servant; or anyone's servant anymore.

Cassiopée looked up as Aurore staggered into the flat.

"Big sis!"

And then she saw Aurore's face, and rose—a slow process requiring clinging to the shelves by her side. Her legs, broken multiple times that night in Harrier, hadn't healed properly and wouldn't bear her weight for long periods of time.

"Don't!" Aurore said.

"Don't be silly," Cassiopée said.

She reached for her cane, leaned on it to cross the room and walk to the table. Her long, graying hair fell down her back: it wasn't tied in her usual topknot, and strands of it were curving away in all directions.

"Here." She laid a small box of unguent by Aurore's side. "Camphor, and a touch of *khi* fire."

From the last time Philippe had visited, for her daughter Marianne's fever.

Aurore laughed, bitterly. It was going to take more than a touch of *khi* currents and traditional medicine to overturn Asmodeus's spell. She found a chair, with shaking hands, and sank into it.

"I'm going to need a knife," she said. "And some boiling water and whatever clean cloth we have."

Cassiopée stared at her. "What happened?"

Aurore glanced at the back of the flat. The partition with the other room—the thin, patched curtain with colored splotches of ink—was closed.

"Marianne is sleeping," Cassiopée said. "It'll be fine."

Not if Aurore managed to do what she needed to do.

"The knife, lil sis. Please."

Cassiopée handed it to her. In silence, she set water to boil on the stove, and brought back a slightly grubby cloth from the scraps basket. When Aurore bared her skin and raised the knife to the disk, she looked alarmed for the first time.

"You can't possibly remove something that large ..."

Aurore cut into her skin, below the disk. Or tried to. Because, as soon as the knife touched the wood, the pain rose a hundred-fold, a thousand-fold. Her hand opened, sending the knife clattering to the ground, and she fell, convulsing and clutching her chest, breathing through burning tears and struggling to pull herself to her feet.

The clatter of the cane on the floor.

"I can ... get ... up," she said, as the pain lessened—going from utterly unbearable to merely agonizing.

"You don't look like you can."

Cassiopée held out a hand. Aurore got up without touching it. She picked up the knife again, stared at it.

"The disk," Cassiopée said.

"It didn't work." Aurore sat down again. She raised the knife again—felt a hint of the same pain she'd feel if she tried to cut away the disk again. "I got caught. I barely had time to get oriented in Hawthorn, and certainly not to find the building on your map. Deer antlers on the doors. It couldn't be that easy, could it?"

She closed her eyes. Below her eyelids, in the darkness, blood-red flowers blossomed, limned in terrible, distant light.

I could die there.

It'd be such a shame, wouldn't it? But mostly for you.

"Never mind the map. He branded you."

Cassiopée's voice was flat, angry. She reached out with her free hand to touch the disk. As her hand brushed it

Aurore felt the pain squeezing her insides, cutting off her breath. She pulled away before it could send her sprawling to the floor again.

Cassiopée said, "I told you to be careful—"

"We agreed." Aurore breathed in, and it burned in her lungs. "It was the only way."

Get in. Find the building. Follow the map.

Cassiopée grimaced. "I can't even be sure that the artifact is still there."

"No one looked for it, did they?" Aurore thought it was the kind of thing Fallen would try to destroy. "I don't even understand how it still exists."

Cassiopée shrugged. "A whim of a Fallen, it suggests. One who loved a mortal very, very much, and didn't want them to feel powerless."

Aurore snorted. "As if that ever happened."

As if Fallen ever wanted mortals to gather power enough to challenge them. As if it wasn't in their interest to keep mortals dependent on their magic.

"Don't judge." Cassiopée's voice was gentle. "Fallen are just like the rest of us. Anyway, saying that artifact is obscure is probably an understatement." She was a scholar's descendant through and through, hunting down rare references in books and wrestling with ancient, fragmentary texts with dogged tenacity. "Insofar as I can tell, the key text was destroyed, and the only extant copy was made by an Annamite servant of Hawthorn with a grudge against his masters. It's unlikely the Fallen speak Viet, or are going to bother with it. So I think it's still there."

But they had no way of finding it.

"We could . . ." Cassiopée stopped, then, "Philippe . . ."

"No."

They could ask Philippe to teach them magic, but, even if he said yes to students beyond the one he already had—which was unlikely—the *khi* currents he wielded were insufficient. His magic lay in small healings, spells to make life easier: nothing that would stand up to a House.

"We've been over this before."

"I know," Cassiopée said. She looked tired. "But it's not the only way."

"You want us to remain here?" Aurore asked. Everything hurt, and she didn't have the energy to be gentle or kind anymore. "Wait for Harrier to get interested in us again?"

"They threw us out."

"They *killed* us," Aurore said.

The only reason Harrier wasn't interested in them anymore was that they had been left for dead—and they would have died that night, if Aurore hadn't found the broken pieces of a mirror infused with Fallen magic in the midden heap. She tried to remember what it had felt like, to inhale that power. To have fire coursing through her, a manic energy that had helped her rise despite her pregnancy. To stagger to Cassiopée's unconscious body and lift it, and run into the streets of Paris, her breath coming in short, shallow gasps, everything limned in trembling, decaying light. To run, through street after street after street, every step taking her further and further from the House that had cast them out. She tried to remember what it had felt like when Marianne had been born: a pregnancy carried to term despite all of her injuries, her very own miracle, the kind that squeezed the breath from her lungs. But all she could find was pain: that endless hook pulling her away from their home, and back towards Harrier.

Cassiopée laughed. "House Harrier has other problems."

House Harrier blew up, Asmodeus's amused voice said in Aurore's mind.

Bastard.

"But we'll always have to bow and scrape to them," Aurore said.

"I'm not reneging on the plan." Cassiopée watched Aurore for a while. "But I still don't understand what happened."

It came out in halting, fragmented sentences—interspersed with that growing, sharpening hook within her: the cells, the torture, the hospital room. The disk. The long, endless way home, with only the red haze of pain stretching across her entire world. After a while she got up and paced the flat. It helped, but the pain remained within her, like a tiger biding its time before it struck.

Cassiopée was silent for a while. Then she walked back to the chair she'd been sitting in, putting the books she'd been reading on the shelves and painstakingly lowering her body into it.

"You can't stay here."

"I have to." Aurore wasn't going to give Asmodeus the satisfaction of doing his bidding. "But how are we going to find what we want, if I go into Harrier?"

Cassiopée sighed. She'd been the one to find the old, old legend in the ruined books she collected, painstakingly piecing back together rotten fragments of texts, trying to make sense of words that time and war had blurred. An inexhaustible source of magic: an artifact that didn't need to be recharged by Fallen breath or blood. An object hidden in Hawthorn and lost a long time ago. A promise of something that would make them more than magicians, that would give them power to be reckoned with.

"A day and a night," she said.

"You forget." Aurore rubbed the disk. It bent under her touch, as if hungering for the warmth of her hand. "I have to go back to Hawthorn once this is done."

"Where you'll be free to search."

Of course she wouldn't. She didn't even know if she'd be alive, then; or back in the cells of Hawthorn, where it had all started.

"Lil sis."

Cassiopée sighed. "I know. But ..." She paused, took in a deep breath. "Do you really think you have a choice?"

They'd never really had one. They'd been servants in Harrier since birth, raised to cringe and bow to Fallen—given to the House's summary justice for failing to make way quickly enough for a Grand Secretary of the Great Interior. A path ringed by threats and punishments and pain, and Aurore had had enough of it.

"I don't know," Aurore said, but they both knew the answer to Cassiopée's question.

Cassiopée glanced at the window. Its oiled paper was halfway gone, leaving a large, gaping hole through which whistled the evening wind: they'd have to fix it before winter. Outside, in the street, traffic was thinning. It was late summer: people were bringing out tables and chairs, and congregating around them to eat, play chess, or trade gossip with the street sellers headed home. Aunt Thuy, the midwife, was down there with a few other aunties, laughing. She waved at Cassiopée. Thuy had sewn them back together when they'd reached the safety of the community. Aurore would always remember the long, long nights Aunt Thuy and Aunt Ha had spent over Cassiopée and her, forcing them to swallow water and medications, and grimly waiting for the dawn of another day.

For a moment—a hopeless moment of weakness—Aurore wanted to go down there into the street and beg for their help. They'd understand what she and Cassiopée were doing. They'd know, all too well, that their community existed only on the whim of people like Asmodeus.

No. Even if they did understand—even if they did approve—they wouldn't be able to help her. No one could, anymore.

Cassiopée said, "There's food on the table—I kept dinner ready. Try to stay here a while. Until daylight, at least. The streets outside our community will be full of gangs at night."

The lost youths, roaming the streets and hoping to find Fallen they could rip apart before the Houses could step in; but in the absence of Fallen they would quite happily turn on their own.

Aurore rubbed her chest, trying to find a position that would be free from pain—obviously there was none.

"Let me see that dinner."

The meal was rice dark with grit, a drop of fish sauce to hide the blandness of grains that had grown in poisoned fields, and a scattering of dried fish, from the large jar that they'd been sparingly taking from for months.

Afterwards, Aurore went into the bedroom.

Beyond the curtain, Marianne was sleeping with the abandon of a three-year-old. The tattered blanket she'd been sucking on lay by her outstretched hands. Aurore bent, slowly, gently—the pain made it hard to do so, sending little jerks of fire under her ribs, into her heart—and kissed her on the cheek, breathing in the smell of youth, if not of innocence, in a city that had long since corrupted everything from the air they breathed to the stones they walked on.

Then she sat on the floor, on the broken tiles by the bed, and tried to sleep.

In her dreams, she ran away from the blurred shape of a Fallen with horn-rimmed glasses, and with the shadow of great, black wings at its back. She woke up, gasping for breath—fell back into sleep—and they were there again, chasing her. And again and again, each time deeper into the dream. And as the Fallen got closer and closer her heart burned fiercer and fiercer, and when she looked down she saw it, tearing itself free from her chest, trailing bleeding stumps of veins and arteries, and shards of bone and skin ...

She opened her eyes, and everything hurt. The hook had spread from her chest to her belly and it was tearing her apart, driving her to her feet, scrabbling and biting her lip not to scream—anything, she'd do anything to make it stop, even to make it abate, only for a moment.

Outside, it was almost dawn: that familiar grayness to the polluted sky, in the moment between dog and wolf, as Mother had said—the time when workers congregated into the streets to go to the factories for another day that would wear their fingers to the bone. She could barely think through the pain. Cassiopée slept on, sprawled in her own bed in the other room that served as bedroom, kitchen and dining room all at the same time. Aurore had to be silent. Had not to cry out—she would worry them for nothing, and they could do absolutely nothing to help her.

Fine. Hawthorn had won. Asmodeus had won. She tried to bend down to kiss Marianne goodbye, but she was shaking so much she'd just wake her daughter up, and she didn't want Marianne to see her like that. She'd worry, or have outright nightmares for the rest of her life.

For that, too, Asmodeus would pay.

Cassiopée had left the map of Hawthorn on the table, the one that was supposed to lead them to their goal. Aurore reached out to grab it, stopped herself. She'd learned it by heart, because it was too incriminating to keep; she could have recited it even in the throes of the current pain.

She staggered down the stairs and into the streets, stumbling towards the distant House of Harrier.

When they got back into the Harrier streets, Darrias went ahead, carefully scouting the way. Louiza and Jamila followed. Emmanuelle had tried to suggest they could remain behind, but the glare on Darrias's face had discouraged her. Did she feel guilt or responsibility for them? She'd judged Harrier untenable for herself. What did it feel like, to see others left behind—the mortals, their inferiors according to Harrier's twisted ideology?

Louiza was hovering beside Emmanuelle: at the next muscle spasm, she set her shoulder against Emmanuelle's. "Here, Mistress. Let me."

The sun had already sunk down but its dim, gray light remained. Everything seemed leached of color and they had perhaps another half-hour before they needed to find shelter. And then Emmanuelle realized they couldn't afford to think that way. She was too used to night outside—especially outside the Houses—meaning danger, but they were in danger so long as they were inside Harrier. They'd have to go on in the darkness, and hope that angels—the un-Fallen, the favored ones—were indeed watching over them.

Lead us not into temptation, but deliver us from evil...

"Not 'Mistress'," Emmanuelle said, wearily.

She'd eaten the bar Jamila had found, and the food had stayed down. She'd half-feared she was going to vomit again when she woke up, that feeling of retching again and again, continuing to drag bitter bile up from her stomach long after it was empty. But even food didn't make her feel better. If she was right about her brain injury, there wasn't much she could do that would.

They were going down a straight street: it was that part of the House where everything seemed to intersect at sharp, clean angles, reminding Emmanuelle of nothing so much as the western area of Silverspires, those places around what had been the Préfecture where everything was rational and orderly. Or had been: no one had lived in those areas for many years. Emmanuelle turned, briefly. In the direction of Dupleix the smoke had become dark clouds, barely distinguishable from night in the dimming light. Whatever was burning had exhausted itself, but there wasn't enough wind to scatter its aftermath.

They started going east, but soon they turned to the

south, towards the gas factory that marked the boundary of Harrier. She saw fewer and fewer bodies in the street—which wasn't a good sign, because it meant people had been collecting them. Everything was silent again, only broken by distant screams. Ahead, she could see—distantly—the walls of the Great Interior and the occasional light of a spell illuminating a window or balcony.

They passed a deserted market. The roof and walls had held, but its brightly colored stalls were empty, with fruit and vegetables glistening on unsteady trestle tables. Darrias was still scouting ahead, a few paces from them, when a distant scream broke the silence, followed by the sharp sound of rifle fire.

Fighting. It came from the other end of the street, but Emmanuelle couldn't see anything.

"Wait here," Darrias said, and slipped on ahead.

Emmanuelle found herself alone, leaning on Louiza. There'd never be a better time to talk to her in private; Emmanuelle liked Darrias, but trusting her was another matter. Her brushing off looking for Morningstar had been reasoned, and reasonable on the face of it; but it still left Emmanuelle reliant on someone who belonged to another House and had vastly different priorities from hers.

Emmanuelle remembered the evening she and Morningstar had arrived in Harrier—the party for the House envoys, an uneasy, cramped affair that thinned as envoys left, each conversation growing more and more uncomfortable.

Darrias had found her by the buffet, and dragged her to a table.

"Here," she said, pouring champagne into a glass.

"Getting me drunk for Silverspires' secrets?"

Darrias snorted. "Getting you drunk so you can forget where you are."

"I'm not—"

"You look like you'd jump if I said 'boo'," Darrias said.

"You're honestly going to tell me it's not that bad?"

Darrias looked at her for a long, long while, and then shook her head.

"You don't want the lie, do you? You were never one to bury your head in the sand." And, then, more slowly, "It's bad, and tomorrow is going to be worse. Guy isn't going to waste a single opportunity to humiliate us."

Emmanuelle hesitated, and then forged on.

"It must be worse for you."

It had been Darrias's previous House, and she didn't even understand how Asmodeus could be cruel enough to send her there. But, of course, she was the ideal envoy from his point of view, already knowing the lay of the land.

"Oh, I'm already drunk," Darrias said sharply. She stared, moodily, at her glass, and then downed it. Nothing in her voice or demeanor suggested drunkenness. "I'm going to need this to get through the day."

"You didn't have to come," Emmanuelle said. "I know Asmodeus wouldn't have left you much choice—"

"Oh, I asked to come," Darrias said.

Emmanuelle opened her mouth to ask why, but before she could Morningstar was there.

"Anything the matter?" he asked, smiling at Darrias with a mouth full of teeth.

Darrias flinched, visibly. Morningstar wasn't his old self any longer—not the cruel and mercurial ruler of the

House who'd done anything, sacrificed anyone, for the good of Silverspires. He'd died and been revived in murky circumstances and remembered nothing of the days before his death. He had changed immensely. He had become a friend. Someone she could rely on. Though Darrias couldn't know any of that.

"Darrias is a *friend*." Emmanuelle knew what he'd say about friendships between Houses—that it was an unattainable, unreasonable dream. "She means me no harm."

Darrias had looked startled, then, staring at Emmanuelle.

"Of course I mean no harm," she said, and something in her voice—some barely hidden steel—had suggested that all the harm was reserved for someone else.

Emmanuelle had meant to track her friend down and ask, but there'd not been an opportunity. Or perhaps there had been, and she didn't remember? She felt herself, once again, probing at the edges of that missing chunk of time, steeling herself against a flood of memories that couldn't possibly be true. She was following a Harrier envoy through a long, darkened corridor—towards a room that filled her with slowly mounting dread—and there was a sound in the background she couldn't quite make out, something that tightened around her heart and squeezed until it beat faster and faster, desperate to escape, the same sound she'd already heard whenever she tried to reclaim her lost memories. And, finally, large cream-colored double doors opening on a dimly lit room.

"Lord Guy is expecting you," the Fallen said.

And then the memory ended, and she was back on the streets of a devastated House, staring at Louiza and shivering. Another person she couldn't be sure of, but that didn't matter right now. Darrias did.

She considered, for a while, the best opening.

"You've known Darrias a long time," she said finally, as it was close to the only thing they had in common.

The air was colder now, with that bite that promised autumn.

Louiza cocked her head. She was obviously deciding how much to tell an outsider, even if that outsider was Fallen.

"Everyone knows Mistress Darrias," she said. "Nothing would stop her, once she got started."

She sounded *proud*—all that went through Emmanuelle's mind was what kind of things Darrias would have started and taken to an end.

"I've known her for a year," she said, curtly.

Her arm spasmed, hitting Louiza in the face—and when she tried to stop it, her leg did the same, sending her sprawling to the ground, debris digging into her skin.

"I'm sorry."

Louiza pulled her up, with visible concern on her face.

"You're sick, Mistress," Jamila said slowly, softly, her small face creased—bracing herself for a rebuke. "You should go to hospital."

If there still was one. Emmanuelle laughed, bitterly.

"When I get back to Silverspires . . ."

If she ever got back to Silverspires. She wanted to dive into her library and never emerge—far away from fighting, screaming and smoke. She'd never really appreciated the value of it before.

"Where did you meet her, Mistress?" Jamila said. "On the streets?"

"Jamila!"

"I want to go out," Jamila said, a little plaintively. "Chase down the enemies of the House. Fight gangs and scavengers. Cool things."

"Excuse her," Louiza said, with a sigh. "We're seamstresses, Jamila. That's our future." Her face was pinched.

"I don't want that future!" Jamila gestured towards the ruined streets. "Everything has changed."

"No," Louiza said sharply. "Nothing has."

"There's nothing left …"

Which just meant things would get worse. Emmanuelle clamped her lips on the words.

"We have to hide."

Louiza grabbed Emmanuelle's arm, and ducked into the market.

What? Emmanuelle wanted to ask, but then she heard the sound of fighting, moving closer to them. No. No. Shouts, and the clamour of a crowd—grunts, the moans of the dying. The sound of metal on metal. She looked out, and caught a glimpse of Darrias fighting a Fallen wearing Harrier colors, before Louiza caught her and slammed her against the market's walls, well away from the fighting.

"Stay down," she whispered.

All Emmanuelle could hear was sounds: sword against sword; the slow whoosh of indrawn breath; the occasional thunder of rifles; the shifting crinkle of debris; and then a scream, turning into low moans—and the sound of a body striking the cobblestones.

Footsteps, getting closer.

Louiza's grip on Emmanuelle tightened. She was whispering the *Shahada*, very fast and over and over. Emmanuelle tried to look for the words of a prayer, found her mind scoured clear of almost everything.

Our Father, who art in Heaven …

She gathered magic to herself, but she was so exhausted she could barely think of a spell.

"It's over," Darrias said. She tossed a long knife onto the debris. The clattering sound startled Jamila, who was making calf-eyes at her. "Come on. We'll have to be a little careful—we're skirting the Great Interior."

In the main street, two bodies lay with blood pooling under them—and then, as they moved closer, a handful more, hanging over the wrought-iron railings of a small park with diseased trees and darker grass that looked mostly intact. These last bodies had been torn apart.

"Darrias …" Emmanuelle said.

"Not me." Her voice was cautious.

Ahead of them was a huge, dark building, shimmering with the light of wards: the Great Interior. The section they were facing had been a church at one point, but its three-lobed entrance was now sealed, and the belfry was burned, with only charred emptiness where the bells should have been. There were no soldiers or guards anywhere, and only silence around them. That wasn't normal, but what else could they do?

Darrias pointed left, making a gesture for them to remain low. Emmanuelle, Louiza and Jamila crouched as they went around the wall. Overhead, people moved behind the windows—dark silhouettes that didn't seem to slow down or point. The light was dim, but not dim enough: they must still be extremely visible against the cobblestones, but no one screamed or pointed. That was wrong. And something had torn those bodies apart.

They were halfway along the church's entrance when the sounds started.

It was low whistles at first—a series of plaintive calls echoing all around them, barely noticeable at first. Ahead, Darrias reached the corner, and knelt by another body. This one had their eyes open, staring at her. Their hand still clung to a useless, broken rifle.

"Asérimée," Darrias said.

The person looked mortal, but it was hard to tell because so little was left of them, just torn, bloodied skin, and face blackened with marks.

"Darrias ..." Asérimée laughed, and coughed wetly. "Come back for them?"

"My family is none of your business," Darrias said sharply.

Family. Emmanuelle looked at Louiza in rising horror. Inside the House. Inside Harrier, where Guy would have had all the time to hurt them as he wished.

"Darrias, you never said—"

Darrias had risen in one single fluid leap, her knife bloodied where she'd drawn it across Asérimée's throat. She stared around her, breathing fast. The plaintive call had become high-pitched screeches and silhouettes moved across the ruined church's walls—the shadows of small birds of prey, getting closer and closer.

"Run," Darrias said. "Now!"

When Emmanuelle stayed frozen she began to push her away from the church.

"If they catch you, you're dead. Now, Emmanuelle!"

The birds *detached* themselves from the church. One moment they were flat shapes on the darkened limestone, the next they were wheeling in the air, screeching and squealing triumphantly, except she could still see the outline of the limestone bricks on them—as if someone had cut them from the fabric of the building. The birds dived for them, unerringly, their talons and claws out and glinting in the evening air.

If they catch you, you're dead.

Emmanuelle turned, stumbling over debris, and ran.

There was nothing in the world but her body: her feet, catching on cobblestones; the air burning in her throat and lungs; the tight feeling of fear that made her head feel too large, too exposed to the night air. She wasn't going to make it—any moment now a spasm would come, and she'd sprawl again, an immobile target for the birds when they dived.

When she dared to peek back, just for a moment, she saw there were more of them: an entire flock emblazoned with the colors of broken buildings, shattered windows, and some of them coming from the armory further away, the dark red of flames and smoke, shimmering in daylight. They screeched like birds of prey.

Harrier.

Hawks.

To her left was the dark, deserted shape of the Great Interior. She should turn, go back up the street they'd come from—or at any rate not become hopelessly separated from the others—but all she could do was move forward, tensing at every moment, imagining the rush of air as they finally caught up with her. Night was falling now, and she saw less and less, everything reduced to gray, blurring shapes. *Run run run.* She needed to—she had to—she didn't know where safety was anymore. Ahead were the factories, and the Seine, and the bridges to Hawthorn, and Asmodeus's mocking voice. She could imagine all too well his delight at holding such a prize. What could he not make Selene do, if he threatened Emmanuelle, if he sent her back piece by bleeding piece back to House Silverspires . . .?

Screeches, behind her, getting closer and closer. And a wind of beating wings, rising at her back. Feathers swirled to either side of her, tinged with all the colors of the ruined House—fragments of debris and flame and smoke.

She'd heard that sound before—it was the one of her nightmares, the one of her vision of that dark corridor. Not billowing cloth. Just wings, rising in the emptiness. Her worst fear—but why?

If she could just duck into an empty building—just find someplace they couldn't fly—but there was no shelter anywhere, just emptied parks and plazas with ruined, rusted fountains. Ahead—impossibly far away—was an intersection of streets by a large triangular building, its wrought-iron windows all shattered.

She paused, panting. It was unwise of her, but she couldn't even breathe anymore, and every step sent pain into her legs, alongside the deeper, sharper pain of a stitch.

When she looked up, the birds had moved in front of her, cutting her view to the square she'd hoped to reach, a wall of beating wings and screeches and sharp talons darkening the sky. One of them detached itself from the flock, moving with its wings spread, as though soaring on thermals. Its wings were the color of ashes, patterned with fragments of wrought-iron railings and fogged-over glass.

Emmanuelle cast her spell—bringing her hands together and emptying all the magic in her body, willing the birds to burn, to fall into a thousand pieces. It felt like sinking into a cloud of dust. The birds at the center of her target flew away, shrieking; but others took their place—and the one hovering in front of them all didn't move.

This was how it ended, then.

Her exhausted body was bearing her down, on her knees in the street, but she wasn't going to give them that satisfaction. She forced herself back up—ignoring the aches and twinges in her body—and was betrayed, again, when her leg spasmed and left her sprawling in the dirt.

"You will stop."

It was a sharp, loud voice—one with the commanding assurance of a woman used to power.

"Stop, in the name of the head of the House!"

When Emmanuelle managed to look up again, she saw the woman facing the birds. She was small and slight, and wore the cloak of Harrier—the uniform of the House's magicians, without the collar ribbon that would have marked her rank outside the Great Interior. The bird had shifted, to face her.

The woman threw back the hood of her cloak. She wasn't small—she was *young*, a teenager at most, flush with Fallen magic but in perfect control of it. Her hands were weaving the pattern of an unfamiliar spell—something to stop the birds?

The world was swimming and folding into a hundred

different fragments. Emmanuelle struggled to keep her grip on reality. As she tried to push herself back to her knees, the foremost bird dived towards the woman. It went through her face as though she wasn't there, except that she gave a little low moan as it did so, and that, when it finally emerged from her back, it was heavier, struggling to free itself from her flesh as though the girl was holding it fast—head and beak, and wings, and with every fragment that emerged, color drained from the girl's face, and her eyes grew darker and darker, the color of smoke and winter evenings.

As the bird's talons finally pierced her skin, she collapsed—not like a living body or even like a corpse, but limp and boneless as though every bone and every organ in her body had been broken or liquefied, leaving only a cloak of cloth over a cloak of skin.

The bird gave a long, triumphant screech. Emmanuelle pressed her hands over her ears. She didn't even move when the birds slowly faded away, or when guards in the blue and black of Harrier came, cautiously sidestepping the remains of the magician, to drag her into the Great Interior.

6

Wounds Old and New

Thuan was thinking on House Harrier.

It was late, and he should have been going to bed. He'd dealt with all his non-conflicting obligations: he'd read the reports from the various courts; dealt with the curt message Second Aunt had sent, expressing sympathy with his situation but subtly reminding him the kingdom wouldn't intervene.

Which left only his ongoing and larger troubles. Asmodeus still hadn't woken up, and Iaris had blocked all of his accesses to the hospital. So he'd settled for the backup plan of taking a serious look at the House Harrier business.

He'd spread a map of Paris on his desk, and had laid a finger on the Grenelle bridge, the one that separated Hawthorn and Harrier. The thin sliver of l'Île aux Cygnes, the land that was neutral in principle, but was in practice claimed by neither of them, because the dragon kingdom's soldiers would drag anyone on the islands down into the depths of the Seine.

The kingdom wasn't going to intervene.

He'd known this for a while. The kingdom had been

embroiled in civil war, and Second Aunt's authority was too badly shaken. He'd have liked House Hawthorn not to intervene, either—and if it were any other House they might get away with it. But Harrier was their neighbor. All the reports said the House had descended into civil war, with different factions fighting each other for dominance over the ruins of the House. If it convulsed and collapsed, it was their own border sinking into chaos—and chaos had a habit of not being neatly contained.

He traced, idly, the lines from the other Houses: Silverspires, on Île de la Cité, too far away and too powerless to embroil themselves in anything; Lazarus, always eager to sow discord; Shellac, a minor House in the southeast, hungry and desperate to be larger; Mansart, Fontenoy and Solférino, the three small Houses closest to Harrier, and the first who'd swoop in to fill the void if House Harrier became irretrievably diminished.

That was assuming the fighting remained contained in Harrier.

Having a war zone on their doorstep was going to be a problem, and he couldn't see a path that didn't embroil them irremediably in Harrier's succession. Which they couldn't afford. As for an alliance with another House ... even if they'd wanted to, trust would be a problem. A House that was half-dragon and half-Fallen was a new and unknown quantity in Paris, and that meant the other Houses were steering clear of them, unable to predict by which rules the new Hawthorn would operate.

He had his own troubles in the House; but this would blast them into insignificance, if it happened. If only he could make Iaris see it.

Thuan became aware someone was watching him.

He looked up, and saw Asmodeus leaning against the door jamb. The smell of bergamot and citrus fruit wafted into the room, alluring, intoxicating. He wanted to close the distance between them both and kiss his husband, hard—to bear him against the door where he couldn't escape, and take in all the glorious proximity of his body. But the other smell—the one his dragon senses couldn't ignore—was blood. Thuan would have said not Asmodeus's, but the way Asmodeus leaned against the door jamb was characteristic—a little too slouched, a little too tense. He was using the wood for support, rather than for effect; which meant that he was still weak.

He didn't ask how Asmodeus was doing. *That* was never going to get him any kind of useful answer.

"We missed you earlier," Thuan said. "When House Harrier tore itself apart."

Asmodeus smiled. He moved away from the door jamb, and into the room. Thuan was impressed, because there was barely a shake in his legs, or even a hint that walking unsupported was a problem.

"Or when you got into a shouting match with Iaris and Phyranthe?"

Thuan winced. "I see news travels fast."

Asmodeus snorted. "It's a wonder Iaris wasn't sitting on my bed with a checklist of grievances when I woke up."

He reached Thuan, grabbed him. Thuan felt the way Asmodeus's hands used him for support, but that didn't matter because Asmodeus's lips were on his, pressing down hard enough to draw blood. Desire rose, trembling and unbearable, just as magic stroked his spine all the way down.

Asmodeus smiled. "Well, isn't it pleasant to see you."

He pulled away, sat on the desk, on the edge of the map of Paris, playing with a knife that seemed to have come out of nowhere. He was watching Thuan, his green-gray gaze lambent with Fallen light. Thuan ached to kiss him again.

"About Iaris ..." he said.

Asmodeus bent a fraction. "Do tell." He still sounded more amused than angry.

Thuan shrugged. He could be detailed, but clearly that wasn't what Asmodeus was after.

"I made some decisions. Iaris thought they were poor ones. Some of them concerned the Court of Persuasion."

"Hence Phyranthe." And, in that same light, amused tone, "You do know Iaris doesn't run the House."

Some days, Thuan wasn't sure he did, either.

"But you do."

"We do." Asmodeus's voice was sharp. Thuan couldn't tell if he was pleased or not.

"You know it doesn't work that way."

Another snort. "To say the least. One of the ways it works is that those who show loyalty are rewarded. That's not something I plan or want to set aside anytime soon. Are we clear?"

All too clear. "Yes."

A pause. Asmodeus cocked his head to watch Thuan, in a way that suddenly threw Thuan back to Phyranthe's office, with the smell of smoke and Vinh Ly on the carpet, shivering and trying to move away from them all.

"All the same, things have changed in the House, and

those once loyal would do well to remember the new order of things."

Thuan threw caution to the winds. "I need to know if you approve of what I'm doing."

Laughter, genuinely amused. "In need of reinforcements?"

Given the situation with Phyranthe … But Thuan knew Asmodeus didn't like weakness, and would only laugh if he admitted to it.

He weighed his possible answers, and found only the truth.

"We have something," he said. "I don't want to see it destroyed."

He must have looked away—because suddenly the chair was empty, and Asmodeus was by his side, one hand running on the line of his jaw, until it rested on his lips. A pleasurable tingle, that ended when Asmodeus withdrew his hand.

"My sweet dragon prince," he said, slowly, almost gently, "of course we do have something."

A shiver ran up Thuan's spine. He clamped his lips on a moan, and instead kissed Asmodeus, drinking in bergamot and citrus, on the verge of a chasm that would engulf both of them whole.

He was the one who pulled away, gasping for breath. Asmodeus's shirt was half-open, revealing soft skin the color of milk. Thuan ached to drink it all in.

He said, finally, "You must think I spent my time getting into fights."

Asmodeus's lips tightened. "It takes two sides to have a fight. I'll have a word with Iaris. And you will keep your dragons in check."

A sore point, there: he'd grudgingly admitted their presence, but he was more disturbed than he'd like to admit by having near-unkillable beings in his House, ones that only owed loyalty to Thuan rather than him.

Thuan nodded. "On it."

"Good." Asmodeus turned, to stare at the map of Harrier. "You have rather dry bedtime reading."

"Harrier is mired in a succession war. I'm trying to see where we stand."

Asmodeus ran a hand along the Grenelle bridge, following its lines until he hit the midpoint: the place where their boundary to Harrier was.

"An interesting turn of events, isn't it."

Not the tone Thuan wanted. He took in a deep, shaking breath.

"Asmodeus. Please tell me we're not going to involve ourselves in it."

"They *are* our neighbors, in case you failed to notice."

"I did notice," Thuan said, mildly. "I also noticed that we're not in the strongest of positions right now."

A gentle touch of magic on his lips, like a prelude to another kiss; and Asmodeus's hand, moving to hold his, sending a shock of warmth through his body.

"Dragon and Fallen united? You think that's a weakness?" Asmodeus asked.

Thuan forced himself to focus on the matter at hand.

"It was a costly union. The dragon ice killed off part of the House, and a lot of dependents. And now this happens, when we have forty wounded dependents in hospital, in case you hadn't noticed, from the shock wave."

Asmodeus's face hardened, almost imperceptibly. "I did notice."

"Asmodeus. They're not *harmed*." There was no need to hound House Harrier to the end of the earth because something or someone that belonged to him had been touched. Thuan said quickly, "It's a regrettable business and it will weaken them, but the best thing we can do is to stay out of it. There's no gain from rushing in."

"You forget. We have dependents inside Harrier."

"I didn't forget. But there's a difference between recovering dependents in danger, and deciding we need to intervene to designate the new head of the House, or support the old one, or whatever else you have in mind."

"I don't have much in mind." Asmodeus's hand still held Thuan's, and his other one was on Thuan's neck now, gently trailing along his jawline, sending a small shiver of pleasure up Thuan's spine. "Not in the matter of politics, at least."

And *that* was very clearly a lie.

"Who is in Harrier?"

"Darrias."

Thuan took Asmodeus's hand and held it immobile against his neck.

"Darrias? In Harrier? Are you *trying* to start a war between Houses?"

"She asked." He sounded amused again. "I told her she'd bear the consequences."

But he'd still said yes. Typical. Always go for the dramatic and explosive option.

Thuan said, more forcefully than he'd intended to, "The

consequences are a war on our doorstep. It's going to change the balance of forces in Paris."

Asmodeus paused, for a moment. "Afraid?" he asked, and his eyes glinted behind his horn-rimmed glasses.

Thuan stared at him. "Yes."

Asmodeus's smile was fond. "That's you all over, isn't it. Always overcautious. Getting involved doesn't mean fielding an army. The time for war is past."

How desperately Thuan wanted that to be true.

"But I agree with you on one thing," Asmodeus said. "It's too early. We don't know where the points of pain are, yet. We can afford to wait."

"You think so?"

Asmodeus's smell trembled in the air; his presence was beside Thuan, a palpable warmth.

"Of course. In the meantime, you can get on with your ... reforms."

"You indulge me," Thuan said sharply.

"Oh, believe me, I don't. I do trust you to get the House where it needs to be."

Asmodeus's hand climbed up—now they were either side of his neck, long, graceful fingers trailing over the planes of his face, ending each time with a soft, long stroke at his collarbone, like raw, naked heat on Thuan's skin.

"And I trust you in other matters, too."

Thuan shuddered. Asmodeus merely went on, slowly, each touch unbearably warm—making Thuan's entire being ache, everything sharpening and folding around him until the entire world seemed to be in the gentle, deliberate sweep of these fingers like fire on his skin, each touch filling more and more of him until he thought the intensity of his desire would tear him apart. There was nothing left but his imperious need.

"Other things." Thuan struggled to breathe. He reached out with both hands, drawing Asmodeus closer to him. "Your private business."

A sharp, wolfish smile, and the heat and hardness of his body closer to Thuan's.

"A significant part of it." The smell of bergamot and orange blossom trembled in the air, and the room felt cramped and stifling. "Wouldn't you say?"

Thuan tried to speak, but the same gentle touch of magic that had stroked his lips now silenced them, pressing itself against them with the slow and fierce intimacy of a kiss. All he found was an incoherent moan.

"Asmodeus," he said, drawing his husband closer for a kiss, a long, drawn-out one that made his entire being tremble and ache.

"Ssshhh," Asmodeus said, pushing him back in the chair, holding him down, searching for the buttons of his shirt even as Thuan pulled away the swallowtail jacket and opened Asmodeus's own shirt, revealing skin as pale as alabaster and swirling with magic—and the world shrank down to the shivering heat of pleasure.

Thuan woke up to someone frantically knocking at the door. It took him a moment to orient himself: they were in his bed, in his rooms, with him pillowed in the hollow of Asmodeus's broad shoulder. As he got up to hunt for clothes and a quick way to make himself presentable, Asmodeus stirred, opened his eyes, and immediately went from vaguely awake to knife-sharp.

"My lord, my lord." It was Sang's voice, high-pitched and panicked.

Great.

Thuan located a dressing gown and hastily wrapped himself in it.

"You have clothes in the bathroom—"

He turned to see Asmodeus already dressed in pajamas and a startlingly colorful dressing gown that mingled thorn trees and roses with the antlers of deer.

What was happening?

He glanced at Asmodeus, who raised an eyebrow. *Your room, your rules.*

Thuan threw the doors open—and was all but bowled over when Sang swept into the room.

"Your Majesty, there's an emergency."

With some difficulty, Thuan managed to pull away from the panicked dragon.

"Sang? What are you doing here?"

Sang had just seen Asmodeus—who'd pulled up a Louis XV chair and was sitting in it with steepled hands.

"I'm sorry, my lord, I didn't know . . ."

So whatever she wanted to say, she didn't want Asmodeus to hear. Unfortunately, it was too late for Thuan to throw Asmodeus out of his rooms. Great.

"Tell me," Thuan said.

Sang paused, for a bare moment. "Ai Nhi just lost control of her powers. She's scalded another child in the school with *khi* ice. And Phyranthe arrested her."

Thuan stared at her. He'd misheard. He must have, but the words didn't go away.

"She did what?"

Sang looked forlorn. "The other child is in hospital. Iaris refuses to let us help with the healing. And Vinh Ly …"

Thuan didn't think it could get worse, but apparently it could.

"Vinh Ly argued with Phyranthe about Ai Nhi's arrest, and it turned badly, so Phyranthe arrested her too. For disrespect of her superior."

Arrested. His oldest and most respected dragon, and a child. A five-year-old.

"Where are they both now?"

"Ai Nhi is in the cells. Vinh Ly is in her room under guard—Phyranthe said her offense wasn't as grave …"

The cells. And Vinh Ly had decided the best course of action was to try and plead with Phyranthe, rather than immediately go see Thuan. Which would have given Phyranthe ample time to devise punishments for Ai Nhi—and for her interrogators to get started. Because of course Phyranthe wouldn't waste an opportunity like this. No wonder she'd been content with locking Vinh Ly in her room: Ai Nhi herself was opportunity enough.

Thuan turned, to look at Asmodeus—who was looking at him with that same amusement. No, not amusement. Anger, and ill-disguised at that.

"She didn't mean …" he started, when he saw Asmodeus's face harden.

"I did tell you to control your dragons, didn't I?" Asmodeus rose from the chair. The shadow of black wings clung to his back. "Instead, they decide to create a diplomatic tangle in this House that will take me days to sort out, and make me look weak by making it apparent I can't teach my own husband's court the basic rules of good behavior." His voice was flat. "You will stay here. I'll get your dragon child back from the cells, where she should never have been locked in the first place, and make sure she's appropriately disciplined. Your other dragon dependent is your own business to sort out."

He made for the door without a single look at Thuan.

"Asmodeus …" Thuan started, but Asmodeus was already gone, and the doors slammed shut behind him.

Thuan tried to think of the political ramifications—of Iaris's and Phyranthe's sheer *glee* at the way things had turned out—and felt as though someone had cut the blood from his legs.

"Disastrous" was probably too weak a word for what had just happened.

Philippe carefully bound Hoa Phong's wounds, ignoring her grimaces as he touched suppurating skin. They looked, if anything, uglier than before: the *khi* elements shriveling and dying in the crevices of skin, and everything swollen and red. When he ran his hands over them he could feel waves of am: they were unbalanced, the *khi* stagnating and gradually strangling them.

They were back in the flat—they'd run from Diamaras and whatever was lurking in the Trocadéro fountain and gardens, all the way to Boulevard Barbès and Philippe's house.

"Alcohol," he said.

Isabelle handed him, in silence, the disinfectant—in reality the flask of rice alcohol they used for festivals and anniversaries. He applied as much of it as he dared to the wound, though of course it was adulterated stuff, the only thing the Houses had left them—the Fontaine and Calmette process, tasteless and still way too expensive, but all that could be found in the ruins of Paris anymore. He wove the *khi* fire and *khi* water into a loose spell, one that would force the *khi* to circulate around the body and promote healing—but noticed, as he did so, that the skin under his hands kept crumbling into the scattered shapes of *hoang mai* flowers.

When he was done, he stared at his fingers for a while—and finally ignited the *khi* fire in the air, burning away any contagion there might have been.

"I don't know how to heal you," he said.

A flash of something that might have been anger on Hoa Phong's face, swiftly gone.

"You don't have to." She flowed from the chair. "I'm Immortal. I'll heal."

Isabelle was sitting on the table, dangling her legs over its edge. She grimaced, but didn't say anything. Philippe pulled out a chair and sat, feeling drained.

"House Silverspires," Hoa Phong said slowly, thoughtfully—as if considering a challenge. "Morningstar."

Isabelle looked both fascinated and scared. She remembered, obviously, where she'd come from, enough to realize the House would never take her back in her current state. Philippe closed his eyes, remembering bones in a crypt, remembering the promise of power dragging at his being, remembering Isabelle lighting up with dreadful magic.

"He's the worst of them," he said. He'd been gone for a while, but now—through an unexpected, unexplained miracle—he was back in House Silverspires, ensconced as though he'd never left. "And you just can't walk into Silverspires."

Hoa Phong gave him a hard look. "Why not?"

Because he'd tried—or rather, because they'd kidnapped him once, taken him from the streets and kept him like a curiosity. Because he still had darkness lodged within him, a living reminder of what he'd done. Because it had only brought death and corruption, and Isabelle was only alive because of the mercy of Quan Am and a miracle. Because they couldn't hope to do anything more sensible than keep their heads down, and make the best lives they could, out of the shadow of the powerful.

He said, finally, "Because they'll kill you. Or take you and twist you until only a shadow of yourself remains. And because Dân Chay isn't in Silverspires and never has been. I know how Lucifer Morningstar worked."

He didn't say it was because of the darkness within him, the curse of the House.

Hoa Phong raised an eyebrow.

"They held me once," Philippe said, lightly. "It's always better to know how your jailers work. Dân Chay was dangerous, and Morningstar wouldn't have wanted him in his House, weapon or not."

Isabelle said finally, reluctantly, "He's right. Morningstar valued the well-being and safety of his House above all else. He'd have moved Dân Chay elsewhere. In the other House."

"The other House was Draken," Hoa Phong said.

Isabelle said, carefully, "That's ..."

"The one who imprisoned me? Yes," Philippe said. "It's dead." He'd felt it die, as the other Houses overwhelmed it; had lost his squad and his friends one by one. “It’s a ruin now. But we can go there and search it.”

Isabelle’s gaze rested on him, mercilessly clear.

“It’s not a ruin, is it? It’s a grave. The grave of your friends.”

Ai Linh. Hoang. Relaxed nights in the barracks, listening to folk tales and ghost stories and trying to forget that some of them might be their own, all the conscripted natives who’d died for the good of a House who’d never seen them as more than vermin.

“I’ll deal with it.” Philippe stared at his hands, willing them to stop shaking. “It’s just a place. We’ll leave tomorrow morning—we can be back before sundown if we get an early enough start.”

Isabelle grimaced, but didn’t protest.

“Tomorrow,” he said firmly. “It’s the middle of the night. Let’s sleep first.”

Hoa Phong opened her mouth to say she didn’t need sleep—he knew it was exactly what he’d have said, centuries ago, when he’d still been part of the Court.

“You need to heal,” he said.

“You’re not—”

“A doctor? I work as one, as a matter of fact,” Philippe said flatly, using the pronoun of a superior to an inferior, a scholar to an uneducated person. “Go to sleep.”

Philippe woke from a confused nightmare of running through House Draken as it was burning—desperately trying to find an exit through corridors overrun with fire and soldiers and the smell of smoke choking his lungs—and turning a corner and seeing the crest of House Draken flutter in the wind, the wyrm at the center detaching itself from the arms and moving towards him, extending burning fangs ...

He sat up for a while, breathing hard.

It's just a place.

He repeated that to himself, over and over. It was a burned-out ruin and nothing more. He could bear it. He had to.

It's just a place.

Just one day. That was all. It had no hold on him anymore. But nevertheless, he found himself saying the names of Manh Ba and the Earth-Store bodhisattva, over and over, a beseeching for mercy on long dead souls.

He could do this.

It's just a place.

Hoa Phong was sleeping on Isabelle's stained and flattened mattress. She'd undone her elaborate braids, and her long flowing hair lay beneath her like a cushion, shimmering with the faint golden sheen of flowers.

Isabelle was already up, ensconced in one of the chairs, while on the stove a saucepan simmered with steam.

"You went down to the pump?" he asked.

Isabelle didn't answer. He realized she was reading the papers he'd grabbed from Diamaras's office—in the confusion after they'd come back, he'd forgotten that he'd dumped them on the table while he cared for Hoa Phong's wounds. Isabelle was reading them with rapt attention, setting each one aside after taking notes on a piece of separate paper—he wasn't even sure where she'd found *that*. She'd drawn little sketches in the margins of her notes: those clouds again, those sweeping shapes that always looked as though they were about to burst into something dreadful. Except that they weren't flowing, but jagged and angry, their lines forcefully broken in several places. She was upset.

He peered into the saucepan, and saw the buns from the day before, dried and wizened. They'd perk up, soon enough. He picked up the papers, and glanced at them. They appeared to be a journal written in multiple hands, all of them competing to be the most illegible—and to be mostly fragmentary notes and diagrams.

It appears to be impervious to fire, but not to acid. Prolonged immersion in water didn't kill it, but it wailed when forced to swallow it, clawing at its throat and stomach—all for show, since of course it regenerated as soon as the water was gone.

All for show.

That dry, emotionless tone; the cataloging of horrors; and then a little further on, the measurements. The charts, showing how much water and how much pain. The knives: the detailed descriptions of the cuts, of how fast they healed.

The water, of course, isn't of much help in controlling it. But a suitable vehicle for acid could be devised . . .

The diagrams.

They weren't random drawings. They were dissections. And the notes were experiments: on how much pain a body could bear, before it knitted itself together—or before it gave up altogether. They'd handily labeled the corpse, too.

"Isabelle . . ."

Isabelle didn't look up. "They were trying to find out how spirits worked. We. *We* were trying to. My House."

"You don't know that," he said.

Draken, or Silverspires. The House he'd been conscripted into—but did that make him less guilty, that he'd been blind to what was happening?—or the House that had been her home. And really, what had he expected? They were building a weapon at a time when anything and everything was justified, if it could win them the war.

And then, more quietly, "Who was it? The . . . person they were experimenting on?"

"It doesn't say," Isabelle said. "But it was more than one. The things they did . . ."

She looked crestfallen. He hadn't realized how attached she still was to Silverspires—the House that had separated them, that had turned her into a distant, ruthless monster ready to pay any price for its survival.

He said finally, "It's not your House anymore."

"I *remember*, Philippe. That time isn't magically going away. They're my friends."

Philippe sat down. He struggled for words. He hadn't thought—he hadn't been paying enough attention. A chasm opened in the pit of his stomach: a sense of never-ending danger, like a bell tolling in the distance. Bad enough when they'd taken him and made him a prisoner, but if they took Isabelle . . .

"They can't be your friends anymore," he said. "You died."

A sharp, weighing look. "I remember that, too."

She didn't remember her rebirth. He hoped she didn't—hoped she never realized that she was only mortal because he'd failed, because he'd been scared of her powers … because an ugly part of him had preferred her weak and scared, not the fey and distant Fallen who'd barely hesitated before suggesting the House commit atrocities.

He was teaching her magic because she'd asked, but also because he needed … to make things right with her, even though he knew the only true way to do that was to ask for her forgiveness. But if he told her, he'd lose her. And not only that, but she'd go straight to Silverspires, where they'd have no pity and no consideration for who she was. She'd just be a means to an end, the result of a spell they'd desperately want, no matter the cost that had to be paid for casting it.

"Isabelle."

She made a face. "I know. I'm not welcome there anymore. But …"

He forced himself to remain still. "But?"

She was silent, for a while.

"They're not all bad." She raised a hand. "I know what you'll say. Lady Selene would have me dissected in a heartbeat. But she's not the only one in the House."

"She's not your friend."

"Other people were! You're the one who's always going on about compassion and being kind. Is letting them think I'm dead kind?"

He'd seen her turn cruel and fey once; because he'd seen how power had eaten away at her until she'd thought nothing of harming others for her own sake. He had to try to teach her what it meant to see everyone else as people, rather than things to be used.

"No," he said finally. The last time he'd been a parent was a thousand years ago, and he still felt inadequate now. "But it's for your own survival."

"So harming others is fine, then? Where do you draw the line?"

She was always effortlessly running rings around him.

"You weigh the harm you cause to others against the harm you might cause yourself. You don't kill someone just because you can. You don't slaughter hundreds for your own life. But in the scale of things, letting others grieve so you can live? That's a line I can accept."

"Perhaps I can't. Perhaps I'd rather tell them. Perhaps I can trust some of them. Unlike you."

"All it takes is one ruthless person learning the truth. You read these papers," he said.

"That was—"

"You're going to say that wasn't you? That their subject was *native*?"

"No! That's not what I meant!" Isabelle stopped, pressing her hands against her eyes, frustrated. She paused. "Laure wasn't bad, either, in the kitchens. You know what I mean. Emmanuelle helped us."

Only because helping them hadn't stood in Selene's way. But no, he was being unfair. Out of all of them, Emmanuelle was an oddity: almost as concerned with what was right as with the House.

"I know," Philippe said. "But if you go back into the House, Selene will know. Draken is where we're going next."

"It could be outside the House. I could ask one of them to come here."

Now she was really scaring him.

"No one is ever going to go into the Houseless areas. Isabelle—"

"You don't understand." Her face was hard. "It's my past, Philippe. You may be happy cut off from yours, but I can't live that way."

"I'm not cut off by choice."

It was a House—House Draken—that had taken him.

"Be honest. You'd left the Court of the Jade Emperor before, hadn't you? You were *wandering*. You'd already left. No ties. Immortals don't have these anymore, do they?"

She couldn't. No one addressed him like this. Power surged in his hands, all the *khi* currents gathered to bring her to her knees. And then he realized: she was Western. She had no idea of the respect due to teachers. She wasn't being flippant, or deliberately insolent.

He took in a deep, shaking breath, composing himself for a suitable answer, and was stopped by a knock at the door.

At dawn? An emergency?

Philippe got up, opened the door, and found Grandmother Olympe on the threshold.

"You never come here," he said, shocked.

Grandmother Olympe pushed past him, into the room—just as Hoa Phong pulled herself up, stretching. For a fraction of a second as the light hit her, the outline of hundreds of flowers was superimposed on her skin, and then it faded. Philippe held his breath, but Grandmother

Olympe appeared utterly unperturbed or unawed. She must have missed it.

"Other people come here," Grandmother Olympe said. "As I see. You have a new patient, child?"

"Are you keeping an eye on who sleeps here?"

"Hardly," Grandmother Olympe said. "I've come because we have refugees, and some of them are wounded and need a doctor." She glanced at Hoa Phong. "Your other friend who's not your assistant can come, too."

"Refugees?" Philippe couldn't see ... He stopped, then, because he knew. "Harrier," he said. "We can't possibly take in House-bound ..."

Grandmother Olympe's glance suggested that she wasn't going to let the small detail of a link to a House stop her.

"They're not House dependents. They're the small folk—the servants and the day laborers with nowhere else to go." She grimaced. "They want to go to the Halles, but I've forbidden it."

The Halles, the food belly of Paris before the war, now hosted a far less savory market: one where the desperate offered their services—and didn't always come back from the tasks allotted to them, as many who cruised the market were there solely for harm and pleasure in inflicting pain.

"How bad is it?" Philippe asked.

Olympe's carefully composed face was enough. Of course it would always be those in the most precarious positions who lost everything, even within the Houses. He'd said he wasn't going to meddle in House affairs again—what a promise, broken twice in as many days. First Hoa Phong and the Trocadéro business, and now this. Philippe sighed, and reached for his doctor's bag.

"We're coming."

House Draken could happen another day—and in truth he was half-relieved for the respite before he walked into the ruins of his old life.

Hoa Phong opened her mouth. She was going to say something about her mission and its importance to Vietnam—to the kingdom that had been, before French Indochina—but Isabelle cut her off.

"You can surely spare half a day for those who've lost everything, elder sister?" Her Viet was peppered with errors, but still blistering.

Hoa Phong stared from Isabelle to Grandmother Olympe. The face she made was fleeting, almost imperceptible.

"Of course I'll help," she said, with visible ill-grace.

7

The Past Casts Long Shadows

As the omnibus traveled the devastated banks of the Seine, it became easier to breathe. The sharp feeling pulling apart Aurore's ribs gradually became a stitch, and then a simple discomfort. They crossed the Alexandre III bridge and Aurore found herself whispering a prayer to her ancestors as the Seine churned, oily and dirty, below them, always hungering to grab people and drag them under. The nymphs and extravagant statues of the bridge had been torn away, revealing only black and diseased stone, and the street lamps were sharp spikes pointing towards the roiling heavens.

They skirted the territory of the Houses: Solférino, Mansart, Fontenoy. As they reached the emptiness that was the Champ de Mars, the plume of smoke in the sky became a cloud that loomed over them. Just as Asmodeus's spell eased and Aurore finally became able to breathe, the omnibus stopped.

"Can't go any further," the driver called. "We'll have to turn back."

Everyone stared at Aurore as she, alone of all the

passengers, clambered down from the bus. An old woman grabbed her hand as she passed, shaking her head.

"You don't have to, dearie."

Aurore breathed in—smoke and burning, and the faint, distant claws of Asmodeus's spell, a hook that had almost stopped pulling. The disk on her skin was cold, quiescent. One day, she'd have enough power to make even Asmodeus take notice.

"I do," she said, and gently took the hand away. "But thank you."

Outside the air was fogged, with the faint taste of smoke. As Aurore walked towards Harrier, it became … faintly harder to breathe, but almost nothing compared to the pain that had driven her there. She wrapped her scarf around her mouth, and tried to walk as slowly as possible, to not choke on smoke as she ran. She walked by the smoldering ruins of the Exhibition Palace, and the shadow of the broken Eiffel Tower at the end of the Champ de Mars—the knife-slash of monumental buildings and greenery that had once marked the splendor of the city.

Halfway through Place Joffre she saw the dim shape of the North Gate, and tried to breathe through choked lungs. There'd be the guards, and the flat cages—and the casual reminders of the House's indifference or outright cruelty to its mortal dependents. There would be …

It was different. It was *gone*—no, not gone, diminished. Look, here she was, almost to the House, and everything was choked with smoke, and she couldn't see any guards or any people. It couldn't harm her anymore. It …

Her hands shook. How was she ever going to get to power, if she couldn't even walk up a street and into a

House? It had seemed an easy decision to make, back in la Goutte d'Or, but now every step cost her. Every step changed and shrank her—made her eight years old again, barely out of training. Standing, shivering, with eyes lowered as the Fallen and the members of the Great Interior passed them by in the streets, made her ten years old again, standing unmoving and silent as a Fallen held Cassiopée's wrist tight enough to bruise, pinching the skin and watching her struggle not to cry out, for pouring a drop of wine on his sleeve.

All the small, casual cruelties; all the mountainous indifference of the House. Of Pellas, the Master of the Baths, who'd beat any servants who stumbled or didn't come fast enough when he called. Of Corinne, who ran the building while high on angel essence, and never missed an opportunity to assert her power by assigning extra chores to her and Cassiopée. Of stumbling into Cassiopée one final time, the piles of soap-holders they were carrying tumbling on the parquet, the sound of breaking thunder in their ears. Waiting, her stomach tied in knots, for her master's judgment and bracing herself for a whipping—until Pellas smiled and said he was remanding her and her sister's cases to the enforcers ...

All behind her. She'd gone. She'd escaped. She'd *survived.*

A day and a night. All she had to do was get into the grounds, and keep her head down, and ...

She thought of the hook dragging her back to Hawthorn, to Asmodeus's mocking gaze, of his taking the knife to her once again. If he did that—if he tortured her again, after her brief, poisoned taste of freedom—she wasn't sure how much she could hold from him. Best lay low—give him what he wanted and pray for mercy. She'd have laughed, if she still had the capacity to laugh about the business of Houses.

Movement, to her left. Aurore braced herself for an attack, but nothing happened. No, not quite—there was someone moving, except they were too small and too agile to be an adult. A child, here, on the outskirts of the House? She stopped moving, and waited.

Presently, the figure moved again—running through the ruins of the École Militaire on her left, away from her. There was nothing that way. There'd never been anything: the École had been ruins since before the explosion, and the streets behind it, covered with a sticky charred residue, were not desirable enough to go to the trouble of cleaning them. Harrier had all but cut them off, as they always cut off the undesirable.

She was supposed to get *into* the House, if she was following orders.

Demons take Asmodeus and his arrogance and his orders. Aurore shifted position, and moved to follow.

There was plenty of shelter—the tricky part was moving over debris without making too much noise. The explosion didn't seem to have done much to the area except throw a layer of charred fragments over everything. The smoke thinned. She was moving away from wherever the explosion had happened. Still no one. No guards. No hawks, either, as if the House itself was sleeping, or blind. Or both.

She kept a wary distance between her and the child, and finally saw them slip into the Grenelle slaughterhouse—a series of large, disused buildings that had fallen into ruins after the slaughtering of beasts had been moved southward.

Inside, the main yard was a quincunx planted with linden trees. The trees were still there, their large trunks threaded through with the whitish strands of fungus, their leaves mottled by rot. Where had the child gone ...?

There. Movement again, in one of the buildings. Aurore walked to it; and found a Fallen holding court under the metal rafters.

There was literally no other word for it. He sat at the center of a rapt circle that included one small child and two adults, speaking in a low, grave voice that she couldn't make out. The child who had just run into the building was perhaps eight or nine, standing at rigid attention as if making a report, desperately eager to please.

Aurore must have breathed, or done something she shouldn't have—because although she didn't remember moving, the Fallen lifted his head to stare straight at her.

His hair was a bright, vivid yellow—the color of gold, of corn in the books she and Cassiopée had trafficked as children, the ones that showed countryside with plump cows and green grass. His eyes—they transfixed her, intent and bright, a sharp, unreal color of blue, swirling with so much magic they shone translucent.

"A visitor. What an unexpected delight. Come in."

Not an order—not even a spell—but she found her feet moving of her own accord, drawn like a mouse to a snake. He wasn't only Fallen—not only the smooth, graceful, deadly beings she'd grown up bowing down to—he was the quintessential incarnation of them, power made flesh.

Everything she desperately wanted for herself: the magic that would keep them all safe.

"I'm Morningstar," the Fallen said, smiling, as Aurore reached the circle of Harrier dependents. He wore a formal swallowtail, black with a red sheen, and a touch of silver at his throat, a cravat with ruffles—and the insignia of House Silverspires on both shoulders, overlaid with the domes of a city she'd never seen. "And you are?"

"Aurore." And, because he was still staring at her, because the words wouldn't stop coming, "My lord."

She wanted to kneel; or at the very least to look down, as she'd done so often in the House. But that time was past. She wasn't anyone's servant anymore. Not even if that someone was the first and most powerful of the Fallen.

Morningstar looked at her, as if waiting; and smiled when nothing happened.

"This is Virginie," he said, pointing to the child who'd just entered the building. "Frédérique and Nicolas"—who looked to be Virginie's parents—"and Charles ..."

They looked to be two young children—Charles was a toddler still, with baby fat clinging to his cheeks—and their parents. Except ...

She stared at Virginie, hard. The child was wearing a nondescript Harrier uniform, but when she moved, magic shone faintly through the planes of her face. Nothing so obvious as Morningstar—a candle to a sun—but still ...

"You're from the Warded Chambers," she said slowly, softly.

Magicians in training, with no Fallen parent nearby to bathe them in their magic and keep watch over them?

"You shouldn't be here."

The urge to look down was becoming overpowering:

a Fallen from another House was one thing, but people from the Great Interior?

Frédérique, Virginie's mother, said, "We could have remained in the Great Interior, and fought to the death."

She wore men's clothes, and her hair was cut short—so short it looked almost shorn. She had swarthy skin and light hazel eyes: a distant ancestor from the Mediterranean basin, the way it sometimes happened in the Houses. She sounded angry. Bitter. Aurore had always thought people called to the Great Interior would be less … She struggled to find words. She'd always assumed they'd be happy, at least—mortals able to lord it over everyone else in the House.

"I'm sorry," she said.

Frédérique smiled, and it was suddenly dazzling.

"Don't be. It's been a hard day."

"It was hard before today," Nicolas, Virginie's father, said. He had a bandage over one eye, and a huge gash that ran from it to his lips, a raw, shining wound that didn't look good. "Lord Guy was losing." He grimaced again. "And you know Niraphanes …"

Virginie said, in a small voice, "I want Niraphanes."

Frédérique grimaced. "She can't be with us right now, sweetheart."

"We could have stayed—"

"There are bad people," Frédérique said. "Very bad people. That's why we need to keep ourselves safe." Her face was hard. "She'll understand."

Nicolas shook his head. "You know—"

"I know she wanted to drag Virginie into this," Frédérique said.

"I can fight!"

Frédérique's mouth opened, closed. Then she said, in a much softer voice, "I know you can, sweetheart. That was never in question." Her face said the rest. *You shouldn't have to.*

It was none of Aurore's business—had never been. She'd never had the chance to try for Warded Chambers. Her pregnancy hadn't been visible when she'd left the House, and menials such as her never caught the eye of the Fallen anyway. Her child would never have grown up bathed in Fallen magic, or become a magician—or had any of the things Frédérique and Virginie took for granted. But Frédérique looked so heartbreakingly afraid. She reached out, and touched Virginie's hand lightly.

"It's all right, sweetheart. It's all right."

She felt small and inadequate—and so very very angry at the way the world was.

"Guy won't be able to reach you within Silverspires," Morningstar said. "I can promise you that."

Aurore let go of Virginie's hand. "You ..." The words were out of her mouth before she could think. "They're Harrier *dependents.* You can't just steal them."

Morningstar raised an eyebrow. "Can't?"

It was none of her business. It really wasn't, and she had enough problems of her own. She fingered the disk between her collarbones, feeling the imprint of Hawthorn's arms.

"Lord Guy will never forgive you."

"Guy will be in no position to forgive much of anything." Morningstar's eyes narrowed. "Lord Guy, is it? You're not wearing the uniform of Harrier." Magic flowed beneath his skin, lazily, probed at Aurore's chest and belly—the disk warmed imperceptibly, and it felt as though Morningstar's spell was sliding off it. "And not linked to any House. Come here to scavenge?"

Aurore opened her mouth, and then closed it. She'd had time to think of a plausible lie on her way there, but something in those blue eyes invited … trust. Confidence.

She wasn't that naive.

"My sister and I were thrown out of Harrier three years ago. It's been … hard."

A sharp look from Morningstar, but Aurore had, by now, had plenty of practice at dissembling to Fallen.

"You'll be far better off with us."

A day and a night in Harrier.

"You're headed back to House Silverspires, aren't you?"

Morningstar shook his head. "Not quite," he said. "There's … something I want to see first."

Frédérique looked tense again. "We shouldn't tarry here."

Morningstar's voice was reasonable and calm, but Aurore could hear the unspoken edge.

"I'm here for a reason. I'm quite willing to take on … extras"—his voice was low and thoughtful— "but my primary purpose isn't to poach magicians from Guy. I have a head of House who'll be very unhappy if I don't finish assessing the situation here." He shrugged. "You can go, if you want to. I'm not forcing you to stay."

But he was their only chance of escape. As if they'd leave.

And he was staying in Harrier, for a time. *You'll be far better off with us.* As it happened, Aurore was thinking the same thing. She wasn't Fallen and couldn't afford to pay for any reserves of magic—the little charged mirror she'd had with her in Hawthorn, worth a year of savings, had been confiscated when Hawthorn's guards had arrested her. Still …

"Why would you find me worthy of regard?"

A sharp look. She was failing to be sufficiently servile.

Morningstar said, "I'm a lone dependent of another House, trapped in a burning one in the middle of a succession war. I can use any help."

It wasn't that. It was … vanity, or something similar? A desperate need to collect broken things—to break them himself, if it came to that. She'd met his kind before.

A day and a night. She could tag along with them, and attempt to learn what was happening in Harrier from Frédérique and the other parents, uncover the kind of politics that would keep Asmodeus happy—or at any rate, not displeased enough to hurt her again. He'd expect her to explore the House, lying low, but would certainly never approve of what she was doing. His fault. He should have been more specific when setting the spell that had dragged her here against her will.

Being with Morningstar and the escapee magicians wasn't the *safest* place, but was there really anywhere safe, right now?

"All right," she said, feeling as though she was dancing on the edge of a chasm. "What now?"

Her captors marched Emmanuelle to a room underground: some kind of cellar, at the end of a maze of damp, dark corridors holding closed doors and cells. They left her there, without a word, to stare at the inside of her cell.

There was stone under her, and light coming through a grate. She waited for her eyes to make out shapes: the bench on which she was lying, the darker shape of the closed door.

She remembered the birds, and the magician—and the way the hawk had passed through her as though she were just a wall of water, or thin paper that crumbled under its touch. Remembered the soft, wet sound of her crumpling, the coat floating down to the ground. Harrier had sent guards to retrieve Emmanuelle instead of killing her. Why would they bother with her, when they were already busy with their own succession war?

And where were the others?

Darrias.

She remembered Darrias's taut face as she drew the knife across the Fallen's throat.

My family is none of your business.

Darrias was jewel-hard and taciturn: Emmanuelle had always assumed that she'd walked out of her Harrier life with no regrets, as lonely as she'd been in the House. She'd never thought she had a family. Who had she left behind? One or several spouses? People seldom said "family" unless children were involved.

Which meant . . .

Emmanuelle hated playing political games, but that didn't mean she was *bad* at it: she'd had ample time to learn, standing by Selene's side. Her partner was, after all, head of House Silverspires, and the intrigues she breathed in every day had rubbed off on Emmanuelle.

Fallen were sterile. They could adopt mortal children, and some did—but in Harrier that could only mean one thing.

A magician.

Which meant …

Darrias hadn't just been an outcast when she'd walked out of the House. She must have lost a power struggle—because there was no way the Fall-mother of a magician would have been sent into the streets as an envoy. Magicians *lived* and *breathed* with their Fall-parents, long after their formal presentation to the House.

She had never breathed a word of this to Emmanuelle. Not once, in their long, barbed drinking sessions in the cafés House members considered neutral territory, staying all afternoon, remaking the world in their cracked glasses. She … she could have told her. Emmanuelle tasted the thought, carefully, again and again. They'd been … acquaintances, no more. Not friends. There could be no friendships across the dividing lines of House loyalty. Why did it hurt so much, that she hadn't been confided in?

And—more importantly—where was Darrias's family now?

The door opened. Emmanuelle scrabbled to her feet, fighting a wave of dizziness. Two guards in the colors of Harrier, who gestured her towards the door.

"Where are you taking me?"

No answer.

They walked through damp, dark corridors holding more cells, and moaning prisoners—where had they come from, had they always been there?—and then up a flight of stairs, and into the early morning light. Emmanuelle's eyes burned, but her guards didn't even slow down. The corridors opened up, widened into chevroned parquet—not decayed or cracked, but brand new, a staggering display of opulence and power. The wallpaper was only lightly mottled, its pattern of hawks in flight exquisite. The furniture was so polished it *gleamed*, the upholstery a dark, deep green, the marble chimneys pristine. In the distance was the faint sound of a grand piano. Emmanuelle felt she'd woken up in a different universe, one that had nothing to do with the devastation of the House, or the even older one of the Houseless areas.

The corridor felt familiar, but she couldn't place it. Not until they reached the end, and she saw the double doors—the cream-colored doors with handles shaped like leaves. The exact ones she'd seen in her memories.

Which meant this part—this specific part—of them wasn't false. It couldn't be. Because the Great Interior wasn't open to foreigners; and how could she remember a door and a room if she hadn't already been there, if she hadn't already seen Guy?

It didn't help. Because she still didn't remember what had happened, not a word. Just dread, and the birds, and the fear.

Useless.

Beyond the door lay a reception room, the ceiling of which was overwhelmed by stucco and moldings of acorns and lily flowers. Huge mirrors alternated with curtained alcoves—the illusion faded with the curtains, whose deep purple was faintly tinged with mold. In front of each mirror was an ornate table with an alabaster bust. Emmanuelle couldn't recognize their faces. People important to the House, presumably?

A Fallen was waiting for her, sitting in a gilded chair with blue upholstery. By his side, on the low table, was a tray with a cup of coffee in cracked porcelain. He raised his eyes, but didn't otherwise move when she entered. A familiar face: slick brown hair, reddened cheeks, deep-set hazel eyes suffused with easy, insufferable arrogance. Behind him were four young people standing at attention, with the cloaks of magicians over their shoulders.

Guy. The beleaguered head of House Harrier. He wouldn't have looked beleaguered at all, sitting in the untainted heart of his power, except that his magicians were far too young, barely out of childhood: their confidence was hollow swagger and ignorance. Also, his wife Andrea was nowhere to be seen, which was ... not a sign of weakness so much as odd, because Emmanuelle had always seen the two of them together.

"Hello, Emmanuelle," Guy said.

On the sofa behind him, between the magicians, was a prone body. No, not a body, a corpse: an older boy with ginger hair with a bleeding mess where his chest should have been. The magician's cloak he'd been wearing should have covered it, but it had slipped away and no one had bothered to set it right. He didn't wear a ribbon at his collar: not merely a magician then, but a warded one, the most powerful and reclusive of Harrier's magic-users.

He was a *child*. Twelve or thirteen, at most? This ... this was what the House did to its own children.

"Benedict," Emmanuelle said, aloud.

Guy's last and most powerful son—the one who'd died

and set off the succession crisis. She felt, once again, that nebulous fear—a feeling of her head being too large for her, a fleeting memory that should have made sense.

"As you well know." Guy didn't move from his chair. "I'm surprised you're still here."

Emmanuelle didn't move. She forced herself to remain casual—her tone light, banter filled.

"It's a little hard to get out of your House at the moment. As you well know."

A tense, taut silence. She threw a glance around the room. Something else wasn't quite right, but she couldn't put her finger on what.

Guy said, mildly, "I would suggest you learn respect. Silverspires is no longer your shield."

"It's not my House that's burning."

Emmanuelle couldn't help herself. Silverspires was so weak it barely counted as a House anymore, and it afforded her no protection. But it had been a long, exhausting day, and the little sleep she'd managed in the cells hadn't really improved her mood.

One of the guards forced her down, twisting her arm upwards as they did, and standing with a foot on her wrist to keep her in that position, flat on the carpet. Pain shot up her arm. She bit her lip until she tasted blood, because she wanted so badly to cry out, and she wasn't going to give him that satisfaction.

"As I said," Guy said, rising and coming to stand over her, "I suggest you learn respect."

The pressure on her back eased and she managed to pull herself up. She knelt, slowly, carefully, praying that there would be no unwelcome spasm to bring her down. Guy was watching her—still trying to make sense of her? But no, he was barely disguising cold fury.

She kept her voice icy and calm.

"Do you really think you can afford a war with Silverspires?"

Guy stopped in front of her. All she could see were the tailored trousers, with the blue-and-black tracery of hawks on the cloth.

"You're the one who started it, Emmanuelle."

"I did not."

Guy went on as if she hadn't spoken. "I warned you to stay out of this. Quite explicitly."

She couldn't admit to missing memories. It would be the height of recklessness—she might as well roll over and show him her throat to be torn out. So she said nothing. He was angry—losing his hold over the House he'd ruled, shut in a room with the corpse of his child. He would never remain silent if he could gloat.

"I warned you, and yet you keep associating with Darrias," Guy said.

"I haven't—" she started.

"Don't lie," he hissed. "I saw you together in the streets."

That startled her. How? The windows of this room opened on an interior courtyard with cobblestones. But of course he'd have left the room …

"I have *eyes*," Guy said, softly, and that was when she saw them.

They'd been there, unmoving, sitting on the ornate furniture, on the busts, on the low tables, half across the surfaces of tarnished mirrors—everywhere. The translucent images of birds of prey: hawks at rest, with folded wings and cocked heads, turned towards Guy. It was like a trick of the light: blink, and they became visible, outlines waiting to detach themselves from the furniture and make for their prey.

The girl-magician, standing very still as the bird went through her—the sound of her collapse, a wet, gurgling thing with no bones or blood anymore, fused flesh and muscles turned to mush. The cloak, fluttering in the breeze, falling over what was left of her. The sound of beating wings, rising and rising until they filled her entire universe.

She couldn't stop the shiver that ran through her; or the spasm of her left leg that followed it.

"I'm going to make an example of Darrias, when I catch her. Thinking she can walk in here and steal people from me. I don't need more chaos in this House, Emmanuelle."

All she could see was the parquet floor, and the points of his shoes. And, as he spoke, a rising, raucous whisper—a flutter of beating wings, the twisted, empty places in her memory.

"As I told you—I know exactly what Darrias's game is. I've always known, even when she pretended to walk back into Harrier as an envoy from her new House. She's always believed she could have what was mine." Laughter that had absolutely no mirth; only dark delight at others' suffering. "I was going to take her apart at the dinner after the Great Presentation, and the most beautiful thing is that Hawthorn couldn't have interfered—she was the one who'd have started it, poking her nose into the affairs of another House. Asmodeus would have her broken, bloodied corpse back, and not even been able to ask for reparations. That would have taught him." He knelt, peering at her. In his eyes danced the flames of someone who had long, long since lost touch with reason or balance. "It would have been such grand entertainment, wouldn't it? All those exquisite courses served against a background of her screams. And even Niraphanes couldn't have protected her—"

"But you don't have her."

Emmanuelle said the only thing that came to mind. He'd told her about Darrias's plans. He'd warned her to stay out of it. He must have gloated about it back then, as he was now. How much *else* did she not remember from that night?

"I have *you*." He was breathing into her face now, and his eyes were the round, unblinking ones of his hawks—his face illuminated by the smoke and fire of his House. "Perhaps you'd serve as well."

He'd take her apart in a heartbeat. He had nothing left to lose. She could talk about Selene's ire all she wanted, but it wouldn't mean anything to him—he was losing his grip on everything he'd taken for granted. She forced herself to remain calm.

"You no longer have an audience, I fear."

He smiled. It was slow and lazy and utterly bone-chilling.

"At the moment, no. But I'm sure I'll think of something."

He snapped his fingers—the guards dragged her up. Around the room, the birds had spread their wings and were looking straight at her.

"Get her back to the cells."

8

Things are Changing

"Here you go," Iaris said, in a firm voice that barely allowed keeping the door open for Thuan. She thrust a dejected and trembling Ai Nhi into Thuan's arms. "Your child."

Thuan wanted to protest Ai Nhi wasn't his, but with Vinh Ly under guard, he guessed that it was as accurate as it'd ever be.

"Unka Thuan." Ai Nhi was shaking. She didn't appear harmed. But her wounds would have closed much faster than a mortal's. "I'm sorry I didn't mean to I won't do it again." It came in a breathless, scared jumble of words. "I swear."

"Sshh, child," Thuan said. "It's all right. You're safe now." He'd ask later the question he dreaded, about what had happened to her. He said, to Iaris, "I need to see him."

Iaris's face was a sliver of pale skin through the door she was barely bothering to keep open.

"He won't be disturbed," she said.

Behind her, Thuan could just see Asmodeus—he had his back to Thuan, and was pouring Phyranthe a whiskey from a decanter in the cupboard, a prelude to a talk Thuan couldn't even guess at. Was it going to be a dressing-down?

It was looking more like two old soldiers sharing a drink and comparing experiences, the kind of rapport he and Phyranthe would never have. Easier to quietly say to Phyranthe she'd gone too far, and not to have her bristle because she thought he presumed.

"The child," Thuan said.

"You have her."

"The other one. The …" He swallowed. "The one Ai Nhi harmed. How is she doing?"

A raised eyebrow. "Oh, so you are taking responsibility for your dragons? Mélanie has been burned extensively. We're doing all we can to make her comfortable."

Which didn't sound comforting at all. Mélanie. A name Thuan could feel now, in his mind, with the other dependents of the House—young and scared and struggling against wounds that would, at best, leave her crippled.

"Let me heal her," Thuan said. "Or, if not I, another member of my court."

That was the wrong word to use. He saw her stiffen.

"You have no court."

"So you'd rather let Mélanie die to sate your pride. I shouldn't be surprised, I guess, after what you did to your daughter."

Iaris's daughter Nadine had been exiled from the House after intriguing against Asmodeus; and Iaris had never attempted to intervene on her behalf.

Her smile became a rictus. "You won't speak of Nadine here."

Thuan kept his face expressionless. He didn't much like to speak of Nadine either. It brought back unpleasant memories—she'd been his teacher inside the House, and he'd believed her his friend.

"I will say what I want. And it's only the truth, isn't it?"

Iaris's face didn't change. At last she said, "She was a traitor," but her voice was a fraction less assured.

"I'm sure you'd have said that to her face, and found only happiness when Asmodeus punished her." Thuan kept his voice emotionless. "Applauding every cut and every broken limb."

In truth, Asmodeus probably wouldn't have done it. Not for Nadine's sake—but because Iaris had been with him long enough that he was unwilling to reward her loyalty by killing her only child.

A silence. Iaris's gaze on him was burning. She wouldn't have borne it, and they both knew it.

"We all have our weaknesses," Thuan said.

Iaris said nothing. At last, "You may see to Mélanie's wounds." She raised a hand to stop Thuan from speaking up. "You personally, and no one else. And Ai Nhi will watch you do it."

Thuan nodded. It was only fair.

Iaris went on, as if she hadn't seen him nod, "Under supervision."

"Wait," Thuan said.

Iaris gestured, and Mia, the Fallen Thuan had already met, came to stand by her side. She'd dropped the kittens and was now doing her best to look ferocious. That she managed it in a vivid red dress laden with sparkles and sequins was impressive.

Thuan stared at her. "I have plenty of dragons. I don't need a bodyguard."

Or a busybody. It was going to be hard enough to do a healing—he was more a scholar of magic rather than a magician per se—without adding an omnipresent agent of Iaris scrutinizing him for any weakness they might later use against him.

Iaris's face was all fake concern. "I have every confidence you can take care of your own. This is about how it'll look to the dependents of the House."

Only because she was making the most of it already, spreading and fanning rumours about dragons' betrayal. But he couldn't say that out loud.

"I'm sure they're intelligent enough to separate truth from malicious rumours."

He kept his voice light, as sweet and as cutting as hers. She wasn't the only one used to court intrigues.

"Not everyone is as well-informed as you'd like to be." Iaris laid a hand on Mia's shoulder. "This is for your own good, and the good of the House. For the sake of fairness."

Fairness. The word tasted like ashes in Thuan's mouth.

"All right, I'll take Mia with me. About Vinh Ly . . ."

Iaris shrugged. "I can't help you with Vinh Ly. Her offense was against Phyranthe."

"And we don't run a personal tally of grudges, do we?" Thuan asked softly. "Is this really the way you want the House run?"

It was, by all accounts, the way it had been run under Uphir, Asmodeus's predecessor. Asmodeus ruling the House on his own had been bad enough, but at least he'd protected his dependents, even risking his life for them. Uphir had just used and discarded them for his own pleasure.

"No, not the way I want it run," Iaris said. He'd annoyed her again. Too much, perhaps. A fine line to walk between standing his ground and angering her. She made, again, that sigh of fake concern. "But Phyranthe is like Lord Asmodeus. Slow to forget grudges. I'd advise you to take it up directly with her."

And wasn't that going to be a pleasure. He was angry at Vinh Ly—because she should have gone to see him, because she was at least partly responsible for Ai Nhi's stay in the cells—but that was no reason to leave her in Phyranthe's hands. This time, she had an offense against her, rather than mere sloppiness in the course of work. This time ... he didn't know what Phyranthe would come up with, to crush Vinh Ly utterly.

"Of course," he said, knowing he'd lost.

Ai Nhi, when Thuan spoke to her, clammed up. She wouldn't say anything about her time in the cells, or whether Phyranthe or anyone in the Court of Persuasion had harmed her.

"Asmodeus," he said, and got only a scared-looking five-year-old parroting that she hadn't meant to, and wouldn't do it again.

Discipline her, Asmodeus had said. What had Phyranthe done? What had Asmodeus done? What were they doing now?

Thuan had fought the urge to ask Ai Nhi to undress so he could check her body—it would not have been right, and only upset her further. At length, exhausted and imagining the worst, he gave up.

"Come on, child. Let's go heal your friend," he said.

It was the midday break, and the corridors were quieter than usual, though people stopped and stared at him. Word had gotten around: he wasn't sure what kind. Sang and the others would not be without friends, but Iaris and her ilk had more hold on the House. He'd gotten Ai Nhi a ham sandwich from the kitchens, which she half-heartedly nibbled. Mia had used the opportunity to grab a glass of sparkling wine and an apple, which she consumed with absolutely no hint that anything was wrong. It would have been impressive in other circumstances.

The ward reserved for the Court of Birth was almost separate from the rest of the hospital. To get to it, Thuan had to take winding corridors with faded, rotted wainscoting and sad-looking orange trees that bore only wizened fruit. The door was wood, with round ivory handles and a frieze of painted thorns running around the panels. He scowled at it. He hated casting spells, and this one was going to be neither easy nor short.

Something brushed across the nape of his neck, below his topknot. A touch of wind, except that it felt like the fingers of a thin and wasted hand. He turned. Nothing. Just a faint creak of parquet floor. He was imagining things, but it felt as though the House was watching him as he laid his hands on the door handle.

"Let's do this," he said.

The ward was almost deserted as well. He supposed he should be thankful for that. It was a large bedroom with faded wallpaper and a cracked tile floor inlaid with gold. The chairs were mismatched and made with chipped wood, put together inexpertly by someone with too much glue and not enough time, and the beds were simple metal frames painted the silver and gray of the House, with the crest of Hawthorn on the curtains.

Mélanie was at the back of the ward, so small against the bed that it felt it had entirely swallowed her. Her arms and neck were covered in bandages, beneath which protruded ice crystals and the pearly shape of blisters, a constellation of them on every part of her skin he could see. Her face was pale, almost obscenely so in comparison to the redness of her burned skin. The sharp smell of *khi* ice hung in the room, and didn't quite disguise the animal one of waste.

Ai Nhi inhaled sharply. Thuan started to say she didn't need to be there, and then saw Mia watching them, leaning against the wall. Behind her were two nurses, watching him intently. Under supervision. He felt like a performing animal at the circus.

"It'll be all right," he said.

He felt useless, and inadequate, because everything was so far from all right.

He knelt, to look at Mélanie. They'd done their best to remove the *khi* ice with Fallen magic, but more as a side effect of trying to soothe down the burns, rather than as a systematic effort. So far, only dragons—and possibly Berith, Asmodeus's Fall-sister—could see the *khi* elements. He didn't think Iaris had called on Berith.

He exhaled. Long, thin chains of *khi* ice clung to Mélanie's hands and arms, digging into her skin and constricting her blood vessels. He could see the fine lattice of ice crystals that kept building under her skin, kept trying to propagate itself.

Ai Nhi said, in a small voice, "We wanted to build an ice castle."

Thuan nodded. "All right."

Normally, *khi* earth was the element that counteracted water; but if he wove only *khi* earth, he was going to kill Mélanie. The ice would be destroyed, for sure; but her body couldn't take the shock.

"What did you do?" he asked.

One of the two nurses detached himself from the wall. Ahmed. His face was grave.

"The usual. Bathe in warm water, basic analgesia. Some magic to relieve the burns." He grimaced. "The blisters were too extensive for treatment. And they kept coming back when we tried to remove them."

Because of the *khi* ice.

"I see," Thuan said. "I'm going to need everyone to take a step back."

He closed his eyes—remembered the spells of healing in the books he'd used to read in the palace's library, trying to find some calm and order in the cut-throat environment there. Right. First remove the ice, then use a lattice of *khi* fire and *khi* earth to soothe the burns. Easy.

He bit back a hollow laugh. Who knew that skimping on his magical lessons would lead him there.

He made the weave slowly, carefully: *khi* earth and *khi* wood, just enough of it to dampen the effects of the earth. Then, in that same suspended moment when everyone and everything receded into an impossibly faraway distance, he started applying it to Mélanie's skin.

It was slow and painstaking work: crystal by crystal, fragment by fragment of *khi* ice, to make sure that his impact was as small as possible. Halfway through—or maybe less, maybe more—he'd lost track, Mélanie shuddered. He stopped, heart in his throat. What if he'd damaged her body past healing? But she subsided, her breathing ragged and slow. One of the nurses, who'd started to approach with a syringe, slowly backed away. Thuan resumed chipping away at the *khi* ice.

He didn't know how much time had passed when he looked up. In the gardens beyond the barred windows, the sky had turned the red and pink of evening. Ai Nhi was curled on the chair, watching him. The sandwich had been replaced with another, which she barely nibbled on. She looked miserable. Mia was still watching him, and the two nurses had been replaced by a single one, who watched Thuan unblinkingly.

He exhaled, slowly, softly. It didn't seem like there was ice anywhere. He rose, wincing at the way his body cramped, went around the bed to check. Once, twice.

"May I touch her?" he asked.

The nurse nodded.

Thuan lifted her arms slowly, carefully. Bandages crumbled into dust and dry, iridescent scales like a snake's. Mélanie didn't even stir. No ice left.

Good. He settled on his haunches again, and wove the lattice for healing, slowly looping it around her arms like a woven bracelet, strand after strand—and then around her chest and back, covering every burn he could see or guess at.

There.

Her breathing was still slow and ragged, but the burns were fading into puffed, raised scars, the kind that would subside with proper care. He exhaled again, got up.

"It's gone," he said. "You can bandage her again."

And met the eyes of Phyranthe, who was leaning against the door jamb.

His entire body tensed, drawing on reserves of energy he no longer had. He almost tripped over his own feet.

"You," he said.

Mia was gone. Ai Nhi was asleep in the chair.

Phyranthe's smile was incandescent. "Very nice healing," she said.

"Have you come to gloat?"

Thuan was exhausted, his body racked by the cramps he could no longer keep at bay—and in the worst state possible to fence with her. But she must have known this.

"I'm impressed, actually. You didn't have to care quite so much about a mortal child."

Thuan's eyebrows shot up. "Was I supposed to let her die?"

"Some people would have," Phyranthe said, and he knew with absolute certainty that she was talking about herself.

Some of what he felt must have shown on his face. Phyranthe laughed.

"You must know by now what I'm capable of."

Capable of, yes. But something about her behavior was off. She was taunting him. Waiting for him to say the irreparable. Like Asmodeus, Iaris had said, but Thuan didn't think that was true. Asmodeus freely described himself as a sadist. Thuan would have bet that Phyranthe didn't feel quite that inhibited.

He said, finally, "I'm capable of killing people. It doesn't mean I'd do it."

Laughter, almost good-natured, from her. "You're sharp." She sounded almost pleased. "I came to see justice done."

Phyranthe showed him pointed, shining teeth. Her red dress shone against the grayness of the tiles. She turned to look at Mélanie, the dress slowly following her movements until she seemed surrounded by a whirlwind of red cloth.

"You don't care about justice," Thuan said.

"You malign me." Her voice was sharp. "Of course I care. Punishment to fit the crime."

"So that's why you took a five-year-old into the cells." Thuan knew he should have been nicer, less abrasive. More willing to find ground they could meet on. But he had one scared child, and another he'd taken from the verge of death. "Very fitting. Very … apt."

Phyranthe threw a glance at Ai Nhi on the chair. Something passed across her face he couldn't quite interpret: anger, and that same expression she'd had when telling him what she was capable of. She turned back to Thuan.

"Iaris tells me you were inquiring about Vinh Ly."

Ah. Gloating, then. Thuan bit back the fantasy he could plead on Vinh Ly's behalf.

"Punishment to fit the crime," he said, slowly. "What do you think would fit the offense of standing up on behalf of her niece?"

"I was under the impression parents were punished for their children's offenses, where you came from. A life for a life, or sometimes more, if the victim's life had value." Phyranthe's voice was level. "The nine kinships exterminations."

Thuan couldn't help it. The laughter welled out of him, sharp and desperate and uncontrollable.

"You malign me. Not every old-fashioned tradition has to be blindly followed."

A raised eyebrow. Phyranthe moved back to stand in the door frame, backlit by the lanterns in the ward. Thuan didn't know how long he could sustain that conversation before he fell flat on the floor.

"Old traditions. You know," she said, almost conversationally, "back in Uphir's day, he didn't really care about who was harmed, or how. People like me were given license to indulge their wildest urges." Again, that odd expression on her face.

And had the House changed that much, really? Asmodeus allowed no one else to harm his dependents; but he'd torture the guilty and make examples of them without a qualm. Thuan said nothing, exhausted and angry.

"You're lucky that times have changed." Phyranthe sounded amused again. "And that I was never the kind to take advantage of that. I keep my … less savory urges under strict control. I won't kill your dragon." She moved away from him again, looking at the still shape of Mélanie on the bed. "A fitting punishment." She pursed her lips. "I'll let you know how I get on with her, shall I."

And then she was gone, and Thuan finally fell to his knees, trying very hard to pray to his ancestors for mercy.

When Thuan finally walked out of the ward, he found Mia waiting for him at the doors.

"Here."

He handed the sleeping Ai Nhi to her, because he didn't think he was capable of carrying her further. His weakness stung. He turned to close the doors to the ward. As he laid a hand on the ivory handles, he felt that cold touch at the nape of his neck.

This time, he definitely hadn't imagined it. And he didn't think he'd imagined it before, either.

"Mia?" he asked.

The Fallen looked ill at ease. "Yes?"

"Stand a little further away."

"I have orders—"

"I'm not going anywhere," Thuan said darkly. "And you have Ai Nhi, in any case."

Mia stared at him. She must have thought he was joking, and then she saw the intent fear in his eyes.

"I don't understand . . ."

Thuan stood in the corridor, watching the swollen parquet floor. Every step they'd taken had released a little cloud of mold, increasing the humidity in the air. It almost felt as though he were back under the Seine. The wallpaper was peeling—opening up the ceiling through a dozen wounds like flowers.

"I know you're here," he said.

Silence. The creak of parquet floor. The sigh of the wind through the branches of trees, in a grove with blood-soaked earth.

"Thuan," a familiar voice said.

There were three of them: children with bodies of woven thorns. One of them, the one speaking to him, was smaller than the others, with the antlers of a young dragon. Thuan had a flash of anger.

"Don't ape her," he said.

The child's head cocked towards him. "Aping? We merely choose the shapes which hold meaning for you."

Thuan's fists clenched. He unfolded them only with an effort of will.

"Find another one," he said.

Another of the children—one that didn't look so much like a parody of Ai Nhi—moved towards him.

"What do you want?"

"Answers," Thuan said. "You were standing watch outside the door."

Once, before he'd become head of Hawthorn, they had touched him. Once, they had drawn him deep into the House, trying to subsume him into the wards so that his magic could be Hawthorn's, now and forever. They hadn't foreseen that one day he would bind himself to the House more thoroughly and more tightly than through them, willingly, and for … not love, perhaps, but out of desire, and in hope of a better future.

"What's so special about here?"

A silence. The children stared at each other.

"Nothing more and nothing less than any other place."

Obviously. That would have been too easy. They weren't children, weren't even human: just a mask the House chose to wear.

"Then tell me this—will Harrier's devastation touch us?"

A moment of hesitation. The children stared at each other.

One of them said, "No," at the same moment the other said, "Yes."

"That's not helpful."

"We're not here to be helpful."

The children had regained their composure. Their fingers danced gently in the air, as if they were pulling the strings of some vast puppet, and trails of light hung from their tips, fading into nothingness before they touched the floor. But nevertheless the parquet under Thuan shivered and danced, too.

"This is where the children of the House go, when they are wounded and sick—one of the many places where the future of Hawthorn hangs in the balance."

Thuan struggled to keep the weariness from his voice. "That's not exactly reassuring."

Laughter, which sounded like thunder shaking the branches of trees. Bluish, sheeny petals fell from the children's bodies onto the floor.

"Beware, Thuan. Things are changing, and we are weak."

"Things are changing?" Thuan asked.

He hadn't looked away—but the children were gone, snuffed out as if they'd never been, with only the distant sound of wood creaks to mark their departure.

Beware, Thuan, the House whispered.

Beware of what?

Grandmother Olympe and the aunts, with their usual ruthless efficiency, had set up a triage station for refugees. For a brief moment as he saw the tables under the vast rafters of what had been Gare du Nord, and the queue of haggard, shocked people, Philippe was back in House Lazarus, trying to keep his head down, to be nothing more than a starved mortal in a sea of starving mortals. And then it passed—he was sixty years older, and Isabelle was a reassuring presence by his side. And it was a single queue—forty to fifty people, not the hundreds and hundreds Lazarus had attracted each morning.

The large trestle tables had been set on the ruins of the platforms, and people queued from what had once been the station's marshaling yard to the departure concourse—the hall of wasted steps, as they'd called it back then. Beneath the ruined three-lobed glass windows of the entrance, three aunts were questioning people, most of them covered in soot and blood and other unpleasant fluids, and holding young, screaming, exhausted children. They were then directing them to various areas. One was for food: Aunt Ha was ladling warm soup into bowl after bowl. One appeared to be for lodgings, and one—the one on the mezzanine floor—was the hospital.

It had once been the buffet—a small salon with luxurious sofas and a large dining room, serving meals unaffordable to the working class. But now the dining room had been hastily cleared of debris, leaving small gray canvas tents spread across the floor to provide a modicum of privacy—where had they found these?

At the entrance, harried Annamites triaged people. The smell of chlorine hung in the air, overwhelming the scent of fish sauce from the platforms.

"Philippe!"

A middle-aged Annamite woman with gray hair: Cassiopée, the bookish one of two sisters. She was sitting at a low table, her cane propped against the edge. She had her hands full of bandages and gauze.

Philippe asked the question on the tip of his tongue. "Lariboisière . . .?"

The hospital was about a ten-minute walk.

"Understaffed, underequipped and already full of patients." Cassiopée's voice was grim. "Not to mention the risk of sharing infections. They sent us the people they could spare. We're going to do the basic bandages, and we could use an operating room." Her smile was mirthless. "A lot of them have eye injuries from the debris."

"Water—" Philippe started.

"This was the dining room. The pump and pipes are still working. Come on."

Hoa Phong's gaze went from the people huddled in corners against the gray canvas of the tents, and then upwards, to a distant Heaven that did not contain the Jade Emperor.

"This is—"

Isabelle's face was hard; when she spoke, he felt pride flutter in his chest.

"How can we help?"

"There," Philippe said, carefully laying down his scalpel in the bowl. It clinked, the noise like a rifle shot in his mind.

Everything seemed drenched in blood or gore or both. He realized he was still holding on to the amputated eye—he put that down too, and then called *khi* fire to burn the contagion on his hands. Flames danced over his fingers, illuminating the darkening corner of the hospital. His patient—a thin, starved teenage girl called Morgane—stared at him, eyes wide.

"You'll get used to it," Cassiopée said. "He's our … good luck charm."

Which was embarrassing but not as much as being called a tutelary deity or whatever other nonsense half the community believed.

Cassiopée had moved from her original desk to assist Philippe. Isabelle could have done it, but her nascent skills with the *khi* elements meant that she could boil water for another operating table, set up by Aunt Rochita—whose Viet name was Xuan Yen, but who breathed fire on anyone who even suggested she needed to use it. Isabelle couldn't do complex work, but gathering *khi* fire didn't require much subtlety. Hoa Phong … He didn't know what Hoa Phong had done, or what skills she'd admitted to. Perhaps she could heal just as he could, though his healings were small, slow and pathetic compared to a dragon's touch.

"You're not House," the girl said.

"No." He smiled, but it took an effort. "I'm something else."

"Come on." Cassiopée finished bandaging the eye, and watched as the girl walked unsteadily from the room. "There should be someone waiting for them." She gestured at her cane. "I can't help them out."

Philippe grimaced. "Everyone is busy. And they need the bandages more than a friendly arm."

"Mm." Cassiopée didn't sound convinced. She said, "It's the middle of the night. Isabelle and your … friend left a while ago."

By which she meant no one would blame him if he did, too.

He didn't need to look into the corridor, though, to know that there would be more wounded people, and that dealing with them would be slow and involved.

Philippe held his hand in front of him. It was still steady. He felt worn, but not so tired he'd make mistakes. Or perhaps that was just sheer optimism.

"Do you remember how many people we still have outside? Don't get up," he said, realizing what he'd done. "I'll have a look if you can't remember. It's been a long day."

"Four, five?"

Aunt Ha had left some cold rice cakes. Philippe took off his work clothes, stretched, and grabbed two, one of which he proffered to Cassiopée. He dipped his in some of the fish sauce—the over-salty, under-spicy concoction that was the best Paris had to offer. Literally the best: that looked like Olympe's bottles, not the ones cut with soy sauce and salt that were traded between the poorest residents.

"The good stuff," Cassiopée said ironically, lifting her own rice cake. "Rewards of virtue."

"Community," Philippe said finally, a word that tasted unfamiliar and strange.

"You've been listening to Olympe too much."

"It's not optional."

"Maybe not," Cassiopée said, clearly suppressing a smile. "She gets like that."

Philippe finished his rice cake, and brushed his hands on his clothes.

At length he said, "Half of them will get infections. If we're lucky."

Cassiopée's voice was sharp. "We do what we can with what we're given."

He didn't really know her or her sister Aurore. They'd run from a House, hadn't they? And then he remembered the House was Harrier.

"It must be odd for you, helping your former House."

A flash of something he couldn't interpret. Cassiopée said, levelly, "The wheel of life turns, and everyone gets what they deserve."

"Do they?"

Cassiopée didn't answer for a while.

"They will. One day."

It sounded sharper and more personal than it ought to have been. It was none of his business, and he'd sworn not to get involved in Houses' affairs. But that was hypocrisy and cowardice, because helping Hoa Phong and the court of the Jade Emperor made running into Houses a certainty.

"Is anything the matter?"

He could feel her weighing him—deciding whether to trust him. He didn't move, and tried to project the same face he had for his patients—calm, competent, concerned.

At length, Cassiopée said, "Aurore is in Harrier."

That stopped him. He hadn't been there when the sisters arrived, but he'd heard Aunt Ha—what she had said, and what she wouldn't admit.

"Regrets?"

Cassiopée snorted. "In a manner of speaking." She said, finally, "I'm worried about her."

And no wonder. Philippe considered and discarded the first few answers in his mind.

"Is there anything I can do?"

"Can you fight a House?" Cassiopée's voice was bitter.

No one could. "Is she … Is she in trouble?"

Cassiopée didn't answer.

She said, finally, "It's funny, isn't it. I can trace the lineage of my ancestors all the way to the first scholars"—she used the Viet word, the one that implied knowledge and power and magic—"and we end up here, in the gutter."

"Bloodlines don't mean much."

"Said like an Immortal." She snorted. "For some of us,

they're the only wealth we have. The comfort of our kin. The flesh of our fathers, the blood of our mothers."

She was speaking archaic—the language of the court in Huê, of the Chinese colonizers who had preceded the French ones. A scholar, indeed. It was jarring to hear that here.

He said, finally, "No one can fight the Houses. You have to know this." Her face closed. He should have left it there, but something in him had twisted past prudence. "I was in a House. Twice. Held against my will, both times."

"But you escaped."

Once, because the House had died. And once … He closed his eyes, remembering broken fingers and ribs and wounds, and the glint of the knife in Asmodeus's hands, and Selene's voice telling him that he had gone too far.

"I was lucky. You can't count on that happening every time. They …"

He paused, trying to put things into words, flexing his fingers again and again, reassuring himself that they worked. That he could breathe without pain or the bubbling feel of blood in his mouth.

"The Houses hold all the power in Paris. It's always been that way. And every time someone with the barest hint of magical talent rises, they take them. Or kill them. Or both." He was keeping out of their sight, hoping they'd forget him—especially Asmodeus, who had never willingly let go of what was his. "I'm sorry."

Cassiopée's face was closed. He fought the urge to shake her. To make her see.

"Yes, I know, the world has always worked this way. You don't need to tie yourself in knots justifying it to me."

She put her cup of tea down. "We're going to change the rules of the game."

An odd remark, but he forgot it because a scream came from just outside the room. Philippe was on his feet and running before he could think, grabbing his apron from the table just in case. He took the staircase leading from the hospital floor to the ground floor at full speed. It was completely dark outside, and the refugees seemed to have been herded elsewhere to sleep. A man of perhaps forty years old had collapsed, writhing, at the foot of Aunt Ha's kitchen station. His shirt was soaked with liquid. He was the one screaming, but the scream didn't seem to be human anymore.

The air was saturated with *khi* currents—a tangled mass like an angry swarm, flowing into Philippe's hands and driving spikes deep into his flesh, again and again. Each of them stung like an insect bite. By the time Philippe had reached the trestle table, elbowing an aunt who wouldn't move fast enough out of the way—a sin of impropriety he would pay for later—his hands were dripping blood from a hundred pinprick wounds. The air was taut and heavy, like the moment just before a storm.

Aunt Ha was kneeling with her hands on the man's chest. Trying to stop the flailing? No, her eyes were wide and dark, her teeth gritted, and her entire body was arching, as if on the verge of convulsing as well.

Tade, the burly Yoruba dock worker who always worked night shifts, said, "He was already shaking when he came up to Aunt Ha."

He had his sleeves rolled up, one arm heavily tattooed, and the other one with a small, simple pattern of sketched lines, and his lithe body was tense, ready to jump into battle.

"No one touch him," Philippe said, sharply. "Or her."

A bowl of soup had spilled on the floor, spreading noodles redolent of star anise everywhere in the midst of rubble.

"He collapsed when he took the meal?" Philippe asked. "They're *noodles*. It's not like ..."

He didn't see the connection—it was hard to focus, with that endless screaming in the background, and Aunt Ha's dark, frozen gaze. He wiped his hands on the apron he'd grabbed when he'd left the room and grabbed the *khi* currents—struggling with them as if he was wrestling panicked beasts that kept clawing and biting—and wove a quick spell of protection, something to soothe panic.

He felt like he was throwing it—not at a wall, but at something sharp that shredded it into nothingness. He tried again. Again, his simple spell was cut into shreds. But it wasn't like Diamaras—the *khi* currents weren't cut.

No.

They were fleeing, as if something or someone at the center of the conflagration was driving them away. All but one: around Aunt Ha and the writhing man on the floor, a single set of lines, tangled and chaotic, remained, colored the red of heart's blood.

Khi fire.

That made no sense. They were *khi* elements—the breath of the land under them, the warp and weft of the universe. They couldn't get *scared*.

Behind him, he could distantly hear Tade screaming at people to stay away and not touch anything. Good. That gave him time. He wove the spell of protection, not around Aunt Ha or the man, but around himself—*khi* water, because it was the element opposed to fire, and wood, which gave birth to fire and could thus control it. The stillness and weight of old age. All his years and all his memories, from the very early, bright ones of his parents holding him before incense sticks burning on the ancestral altar, to the more recent past—the Houses, Isabelle, Hoa Phong and Diamaras in her decrepit refuge, refusing to believe that time had reduced all she held dear to worthless curios. The rough and cold feel of a dragon's scales, of a fish held in both hands, in that single suspended moment before it slipped away into the river.

Then, carefully, cautiously, he reached out and touched the man's skin.

It burned, as if he'd grabbed a live coal. His spell of protection was overwhelmed and reduced to cinders in a moment, and then the fire looked for something else to burn, too—digging into his chest in search of his heart.

Isabelle, standing in the darkened corridor of a House, telling him anything was justified if it ensured the House's survival—and the flash of anger and disappointment he'd felt then, knowing they couldn't possibly remain friends.

Asmodeus, rising from behind a mahogany desk and smiling, and a noose of Fallen magic tightening around Philippe's neck, with nothing—no *khi* currents, no stolen magic—that could possibly save him …

Fleeing in the darkness after the fall of House Draken, walking the streets looking for food and drink and knowing the Houses held it all.

They deserved to burn. They'd always deserved to burn,

the Houses and all they held dear. As the thought filled his mind, the fire found something else within him—the dark shadow of the curse he'd once found in House Silverspires, the never-ending, never-sated hunger of a dead woman.

No.

He'd left all anger, all grief behind him once. He'd carried that curse within him for over a year, a penance and a reminder, but he had never given in to it. That wasn't him. That had never been him.

He opened his eyes, and found himself facing the man—who had risen, tossing the limp Aunt Ha aside like so much chaff. His hand was clenched around something, which he slowly unfurled: a translucent paper like the one Hoa Phong had shown him, except the Southern characters on them were elongated and sharp, traced so roughly they'd torn the paper. At the bottom was a seal so stylized he almost didn't recognize it, but then he remembered the language of the court.

"Dân," he whispered. *Tiger.*

"Annamite," the man whispered, and his teeth were no longer blackened and broken, but long and curved and sharp. "A message for you, from the ruins of a House."

"Who are you?" Philippe asked, but the man wasn't looking at him.

"You *knew*," the man whispered. "All of you who cooked the food and fought in the war and tended the cages. You *knew*, and yet when your Houses cut you loose, you did nothing."

Tiger.

"Dân Chay," Philippe said, but the man was speaking over him, not even acknowledging his existence. A message. Recorded words, nothing more. Nothing he said or did would change them.

"But everything is afire now. I've burned down the House that imprisoned me, and I'll burn everything else in the city, Houses and mortals alike. I'm coming for you all." The man shifted, and bones cracked, as if they were as fragile as kindling. "Because you didn't harm me directly—because you're the least guilty of them all—I'll give you a warning. All that makes you proud—your little community of fragile hopes and dreams rooted in the blood of others—I will destroy." He smiled again, and it was a horrible expression, the lower lip pierced with the bloodied holes of fangs. "Abandon it all, and you may live."

He collapsed like a puppet with cut strings.

Philippe knelt—not by his side, for there was nothing to be done, but by Aunt Ha, trying to find her pulse with shaking hands. Once, twice, his fingers slipping on what should have been the small area of skin.

"Philippe, Philippe!"

It was Isabelle, out of breath, followed by a dark-faced Hoa Phong.

"We found something." She ignored Hoa Phong's attempts to stop her. "Diamaras got the wrong House. The second one, the one that actually held Dân Chay. It wasn't Draken."

"I know," Philippe said.

You knew. All of you who cooked the food and fought in the war and tended the cages.

By his side, the blue and black of the man's uniform peeled away in a rising wind that carried the smell of charred meat and smoke to Philippe's nostrils. Beneath, the naked body was marbled with what looked like bruises—dark, purple skin in sharp, mercilessly clear patterns, spreading on either side of the spine and turning into rings encircling the arms and legs: the thickened, fuzzed lines of a tiger's stripes.

A message, from the ruins of a House.

"It's not Draken. It's Harrier. Dân Chay is in Harrier. He's the one who destroyed the House."

Abandon it all, and you may live.

And, now that House Harrier had split open like a skull cloven by an axe—burning, burning, always burning, a cage Dân Chay had charred into cinders to get free—he was coming for those he thought had failed him.

9

A Box of Smoke

Morningstar's errand took them straight to the edge of the smoke that was still billowing from the source of the explosion. As they neared it, Aurore's chest began to ache, and she slowed down. Morningstar was walking ahead of them in great strides, unconcerned by whether they were following. Charles, the toddler in Nicolas's arms, began to cry. He rubbed his hair and whispered to him and after a while the screams became whimpers. Virginie, the eight-year-old with the uniform, strode ahead, with that determined air of all children pretending everything was fine.

Aurore had had enough, by then.

"Morningstar!"

"Yes?" He barely slowed down.

"The children." She ought to have toned it down, but she wasn't breathing very well either. The smoke had gotten in her lungs, and it felt like something stuck in her throat that wouldn't go away no matter how often she swallowed or took deep breaths. "They're going to choke."

He paused. She couldn't see his face.

"Very well."

Lambent light streamed from him: he turned and walked, in turn, by each of the refugees, laying a hand on their shoulders. When he lifted it, the light still clung to them—patches of translucence that swam under their skin, throwing veins and muscles into sharp relief as they moved upwards, to settle around their noses and mouths, descending all the way to the chest, a luminous thread splitting in a butterfly-shape blob at the level of the lungs.

When he reached Aurore, he paused. He towered over her, and the shadow of large, radiant wings hung behind him. Her knees wobbled—she ached to kneel. *No.* He was Fallen, but no more extraordinary or valuable than her or Marianne. Anyone with magic could be as powerful as him.

The hand he laid on her shoulder was warm, and the magic roiled as it passed into her—an odd, unsettling sensation of bubbles climbing through her arms, filling her mouth with something warm and sweet, but beneath it she could feel the sourness, a sharp taste like mold, a reminder that everything he touched would rot and become corrupted. When it reached her lungs, she thought she'd gag. It felt like inhaling sweet-smelling smoke, and only realizing afterwards it evaporated into bitterness.

"There," Morningstar said. "Let's go."

When they started walking again, Charles was wailing ceaselessly. Nicolas was attempting to calm him, looking increasingly frazzled and desperate, until he got the idea of bouncing him up and down, slowly. Charles laughed, and nuzzled against Nicolas's shoulder, bright eyes watching everything within the smoke.

Aurore caught up with Frédérique, who was watching

her daughter Virginie with the attentive gaze Aurore knew all too well: that desperate attempt to watch over her child while knowing it was futile and any protection she could offer was hollow.

"Do you need help?"

Frédérique shook her head. "Just keeping an eye on her, that's all."

Her gaze rested, for a moment, on Nicolas and Charles. "Poor thing. I wish his parents had survived."

Aurore almost stopped. "I thought—"

Frédérique laughed. It was almost carefree. "That he was ours? Only one magician per family until they're presented to the House. Or thrown into battle." Her voice was carefully casual, balanced on a knife's edge. "Charles's parents both died in the explosion. We thought …" Her voice trailed away. "It didn't feel right to leave him all by himself."

"No," Aurore said. No wonder he had been wailing. Unfamiliar people in an unfamiliar setting, and a tension to the air he had to feel. "Are you all right?"

Frédérique rubbed her chest. "I guess." She didn't sound convinced. "It doesn't feel quite right."

"Like being underwater?" Aurore said.

Like they were choking all the time, except with a sweet aftertaste. At least they were still breathing. At least they were upright. She felt a ghost of Hawthorn's tug in her chest: a reminder that she was bound to a House as surely as Frédérique was.

"You said you used to be House," Frédérique said.

Aurore tried to keep her shrug casual. She didn't know much about Frédérique.

"My sister and I were menials. We worked in a number of places—the hospice of Dames du Calvaire, the household of the Master of Baths. We made a mistake."

Too many mistakes. *Lazy, untrustworthy servants*, Pellas had said, before washing his hands of them. *But then, what can I expect from mortals?*

"The House doesn't forgive."

Frédérique's gaze was bruised and haunted, as it had been in the slaughterhouse. Aurore fought the urge to reach out to her.

Keep her head down. Wait. Go back to Hawthorn and pray for Asmodeus's mercy—and start her quest for power again. That was the wise thing to do. But she was so tired of being the plaything of the powerful; of failing, time and time again, to be listened to instead of manipulated.

Instead, she said, "I always thought being Great Interior would be ..." She stopped, then. "Would change your life. Would keep you safe."

"Nothing is safe." Frédérique's face didn't move.

"Factions," Aurore said flatly.

"The losing side." Frédérique laughed bitterly. "Niraphanes ..." She shrugged. "We used to be with a Fallen called Darrias. She was one of Guy's enforcers. The one who noticed me, originally. Who took me from being a menial into the Great Interior."

"I don't know her," Aurore said.

Had Darrias been one of them—one of the enforcers who'd come for her and Cassiopée, bearing the swift justice of the House? She'd remember their faces, surely—and she was surprised to realize she didn't care anymore. She didn't want revenge. She just wanted her family and her community to be safe.

"She wasn't a saint." Frédérique sounded … regretful? "But Guy is worse."

"He doesn't like you."

"He doesn't like Darrias. Darrias walked away from Harrier."

"She …? I didn't know that was possible."

"She walked away, but we stayed." Frédérique's face was carefully closed.

"That must have been hard." Aurore said. "Sorry. Platitudes."

She'd faced the House's harsh justice herself—what could it bring to bear, against the family of someone Guy would have considered a defector and a rebel?

Frédérique shrugged. "We've survived. Niraphanes was Darrias' friend, and she's been looking out for us. She's … decent."

Looking out for them. Replacing Darrias. A complex tangle of relationships Aurore wasn't privy to.

"But she asked for more than you could give."

"She needs magicians." Frédérique's voice was quiet. "Most of the House's magicians are in the Great Interior with Guy, regardless of how loyal they actually are. Niraphanes doesn't have much choice, if she wants to win." Her voice was bitter. "She's an idealist. She believes in that House more than her own children."

Family business. Questions Aurore had never had to ask herself, because Marianne was a toddler with absolutely no affinity for magic.

"You don't have to tell me any of this."

Frédérique's gaze was sharp. "I saw your face when you said you'd been thrown out of the House. There's more to it, isn't there?"

Aurore stared at her for a while.

"They beat us and left us for dead," she said finally. "I carried my sister through Paris, as I swore it would never happen again."

"Hiding."

"No," Aurore said. The words came welling up before she could stop them. "I want to stop hiding. I want to be what they are."

Frédérique gestured at the dim shape of Morningstar, striding ahead in the cobbled streets.

"Like him?"

Aurore ran a hand over her chest, feeling the disk there, remembering Asmodeus's mocking smile.

"Power is what you make of it."

They were cruel because they chose to be. She wouldn't make that choice. What she found, she and Cassiopée would use to defend themselves. To keep everyone safe.

Frédérique was silent. The smoke rose in billows around them, a dense cloud that slowly obscured everything until all they could see was each other, and even Morningstar and the others seemed distant figures, though he still shone like a beacon. How could anything still be burning in there? Surely it had spent itself by now?

"Virginie!" Frédérique said sharply.

The child—a ghostly silhouette—turned and walked back to them, gradually gaining focus. She was silent and taut.

"Mum—"

"I know," Frédérique said. "Has he said what he's looking for?"

The light was turning towards them: Morningstar was walking back.

Virginie said, "The explosion. Whatever caused it."

"Yes," Morningstar said. Aurore had seen his light walk back, but even so he seemed to appear out of the smoke. "All that raw power harnessed the right way … It could have achieved so much …" He sounded almost regretful.

They were standing between two large buildings with wrought-iron gates closing the space between them—except that the gates lay twisted and destroyed, and one of the buildings had been completely razed, reduced to rubble. Ahead, in the semi-darkness, loomed pairs of long, flat buildings.

"It was the barracks." Virginie's voice was taut. In Nicolas's arms, the toddler wailed again.

"We're close," Morningstar said.

His eyes were two pits of darkness, the cornflower blue almost dispelled. Light flowed to him. As it did, the disk against Aurore's chest contracted into a pinprick wound—she gasped, bringing a hand to her chest. Virginie was watching Morningstar intently.

The radiance grew stronger. For a moment as Morningstar stretched, Aurore saw the shadow of sharp, great wings, and an even fainter shadow of domes and churches, and a hint of a great, golden presence, an absolute and utter certainty that all would be right, and then it was all gone and there was a wound at the heart of the world, an emptiness that nothing would ever fill.

The smoke lifted, for a moment. The ruined barracks

stretched all around them: the large, squat buildings ahead, parallel to the two around the gates, one group of buildings lying diagonal to the left. And, to the right, rubble lit by the orange glow of flames.

Virginie said, in a small voice, "There was a building there. A large one, with a metal awning."

"The armory?" Morningstar asked.

"I don't know."

Frédérique said, "The barracks haven't been used since the war."

But they'd still have stored ammunition in them. The House threw away useless things, but weapons and offensive spells were always useful: a way to deter others, a way to fight another war if it came to that.

And now it looked as though it wouldn't be used again. Aurore stared at the flames—they pulled at her in some undefinable way, not the sharp painful reel of Asmodeus's spell, but like a familiar, beloved thing she wasn't even aware she'd lost. In the swirls of light a dim, elongated shape danced and turned, a memory tugging at her. She'd seen this before. But how could she have? As a child in Harrier?

"Morningstar."

He turned, the light streaming from him merging with that of the flames.

"Is that safe?"

A raised eyebrow. "Is anywhere safe?"

"For the children?" Aurore said sharply. "They can stay here, surely."

It didn't look like much, but whatever was at the center of that conflagration had destroyed a House.

"She's right," Nicolas said abruptly. He'd put Charles on his shoulders, and was attempting to stay upright. "They're too young. Both of them."

Morningstar cocked his head. Aurore could have sworn he didn't look happy.

"I can help," Virginie said. Her face seemed sharper in Morningstar's radiance.

"Sweetheart—" Frédérique started.

"I'm not a child!" Her face was harsh. "They teach us wardings in the Chambers. For battle." She knelt and peered at the cobblestones, wincing as she ran her fingers on the warm stone. "The House is weak, but I can draw one here."

"It won't hold against the fire," Morningstar said.

"It'll be better than nothing, won't it?" Aurore asked. Why did he seem to want to drag children into the most dangerous zone in the House? "Or you could draw one yourself, surely."

A pause. It was hard to tell because the radiance obscured the features of his face, but Morningstar looked to be biting down on something.

At last he said, and it sounded like it had cost him, "Of course. My apologies. Do go on." And, almost as an afterthought, "There's not much I can do in the way of wardings here. I'm away from my House, and drawing protections against another House is always tricky."

Virginie was tracing the beginnings of a circle on the cobblestones, her small face screwed up in concentration. As her fingers rested, briefly, on each stone, they left blackened imprints behind, and her clothes billowed as though in an invisible wind.

"Do you need help?" Aurore asked Frédérique.

Frédérique's face was a study in politeness, but she clearly thought Aurore would be useless. One day. One day people wouldn't dismiss her or Cassiopée as harmless or meek.

"It's all right," she said.

"I've got it," Virginie said.

Aurore left them to it, and walked behind Morningstar. He had the grace to stop and wait for her.

"Curious?" he asked, a little too sharply.

Aurore ignored the spasm of fear that seized her. She'd survived Hawthorn and Harrier and there was nothing he could do to her.

"I'd rather run towards danger than wait for it to reach me."

"A sensible woman." There was a faint trace of irony in his voice. "Or perhaps just a scavenger."

Judging her?

"And why would that matter to you?" Aurore tried, unsuccessfully, to keep the sharpness from her voice.

"There's no time for petty interests," Morningstar said, mildly, but even the soft rebuke was strong enough to make her knees wobble.

Close by, the flames seemed to enfold the universe. The smoke was so thick Aurore couldn't even see the ground. Everything was black and dark, and Morningstar's spell of breathing felt like a leaden weight in her lungs, constricting every breath she took. Debris clattered underfoot—she tripped more than once when the ground seemed to slide away from her, and caught herself on sharp stone. Everything was covered with a thin layer of ash. She didn't want to think about what had burned, though during one stumble she found herself staring into the eye sockets of a charred skull.

There was nothing but darkness and fire, and even Morningstar's radiance paled beside that last. He knelt as he reached the flames, which flickered and bent as if bowing, and then snuffed themselves out like a blown candle.

In the center, where the fire had been, was a box. No rubble there: it had been vaporized in a circle about five meters wide. The box itself was an oddity: old and battered, but its surface *glowed*—and abruptly Aurore was five years old again, watching Mother take her turtleshell combs from a similar box. Its lacquer shimmered, not with the reflection of the fire that had snuffed itself out, but with an inner radiance from inside the box itself, and on its lid was a vaguely familiar shape, a large oval outlined in flickering light.

Paris.

It was a map of Paris, with lines radiating from the southwest, connecting Harrier to places—no, not places, Houses. These were all the Houses of Paris from Solférino to Hawthorn, from Stormgate to Lazarus, every one of them caught in a spider's web of gently pulsing light.

On the front of the box were two faded characters, but Aurore could only read one of them. She thought at first that it was an odd scribble, and then an old script character, Chinese or *Chu Nom*, the pre-alphabet Southern script—and then it shifted, and became a single Viet word.

Dần.

Tiger. Not the animal, but the zodiac sign.

"Dân." The word tasted like smoke and ashes on her tongue.

And, abruptly, the darkness around them took on the vague, shadowy form of a man.

He was dressed as an official from some faded painting: a tunic billowing in the wind, a square-capped hat with a vermilion pearl atop. His skin was tawny, with the faint outline of stripes on his cheeks; his eyes were the color of lucent amber, and his fingernails so long and sharp they had nail guards, ornate things of woven white metal with a delicate filigree pattern.

He smiled, and the teeth in his mouth were long and pointed.

"Morningstar," he said.

He bowed, only a fraction—only for show. His gaze raked both of them. Aurore forgot, for a moment, that she could breathe when it rested on her: large, luminous eyes in which danced the heat of the flames. They promised … surcease. Rest. A time when all the world would be ashes and dust.

"What a pleasure."

Morningstar watched the man, warily. "Dân Chay."

Dân Chay? Aurore couldn't tell what the second word was meant to be, with Morningstar's atrocious butchering of the name.

"I must admit I was half-expecting you not to come," Dân Chay said.

"I always keep my promises."

"Do you?" Dân Chay smiled again. He knelt by the box, one hand resting lightly, on the map of the Parisian Houses on its lid. "You'll excuse me for not thinking much of Fallen capacity to respect the treaties they pass."

Morningstar walked, slowly, to face the man. He wasn't smiling as broadly as he had been.

"Treaties, perhaps not. Bargains I make for the sake of friends ..."

"Ah, friendship." The box lit up briefly, enough for Aurore to see that it contained bones. "A most laudable goal. Yes. You made a bargain with me because you were worried for your little Fallen friend, and the trouble she'd got caught in within Harrier. You wanted Guy stopped before he could hurt her, and you were desperate enough to come to me in my prison, and promise me my freedom in return for helping you." Laughter. "I did stop him, didn't I? I burned the entire House and ground Guy's power into dust. Is she happy now, your friend?"

Morningstar's face was hard. "You won't speak of Emmanuelle here."

"Such a sweet devotion to her. You may not be willing to hurt her, but *I* am."

He spread his arms wide, and the shadow of flames outlined him, and the network of red lines spread from the box to the ground. It came up against Morningstar, where it broke as if it had hit a wall.

"Never." Morningstar's face was set.

"Oh, I forgot. Our bargain." A laugh. "Perhaps I'm a Fallen, too, just as disinclined to keep my word."

Morningstar spread out his right hand. There was something resting in it: threads of light converging into the familiar shape of a whip.

"Silverspires still owns you, in the end. The old ... punishments still hold sway."

Dân Chay looked at him warily. Morningstar grabbed the whip—he didn't even wield it, but Dân Chay's face contorted in pain, and blood pearled up on his tunic. Morningstar walked forward, raising the whip, and Dân Chay fell back, snarling and roaring. One, two sickening thuds against flesh, and red, luminous sprays falling on the earth. Dân Chay screamed, a sound that tore at Aurore's guts. She'd been there. She'd been the one driven back step by step until pain froze her and they did whatever they wanted with her.

Dân Chay had burned the House. He'd destroyed everything—not only Guy and his enforcers, but the lives of the servants and menials. Aurore dug her nails into the palms of her hand to prevent herself from stopping Morningstar.

By now Dân Chay was curled into a ball, and Morningstar stood over him, not even breathing hard, not even smiling—merely looking faintly annoyed.

It was too much.

"Stop," Aurore said.

Morningstar looked at her as he would an insect that had learned to speak.

"Stop? You would tell me what to do?"

Always more heart than sense, Cassiopée had said. If only she'd had power, any power, to back up her hasty decisions. Aurore looked Morningstar in the eye, refusing to back down.

"He's cowed. There's no need for this."

"Is he?" Morningstar's smile was wide, amused once more. Behind him, Dân Chay lay in a pool of that thick, luminous blood, pouring from multiple wounds. As Aurore watched, he pulled himself to his knees—his face drawing together as he did so, changing to something huge and dark and hungry, not only the tiger in the night, but the predator at the heart of all the nights. Then it was back to that undefined, wavering middle age, the emotionless face of an elder uncle, of a trusted official.

"Tell me what you want," he said. Every word made the earth shake underfoot.

Morningstar turned away from Aurore, and faced him again. He held the whip lightly in one hand, toying with it as though he might lash out again at any moment.

"Will you honor our bargain?"

Dân Chay shrugged—wincing as his shoulders moved.

"Free me, and I won't touch your friend, or House Silverspires." He smiled. "I can live with that. I noticed you haven't tried to exempt yourself from harm."

Morningstar's face didn't move. "Would you have accepted, if I had?"

"Of course not." Dân Chay cocked his face. His pupils were two slits. "Now free me."

Morningstar shrugged. He knelt, and laid a hand on the lid of the box. The lines on the map flared red, and his own radiance grew and grew until Aurore saw the shadow of wings at his back again. A faint song spread over the ruins of the barracks, until the ground seemed to hum with it: a distant thing of alien beauty and grace that Aurore had no hope of understanding, and for a moment only she saw him as he must have been a long time ago. Not an arrogant Fallen, not a frightful being of magic, but *something* that was beyond all of this. Something … sated. Content.

And then it passed, and it was just Morningstar on

his knees. The box was gone: only the character for *tiger* remained. Dân Chay stretched. Flames played beneath his face, his fingernails, the whites of his eyes—as if all it would take for him to scatter into fire was a breath. His skin was cracked like celadon, and beneath it was the shimmering gray-red of glowing embers.

"Thank you," he said. And laughed.

He spread his hands: between them was the lid of the box, with the map of all the Houses. He flicked them, and it was … not gone, but superimposed on the ground, and spreading, fading as it went, until the lines were the faintest of shadows.

"I'll keep this, I think. Such a handy link to all the Houses of Paris, all the ones you and Harrier wanted to destroy, back in the war. And now …"

Morningstar rose, stretched. "You want to fight me?"

"Your … tricks will no longer work," Dân Chay snarled.

"We shall see." Morningstar turned, and looked straight past Aurore. She turned—she couldn't help it—and saw Virginie, standing guard beside the circle she'd drawn, the one that enclosed her mother and the others.

Dân Chay was looking at them too, intently. He laughed, and the ground danced and trembled under Aurore's feet. She had to get away. She had to run, but where could she get to before their fight lit up the entire House?

"Using children? You're growing sentimental in your old age, Morningstar. You think I haven't hunted and eaten my share of them?"

"These are special children," Morningstar said. "The House's magicians. Raised and shaped to be living weapons. I'm sure you're intimately familiar with the methods."

Dân Chay moved, fluid and inhuman. Orange threads lit up under his feet. Before Aurore could even open her mouth he was standing before Virginie. The child stared at him, eyes wide. The light of Fallen magic trembled on her hands.

"Stay away," she said.

Within the circle, Frédérique was moving—as was Nicolas, one step behind her, face twisted in anguish—but whatever Virginie had done had sealed them off. All they could do was bang their hands on an invisible, transparent wall between them like a pane of glass.

"Stay away from my family. Or I'll kill you."

She looked absurd. A seven- or eight-year-old, standing up to whatever Dân Chay was—and to the other monster behind Aurore, the first Fallen who'd casually destroyed House Harrier just because he could. She was small and pathetic, and there was no hope, no hope whatsoever, that she'd be a match for the magic involved.

"Virginie!" Aurore said, and started to run.

But Dân Chay was already reaching out—threads of fire climbing up Virginie's legs and arms and chest, all the way to her neck, entangling her more surely than a spider's web. Before Aurore could even get close, he'd tilted Virginie's face, and was staring into her eyes.

No no no.

Something passed between them. The threads, tightening; Virginie, struggling to breathe, her mouth opening into—no, not a scream, but her entire face was stretched as though remembering something unpleasant.

"You can be more," she whispered. "You're mortal and tainted and so much less than we'd hoped for, but you can transcend that. You can be more." And, in a smaller voice, "It's just blood and pain. It will pass. It should mean nothing to you."

Behind the invisible glass pane of the wards, Frédérique had sunk to her knees, head bowed, weeping. Nicolas was still standing, staring at them with the hollow gaze of a man whose heart was being torn out of him.

Blood and pain. It's nothing. Oh, Ancestors.

Dân Chay let Virginie go. The orange thread faded. She fell, gasping, to her knees—his hand briefly brushed her hair.

"Ssh, child," he said. "It's over. They're dead." A touch of anger in his voice, but a very different one. "I made sure of that."

He turned, snarling, to Morningstar, who was walking back through the rubble with exaggerated care.

"And you dare reproach me for hunger? At least it's *clean*, Morningstar. There are no lies in the hunt."

"You're hardly in a position to reproach me. I understand tigers eat their young." Morningstar's voice was malicious. "Do you want to fight? It wouldn't be contained. There would be … casualties."

That was why he'd wanted the children. Not to protect them. Not even to recruit them for Silverspires. To use them as shields. That was why he'd been determined to bring Virginie all the way into the fire's heart: because she was the safeguard he'd planned to play all along.

Aurore dug her nails into the palms of her hand. She couldn't do anything. She could speak up; she could face them, and die. She had no magic, no spells, no power. She had nothing.

Nothing, or she'd have struck Morningstar dead where he stood.

"You have to understand," Morningstar said. "I have a duty of care to my own, and no intention of leaving them bereft. It doesn't have to get messy."

"Oh, but it will," Dân Chay said. His smile was fractured, incandescent. His corporeal shape was wavering—and Aurore saw, suddenly, that his body was woven of threads, the same ones he'd flung to the ground. "I'm not an animal, Morningstar. I'm exactly what you made me, and there will be a reckoning. They won't always be here to protect you."

Morningstar's face didn't move.

Dân Chay shrugged. "Arrogance, in the end, was your downfall, wasn't it? No matter. All I need is a little time." He spread his hands—the nail-guards caught the light and shone like molten gold. "After all, I have a revenge to exact. A city to burn."

"The other Houses?" Morningstar said. "Suit yourself." His gaze was hard. "It'll only make us stronger, in the end."

"A busy day," Dân Chay said. "The Houses. A stray Immortal. The mortals."

"No," Aurore said. *The mortals* meant them. It was the Houseless. It was the Annamites. Cassiopée. Marianne. "No!"

They both completely ignored her.

"Go," Morningstar said. "You're no longer needed here." His gaze turned, sharp and angry, towards Aurore. "And neither, I think, are you."

Of course. At best, she was an embarrassing witness, the only one who'd heard everything between Morningstar and Dân Chay; at worst, she was completely useless, for she provided him with nothing that he valued.

"Morningstar . . ." she said.

Dân Chay had started to fade, unraveling into threads that joined the network on the ground—lines that shone even through the rubble and burned wood and metal. Links to the other Houses. To the Houseless.

Aurore moved; too slow, too late. Morningstar threw something at her. She raised one hand to ward him off, and pain flared into her palm, clenching her fingers together and sending her to her knees, gasping to breathe. The disk on her chest flared harsh and painful, and then everything fuzzed and went dark.

10

Tastes of Home

Emmanuelle spent her time in the cell thinking on how she could get out.

The grate was the most likely exit, or the best way to send out a message, but it was heavily warded: she couldn't even put her hand close to it without getting a jolt of pain. She could see cobblestones through its bars, but no one had walked across them. Likely, it opened on rue des Entrepreneurs, and she'd seen first-hand how deserted that was, with the devastation in the House.

They'd taken almost everything from her, but the disk Darrias had given her was still there. It was quiescent now—enough time on her and that would change, Darrias said, but of course it had barely been there for a few hours. And even if it did start working, it was a safe bet it wouldn't work within a heavily warded room.

How could she contact Darrias? Assuming Darrias had even waited for her—and why would she? She'd never trusted Emmanuelle, why would she now risk herself for her? No, Darrias's best plan would be to go on as they'd planned: to find Niraphanes and her faction, negotiate a safe passage back to Hawthorn. She'd know, all too well, not to embarrass herself with dead weight.

She's always believed she could have what was mine.

Darrias had come back for her family, but hadn't told Emmanuelle. It was Guy who had—assuming she could trust Guy, assuming this wasn't some twisted game he was playing. But why would he bother lying about something they both remembered?

Or both ought to. Annoying brain injury.

So Darrias had come back to House Harrier to get her family out, under the guise of being a Hawthorn envoy. And Guy, never fooled by Darrias's pretense to be there under Hawthorn business, had made plans to publicly torture and execute Darrias at the banquet all the envoys would attend. And because he'd always been the kind to gloat, he'd told Emmanuelle, secure in the knowledge she was powerless against him.

Except … Except Darrias was alive and not markedly hurt. Certainly not dead or badly tortured: she had a habit of brushing off wounds to appear tough, but she would not have been able to hide something of that magnitude.

What had happened?

The House had exploded, and Guy had never found time to harm Darrias. And Emmanuelle—she had a stubborn hole in her memory, shot through only with glimpses of unbearable fear.

Not that it mattered much, currently. Darrias wasn't going to walk into this much danger for anyone's sake.

That left Emmanuelle with herself. Or Morningstar.

She closed her eyes. A memory, bright and unbearable, of an evening before they'd left for Harrier: Morningstar, standing at the door to her refuge in the library, the area where she stored all the spare books along with those in need of more advanced repairs. The lantern on her desk threw trembling light over the cornflower of his hair, and created hulking shadows at his back, like a memory of his lost wings.

"Working late?" he said.

Emmanuelle put down her book. "You're going to tell me it's not reasonable."

Morningstar shrugged. "It's your business." He pulled up a chair and sat down. "Selene wanted to make me responsible for the delegation."

"And you want my approval?" Emmanuelle said, then realized that wasn't what he was saying. "You said no."

He'd died and been reborn. None of them were sure how: it had happened in the mess of Silverspires' collapse the year before. Selene was reasonably sure Asmodeus had had a hand in it, but they couldn't prove anything.

Whatever the case, the bewildered Fallen they'd found wandering the corridors wasn't the old Morningstar, the cruel, fey Fallen who had ruled the House with a fist of iron. The only thing he'd kept from that time was the stubborn, boundless desire to do what was right by the House no matter the cost, and the unthinking arrogance of those who believed themselves indispensable.

"You have the most experience."

Emmanuelle laughed. "Do you want tea?"

When he nodded, she moved to her small stove, and pulled out some of the water she'd kept warm along with the flecks of the black tea that was the best the House had to offer. He wanted milk; she took hers plain. They sat, warming two mugs and staring at each other.

"My main experience of these things is going to them."

"Which is more than I have." Morningstar grimaced.

He had very few memories of what had happened before—as if he were a newly born Fallen. Not an easy thing, in a House where every memory of him weighed as heavy as flung stones.

Emmanuelle said, finally, "She's right, you know."

"Selene?"

"I'm not sure I can go," Emmanuelle said.

Among all the Houses, Harrier was the hardest. It had become harder and harder to go there, knowing what was happening. Knowing that the foundation of the House was that sheer, blind-headed worship of Fallen superiority. Knowing she had to be silent, and not interfere.

"It's always exhausting, and all for what? So we can reaffirm Guy's opinion of himself?"

If only she believed that whoever came after Guy would be better, but they wouldn't be.

"And … it's going to be nasty, this time around."

"Hmmm," Morningstar said. "Trouble?"

"I don't know," Emmanuelle said. Guy always looked at her as if she'd been dragged in with the trash. She was Fallen, but in his view she consorted too much with mortals. And, of course, she looked like a native. "I don't know if I can do what's needed."

Morningstar laid his cup on the table. "You can."

"You're just saying that to make me happy."

A laugh—and he rose, and for a moment he was tall and overpowering, the Fallen who'd been so disappointed in her lack of hunger for magic and power. The Fallen who'd protected the House from decay.

"Emmanuelle—you and Selene *always* do what's needed. And I'll always stand by you. I'll be there. I promise."

Except nothing had gone to plan, and he wasn't there—not in her cell, perhaps not even in Harrier. Nevertheless . . .

Morningstar.

It felt blasphemous, to call on Lucifer Morningstar with a faith akin to prayer. But she knew she could trust him—a thought that enfolded her like huge wings.

Emmanuelle rubbed the hollow between her collarbones, wishing again and again that she'd thought of taking a tracking disk from Silverspires. Or something, anything that would make her feel less isolated. Less scared about what the future held.

Within her was the link to the House: the quiescent thread that tied her back to Selene, and to all the other House dependents. It would light up like a beacon if she was in immediate danger, drawing Selene and any other dependents to her aid.

She could put herself in immediate danger—no, there was nothing sharp in that cell, and there was no gain in being near death. Even Morningstar—who had to be the closest Silverspires dependent to her—wouldn't be able to walk or break through walls.

Selene?

Nothing. A sense of Selene's presence through the link—distant and preoccupied, mind busy with the business of the House, the need to appear strong.

Selene?

A flicker, perhaps. A ghostly touch on her shoulders, the way Selene would wrap her hands around her at the end of a tiring day. She was lost and exhausted and thirsting for anything that would bring hope. There was none; but perhaps she could take comfort in memories, and the unalterable, unbreakable past.

There had to be a way. Some sign she could send. She stood up on the bench by the wall, and looked at the wards on the grate. Magic flickered and bloomed into being, a rippling light that illuminated the darkness of the cell. The wards were old, anchored in the roots of the House—a spellcasting she wasn't familiar with, whose patterns were meaningless to her.

Except that they held meaning, after a fashion. She couldn't read the spell or make out its details, but everything was slightly out of kilter, slightly too loose—bent inwards towards her. From the force of the explosion, no doubt.

She could chip at it, layer by layer. Undo piece after piece with fingers that felt like lead—cursing, from time to time, as the magic earthed itself through her.

Halfway through, her arm spasmed. She held herself still, breathing hard and heavily, as the wards dug into her back. Again and again—it didn't seem to be stopping, but she needed to stop and rest. She'd been running on too little energy, and her body was going to present her with the complete list of unpleasant consequences soon.

Rest was for the dead. And dead was what she'd be, soon enough, and worse: a pretext for embroiling Selene in a war House Silverspires couldn't win.

Emmanuelle gritted her teeth, and undid another thread of spell. And another and another. Everything ached. Her hands clenched of their own accord, fingers shaking. The little hole she could see between the bars wasn't even a free space: when she pushed against it, it pushed back—only not with pain or burning, but with the yield of an elastic surface. Enough of a push, and it'd crumble completely …

The door opened.

What—?

No time. Emmanuelle reached for Darrias's disk, and wedged it in the small space she'd opened, pushing hard until her wrist felt stretched out of shape altogether. As she did so, she put all the magic she could pull from her body into its opalescent surface. A faint, weak burst answered from the disk as it clattered to the cobblestones, tearing the edges of the wards in the process. Pathetic. A distant, clouded star, not a bonfire. But it was all she had.

Lord in Heaven, help me get through this.

Then, and only then, she turned, clambering away from the grate, making herself look as though her attempt to slither through the bars had been interrupted.

"Leaving us so soon?" The voice was mocking.

"Andrea."

Guy's wife stood limned in light on the threshold. She wore the colors of the House: a deep, midnight blue on the hem of her dress, and black everywhere else, down to the gloves on her hands and the cigarette holder in her hand—an affectation, or the real thing? The Warded Chambers had seemed flush with things from before the war, so why not tobacco?

"I was surprised not to see you up there," Emmanuelle said.

"With my husband?"

Andrea walked into the room. The emphasis she put on the last word was … tentative.

Emmanuelle had never dealt with Andrea. She'd grown

used to seeing the two of them together, husband and wife, Guy full of bluster and grating arrogance, and Andrea interjecting to support him. She'd thought of her as no more than an extension of her husband—an altogether unworthy and uncharitable thought.

She looked at Andrea again. Deep, shadowed eyes that looked bruised—she wouldn't have been surprised if Guy were abusive, but he seemed to take his pleasures elsewhere. Make-up that was a little too shakily applied, and of course the black dress.

She thought, again, of the boy's corpse in the reception room. Not a child, but barely out of childhood all the same. The last of Guy's sons—which meant all the others, too, had died.

"I'm sorry for your loss," she said, and was surprised to find truth behind the words.

"Don't be." A long, sinuous shrug; a drawl as Andrea leaned against the door jamb, studying Emmanuelle. Dissecting her. "Children are meant to die."

"They shouldn't have to."

"Oh, Emmanuelle. Are you always so naive? You of all people can't afford it."

"Of all people?"

"Fallen," Andrea said, simply. Of course—Emmanuelle had forgotten she was mortal. "And let's face it—you look like a native."

A fact people were only too happy to remind her of, in myriad little ways.

Emmanuelle said, more sharply than she'd meant to, "That's irrelevant, isn't it."

A wide, bitter smile. "Perhaps. Perhaps not. Let's talk of the future, then."

Emmanuelle thought quickly. Guy was beyond reason—but Andrea might not be. It was all about finding the right words.

"I would like to go home." She kept her voice slow and steady; because if this failed, she wouldn't get a second chance. They would make whatever example Guy had in mind of her. "I have no position in this, and I'm not about to involve House Silverspires in the affairs of House Harrier."

She stopped before she could say "war of succession", because she could guess that insofar as they were concerned, it wasn't a succession question. It was a temporary rebellion, no matter how bad it had got.

Andrea inhaled from the cigarette holder: the smell of something sweet and moldy wafting up to Emmanuelle—she'd have known it anywhere. Not tobacco, but angel essence.

"There's no going home," Andrea said, at last, and she seemed to be talking about more than Emmanuelle. "Not after you got involved."

"Because of Darrias?" What had Darrias done?

"Do you know who she is?" Andrea said.

"A friend." The words were out of Emmanuelle's mouth before she could think, and in spite of all evidence. And then, because she wasn't completely rash, "A traitor."

She's always believed she could have what was mine.

Andrea leaned against the door again. Magic flickered and died on the tip of her cigarette.

"Darrias was always a liability. Houses are built on

certain foundations, and Darrias ... came to doubt them."

Emmanuelle had known Darrias long enough to know exactly what foundations her friend had questioned.

"You mean she thought that humans could be the equal of Fallen? That hardly seems revolutionary. *You're* human."

"But not immortal. Not infused with magic." Andrea's voice was matter-of-fact.

"Fallen aren't immortal. Just ageless, and very long-lived."

"You know that makes no difference."

"That's assuming the things you most value are magic and long life."

Emmanuelle was conscious of the privileges they conferred on her. But it wasn't the same thing as assigning value to an accident of birth. She tried, very hard, to not let that be the rule she lived by.

Andrea laughed. "Look around you, Emmanuelle. Look at your Houses. See who holds the power. There is only one human head of House—Claire in Lazarus—and she's beleaguered and weak, only getting her way by setting us at each other's throats. I'm honest about the way the world works. I know where power is, and how you get it, when you're not its source."

By breeding child after child that she'd watch Guy infuse with magic, and losing them one by one to the House battles? Emmanuelle stopped herself before she could fling the words into Andrea's face.

"He doesn't love you," she said.

"Oh, Emmanuelle. Don't be so naive. We both get what we need from the relationship."

Emmanuelle closed her eyes, because it hurt too much. Because it was all bitterness and political calculations, and watching children die … Her head hurt again—she'd thought that once before, hadn't she? Such a huge, angry thought that had seemed to swallow up the universe.

"Who is Niraphanes?" she asked, finally.

"An upstart." Andrea drew on her cigarette, blew out the smoke in colored rings. Magic pulsed, weakly, in the air. "Someone who thinks she can run the House better than Guy does."

"That's not what I meant. Guy said she'd try to stop him if he killed Darrias."

Andrea laughed. "I doubt she would have. Niraphanes is the one who replaced Darrias."

"Replaced?" Emmanuelle asked with a sinking feeling, suspecting the answer already.

"Every magician needs a Fall-parent. After Darrias was disgraced—before she left the House, when Guy sent her back onto the streets—Niraphanes took her place."

"Took. Her. Place."

It was so clinical, so detached. As if you could take one parent away and replace them with another, and have neither child nor parents notice or care. But then it was what Harrier did, wasn't it? All the blood they spilled and the misery they thrived on, never giving a second thought to the devastation that sustained them.

Again, that pitying head-shake. "Darrias wanted everything back. As if that would ever have been granted to her."

"Guy warned me," Emmanuelle said, slowly, carefully.

Missing memory was bad enough; having to hide it from everyone else was like dancing on the edge of the abyss.

"Next you'll be saying you just happened to meet her in the House."

"I did," Emmanuelle said.

She stopped, then. Had it been truly random, or was this an elaborate plot on Darrias's part? But why would she? No. Not trusting the people who wanted to torture and kill her was the most sensible course of action.

"I saw your face," Andrea said conversationally. "When Guy warned you, back before all this happened. You're good at hiding it, but you were upset. And worried. You went straight to see Darrias, didn't you?"

When in doubt, stay on the offensive.

"What if I did?" Emmanuelle asked. "I think we're allowed friends."

"Outside our Houses?" Andrea's voice was sarcastic. "Very risky."

"Is it?"

It was like fighting with one hand tied behind her back, and she couldn't afford that. It was very uncomfortable defending herself against allegations of interfering with another House's affairs when she had no earthly idea how rash she'd been in the past day or so.

"Things have changed too much. And we can't afford a war with Silverspires."

She should have sounded as though she was going to free Emmanuelle, but it came out very differently. The cigarette holder shone like a beacon in the dim light, and magic bloomed in the room, dragging Emmanuelle down on the floor.

"You're not here to do me any favors," she whispered. "There's no need …"

Silverspires couldn't afford to get into a war with anyone, not even for retribution.

Andrea laid the holder down. It smoldered on the threshold, and when she stood up again she had a dagger out.

"In a manner of speaking," she said with a bitter smile. "It's such a dangerous House, currently. So many things can happen. It'd be so … regrettable if you died in a skirmish and we had to return your body to Selene, but much less so than having you executed in full sight of all the dependents and the rebels."

It felt unreal. Emmanuelle, flopped on the floor like a dead fish, watched Andrea walk into the room—everything slowed down and jerky, time stretched out into molasses, but her own attempts to escape were as through treacle. This was how it ended, and she didn't want it to, so many things to say and do …

Selene.

In her mind, the link to the House *burned*, and she heard her lover's voice, edged with anger and fear. *Run.*

Where …?

It didn't matter where.

Emmanuelle kicked at Andrea, again and again until the magic holding her in place broke. Her first kick was so weak it didn't even lift dust from the floor, the second one landed wide, and the third one hit Andrea in the solar plexus. She gasped, reeling. Emmanuelle kicked again and again, feeling the magic shudder and give way. It should never have worked, but the House was weak, and so was Guy and Andrea's magic.

Andrea was folded over in pain, curled around an arm

that hung at an angle. In shock, though that wasn't going to last long.

The grate.

Emmanuelle ran to it. No time. She couldn't finesse unwinding of the threads anymore, but she had something on the outside, this time.

The disk.

She pulled it in, pulling again and again, the wards shriveling in its wake. Too slow, it was too slow—at any moment now Andrea was going to pull herself together. What would she do, if it was an inner courtyard and not the outside street?

The wards burst. The bars melted. Emmanuelle clambered out, breathing heavily—she expected, at any moment, Andrea to come behind her, but nothing happened. When she finally hauled herself up, she was on a vaguely familiar street: rue des Entrepreneurs, a long, thin line of empty buildings leading up to the greenery of Place Charles Michel. The disk was warm in her hands: it pulsed, not like a tracker disk, but like a stuttering heart. A beacon, Darrias had said, but the tug Emmanuelle felt was stronger than that.

She walked, staggering, into the street. Not much time until someone found Andrea. Until Guy realized what she'd done. Until the birds wheeled in the sky once again. The tug was pulling her west—there was something wrong about that but she didn't remember, any more, what it was. The only thing keeping her upright was sheer adrenaline, and the slow, steady tug in her hand. The street opened up, became a plaza with absurdly verdant trees, and then a long avenue bordered by disused factories—large wrought-iron gates opening on empty courtyards, long hangars with only empty spaces for doors, a chimney still blowing smoke at the sky. And, on the other side, buildings that still stood, covered in soot and fungus, the usual genteel decay of post-war Paris. No corpses, just the glittering of broken shards in the empty window frames, and the air itself was almost clean, almost empty of smoke and so sharp it hurt her throat to breathe in …

Her world was black, shivering and folding back on itself, when something stopped her. All her legs wanted was to keep walking, one foot after the other until she finally reached safety, so she pushed on ahead, stubbornly—she could hear the sibilant cries of the hawks behind her, detaching themselves from buildings, coming for her—but the obstacle, the person, didn't move. Someone moved her hands from their shoulders, pushed her back from their chest.

"Emmanuelle."

"Darrias," she said. "You shouldn't—"

"Have waited?" Darrias's voice was soft, and terrible. "You were hard to miss, Emmanuelle."

The disk vanished from Emmanuelle's hand, the tug finally fading—and Darrias held her as her legs gave out, and the rest of her body followed.

"Like a hook in a fish's mouth," she said, almost tenderly—and held Emmanuelle against her as the world shivered and went completely dark.

"You don't understand," Philippe said.

The small kitchen space in Olympe's flat looked like nothing so much as a court: the dim light of fires in the gray light of morning; the circle of aunts spread behind Grandmother Olympe, their faces unreadable in the dim light. Every available surface seemed to be covered in grit-filled flour, and the air was redolent with the smell of garlic and fish sauce—not the adulterated stuff, but as pure as it would ever be, this side of the Mediterranean—a thick, strong odor that hung on his tongue and reminded him of better days.

Grandmother Olympe was chopping ginger roots with Colette, Aunt Ha's daughter, on a stool and watching with rapt fascination as the rectangular blade made paper-thin slices of yellowish flesh. She put the ginger in a small, chipped bowl.

"I don't understand?" she said, turning to Philippe.

She was using the pronoun for *grandmother* for herself—demanding respect and not acknowledging Philippe's status as older than her.

Not that he'd ever tried to make much of said status. It had been embarrassing—until now.

Philippe closed his eyes, and tried to think of words. He was exhausted: he and Isabelle had spent the night trying to heal Aunt Ha, fighting the *khi* fire that kept rising in her, again and again, tiger stripes appearing on her skin the moment they faltered. He'd left Isabelle there with Hoa Phong—Hoa Phong had insisted her expertise was helping, but she'd turned out to remember some of the more elaborate weaves used by the Court to heal their servants.

"I don't mean any disrespect, but you have to leave before Dân Chay burns this entire place down to the ground. As he's burned House Harrier."

Grandmother Olympe set down the knife.

"No touching," she said, firmly, to Colette. "We can't leave, Philippe."

Was this about their faith in him? He was the last person they could count on for help.

"He's one of Heaven's enforcers."

"Stronger than you?"

Once, perhaps not. But now? He didn't know what the Houses had done to Dân Chay—he could guess, but he didn't have the stomach to ask Isabelle—and he could barely keep Dân Chay's magic at bay in one person.

"What happened in Gare du Nord … that wasn't him. That was just someone he'd touched, once. We'll lose, if we fight."

"And you're saying this with absolute certainty?"

"Nothing is certain," Philippe said. "But the chances—"

"Are minuscule?" Grandmother Olympe smiled. "Still, they exist."

"They might as well not!"

But Grandmother Olympe didn't budge.

"Do you think he'll come back?" Aunt Thuy asked.

The midwife wore a loose tunic over baggy pants, and looked as exhausted as Philippe felt, her topknot almost eclipsed by stray locks of hair. She leaned her back against the counter for support.

"Not this way," Philippe said. He'd burned the scroll the man had been carrying—the vector that had infected Aunt Ha. "He wasn't there. It was just … a memory of him." *Khi* fire honed to a killing edge—elemental stripes that kept reappearing on Aunt Ha's body. "I don't even think he meant to harm Aunt Ha. He burned the man for the fuel so he could speak, and she was just standing in the way. But that's not the point!"

Grandmother Olympe snatched the knife from Colette's grasp.

"No touching, I said! I hear what you're saying, child. But we can't leave."

"Because your life is here? That's just ..." Material things. Houses and furniture and walls. "It can be rebuilt."

And he stopped, because he realized he was speaking as an Immortal to whom possessions had never meant much.

Grandmother Olympe smiled. "There's that, too. But that's not the issue, Philippe. Where would we go?"

"Anywhere!" He tried again. "Grandmother, he's an Immortal who was tortured by two Houses in their attempt to make a weapon of war. He's managed to slip their control, and now thinks most of the city is to blame for what happened to him. He'll burn this area to cinders. He's—like a House, but instead of ignoring you he wants to kill you all."

Abandon it all, and you may live.

"This is our home." Grandmother Olympe sighed, and for a moment she was an old, large and formidable woman who had seen all the decades go by. "You can't understand, child. I wasn't born when the war ended, but I remember what it meant for our parents to be torn from our homes. Those wounds never really closed. This ... we built this. We built our altars and we buried the bones of our ancestors, and every flat that stands is something we made with our own hands, against the indifference of the Houses. This is what home means. And this is where we'll be buried."

"I ..." He stopped, again. The fatigue he'd been keeping

at bay came crashing down, and it was just him, standing in the middle of cracked tiles, struggling to stand, let alone put two thoughts together. "Not everyone will want this."

"You assume other places will welcome us, the dregs of the city." Her voice was amused again. "You assume it is easy to build. People *remember* how much each stone cost us." A short, bitter laugh. "You also assume he would keep his word."

"Who?" And then he realized. "Dân Chay."

"You may live." The words, spoken in the archaic language of the court, sounded almost alien to Philippe. "He burned a man to deliver a message. Why would he not hunt us down, merely for fun or because of his outdated grudges?"

"Outdated." Philippe couldn't help it: the word came welling up before he could stop it.

Olympe's gaze was steel. "Yes. I know in the old country the sins of the father became those of the children, and of their own parents. The nine kinship exterminations. This isn't the old country anymore."

"I won't judge you," Philippe said. The words tasted like ashes on his tongue. "I can't. I fought in the war."

Olympe's voice was almost gentle. She left the kitchen, and folded his hands in hers—and around the hilt of the knife.

"But do you see now? We don't run away. We hold. We fight, no matter how minuscule the chances, because it's the better alternative. Because it's the hope we have." She looked back at the aunts, for a moment. "You can decide, now, if you want to leave. It may make more sense to you. But if you do—you're on your own."

A silence. Not one of them moved.

"You'll die," Philippe said.

"Some of us will." It was one of the newer aunts—a gaunt, tall Maghrebi refugee from Harrier with a singed blue scarf around her head. "But everything dies, in time. At least we know it's coming."

II

Rude Awakenings

Aurore was sitting on something hard—the ground between the two gates of the barracks. The smoke was slowly dispersing, which meant she could see. She wished she couldn't, because skulls and fragments of bones and Harrier uniforms littered the ground.

She was alive.

Everything hurt. Her hand, the one she'd raised to catch Morningstar's spell, felt as though someone had torn it to shreds.

"You're awake," an unfamiliar voice said.

She turned, startled. A Fallen in the uniform of House Harrier was sitting on a pile of rubble, watching her. She had long flowing hair she hadn't bothered to gather in a proper hairstyle—it was tangled and knotted and filled with pieces of dust and smoke. She wore a dress covered with black lace in an elaborate circles-and-flowers pattern—it was lightly singed, but the damage was almost imperceptible. Her clothes were the colors of Harrier, though the crest of the House, the hawk in flight over the burning tower, had been joined by a second bird. Behind her were three guards, standing in a falsely nonchalant pose Aurore knew all too well: if she moved so much as an unapproved muscle they'd slam her to the floor.

She should bow down and grovel—it took an effort to keep her body still, to stare the Fallen in the eye.

The Fallen was unperturbed by her insolence.

"They've gone," she said, conversationally.

"I don't know who you're talking about," Aurore said.

A gently amused snort. "You were unconscious and too hard to carry as they ran away."

They'd thought she was dead, then. Which was good, or Morningstar would have made sure of it before he left.

"I didn't mean much to them, anyway." She shrugged, keeping her voice casual. "I snuck into the House to scavenge and they dragged me along with them."

The Fallen's brown eyes were all too sharply perceptive. "Into all sorts of trouble."

Aurore weighed up what information she could give. It had all been very friendly so far, but she doubted it would remain that. And though she'd sell Morningstar out in a heartbeat, she didn't think the Fallen was looking for him so much as for the children. And she wasn't going to hand them back to their tormentors.

"They wanted to look at the source of the explosion."

Again, an amused snort. "So they could replicate it elsewhere?"

The Houses. A stray Immortal. The mortals.

Dân Chay was going to set fire to everything. She needed to get home, before Dân Chay did.

"Yes," Aurore said.

Morningstar had used Dân Chay to devastate Harrier and then let him loose in the city. Aurore couldn't understand his reasons, but she'd got the rest. Morningstar didn't care if the city became an ocean of ruins, as long as Silverspires was still intact.

"It'll happen again. The explosion. Because the Fallen never really care about anything but destruction."

"Don't we?" The Fallen's face was very still. "We're not all the same, you know. Morningstar is … peculiar. I haven't introduced myself, by the way. My name is Niraphanes. What's yours?"

Frédérique's wife. Aurore blinked, staring at her.

"I'm Aurore."

"Aurore. Pleased to meet you. You've heard of me." Niraphanes smiled. "I'm not surprised."

That seemed, if nothing else, an easy thing to admit.

"Yes."

"From Frédérique?"

"Yes."

Behind her, one of the bodyguards was playing with a knife, staring at Aurore with the familiar contempt of Fallen for a mortal menial. She was exhausted and her hand was a symphony of pain.

I have a revenge to take. A city to burn.

She wanted to go home. To warn Cassiopée. To run, but where would they run to?

"Where are they going, Aurore?"

She didn't know. Silverspires, surely, the children still used as shields by Morningstar. But Frédérique had said something about Niraphanes and the wars of the House, and how she'd wanted to drag Virginie into it.

"I don't know."

The bodyguard moved—no, she wasn't a bodyguard,

because she moved with the easy gait of someone used to power.

"We're wasting our time. Give her to us to play with." A smile that was feral and predatory. "Who knows, we might even get something useful out of her."

Niraphanes looked annoyed for a moment, and then her face was smooth again. She turned to Aurore again, watched her closely.

"Don't mind Lorcid. She gets overeager. They abandoned you. I thought you'd be a little less eager to protect them."

Aurore wasn't even sure why she was doing it—stubbornness, compassion?

"There's a child," she said finally, finding nothing but the truth in the scorched ruins of her mind.

"My child."

"They ran." She kept her voice level, but she was well aware nothing about her manner was humble or servile anymore. She didn't care. The time for masks was past. "They knew it was you and they still ran. If Frédérique is scared enough to leave the House rather than face you, then maybe you don't deserve your own child."

Lorcid moved—one moment she was behind Aurore, and the next pain shot through her cheek and her head whipped back with the force of the blow. She tasted blood.

When the world unblurred, Aurore saw Niraphanes had, effortlessly, thrown Lorcid to the ground.

"No violence," she said, still in that firm pleasant tone.

Lorcid sat up. She didn't look fazed or angry.

"You're too sentimental."

Niraphanes said, "Do you want us to be no better than Guy?"

"Morality will never win you the House."

"Perhaps it's not about winning," Niraphanes said. "But about doing things the right way." She turned back to Aurore. "I'm sorry. You were sharing unpleasant truths. Do go on."

What? Aurore had dealt with many Fallen, but none like Niraphanes. She didn't know on which foot to dance, which was annoying.

"I was saying I didn't feel like betraying a confidence. Even if I knew it."

"Commendable," Niraphanes said. "You do know who Frédérique is running away with, don't you?" Her voice was still amused, but Aurore could feel the steel beneath.

Morningstar. She tasted ashes and dust. He'd keep them alive, because he had to.

"He's powerful," she said. "And it's in his best interest to keep them alive."

"Is it?" Niraphanes' face was expressionless. She reached up, brushed a hand through her own hair, stopped at the first tangle and gently worked out the knot, her gaze on Aurore all the while. "I won't ask how you know. But surely you must have asked yourself what will happen once their usefulness runs out?"

He'd used *children* as shields. He'd bargained with their lives and pain to keep himself safe, because he couldn't envision his House without his own presence.

"I . . ." Aurore opened her mouth, closed it again.

Niraphanes' voice was low and intense. "Frédérique and I may not agree. I understand she wants to keep Virginie safe at all costs, even when the time for safety or neutrality has passed. But I'm not willing to leave her with someone like Morningstar."

She said, slowly, "He said he would offer them the shelter of the House."

Would he? When he was back within his own domain, when he no longer needed the children to shield him from Dân Chay?

"He might. I don't know. Is this a risk I'm willing to take? Of course not."

Niraphanes sounded … frustrated. Angry. Human. A mother, worrying about her child. No. Aurore couldn't afford to think of her that way.

"They're going to House Silverspires."

Aurore was offering nothing to Niraphanes but confirmation of what she already knew, or could work out for herself. Nothing that would keep her unharmed.

Niraphanes was silent for a while.

"I can work with that." She snapped her fingers, and Lorcid was at her side. She appeared unperturbed, though the glance she flashed Aurore wasn't entirely friendly. "Take two people and stop them. Preferably before they reach Silverspires."

Lorcid nodded, and was gone, to confer with the guards at the back.

"You knew," Aurore said. "Where else—?"

"Where else would he go? I couldn't be sure," Niraphanes said. "And I have to be very, very sure, before I interfere with the business of another House." She laughed. It was tense, but still amused. "But I have an eyewitness now."

Aurore's heart sank. "I'm not Harrier."

Niraphanes' look at her, this time, was long and steady and entirely too uncomfortable. Did she know Aurore had been from Harrier once? She couldn't possibly know. It wasn't like Frédérique or Morningstar or any of the others would have screamed the evidence at her as they fled.

"You're not." She smiled. "I'm not going to ask you what you're doing here, am I." It wasn't a question.

Aurore said nothing.

Niraphanes shifted and Aurore flinched—but Niraphanes was simply kneeling by her side, pointing to the hand she kept curled.

"You were wounded in a fight, weren't you?"

She reached out, and unfolded it. Aurore tried to stop her, but Niraphanes' fingers were unbreakable steel. Pain spread through her burned palm and wrist, and she couldn't help the whimper forced out of her mouth.

And then, surprisingly, it stopped—not because Niraphanes was done, but because she was staring at the wound with mild concern on her face.

"That looks ugly. And unexpected."

"I'm not sure what you expected," Aurore managed through gritted teeth.

"Something more sordid. That looks like you tried to catch a spell of shriveling."

"I don't know what you mean."

"If it had worked, you wouldn't be here," Niraphanes said. "Well, your charred body would."

Her chest had burned. The disk, trying to save her? Not out of goodness of heart, obviously, but because Asmodeus would have been disappointed to lose his favorite toy. They were all the same. And Niraphanes, for all her play-acting at concern, was Fallen too. Aurore owed Harrier and the other Houses nothing but blood and pain, and she would never, ever help them save themselves.

"It was the armory," she lied. "I don't know what they kept there."

Again, a long, weighing look from Niraphanes. Lorcid still hadn't left—was she going to call her back? Aurore braced herself. She could bear pain, but at some point she knew her body would betray her.

At length, Niraphanes smiled. "Too many secrets, Aurore. They always choke you in the end." She touched, gently, the charred mark in Aurore's hand. "I'll have my people bandage this, before you leave."

Aurore said, "You're letting me go. Why? You said you needed an eyewitness."

"Mostly as an excuse. It's not like I'll have to produce you for House Silverspires." Niraphanes shrugged. She rose, looking at Lorcid and the devastation around them. "Why? Because every scrap of goodwill has to start somewhere."

An idealist, Frédérique had said. A decent person, but Aurore had seen the light in her eyes when she'd said it. She might not agree with Niraphanes, but she admired her all the same. A naïve child, from Aurore's point of view. There was no room for goodwill in the world, not between those at the top and the bottom of the heap.

"If it makes you feel better," Niraphanes said, "believe I'm saving you in case I need you, further down the line." Her voice was bleak.

Aurore thought, again, over what she'd seen.

Do you want us to fight? It wouldn't be contained. There might be … casualties.

She'd barely met Frédérique and the others, and she didn't have the energy to care about people beyond her own—those she was already failing. And whatever lay between Niraphanes and her family wasn't for her to solve. But there were *children* involved—and children or no, no one deserved to be used that way.

"I hope you find them," she said.

As she left, nursing the hand Niraphanes' people had bandaged, she turned. The smoke was still dissipating, revealing the ruined barracks, the field of debris and bones and skulls all around them—ashes and charred stones, and melted glass. The wind whistled over the emptiness—and in it, she heard, again, Dân Chay's voice.

A city to burn. Houses. A stray Immortal.

She needed to find Cassiopée. She needed to warn her. She needed to stop Dân Chay. But how in Heaven did one stop a being of living fire?

Emmanuelle woke up in shadow, gasping. For a moment everything was limned in edged light, and then it passed. The feeling of dizziness took a while more to do so. What …? Where …?

She was in an utterly unfamiliar room. Dull green wallpaper—that awful olive color that she'd wanted Selene to remove from the west wing of Silverspires. She lay on a four-poster bed with a moldering scarlet canopy—fresh sheets, smelling of laundry. It was, quite definitely, not a room she'd ever seen. Harrier? But the part of Harrier she'd seen had been brash and over-decorated. This …

had been that way, once upon a time, but now it was just genteel decay.

Where was she?

She was wearing new clothes: a set of silk pajamas, the chinoiserie that had been all the rage, with a matching satin bonnet which she took off. She got up, clinging to the bedpost. Her torn and burned Silverspires uniform had been folded and left on the bed, but not patched. A clear statement if ever there was one. There was a door: a huge, two-paneled thing with elaborate wood carvings that were now mostly stubs of creatures with missing heads and limbs. It was locked.

How surprising.

There was a large window with baize curtains in that same shade of green drawn over it—the woven cords of the curtains hung on the walls, flecked with mold. Everything had the same faint smell of humidity.

Emmanuelle drew back one curtain, carefully. It was large and heavy, and she had to pause twice when doing so, once because her hands flexed open of their own accord, and again when her leg spasmed and left her, panting, leaning against the cloth and breathing in the smell of humidity. Wards tingled as she did so: nothing so painful or so barbed as Harrier's, but a gentle touch to warn her away—a softness wrapped in a core of cutting steel.

A vast sweep of lawn, going down to the murky, oily surface of the Seine. Children playing on the ruined gravel, their feet scattering pieces of stone and blackened grit. Dependents in silver and gray swallowtails and top hats, and here and there the sharp features of an Annamite, their faces blurring away to reveal the antlers of dragons.

Hawthorn.

She was in Hawthorn. Darrias's House. Asmodeus's House.

The door opened behind her. She would have turned, but she could barely move, the burst of strength that had propelled her through the room all but extinguished now.

"She's fainted," someone said.

"Not quite. She's conscious, but in no state to stand up," an older woman's voice said. "Come on."

They carried her to the bed: two orderlies dressed in white with the crowned hawthorn arms of the House, and behind them Iaris, Asmodeus's right hand—if she still was that, in the new order of the House—who bent over Emmanuelle with a faintly irritated expression, unwrapping her stethoscope from around her neck. Clearly there as a doctor first, and a representative of the House second.

"Sit still," she said.

It was all Emmanuelle could do to sit. She supposed it was a good sign that they were treating her at all—but it was Hawthorn. The House was not known for random acts of kindness, and everything they did was barbed and poisonous.

Iaris's examination was cursory. She snapped the stethoscope back into place around her neck, asked Emmanuelle a few questions about when she'd woken up, and stared into her eyes.

"Mmm," she said. "Flex your arm for me?" She thought for a while.

"You're wondering if you should tell me," Emmanuelle said. "I can take it. I know it's a brain injury."

Iaris didn't even blink. "I'm wondering what I'm *allowed*

to tell you." She shrugged. It was slow and graceful. Finally she said, "He'll tell you. But I won't leave this untreated."

And with that she and the orderlies were gone, leaving Emmanuelle to wait. There was little doubt who "he" was—but what would he want from her? She must have dozed, or slept, because when she opened her eyes again, the key was turning in the lock.

Three servants, carrying a tray with food they laid on the table. One of them, a woman with long flowing hair, helped Emmanuelle stand up and fold her body into the chair while the others laid a plate and cutlery, and a fine crystal glass into which they poured wine. A thick, golden soup redolent of cheese, a chunk of bread by its side—Emmanuelle stared at the spoon for a while, her hands shaking. She hadn't realized how long it was since she'd touched proper food.

"It's not poisoned," a voice said from the doorway. "Poisoning lacks immediacy. A coward's weapon, I've always thought. There's no pleasure in watching someone die at a remove."

"Asmodeus," Emmanuelle said.

He leaned against the doorway, with Darrias a couple of steps behind him. Darrias was in full House uniform, a masculine swallowtail over a ruffled shirt, and wouldn't meet Emmanuelle's eyes. Asmodeus wore his usual jacket, with a red cravat at his throat and a hawthorn flower in his buttonhole. His gaze, behind the square horn-rimmed glasses, was sharp and amused, and why wouldn't he be? He'd had the lover of a rival House's head delivered straight to him in a neatly wrapped package. With her in his hands, he could make Selene dance to his tune for as long as he liked. Though she didn't know what their weak and devastated House could offer …

"Hello, Emmanuelle."

The servants finished laying the table. The woman left a wrapped package on it, which shone with a faint lambent light. A spell?

Asmodeus came in, Darrias trailing him like a silent shadow, and pulled up a chair, watching her.

"Eat," he said.

One of the servants brought him a glass of wine. They offered one to Darrias as well, but she shook her head.

"And take the medicine," Asmodeus added.

The medicine? Emmanuelle stared at the table. He had to mean the package.

"What is it for?" she asked.

"I've already told you. Not poison."

"There are many things that aren't poison and that I wouldn't necessarily take."

Emmanuelle unwrapped the package. Her hands were shaking—any time now, she was going to knock over the wineglass and break it. Inside was a small vial with round, white pills.

Asmodeus shrugged. "You have a head injury, Iaris tells me. You need rest."

A good thing she was his prisoner then; and locked in a room she doubted she'd leave in the near future. She didn't say the words, because she wasn't capable of mustering the necessary sarcasm. A wave of shakes hit her like a blow to the heart. She wanted so badly to be home, in her little office behind the stacks of books in Silverspires with the smell of paper and glue around her. She wanted to hear Selene's voice, teasing her for worrying too much.

She closed her eyes, so that he wouldn't see her weep. But of course he would.

He was still speaking as if nothing were wrong.

"These are injuries that mostly heal themselves, but you're still weakened, and you might burst a blood vessel, which would have … drastic consequences. Fallen magic can't heal, but these will help smooth your injuries out. Take one now, and then one every morning and evening. You have Iaris's prescription in the package." A pause, then, in the same tone, "This is a prison cell. The walls are reinforced with metal, and the wards around it have been tripled. Thuan has added some spells of his own, a weave of *khi* metal to dry out Fallen magic. I wouldn't attempt anything … extraordinary, if I were you." She couldn't see him, but she could imagine his smile. "Rest is good for you, is it not?"

Emmanuelle opened her eyes, still gummed with tears.

"What do you want?" she asked.

He smiled. "Information. Leverage." He sounded like he was explaining it to a child.

All she wanted to do was sleep, but she lifted the spoon to her lips, and swallowed the soup. It left a burning trail of cheese and onion taste all the way to her stomach, its warmth spreading through her entire belly. She hadn't thought she was hungry before, but now she couldn't have enough of it. She dipped the spoon back in the soup, and before she knew it the plate was empty. The second one they'd left her held cold cuts and some kind of orange purée—squash, which left grit and mold on her tongue. It should have tasted sweet, but the days of sweetness were long gone.

When she looked up again, he was still sitting in the chair. He held his glass of wine, and sipped from it, but it was for only show: the liquid's level didn't change.

"Tell me about Harrier."

"I'm sure Darrias told you everything when she dropped me in your lap." Emmanuelle couldn't quite hide her anger.

"I like to have several sources." Asmodeus's face didn't move.

"I might not feel like sharing."

If he wanted her as leverage, he wouldn't take the risk of harming her.

A smile that was all bright, sharp teeth. "You're assuming you have value as a hostage. Delightful, but I might not need you."

"I'm still alive."

"For now." He took a real sip from his glass. "Silverspires is weak and small. Barely a House anymore, by all standards. You overestimate your importance in this city."

"You want to harm me?"

"I merely want to make sure we both understand where we stand."

He laid the glass on the table by the side of the chair, and shifted. He had to have knives or daggers on him, and she'd expected him to draw one—he'd always been one for the cheap, dramatic gestures, which were a lot less cheap when it was her at the end of the blade.

"At the thinnest, sharpest end of mercy and caprice. I've spared you so far, but I've got very little incentive to continue if you give me nothing of value."

She was so, so tired. All she wanted to do was lay back against the bed and sleep. He knew this, no doubt. He didn't need a knife.

"I don't want Darrias in the room," she said.

"Angry at her?" Asmodeus smiled. "She knows where she belongs, Emmanuelle. And who gives the orders here."

"I don't want her in the room," Emmanuelle said stubbornly.

He shrugged, languid and graceful, and gestured Darrias out with one wave of his hand. Came to stand by her side, laying his wineglass right by hers. There was another chair there, and he lowered himself into it, as if they were having a meal together. The smell of bergamot and citrus choked the taste of food in her mouth.

"Tell me."

She did. In slow, halting words—leaving out the amnesia and her own suspicions of what might have happened that night, of how far she'd compromised herself by interfering in House Harrier affairs. It was none of his business, and he didn't need more weakness from her.

When she was done, he considered her words.

"You have no idea what caused the explosion." His voice was flat, without a trace of sarcasm.

"I woke up in the middle of it," Emmanuelle said.

"Hmmm." He said nothing for a while. "Where is Morningstar?"

Emmanuelle, startled, looked up at him. "I don't know. We got separated."

An amused snort. "Probably busy advancing his own agenda. I understand why Selene felt the need to make a statement by sending him, but there are better people."

He didn't like Morningstar. He never had. Asmodeus hoarded his dependents like treasured possessions; he felt Morningstar had been too cavalier with their lives, back when he'd been head of the House.

"I don't make Selene's decisions for her."

Another snort. "Untrue. If you asked, she'd listen. But you've never had any interest in politics, have you?"

"Is this a review of my personal failures, as perceived by you?"

"Not at all." A sharp smile. "Merely about the location of a powerful Fallen in the middle of this carnage. Especially one who doesn't understand the difference between removing a splinter and setting fire to the hand."

"That's not true. He's *changed*," Emmanuelle said. "Death does that."

He'd died and been born again with no memory of who he'd been, and Selene had always suspected Asmodeus had a hand in his reviving. No proof, obviously: Asmodeus was too canny for that.

Asmodeus's gaze was sharp. "Does it? Power goes deeper than flesh and memories, you'll find. What we are is written in the dust of our bones. No one ever changes. They merely apply themselves a different way." And, in a different tone, "You'll notice he didn't try to rescue you."

It was like a gut punch; because she'd so hoped he would be there, in the cells beneath Harrier. Because she'd prayed so hard for him to come, and he hadn't.

"I told you," Emmanuelle said. "We were separated."

"Did you?" He shrugged. "You're too kind, Emmanuelle. We both know it."

"I'd rather be kind than heartless."

"I have a heart." Another smile. "But never mind my … personal failures. Morningstar wasn't part of any faction that I know of, and I don't think even he would openly engage in another House's politics. Selene would have his head if he did."

"Darrias—"

"Darrias has always been too preoccupied with the life she left behind." A snort. "You take what you have and run with it as far as you can. Though I can understand—her family was hers, in the same way the dependents of a House are its head's."

"Showing me weakness?" It ought to have come out as ironic, but her voice would barely obey her.

"By now you must know how I work."

"I know how you work. Not how you feel."

A gentle nudge. She realized he was pushing her wineglass towards her.

"Don't fake kindness. Please."

She was so, so close to breaking down, and she couldn't be sure how successful she was in hiding it from him. He was a sadist who questioned prisoners in the cells of Hawthorn for his own entertainment: he had seen dozens like her, on the verge of giving him everything he wanted.

When she looked up again, he'd stepped away again. He was on the threshold, watching her, leaning against the door jamb, his smile mocking.

"Sometimes kindness is more cutting than the sharpest knife, isn't it?"

He knew.

She said nothing, braced herself, waiting for the final blow.

"Enjoy the wine," Asmodeus said. "And get some sleep." He turned away, the doors drawing close behind him. But not before she heard him say, "I may, after all, need Selene's kindness in the very near future."

Why—what for?

"Asmodeus!"

But he was gone.

12

Weakness

Emmanuelle, startled, woke up from a nightmare of beating wings and concealed birds to a room bathed in light. She stared at the French windows: the green baize curtains in faded cloth; the omnipresent smell of mold; the sunset over the debris-speckled lawn. Someone had come in, and left a meal: a decanter of wine, a covered tureen, a dish of what smelled like fish and herbs, and what looked like a cherry clafoutis. Expensive, difficult to find things: a clear statement of what Hawthorn could afford to feed its prisoners. The smell enticed her stomach, but wasn't enough to steady her.

She'd dreamed of Morningstar. He'd stood at the door to her room in House Harrier, holding a sword that changed into a spear, then a whip, the radiance of his skin illuminating the four-poster bed.

"What's wrong, Emmanuelle?" he'd asked, and when she'd looked up the world had been blurry with her tears—and the wings had started then, the birds peeling off from the bed and flower paper to find her in the darkness, in the heart of Hawthorn, and run her down.

It was a dream. One of those meaningless visions her

brain kept coming up with to fill the hole, none of which could be trusted. But she'd thought the doors to Guy's reception room were fake—and they had turned out to be devastatingly real.

Guy had warned her. He'd told her he'd kill Darrias.

Surely she'd at least tried to turn Darrias aside from the path she'd chosen?

Not that it mattered—because in the end, Darrias had chosen her own path. No friendship between Houses. Just jailer and jailed.

It shouldn't have hurt so much.

The key turned in the lock.

Another meal tray, another day of forcing herself to eat and desperately wanting to go home.

She looked up, and Darrias was standing in the door frame.

"Emmanuelle."

She'd reapplied the henna markings: an elaborate tracery of letters on her face and hands. Her uniform of House Hawthorn was freshly pressed, her face expressionless. Emmanuelle looked for words—for polite things she could say, as she always did—and found nothing.

"I hadn't thought anyone would be allowed in."

"He'll find out eventually, and then he'll look the other way. He ... indulges me, in that matter, because it makes no difference," Darrias said.

Another way of saying she wouldn't help Emmanuelle escape.

Darrias came in and sat, coiled like a wolf before the final leap of the hunt.

"You're angry at me."

"Yes," Emmanuelle said, because she wasn't in the mood to prevaricate.

"I had no choice. It was cross the bridge or face the birds." She sounded scared, which was … wrong. As if the world had tilted sideways. "You've seen them."

A boneless body crumpling in the street. Dozens of still, silent birds standing on furniture and mantelpieces. She dug her nails in the palm of her hand.

"Yes."

"And once we'd crossed, I couldn't hide whom I'd brought back. Even if you hadn't been wearing Silverspires' colors, you're … distinctive."

Distinctive. Emmanuelle clamped her lips on a wounding reply. Her patience had run out.

"I thought you'd want to know Louiza and Jamila are both safe. Lord Asmodeus was delighted at the prospect of poaching people from Guy, even menials." She sounded almost surprised. Because her head of House had been decent for once? "Jamila has been given to the Court of Birth, and is getting a proper education."

"They were Harrier dependents," Emmanuelle said. "It's impossible to break a link to a House—"

"If you're not its head? The rules have changed." Her face was very still. "Harrier is dying. Links can be snapped, with enough power."

"Dying."

Houses didn't just die. Especially not Harrier. It was brash and unpleasant, and it had always been there. Every few decades it would convulse and present a new face to the world, but it had always survived. It always would.

And, if Harrier was dying—if Houses could die—where did that leave House Silverspires?

Darrias's face was bleak. "There might have been a point, shortly after the explosion, where Guy could have turned it around. But he let it descend into civil war while he tried to consolidate his own power. The House barely answers to him now, I'd think."

"How do you know . . .?" Emmanuelle stopped, because it was an injudicious question. Darrias would never reveal her informants.

"Know with certainty? I don't. I can guess, though. Remember the birds?"

Emmanuelle shivered. "Yes." And, belatedly realizing, "They turned on the magician, didn't they?"

"They're the House itself. The wards became something that takes apart dissenters. The head's eyes in the streets and buildings. And when the magician said to stop in the name of the head of the House, they didn't."

Obvious, in retrospect. Except she'd been too busy trying to survive.

"If you ask me . . ." Darrias's face was still that odd mix of gentle and expressionless. It wasn't Emmanuelle to whom she was being gentle—it was herself. "If you ask me, he'll have to leave anyway. Sooner or later, regardless of whether he wins, he'll realize he's standing in a field of ruins with nothing worth crowing about."

"And go where? There's nowhere inside Paris."

"It won't matter. The other Houses will drive him back into the streets."

Grim satisfaction.

Leave him at the mercy of the Houseless? It would

never happen—he'd still have the power of a Fallen. How much damage would he do, before finally succumbing? Darrias was still thinking like a Harrier dependent: putting too much value on Fallen, and none on the Houseless. Hawthorn, for all that Emmanuelle didn't get on with Asmodeus, regularly recruited its dependents from the streets.

"Dying," she said flatly. She thought of the ruined buildings; of shards of glass glistening on the cobblestones. "You've told Asmodeus."

"Of course."

And of course he wouldn't tell any of the other Houses that this could happen, because it wouldn't give him an advantage.

"I need to tell Selene. We ..." She fought a wave of panic. "We need to cooperate, to neutralize whoever is doing this."

Darrias's face didn't move. "I'm afraid that's impossible."

"Because you won't gainsay him?" It hurt. She said, "I trusted you."

"To be disloyal to Hawthorn?" Darrias sighed. "You know exactly what I fled from, Emmanuelle. I don't want to be cast out from Hawthorn and go back to Harrier. I *need* his goodwill."

"He'd never do that."

Asmodeus would never let her return: in his twisted little world, Darrias was now his to punish, should she err. He would never let someone else exercise that right. Returning to Harrier as an envoy, perhaps—and even then, that had been Darrias's idea, hadn't it? Not his.

"And he let you return to Harrier for your family, didn't

he." She kept her voice light, because if she broke down she was going to say something unforgivable.

Darrias stared at her for a while. This was the source of Emmanuelle's anger—not the betrayal of delivering her to Hawthorn and standing by when she was imprisoned, because she'd never expected Darrias to choose friendship over House loyalty. No, not a failure of trust; but a failure to tell her the truth. To not ask her help.

"You never told me about your family because you thought I wouldn't help you."

A silence. Darrias got up, and paced the room.

"No. I didn't tell you because I knew you would."

"Darrias—"

"You're a bleeding heart on legs, Emmanuelle." It was said softly, affectionately. "Of course you'd have helped. And you couldn't afford to. Silverspires is weak. I don't need Selene's partner dragged into a sordid affair between Harrier and Hawthorn, because I can guarantee you that Asmodeus wouldn't have stood up for you if things had gone badly."

Which they had.

I was going to take her apart at the dinner after the Great Presentation, and the most beautiful thing is that Hawthorn couldn't have interfered—not when she'd started it, poking her nose into the affairs of another House.

"I can make my own choices," Emmanuelle said stiffly. That feeling of fear—of a huge, yawning chasm she was teetering on the edge of—was back, and worse than ever. "Don't treat me like a child."

"Sometimes," Darrias said, "it's not about truth, or choice, but about how to best safeguard those you care for.

How far would you have gone for friendship, Emmanuelle? You'd have thrown away Selene's instructions and entangled yourself in a heartbeat. Look me in the eye and tell me you wouldn't."

Emmanuelle opened her mouth, closed it again. Because Darrias was right. Except that she hadn't learned about Darrias's family ahead of going into Harrier, but later—with hours to spare until Guy had her killed slowly and in agony. What would she have done, knowing sooner? She weighed, swiftly, the price of admitting to something Darrias likely already knew.

"There's an entire chunk of time missing from my mind. The injury ..." She paused. "I woke up, and I was in the middle of a burning House. What happened that afternoon, Darrias?"

Darrias looked surprised. "Nothing. I went to a garden before the banquet to find someone. Next thing I know, the House is on fire and full of corpses." A sharp, weighing glance. "What do you *think* happened?"

Something large and unknowable and horrible.

What's wrong, Emmanuelle? Morningstar had asked, in her dream.

"I don't know," she said, struggling to breathe. "I don't know."

It wasn't her. It couldn't have been her. Whatever had happened to Harrier—however much she'd wanted Guy's smug face wiped off the surface of the earth—she'd never envisioned ... Her mind froze, fleeing again and again.

Darrias's look at her was sharp—but at length she laughed.

"Bleeding heart, Emmanuelle. I don't know what you've

forgotten, but it'll be a book you failed to read or an over-polite, unpleasant conversation you had with someone. You shouldn't worry about it."

"I'm not sure what I should worry about," Emmanuelle said. The feeling of panic had ebbed, but it was still there. Still waiting to be summoned. "Guy—"

"Guy is a snobbish racist coward," Darrias said. "You cannot believe a word that comes out of his mouth. Trust me—I've served under him for years. He'll try to insert all the wedges and raise all the fears he can, and if he has to distort the truth, he will have no compunction about doing so. Insinuation and abuse are second nature to him." She poured Emmanuelle a glass of wine. "Here. Drink this. He got to you, didn't he? I'm sorry."

Empty words. Except that Darrias seemed to mean them. She took the glass, inhaling the wine's scent—a sharp, acid taste of pineapple and grapefruit, followed by a taste like vanilla and honey in the mouth, and a lingering, full-bodied sweetness. Selene would have hated it, but Emmanuelle liked her wines much sweeter than her partner.

"He said . . ."

A beating of wings. A flock of birds on tables and chairs and the mantelpiece. Words shriveling in her mind when she tried to speak.

"I don't want to know what he said." Darrias closed her hands, gently, over Emmanuelle's own—held them for a brief moment before withdrawing. "It'll be too much work untangling truth from lies. If there's any truth, at all."

"You're sure—"

"Emmanuelle. You're the only person I know who insists

on helping the Houseless without expecting anything in return."

"I …"

It was a drop of water in the ocean. A sop to her pride, dispensing charity as though it could make any difference, beyond helping her sleep at night. If she was braver …

Again, her mind stopped, on the edge of a chasm she couldn't contemplate.

Darrias said, "Stop worrying about lost hours. You didn't cause any trouble, and that time won't be coming back anyway. You can't change the past." And, more softly, "I'll ask Lord Thuan if we can open negotiations with Silverspires. At the very least he can tell Selene we have you, so she'll stop worrying about where you are."

Emmanuelle stared at Darrias. Words seemed to have gone altogether.

"And if you want anything, ask. I can get it for you."

Something to make her imprisonment bearable? But it was well meant, no matter how inadequate.

"Thank you. Your family?"

Darrias's face, for a bare moment, was taut with fear.

"I don't know. Frédérique is smart. She'll head somewhere safe." If she's alive, her body language said.

Emmanuelle said, finally, "I don't think Guy had them."

A short, soft exhalation. "No, I don't think so either. Don't worry, Emmanuelle. That's my business. It always has been."

Thuan came back to his room exhausted. He'd spent the day fielding questions from Iaris, reassuring his dragon dependents that nothing was wrong—lying and smiling until his face ached and all his thoughts jumbled in his brain, even as he continued to project the illusion of strength—and disguising his worry that Phyranthe would start sending him bits and pieces of Vinh Ly in neatly tied packages.

His room was dark: it was long past the hour at which the servants extinguished the chandeliers. He could have asked for an exception, but it would have been pointless to make someone stay up just for his sake. A lantern and *khi* fire would do, should he need to read—which he didn't, not tonight. He pushed the doors open and made a beeline for the bed, unbuttoning his jacket as he walked.

"We need to talk," a familiar voice said behind him.

A second of fear, followed by irritation.

"Asmodeus."

Light sprang up in the room: Asmodeus was sitting in one of the armchairs with a lamp by his side, a closed book in his lap.

"Have you been skulking here all evening? There are simpler ways to get hold of me."

Asmodeus unfolded from the chair. He laid the book and the lamp, carefully, on the table, and came to face Thuan. It was dark, even with the lantern—his perfume of bergamot and citrus wafted to Thuan, trembling on the edge of desire.

He'd slammed the doors, the last time he had been in this bedroom, and Thuan had hardly seen him since. Once, briefly, when he'd got Ai Nhi back, but everything else he'd heard was hearsay: drawn from a steady flow of meetings with the different Courts, telling them the House stood strong, unaffected by House Harrier's explosion or the void it left in the balance of powers in Paris.

"What do you want?" Thuan said.

He sat down on the bed, one hand fiddling to button his jacket again. A state of undress wasn't what he needed right now.

"You missed the drama of Darrias's arrival," Asmodeus said. Light glinted on the frames of his glasses.

Thuan, startled, looked up. He'd thought this would be about Vinh Ly and Phyranthe.

"I didn't. There were other fires to put out."

"Apply your mind to this one for a moment," Asmodeus said.

Fine, so he wasn't going to broach Vinh Ly; or how his conversation with Phyranthe had gone, or Iaris's ongoing campaign to weaken Thuan. Typical Asmodeus: weave his way out of the difficult conversations, with sarcasm or grace or both.

Thuan was too exhausted to bring up the subject himself. He closed his eyes, taking time to collect his thoughts. Quynh had been in charge of this, as his temporary delegate to the Court of House. He'd had her report at lunchtime, an eternity ago.

"I know you went to see Emmanuelle." Thuan hadn't sent Quynh, because that wasn't a job he felt he could safely delegate. "What's our position with House Silverspires?"

He hadn't been there for Hawthorn's epic interference in Silverspires' affairs, though he'd got the gist through other people, and surmised some of the rest. A push to unseat Lady Selene had led to Notre-Dame being choked by a huge banyan tree, a weakened House near the bottom of the hierarchy of power in Paris, and a general disinterest from Asmodeus now that he had succeeded in toppling them.

"They're a nuisance at best now," Asmodeus said. "But that may change."

In the wake of Harrier's destruction? That wasn't justification enough for change. Not unless …

"Do you know what caused the explosion?"

A smile. He knew that one. It meant he'd finally caught up with what Asmodeus had on his mind.

"I got Darrias debriefed, too. House Harrier's wards have been shattered, and there's barely any magic or protective spells left in the stones of the streets. I don't know how other Houses work, magically speaking—"

"Assume on a very similar principle to Hawthorn," Asmodeus said. "Pre-dragon invasion."

Thuan opened his mouth to protest at the description of his arrival, and shut it. There were better things to focus on.

"They're dead," Thuan said. "They just don't know it yet. And it's only a matter of time before the other Houses realize it, too. Which means someone blew apart a House," he said, slowly. "I know we've been trying to figure out how to deal with the fallout, but nothing in the war was this bad."

House Hell's Toll's armory had exploded, but even that hadn't ended the House. It had taken armed soldiers, and an agonizing set of ranged battles through the House, until its head had died and the magic had been scattered and pillaged. This wasn't the same. Nothing had invaded the House, and Guy was still alive.

"Someone has found a way to kill a House."

"It might just target a weakness specific to Harrier," Asmodeus said. "But yes."

"And you've been keeping this quiet because . . .?"

Because obviously, who wanted to cause more panic? It was one thing to know another House was dead; but the idea that they, too, could be attacked . . .

A creak as Asmodeus sat down on the bed. He leaned against Thuan's shoulder, the warmth of his body flooding Thuan.

"Someone can kill Houses," Thuan said, desperately trying to focus. "And they didn't do it to Harrier previously because . . ." He paused, then. "Because there was no reason to, or because they only recently got the means." Another pause. "I have to ask. How much do we know about Emmanuelle?"

A laugh. "Emmanuelle? You think she's responsible for this?"

Thuan didn't find it funny at all. "She goes to Harrier as an envoy and it explodes. Now she's here, in our House. Behind our wards."

A silence. Asmodeus shifted against Thuan's shoulder, and said, "Emmanuelle is a bleeding heart. Always trying to make the world a better place."

"That doesn't seem so bad," Thuan said, though he knew Asmodeus would consider it a weakness. Thuan's own ambitions were much more restrained: he wanted to make the House a better place to live in. "Not very compatible with setting fire to things, I'll grant you."

A gently amused snort. "She probably didn't appreciate what Harrier was doing with its dependents, but she wouldn't have got involved. That's the main reason Selene sends her to these things—she'll watch and report. She's loyal and dependable, and it's extremely difficult to make her lose her temper."

"You like her," Thuan said, surprised.

"Hardly."

Entirely too quick to be true. He thought her weak, but he liked her. Interesting. Thuan filed it away with all the other things he didn't quite know what to make of. He stared, for a while, at the carpet—a red and blue Persian floral pattern with barely a trace of patching. *Khi* currents of water swirled on the floor, drawn to his presence—all the other currents were there, but weaker. He reached out, watched one of them climb up to the bed and curl around his arm like a snake—lighting up as blue flame as it did.

"I thought I'd already provided you with a lantern." Asmodeus's voice was sarcastic, but it was mild. "And that your night vision was anyway excellent, as you amply demonstrated while undoing buttons in the dark."

Thuan said, refusing to rise to the jibe, "Fine. So it's not Emmanuelle. So what can we do with this information?" Not much they could do, was there? The thought of the House dying—of the home he'd made for himself, the constant touch at the back of his mind, being torn apart and silent forever—was too much to bear. "Other than panic."

Asmodeus's face was grave, but Thuan could see the fear in him, too.

"Panic is useless. We need to work out who's doing it, and stop them."

"Easier to say than do."

They didn't know anything about the identity or motivation of the person or people behind the destruction of Harrier … People with grudges against Houses were seldom lacking. It was those powerful enough to do something about it they needed to worry about, and *that* was as blatant a display of power as they came. Even the familiar cold touch of *khi* water, raising welts of dragon scales everywhere it touched his skin, wasn't enough to reassure him.

Be careful, Thuan. We are weak, the children whispered in his mind.

People had gotten used to thinking Houses were immortal and unkillable, but that wasn't true. Ice had almost killed the House, a few months before; and of course other, weaker Houses had died during the Great Houses War. But even during the dragon ice episode, the children had not warned Asmodeus about their own weakness.

And if that wasn't scarier than anything that had happened before …

"Darrias gave me a few names in Harrier," Asmodeus said. He sounded … annoyed. Frustrated. "I can think of no one with motive. Or power. I've reached out to my contacts in other Houses, to see if anyone remembers anything useful. It hasn't proved fruitful so far."

A silence. Thuan broke it. "Tell me about Ai Nhi."

A raised eyebrow.

"You said you'd discipline her. What did you do?"

Asmodeus cocked his head towards him. "Accusing me?"

Thuan clamped down on angry words. "No. She won't say what happened, and I can't tell if Phyranthe …"

He stopped then, because he didn't want to make his suspicions real by voicing them.

A silence.

Asmodeus said, "Phyranthe didn't do anything, beyond giving Ai Nhi a rather sharp dressing-down about being careful with her stronger abilities. The same thing I would have done. I didn't add anything to Phyranthe's words because it seemed superfluous, quite frankly."

Thuan opened his mouth, closed it. He thought back to Phyranthe in the hospital ward, and the anger in her face. "I thought—"

"She does have principles, you know. She used to be my student, of sorts, in the Court of Persuasion." Asmodeus sounded amused and weary at the same time. "Taking pleasure in what she does doesn't mean being indiscriminate about it."

"Vinh Ly . . ."

Thuan paused, because something had moved in the room. A shadow, shifting? Probably a flicker of his tired brain.

"You should ask Vinh Ly, when you next get a chance, about how bad things have been between her and Phyranthe, even prior to your little argument with Iaris. As I said—it takes two to make a fight. Vinh Ly has never made a secret of her contempt for Phyranthe and her 'youth'."

Thuan fought down a wave of anger. "You mean whatever Phyranthe is going to do to Vinh Ly, she'll have deserved it."

"Oh, do be fair. Your dragon chose to make herself vulnerable."

"I'm trying to be fair," Thuan said, with increasing annoyance. How could Asmodeus be so . . . glib and detached about it? How could he not care? "I don't see how giving leave to Phyranthe to torture Vinh Ly just short of death for disrespect is in any way fair or just. I thought you wanted the House to be different from that. That we weren't going to build any more on fear and excessive retribution, because it was completely unsustainable."

Asmodeus opened his mouth—to say something sarcastic that would snap Thuan's patience, no doubt—but just as he did so, Thuan's brain caught up with his eyes. It wasn't the shadows which had moved, but the *khi* currents. They were all but gone on the floor—every single one of them moving towards the door in a frenzied tangle. The snake of water still curled around his arm was flailing, cut off from the fleeing *khi* currents of water. And only a single element remained: *khi* fire, getting stronger and stronger.

"Asmodeus."

The sharpness in his voice turned Asmodeus's face jewel-hard.

"What?"

"There's nothing left in this room but fire."

The *khi* fire flowed towards them, circling the bed in slow, lazy circles. Thuan felt the air tighten, as in that instant before the monsoon clouds burst.

He'd felt this once before, but it had been weaker and more unfocused—because he hadn't been at its epicenter, because it had been someone else's problem.

This particular problem was definitely their own.

"Asmodeus!"

A rising, buzzing sound shook the floor under them, a split second before Thuan's link to the House lit up like a bonfire, screaming deadly danger for all the dependents

13
Everything Afire

Philippe went around the boundaries of the community with Isabelle and Hoa Phong, drawing fragmentary wards in the *khi* elements. Weaves of protection against burning in *khi* water; to live to a long age in *khi* wood; for faithfulness and loyalty in *khi* earth—the element that centered all the others, the center of the universe around which everything revolved.

Buildings, in many ways, were simpler. They would burn easier with fire, but *khi* fire wasn't physical fire: it followed the fracture lines of the universe, the easy, downhill path. That meant streets. That meant the breath of hundreds of people drawing grooves in the fabric of the world. Buildings—concentrated, unmoving blocks where mortals stayed put, where they made their homes—were masses of *khi* earth already. For these, he drew a weave on the doors, and watched the *khi* currents slowly and steadily realign around them. He'd offered to do it for Grandmother Olympe and the aunts' flat. The look he'd had would have blistered stone.

"You don't have time. Don't waste it on us, child."

He knew enough not to argue with her dismissive choice

of pronoun: he'd retreated, and sworn never to mention it again.

Halfway through his circuit of the community, he saw the first anomalies.

They were tentative threads of *khi* fire, running under the cobblestones, barely visible in the dim light. He knelt, frowning.

Hoa Phong crouched by his side, thoughtfully staring at the stones.

"That's interesting," she said. "I wonder …"

But Isabelle had already touched one of the threads.

"No!" Philippe said, and braced himself for her to fall; but instead everything lit up like a Christmas garland.

It was a network like fungus, or the roots of some patient tree: the entire street was covered in it, as was every other street as far as he could see. The threads ran back towards a single source; he could guess where.

"Harrier," he said. "This goes back all the way to where Dân Chay was imprisoned."

Hoa Phong's face was hard. "Fire."

Once, man tricked the tiger into waiting, and burned him with fire.

Dân Chay wielded *khi* fire, against which the Houses had no protection: no wonder Harrier had burned like dry kindling. And no wonder they had been Dân Chay's first target, the first people he'd want revenge on for holding and torturing him. But he had finished with that House, and now he was reaching out across Paris.

How dare he? Philippe only kept his hands from clenching with difficulty. How dare he take things meant to protect and heal, and turn them to destruction?

"Not here," he snapped. "Not so easily."

He wove threads of *khi* water like blades, laying them across the street—and watched with some satisfaction as the fire, bumping into them, shriveled and died.

"That won't hold him," Isabelle said slowly. "Will it?"

Not for long, no.

"Let's fight the easy battles first," Philippe said. There would be more streets, more threads to ward against. "Can you help?" he asked Hoa Phong.

She shrugged. "If you don't mind *khi* wood."

Of course. Wind and the first flowers—what else would have been her *khi* element of predilection?

"Good enough. Let's cut him off at the knees, while we still can."

Hoa Phong was walking ahead. Isabelle said, stiffly, "I'm sorry for what I said, earlier."

In all the rush of Dân Chay's arrival, he'd almost forgotten her wounding words: when she'd accused him of forgetting his past.

"It's all right," he said, though it wasn't.

Her gaze was distant. "I shouldn't have said it."

He hesitated. "I'm trying to protect you," he said finally.

And one day soon, he would no longer be able to. It scared him: like dancing at the edge of the chasm. He would lose her again, and nothing he did would prevent it from happening.

"Against a House?"

Against whatever the world offered; against her being used or dying, or both. Was this what it felt like to have children? His had been so long ago he'd forgotten. No wonder parents were afraid all the time.

"I have to try."

Her face was heartbreakingly hard. "Don't," she said.

And she walked ahead, barely looking back.

In Philippe's flat, Aunt Ha turned and tossed on the beaten-down mattress: he'd redrawn the protective net of *khi* elements around her body, but it was being burned up again by Dân Chay's fire, and the faint outline of stripes was already visible on her skin. He'd timed it: three hours each time, a little more, a little less depending on what he poured into her. It wasn't much, but it was enough that they each had some breathing room, with both Isabelle and Hoa Phong taking turns.

Grandmother Olympe had taken her daughter Colette in; though he'd enjoyed the brief satisfaction of watching Hoa Phong's face when he'd suggested they could care for a child. Isabelle was away, visiting one of the aunts and helping them cook for the refugees. She was late, but that wasn't surprising: the aunts had little notion of time when it came to services rendered. It was just him and Hoa Phong, an awkward situation if there was one. He'd cooked some buns, with Hoa Phong clearing away plates almost faster than he could roll the dough.

Now they sat staring at each other and chewing on gritty rice. Hoa Phong's face was drawn and gray, looking as exhausted as Philippe felt. Though in her case it might have been the wound in her side. He should have a look at that, too. When he had time.

"We all need some sleep," Philippe said, with a tight laugh.

Hoa Phong shrugged, and said nothing.

"Tell me about him."

"Dân Chay? I don't know—"

"Try," Philippe said, gently.

He'd read the papers Isabelle had found: a slow litany of horrors on how to turn a person into a *thing*—beatings and cages and the repeated insistence that Dân Chay was worth nothing more than the blood he'd cause to be spilled, the wounds he'd inflict. A dog, a pet, rewarded when he did well and hurt mercilessly when he failed. And the worst was that it was a report, a detailed dissection of what they'd done and how they felt the process could be improved for the next time. It wasn't that it didn't acknowledge guilt, it was that it didn't even seem to *conceive* there was such a thing. Towards the end, he'd felt like setting fire to it all, but it wouldn't have achieved anything except satisfy his own temper.

"Before," Hoa Phong said, finally. "He was on earth, most of the time. Or in the other realms."

Philippe had been an enforcer of Heaven's will, like Dân Chay, a long, long time ago; bearer of the decrees of the Jade Emperor outside of the palace—attending lavish banquets and celebrations only on his way to somewhere else. He had a vague memory of crossing Dân Chay's path—a tall, elegant, taciturn man with the air of someone who'd seen entirely too much. It was hard to reconcile with the primal darkness he'd felt in Gare du Nord, foraging for anything it could use to burn him from the inside.

"I remember he didn't talk much."

"He had a few friends," Hoa Phong said. "One of the dragon enforcers—I can't remember her name." A silence.

"Rong Thi Cam Linh. She was killed a month before he was taken."

Philippe said, "I can't turn him aside."

Hoa Phong was silent for a while.

"I don't think anyone can fight him. That … was the point." Of getting him back. Of returning him to the beleaguered Annam and the Court of the Jade Emperor. Another silence. "I don't think the rules can apply any more. What the Houses did—"

"I know what they did," Philippe said.

Morningstar. Silverspires. Harrier. A flash of anger as red-hot as liquid iron. How they could take something, anything, and eat at it from the inside out until it became corrupted. Just as they'd taken Isabelle—if death hadn't stopped her, she'd have become one of them, just as arrogant and as dismissive of others' well-being.

"So we're just sitting here waiting for him."

He'd done that, in the war—sitting behind a wall and waiting in that nerve-racking silence for the other side to break open the door. He'd sworn he would never do it again.

Hoa Phong said finally, "I hadn't thought it'd come to that."

Why would she? It wasn't her fault.

"The box."

"The box held him, once." Hoa Phong sighed. "It was bones."

"His bones?"

"Of course not. His physical body ascended. The bones of his family." Hoa Phong said.

A silence. What it always meant, being an Immortal:

that others would age and die while one remained the same. Philippe's mortal family had been dust on the wind for so long—their souls passed on to the wheel of rebirth, to make their slow way through the chain of reincarnations towards Nirvana.

"They were the bonds that held him," he said.

"Yes. I don't know where it is now."

In Harrier. Except that House was no longer his jail, was it?

"I know where it is. I don't know if it's still whole. But it doesn't matter. There are threads of *khi* fire reaching all around Paris. He's no longer contained. He's fire." He looked again at Aunt Ha, shivering with her eyes closed—sitting next to her hadn't made any difference, but he was going to do it again nevertheless. Just in case, because no one should burn up alone. "Everything he touches burns."

They'd drawn wards against *khi* fire—trying to be ready for him, but could anyone really be?

"You should have stopped the refugees," Hoa Phong said.

Philippe shrugged. "In case one of them is like that man who burned? That's not a very effective weapon. People burn too fast to pass it on. Aunt Ha happened to be at the wrong place at the wrong time."

Which didn't make it better, of course. But still . . . Still, from the point of view of the community, he doubted Dân Chay would do the same again. He'd wanted to get a message to them, and now the talking was over. Now there was just fire.

"How are you?" he asked Hoa Phong.

She looked surprised.

"Your wounds." He'd not offered to look at them, because she'd say no.

A shrug. Her shoulders started crumbling into rotten *hoang mai* flowers again.

"The same."

He'd tried everything he could think of. Fallen magic was like a canker at the heart of things. This same magic was now in the Court of the Jade Emperor—the rot climbing into the longevity tiles of the roofs, the peach trees covered in blue-gray fungus, the spirits crumbling into flowers or water or fire.

"I'll be fine," Hoa Phong said. "When I'm home."

He opened his mouth to say she couldn't be sure, and then shut it. It would have been thoughtless and needlessly wounding. And … he'd felt the power in the impression of the imperial seal on the scroll she'd carried with her. For a moment, he'd been back in the court's presence, basking in the magic of spirits; for a moment, the past was as vivid and as tremblingly fresh as the previous day. And then he'd remembered the weight of time: the days of wandering Annam; the servitude in House Draken and in House Silverspires; Isabelle's death and resurrection.

He realized, startled, that Hoa Phong had been speaking for a while.

"I'm sorry?"

Hoa Phong looked at him. She hesitated, then said, a great deal more cautiously, "How can you bear it?"

"What do you mean?"

"Being *away*." She set the remnants of her half-nibbled bun on the plate, pushed it away from her with shaking hands. "Everything is wrong here."

"The food?" Philippe asked, though he knew it wasn't just that.

"The sky, the language, the food. Even the taste of the air—there's something that's not right." She laid a hand on her wound, gently touching it. "I wake up every morning and I remember that I'm not home."

"It gets better," Philippe said finally. He hadn't felt homesick in so long. There'd been Isabelle to teach, and then the community to help—and things had blurred and thickened around the gaping nostalgia for Annam until he'd almost forgotten its existence. "You find people."

"These?" Hoa Phong opened her mouth to say something he'd never forgive her for, and then thought better of it. "They can't fill that hole for me."

"In time, perhaps."

"I don't intend to be here long enough," Hoa Phong snapped. And then looked at him. "I'm sorry."

"It's all right," Philippe said.

A small, pregnant silence.

Then Hoa Phong said, "They need every available Immortal to fight, back in Annam. Even the ones they cast out, years ago."

It was like a blow to the gut, delivered when he'd least expected it. He'd made his peace with the impossibility of return; with the idea that when he eventually died—when his agelessness finally ran out or someone killed him—he'd be buried, not with his ancestors in a monsoon-drenched graveyard, but in a patch of debris-covered earth under the perpetual roiling pall of magic. The idea that he might go back—that he might once again breathe in the lemongrass, jasmine petals and garlic, and count grains of rice straight from the paddies . . .

"You don't know what you're offering."

Hoa Phong drew herself to her full height. The outline of petals shimmered on her cheeks and forehead. She was trembling as though she'd disintegrate at any time.

"I know perfectly well. As I know the limits of the power the court vested in me. It is my right and prerogative to offer this."

"Isabelle," he said.

A shrug, from Hoa Phong. "She's your student. The court will respect that." A long, weighing look. She still didn't like Isabelle, but she'd taken the measure of him. "You think whatever she is will stop the Jade Emperor from welcoming her in? He employed Dân Chay."

"Elder aunt—"

"Don't." She raised a hand. "You don't want to talk about it, and I'm not in the mood for lies. But the offer stands."

"I . . ." He was surprised to find a pit of fear opening in his belly. "Let me think about it. We need to survive this first. We . . ."

He stopped, then. "Isabelle," he said.

Hoa Phong had sat down in her chair again.

"I don't understand . . ."

It was dark outside, and the first stars were shining beneath the pall of magical pollution over Paris.

"She's still not home, and it's after dark," Philippe said. "The aunts would have known to let her go." What if Dân Chay had found her—what if he could smell Philippe's magic just as he'd unerringly felt his presence? "Where is she?"

Isabelle had been with Aunt Thuy, the midwife. Aunt Thuy was apologetic as she stood in the door of her narrow apartment, the kitchen of which was crowded with bottles of rice porridge for babies, and baskets of supplies for their mothers. Isabelle had left two hours ago, and she had no idea where she'd been going. She'd looked determined—and Aunt Thuy thought she'd been clutching a piece of paper, but she couldn't be sure.

"Thank you," Philippe said, and walked out, uncertain of what to do now.

Determined meant that she hadn't been snatched by anyone on her way home, surely? But she was, in so many ways, newborn and naive, and the little she knew of *khi* elements wouldn't help her. He gathered a fistful of *khi* earth in his hands—the element of love, of faithfulness—and carefully wove it into a hook: a pattern searching for Isabelle in the vastness of the city.

Nothing. A vague feeling she wasn't far away. It wasn't even strong enough to give him a direction.

Where now?

At this late hour la Goutte d'Or was mostly dockers celebrating after receiving their pay. In a café near Aunt Thuy's house, Philippe caught a glimpse of Tade, the burly Yoruba man who'd tried to help with Aunt Ha. He was arm-wrestling with Sébastien, another of the workers—Tade's simple tattoo on his right forearm shone with a rippling light under the lanterns of the café. They'd drawn in a couple of the refugees, too: a man and a woman still wearing the blue and black of Harrier were watching from the edge of the crowd.

The smell of rice wine and grape wine hung over them all—light and laughter and an utter lack of awareness of the threat hanging over them. No, that was unfair. Why should they not celebrate? It wouldn't change anything.

Philippe pushed his way through the crowd to get to one of the waiters. No, they hadn't seen Isabelle. By then, Tade had finished his bout of arm-wrestling, and came bounding up.

"Expecting trouble?" he asked.

"Not really," Philippe said. "Not yet. I'm looking for Isabelle."

Tade raised an eyebrow. "Here?"

Where was she? What could have happened to her? A message meant a meeting, but there were so many meetings that could end badly.

"I don't think so," Philippe said. "Can you ask around?"

No one had seen her. Tade dropped by the table with the refugees on his way back, and chatted with them for a while. When he left, there was a pitcher of rice wine on their table, and they were cautiously sipping at the glasses he'd poured for them. He came back to Philippe.

"Sorry. Got to break the ice. Not everyone is happy about taking in the refugees, so they're wary. People think we have little enough as we do, and they'll take the bread out of our mouths or some such nonsense."

"But you don't," Philippe said.

He'd been one of these refugees once, except that no immigrant community had wanted to be burdened with him, and the only welcoming ones had been the gangs in the streets. How things had changed.

Tade snorted. "You've all been very friendly to me even though I'm not Annamite. It'd be churlish to be choosy." He seemed embarrassed, and quickly changed the subject. "Come on. Let's try a few other cafés. Maybe someone has seen something."

The tattoo on his right arm continued to glow as he walked. Philippe stared at it, until he realized he was being rude.

"Sorry. Just wondering about that."

"It's a mnemonic." Tade shrugged. "The creation myth. A way of remembering how we came to be here. Not a bad one to have away from home."

"It's glowing," Philippe said.

The strands of *khi* elements had nestled in each of the strokes on Tade's arm, outlining them in rainbow light.

"Yeah. I don't know about that," Tade said. "Something in the air, maybe."

Danger. Death. A time for comfort if there was any; but it wasn't his magic or his business to pry.

"I don't know either," Philippe said.

The next two cafés hadn't seen Isabelle. But the third one they tried—a small terrace on the edge of the raised rue de Jessaint bridge—remembered her.

"She was walking fast. Southwards. Towards the hospital," the owner said.

He eyed Philippe nervously, as if on the verge of prostrating himself. Philippe did his best to ignore it.

Once outside, Tade said, "She wasn't going to the hospital."

"No," Philippe said. Lariboisière was decrepit, overworked, and with a tendency to infect people with bacteria they hadn't had on their way in. "It was getting dark. She's not going to head into gang territory, is she?"

Tade thought, for a while.

"There is a place," he said.

It was a small, almost invisible café on the edge of the Annamite community: in a small street behind Gare du Nord without any streetlamps, a place with boarded-up windows that looked more like a fortress than a place to get merrily drunk. Three steps down from the cobbled street led to a barricaded door.

"Allow me," Tade said.

He walked in front of Philippe, and tapped in a complex pattern of knocks against the door. The judas hole slid open—it was so small Philippe couldn't see who was behind it, and it was dark in any case.

"We're closed."

Philippe had had enough, his searching spell had faded away, and he didn't have the energy to cast it again.

"I think not." He called the *khi* elements in la Goutte d'Or to him; let them glow in all their glory, from the deep red of fire to the green of wood and the shimmering, dark depths of water. "Let me in."

The door opened so fast Tade almost lost his balance.

The owner was a woman with tanned skin and bleached hair the color of pristine snow who looked, aghast, at Philippe as he shouldered his way in.

"I'm sorry, Nene," Tade said. "We need …"

Philippe was already scanning the main room—a

smoke-encrusted affair, redolent of herbs and spices. Waiters carried platters of food, open sandwiches of cheese and glistening marmalade, or pickles and ham. People who'd been deep into their cups scurried to get out of the way, spilling full tankards of brown, spicy liquid. Not all of them were Annamite: some wore, inconspicuously, the arms of Houses on their shoulders or jackets. A meeting place.

By now, the fear that had seized him was a vise of molten metal around his chest.

Isabelle. No.

Yes.

There.

At the back of the room was a door to a small courtyard, where people crowded to smoke pipes of something acrid and unpleasant that couldn't possibly be pure tobacco. Philippe elbowed his way through the crowd, using the *khi* elements to repulse those who didn't get out of the way fast enough. Behind him, he could still hear Tade arguing with Nene about their intrusion. He didn't care.

"Isabelle!"

The courtyard was a small square overgrown by weeds, its walls bending inwards as though they'd collapse at any moment, with a scattering of wrought-iron tables painted in garish colors. It was all but deserted, and the reason why became clear in a heartbeat.

Because, when Isabelle turned, startled, holding a fistful of her dress in clenched hands, Philippe saw the man she'd been with.

Red and silver swallowtail suit, with an embroidered patch showing a broad, two-handed sword against the spires of Notre-Dame; and a clerical collar, and an utterly familiar face from an unpleasant past.

Father Javier, from House Silverspires.

"You're not having her," Philippe said, gathering the *khi* elements into a shield. "She's not yours."

Javier raised an eyebrow. He rose, unhurriedly, from the table he'd been sitting at—it struck Philippe, belatedly, that there was no one else there. Just Javier and Isabelle—and that the table held two cups of tea and a plate of potatoes with herb. Hardly the work of a kidnapper. They'd been …

They'd been talking, which was almost worse.

"Isabelle—"

"I wanted to know," Isabelle said.

"Know what? This is the House that sent you to *die*!"

"No." Isabelle's face was flushed, but her gaze was hard. "I chose to die, Philippe. I remember. I remember everything from the time I Fell onto the city. It was my choice, to defend what I believed in."

He was losing her again. He'd lost her once to the House, their new-found friendship disintegrating as the House made her arrogant, and uncaring, and inclined to sacrifice anyone and anything if she thought it would protect their rule.

"They'll just …" He started, stopped, because he had no words. How could she? After all that had happened, how could she? "They'll just want to know what makes you tick," he said. "You'll be a *thing* to them. A curiosity."

"Because that's what they did to you?" Isabelle's voice was quiet, but its edge was that of a knife.

"Not to me! Have you forgotten Dân Chay already?"

"I have no idea what you're talking about," Javier said

with a frown. "But I'm not here to take Isabelle back. I'm simply ..."

He paused, and in the rising silence Philippe heard a sound like the roar of flames. *What was that?*

"Javier," he said. "What did you do?"

"I didn't do anything," Javier said, peevishly. "As I said, I'm here as a friend. On behalf of other friends who loved Isabelle, and who think her dead."

In Philippe's hands, the *khi* fire flared to agonizing life, burning in the palm of his hands. He threw it to the cobblestones—and watched it light up every single one of the *khi* currents of fire around them, surrounding them in a complex and ever-moving weave of red light. Isabelle stood frozen.

"Duck!" Philippe screamed at her.

A split second later, the world exploded.

Every single window around and above them broke in a tinkle of glass—and the breath of the explosion washed over them, sending Javier and Isabelle flying. Philippe flung the rest of the *khi* elements in his hands at them, anchoring them to the ground and wrapping a dome of protection around them as a storm of wooden shards and glass filled the courtyard. It didn't protect him, but he was ready. As he started flying and his eyes snapped open with the passage of the wind, he wove the *khi* fire into a burning shield around himself. As he did so he felt a mild resistance from afar, and a voice, whispering in his mind.

You're clever. As crafty as a snake, but it won't save you in the end.

Dân Chay.

All the old jails are split open like shattered skulls. Nothing is holding anymore, in the wake of the storm. I'm coming, Immortal.

When nothing hit the shield anymore, Philippe cautiously lowered it, and found himself in the ruins of the courtyard. The tables had flown and embedded themselves in the walls, and the force of the aftermath had ripped the cobblestones away from the earth. Isabelle was on her knees, staring at the ground in shock. Javier was holding her, but he was shaking, and whispering the words of a frantic prayer.

Above them were the walls of the neighboring buildings. They'd always been crooked, but now they seemed to be bending inwards, moments from collapsing.

"We have to leave," Philippe said. "Now."

The café they'd come through was in ruins: one of the floors had collapsed, crushing people underneath. Tade was on his knees in the rubble, trying to dig out someone from the mass of wreckage. Philippe joined him, weaving *khi* wood and *khi* metal into unbreakable nets.

"Philippe."

"Not now," he said.

A few moments were the difference between life and death, for those trapped underneath.

"Philippe!"

He turned, briefly, ready to deliver a blistering lesson on why they should be helping, when he saw what they were looking at. What every single survivor of the blast was looking at.

The blast had leveled half the buildings in the small street they'd crossed, opening up a wide vista on the city. And, instead of a skyline—instead of the usual mass of lights that marked the street lamps and chandeliers of Houses, and the faint remnants of magical pollution clinging to everything in the city—there was nothing but a roiling cloud of smoke, like the one that had been above Harrier. Only this one covered the entire heavens—a black, ominous cloud that cast the entire city in darkness without end.

All the old jails are split open like shattered skulls. Nothing is holding anymore, in the wake of the storm. I'm coming, Immortal.

Emmanuelle was trying not to think of Silverspires, or of dying Houses. She'd asked her jailers to see Asmodeus or Thuan, but the guards had laughed, and said the heads of the House had enough on their minds as it was. In despair, she'd penned a note that they'd agreed to send, but she knew it would end up lost in paperwork on someone's desk.

In the meantime, she was trying to teach herself calligraphy.

The only things of interest in the room were the food, and a fountain pen lying in a drawer. She'd been a bit surprised they'd left it, but she had to admit that as a weapon it was utterly useless, and it wasn't as if she was going to steal it from Hawthorn.

The pen was an old thing: a pre-war artifact with a red-marbled body and a golden finial engraved with an owl and two chicks. The piston turned smoothly and easily, which meant someone had maintained it. Emmanuelle wasn't an expert in pens, but she'd rescued her fair share of waterlogged or fungus-covered books and she knew how quickly things deteriorated in post-war Paris. It had come with a notebook and a small ink bottle: a red that had turned out to be the glistening color of blood. Obviously.

The nib wrote thick, and she was working on her descenders—coming to the slow conclusion that she preferred studying Gothic manuscripts to writing Gothic script—when a low, buzzing sound like a persistent swarm of bees filled the room.

"Asmodeus?" she asked. Was this some new sort of trickery?

She moved towards the great doors, though she already knew the wards on them were so thick she wouldn't even be able to move them.

She never reached them.

Two things happened almost simultaneously. The first was the explosion tearing apart the room, sending her flying into the air, hitting the wall with a dull thump that sent pain flaring in her back and legs. And the second—as she hit the wall and fell to the floor with what felt like everything collapsing around her, the crumbling masonry exposing the metal skeleton underneath—was the link to House Silverspires burning red-hot in her mind. For a moment only—all the dependents of the House in mortal danger; she had to do something, she had to do it now—and then everything was snuffed out again.

She screamed, but the House of Hawthorn was fire and chaos, and no one could hear her.

14

The Margin Between Life and Death

After leaving Niraphanes, Aurore drifted, uncertainly, through the House of Harrier. She was exhausted. Her eyes would close, as soon as she paused, and every time that happened she'd see Dân Chay smiling again, and the firelight spilling from his mouth.

She was on the northern edges. It should have been well away from the fighting, but Niraphanes' faction was spreading through the deserted streets. She was stopped, twice, by Fallen soldiers wearing the two-hawk livery of Niraphanes—but after a glance at her they sent her on her way. Either word had got around, or she didn't look like a threat, or both.

The third soldier who stopped her was a small, swarthy mortal woman wearing amber bracelets on both her wrists, and carrying a rifle that was so long it dwarfed her small frame.

Aurore screwed up her courage and said, "It sounds like you're expecting trouble."

The soldier looked at her, frowning. "You shouldn't be here, little fish."

Aurore bristled at the infantilizing appellation, but

realized the soldier meant well. It was an odd, uncomfortable feeling.

"Why?"

The soldier spat. "It's not a good place to get caught between the games of the powerful. Lord Guy is coming." She pointed in the distance.

Aurore stared. The sky was dark with the remnants of smoke. In the silence she could hear hundreds of beating wings; and the raucous cries of hawks hunting their prey.

The magic of the House. The enforcers of Guy's justice. The birds that not only killed, but sucked away bone and muscle and fat until nothing but a deboned cloak of flesh was left. She closed her eyes—remembering a corpse hitting the floor, remembering how she'd told herself, over and over, that Jeanne had been dead when the first hawk had gone through her, that the screams afterwards didn't count. The words were out of her mouth before she could think.

"You think you're going to lose."

She braced herself for the soldier to grab her and give her a beating, but the soldier merely shook her head with a sigh.

"He has all the magicians of the House on his side."

"You ... You could run away."

The gaze the soldier gave her reminded her of nothing so much as Niraphanes'.

"We could. But everything has to start somewhere." She reached out. Aurore flinched. The soldier's gaze sharpened. "Such as making a world where fear doesn't dictate how we speak to each other. My name is Vida."

She said it with an accent Aurore couldn't place.

"Vida. I'm Aurore."

"Pleased to meet you." Vida handed Aurore a package. "Here. You need this more than I do. Now run."

Aurore didn't run. She walked away slowly. When she looked back, the soldier was still there, and she'd been joined by a couple of squad-mates. They'd put their rifles away and looked to be building barricades. She unpacked the package and ate it. It was fried pork rind, which crunched under her teeth, the taste of meat both unfamiliar and comforting at the same time.

Lord Guy is coming. She thought of Frédérique and Morningstar, of Virginie. No. She couldn't fight every battle. She couldn't save everyone. She had to look to her family first, and save them from Dân Chay before it was too late.

She shouldn't be here. She rubbed, again, the disk on her chest. A day and a night in the House. She'd done that. Never mind that she didn't have any information that would interest Asmodeus—she couldn't dance to his tune forever.

Time to go.

The further away she got, the fewer people she saw. Live ones, that was, because the streets were littered with corpses. Some had died in the explosions—the older ones, the ones in chunks and charred bits. Others were more recent kills: those of Niraphanes' soldiers, stabbed or hacked at or enspelled to death. She wasn't much fazed: she'd known none of them so their deaths were abstract, things that couldn't touch her.

They expected to die, she saw with sudden clarity—Vida and Niraphanes and perhaps even Lorcid. They didn't think they could hold out against Guy, but they'd still try to do the right thing.

The right thing.

As if that had ever kept anyone alive.

At the West Gate—the big, massive wrought-iron edifice that was now torn scraps—she paused. The gaping holes on either side were the flat cages, lying empty and silent. Aurore wasn't superstitious, but she felt her back tense, ready to bow to whatever ghosts lingered. She walked past them with her heart in her throat, breathing in the smell of charred flesh and the faint, nauseating one of quicklime.

Her eyes were on the cage, which was why she tripped, and caught her balance just in time. What was that? The ground had been smooth below her feet. She reached out, cautiously. Nothing. Except … a faint feeling underfoot. She touched it with her fingers. Yes: a faint thread of something that crossed the gates, and then went on.

A thread. Her blood ran cold, but she barely had time to feel fear, because it lit up: a thread with the orange-red reflections of a fire, the same ones under Dân Chay's feet, reaching into the city. For a moment—a flash of suspended time—she saw the entire sky light up in red, as if similar lines had sprung to life everywhere in the city. And then the sounds started one after the other, like distant fireworks.

Not fireworks. Bombs. They went off, one by one, followed by a plume of blackened smoke in the sky, until there was nothing of blue or red left overhead—as if the entire world had become a pall of smoke. The wind carried the smell of charred wood, and another smell she would recognize anywhere: charred flesh and bones, and distant screams.

A busy day. The Houses. A stray Immortal. The mortals.

Explosions. All the Houses blown up by Dân Chay, as he'd said he would. There had been nothing from la Goutte d'Or, had there? Those two plumes of smoke she'd seen in the northeast were House Lazarus, and then House Stormgate. They had to be. Her community had to be safe. It had to be.

Cassiopée. Marianne.

Please.

She ran. Past the gates and away from her old House, through streets wreathed in smoke and the smell of burning. The threads of fire had disappeared, though she could still feel them underfoot. From time to time she'd stumble over something she couldn't see, but there was so much debris, so many things crunching and squelching underfoot and some of them had been alive before it all started and she couldn't afford to think that way. Once, twice, she had to double back because streets were cut off by a mass of debris. She tried, stumbling, choking, to head north without really knowing where north was.

The pain started, then. As she veered towards what she thought was la Goutte d'Or—running across the Iéna bridge between the devastation of the Champ de Mars and the ruined Trocadéro gardens—something started burning against her skin. The disk. Hawthorn's disk. No. She couldn't stop—not now. This was about her family.

She climbed the slope through the Trocadéro gardens, exhausted and out of breath—no one there but ghosts, who had stopped scaring her years ago. Overhead, smoke and darkness; under her, a hundred, a thousand pinpricks of Dân Chay's threads, except that they were now black and dull rather than a shining orange. Spent.

The hook under her ribs yanked hard, once, twice. The third time, as she stumbled on, it sent her to her knees, breathing hard and staring at devastated cobblestones. The world was blurred and refusing to come into focus, and pain grew within her, spreading through her guts, through her lungs. She needed to get up, she needed to walk, now. She needed to be in Hawthorn.

No. No. The words tasted like blood in her mouth. She didn't care about Hawthorn, didn't care if the whole House was blown apart and washed into the river. She pulled herself up, shaking. It was only pain. She could bear it. She stumbled on, through the debris on the Trocadéro square, away from the river—the pain eased a fraction. She could do it. She had to.

And then she realized that the only reason it had abated was because her feet had shifted—because she was now headed down rue Franklin towards La Muette and the distant House of Hawthorn.

No.

Aurore turned aside once more. She heard the distant screams—coming from the Houses, the Houseless areas, both? Ahead, people were scurrying away—not focused on her or on the devastation in the sky, but looking for shelter and food. Life went on, desperately, in the ruins.

The pain sent her to her knees again. Breathing was becoming unbearable—and the tug in her gut was a constant thing, the hook pulling at her innards until they were going to burst through her chest. She laid a shaking hand on her belly, felt the raised edges of taut muscles pushed outwards. It was going to tear her apart and not care one jot.

You're not the master of me, she breathed, but the words were said through gritted teeth. How could she be so weak, so unreliable? She'd carried Cassiopée through the Houseless areas—on those very paths—once. She should have been able to do it again.

Once, twice. Fragmented walks—one foot in front of the other through a rising haze. One street after the other, all a shifting, harrowing blur of cobblestones. She tripped and fell on one of the invisible threads—the jolt that traveled through her calves was suddenly overpowering, a red-hot wave tearing a scream out of her.

No.

No.

Aurore clenched her fists. She stared at the warped cobblestones in front of her.

"I'm sorry," she said to Cassiopée, to Marianne.

For this—and for the previous day and night—there would be a reckoning.

Then, she pulled herself to her knees, her mouth clamped down on further screams, one of her hands wrapped around the pain in her midriff—and walked, one curse at a time, towards the distant House of Hawthorn, and a surcease to her agony.

Thuan woke up with difficulty. He was lying with what felt like a sea of debris digging into his back, staring at the ruins of the canopy of his bed. The last thing he remembered was the blast forcing his eyes open—and clamping down on his wards before he and Asmodeus were picked up and flung away like rag dolls.

Asmodeus.

He was lying unconscious, a few meters from Thuan, thrown away from him when the blast had hit. He'd had the presence of mind, at least, to throw away his glasses. The lenses had shattered along with every window in the room, and he'd be blind if he hadn't. He didn't look good, though: the usual radiance of his body was muted, and . . .

Thuan couldn't feel the link to the House anymore—it couldn't be dead already, could it? He sat up, shakily—his legs barely strong enough to carry him—and closed his eyes, desperately trying to make silence in his mind. Be there. Please be there. Please be alive. Please let me still have a home.

In the darkness, all he could hear was his own panicked heartbeat, and the memory of unbearable light still imprinted on his eyelids. In, out, trying to calm himself—it was going to be all right, they were going to weather this as they had weathered everything else. In, out.

It was still there. It was weak and fluttering, like a drowning man's last struggles, but it was still here—a hint of imperious panic, because so many dependents were dead and he had to help the others and there wasn't much time. He took a deep breath. It was much like an old clock he hadn't been paying attention to. Now that he heard it he could barely focus his attention on anything else.

Thank you, Ancestors. Thank you. A feeling of gratitude so strong it twisted his entire chest.

When he opened his eyes again, Asmodeus was sitting

up. He looked … wrong, and it wasn't only the missing glasses and the debris scattered in his hair.

Weak. He looked weak.

Thuan clamped down on the thought before it could become hurtful. He reached out, and brushed out the debris from Asmodeus's hair. Asmodeus reached up as well—their hands met for a brief moment, held each other tightly. He felt their entwined warmth, like a heartbeat.

"You're alive," Asmodeus said slowly, carefully.

For a moment, raw, naked fear on his face; and then it was gone, smoothed out. He held on to Thuan's hand for a moment more, lowering it to his lips—trembling, pliant skin—before letting it go.

Thuan shrugged. "It was a little uncertain for a while."

"Mmmm."

Asmodeus's gaze took in the devastation of the room: the bed that was little more than splinters of wood; the distant sound of things still collapsing, of moans and pleadings for help. His face didn't move. He rose, with barely a tremor to his legs, and headed for the door with not a word spoken. As he did so, Thuan caught the glint of a blade in his hand.

"Asmodeus!"

No answer. He was moving fast, too—one moment more and he'd just be out of the room, gracefully sidestepping the ruins of the double doors. Thuan tried to force himself up on wobbling legs—gave up and called the last scraps of *khi* water in the room to change shapes and wrap the long, serpentine body of his dragon shape around Asmodeus. There was nothing left in the room: even the *khi* currents of fire he'd seen only a moment ago were stale and weak, as if they, too, had burned.

Asmodeus looked faintly annoyed for the first time.

"This is no time for games."

"And it is time for hurting someone? A knife isn't going to solve anything."

"I disagree. Blades are such a handy way to solve problems. I've been too indulgent, but this ends now. I'm getting the answers I want."

"In the Ancestors' name, who are you going to get your answers from? There's no one here …"

Emmanuelle.

As if what they needed right now was a war with House Silverspires. They could make Selene swallow many things—because she had to, because she was weak—but she would never forgive harming her partner. Thuan tightened his grip around Asmodeus's legs, rearing up to his full and considerable height, his antlers bumping the ceiling and flakes of mold falling around them.

"No."

Asmodeus pushed down—using his strength, not to widen the coils, but to step out of them. Thuan tightened his grip.

"You said it yourself—she always tries to help people. Does that sound like someone who'll bring in a weapon to destroy Hawthorn?"

If she'd even survived. Not everyone in Hawthorn would have. Another thought to be clamped down on, because it was just useless at this juncture.

"She might still be its unwitting agent."

"In which case she wouldn't tell you, would she? She wouldn't even know she had the information!"

His entire body was wobbling. He hadn't thought Asmodeus would still be so strong. Where did he get his energy from?

"Pain would jog her memory, I'm sure."

"And alienate us and Silverspires forever. You *know* this, Asmodeus." He used, not the endearment—but the stern tone of a parent for a misbehaving child. "There's a House that needs our help, right now. That's what matters."

His muscles felt like jelly. If he didn't manage to quell Asmodeus soon, he was going to collapse altogether, adding to the list of people who needed help.

A long, drawn-out silence. Then the pressure on his scales abruptly eased, and the knife in Asmodeus's hand vanished back into the folds of his singed swallowtail jacket.

"You have a point."

Several, in fact. Thuan felt too exhausted to shift back into human shape—the thought of walking was making his coils tremble.

"Let's go see what the situation is."

A sharp, considering look from Asmodeus, but of course his husband had never been the kind to ask people how they were doing, or to drag them to hospital.

"Let's."

It was sheer chaos. The corridor was still filled with smoke, and with bodies, thrown haphazardly against walls and chandeliers. Some of these were still moving—Thuan flew up to disentangle a serving boy who was half folded over the burned remnants of a door, and whose injuries seemed to be nothing more than superficial. The boy insisted on walking, trailing after them with a glazed look of shock on his face.

Not one window was intact, and all the glasses on tables had shattered too, the fragments turned to deadly projectiles. Most of the bodies they saw were pockmarked with wounds.

Asmodeus's face didn't move as they went towards the infirmary, but Thuan could almost taste his mood in the air. The anger. The rising despondency. Not far from what he felt.

"The wards helped," Asmodeus said, as they turned into one of the large dining rooms. "Otherwise everyone inside would have had their brains rattled in their skulls."

And have died almost instantly. Yes. Thuan didn't answer, because he had no words for the magnitude of the devastation. In the dining room, glass shards glinted in the charred remnants of food and chairs. There was still a faint smell of peppers and meat mixed with the sharper, more acrid one of burning.

"Fire," he said.

If every glass had shattered, that meant the lanterns, too. The one in their room had snuffed itself out, but who knew about all the others in the House? This late at night, most of the large chandeliers were extinguished. That was their salvation.

"The kitchens—"

"The armory."

"Wait," Thuan said. "We have an armory?"

Asmodeus didn't rise to the jibe. Bad sign. He normally took to sarcasm like a fish to water.

"Remnant of the war. My predecessor loved to show it off. I think it's garish and sends utterly the wrong message. One doesn't have to show weapons to instill fear. But if it's on fire then we'll have another explosion."

Another two people in the debris. Asmodeus used magic to dig them out, his face showing nothing of the exertion such a spell, unaided, must have cost him.

Thuan carried the one with shattered legs. The other one, a tall, imperious woman who looked to be one of the House's magicians, tried to bow to Asmodeus, who stopped her with a dismissive wave of his hand.

"Not now, Albane."

By now Thuan had four wounded people on his back and was moving much more carefully. He was also keeping a mental tally of all the places they needed to check. The armory. The kitchens. The nurseries. Oh, Ancestors, the children. Ai Nhi. Camille.

"Can you walk?" Thuan asked.

Albane nodded, her face a peculiar mixture of shock and awe.

"The Court of Birth," Thuan said.

Asmodeus said, "I already sent someone."

"Who . . .?"

Thuan tried to turn, but his husband's touch on his scales stopped him. He'd throw people off, if he tried.

"The first person we found." Asmodeus's face was grim. "Come on."

Everywhere the same devastation: people who'd died pierced by shattered glass, by caved-in floors, by bookcases and wardrobes thrown at them with frightful force. People wandering, shocked and dazed, calling for loved ones and not finding them.

"Unka Thuan!" Sang was herding Ai Nhi, the little dragon positively bouncing when she saw Thuan. "Unka Asmo!"

Well, at least she wasn't scared of Asmodeus at all. Thuan winced.

"Child, I've told you not to call him—"

"Leave it," Asmodeus said. "As I said, not now."

Ai Nhi appeared unharmed—or, more accurately, her wounds had already closed up with the customary speed of dragons' healing. Thuan could see faint scars on her face.

"The windows exploded, and then Auntie Sang was so worried!"

Behind her were Asmodeus's sister Berith, her wife Françoise. Berith was holding Camille on her shoulders, and Françoise was clearly nursing an injured arm. Her eyes were caked with dried blood. Camille was staring, wide-eyed, at the devastation.

"Big 'ight, unka. Big big 'ight."

Asmodeus nodded, curtly, at Berith—frowned, when he saw Françoise.

"Can you see?" he asked.

They stared at him. Clearly they hadn't even noticed the blood round Françoise's eyes.

"Hospital," Thuan said. "Now."

That the hospital was working at all was a miracle in a day of disasters. Iaris had lost workers—Ahmed had died in the blast along with half the hospital staff. Mia was moving with a cane until her innate magic healed the injuries she'd sustained, and other doctors were clearly barely in a state to be healing other patients.

When the convoy headed by Thuan and Asmodeus appeared at the door, Iaris's face was terrible to behold—going from despondency to incandescent hope in a fraction of a second.

"My lord! I thought—"

A low, amused laugh from Asmodeus. "I'm a hard person to kill. So is Thuan."

Iaris looked less than happy, but at that moment Thuan couldn't care less about what she thought. He slid to the floor, exhausted, while nurses and orderlies helped slide off the five people they'd managed to cram on to his back.

When he looked up again, Asmodeus had wandered off, but his smell was all over the tray with tea and biscuits that had been left by his side. Mia was fussing over him in a very uncertain way, sticking bandages on as if not quite sure where they should go. Thuan made a low, growling sound in the back of his throat.

"I'm fine," he said. The tea cup was too small for his muzzle, but he managed to gulp down the biscuits. They slid into his stomach, a drop of sugar in a wasteland of emptiness. It would have to do. Food, he guessed, was going to become scarcer and scarcer. "The children—"

"Taken care of." Mia moved away as if he'd bite. To be fair, he probably could. "Ai Nhi was clinging to you and didn't want to go."

"Tell her I'll see her later," Thuan said. If he still had energy—but no, he owed her that. "And ask about Vinh Ly, will you? Is she still in her cell?"

He pushed himself up, coil after coil, changing back

to human as he did so. He didn't mind being a dragon, but the dependents would—and this wasn't a time to remind them he was a foreigner to the House. He paused long enough to sip the tea, inhaling its harsh fragrance. Bergamot. Obviously.

The room he was in was packed with people already, but it was an oasis of quiet compared to the rest of the wards. As he pushed his way through the wounded he caught a glimpse of Lan, organizing what looked like orderlies with hospital trolleys. She was obviously using them to ferry wounded people back to the hospital, loading them with everyone who could sit and putting those who couldn't into their laps. She waved at Thuan, her face breaking into a smile, and then turned back to what she was doing.

"My lord!" It was Alis, a woman who worked in the Court of Gardens.

Thuan stopped, smiled at her in what he hoped was a reassuring way.

"How are you?"

She had a bandage over one eye, and dried blood on her face, a strong, animal smell wafting up to Thuan. A small puppy with white fluffy hair was curled in her lap, barking forlornly at her.

"I'm all right, but we can't find Mother. I don't know how she'll do without us ..."

Thuan tried not to think of the worst case scenarios.

"I'll see what I can find out," he said.

Alis looked at him for a while.

"Ask," he said. He wanted to be gentle and kind, but it was hard.

"My lord—what happened? The House ..."

Thuan stopped, and took time to phrase his answer carefully.

"An attack. We'll find out where it's coming from, and Lord Asmodeus will help me deal with it. You're safe now."

"Deal with it." Alis's voice relaxed.

It was amazing what the mention of Asmodeus had done. It shouldn't have been any way to run a House, but he was their monster—the one who held the dark at bay from them, and savaged those who sought to harm them. And if blood and pain were the price to pay for his protection, they gladly would.

Thuan had words about that, none of them pretty. But it wasn't the time.

"I'll see what I can do," he said again.

She was only the first of a stream of people desperate for news and comfort, all of them relieved that their head of House was still alive. By the fifth one or so everything blurred—which wasn't fair to them, but they needed him anyway, and he continued to mouth platitudes and hoped to Heaven his general fuzziness wasn't showing too much.

By the time he reached Iaris, he was exhausted.

She'd made her office in the antechamber of the morgue—it hadn't been the hospital morgue per se, but adjacent to it, a wealth of mothballed storerooms where nobody had stored anything for years. It was already overflowing with corpses. Thuan could smell decay in the air—and it would get worse.

Iaris looked up when he came in. Her smooth, ageless face was now drawn, showing something close to her true age—thin, translucent skin and the shadow of wrinkles on her forehead and cheeks and wrists. "My lord."

On her left side was Asmodeus, leaning against the desk with the same graceful ease as if it had been his own office. He was deep in conversation with two of the House's magicians.

"I'll need people making sweeps of each wing, telling people to send their wounded to hospital, and to help them dig out those who are still stuck under furniture or rubble. And to clear away the corpses, too. Iaris!"

"My lord?" There was markedly more deference in that tone than in hers for Thuan.

"We should burn the bodies."

Thuan found his voice. "You can't."

Asmodeus turned his way. He'd combed the debris out of his hair, and found a pair of unbroken glasses—how he'd managed the glasses was a miracle in and of itself. "Explain."

His voice was smooth, utterly confident, but Thuan could read the signs. It was his mask on again, and nothing but extreme weariness beneath. He was going to snap, and Heaven help the people nearest to him when that happened.

"Too many people are looking for family members and friends. If they can't find them among the living, they'll look for them among the dead. People need to *know*, Asmodeus." A raised eyebrow. "Perhaps you don't, but most people can't live without knowing if their loved ones are dead or alive. They need closure, even it means staring at a corpse. They need time to grieve. Time to make their peace with it." Thuan was half-convinced Asmodeus would just shrug and move on, rather than be faced with loss. But that wasn't the point. "If you burn the bodies without leaving people time to identify them, the dependents will riot."

"The risks of sickness—"

"Ice," Thuan said firmly. "The dragons can freeze an entire area of the House."

"Oh, believe me, I remember." Asmodeus's smile was sharp. Dragon ice had almost ended the House.

"He's right," Iaris said unexpectedly. She sounded like she was spitting out something particularly sour. "People need to identify the bodies. And we'll need to keep a record, too, to know who is dead and who is simply missing."

"So we can continue to search for them in the ruins?" Asmodeus's face was distant again. "Slim chances. But then, so is the margin between life and death. I agree."

A pause. He was letting Thuan take the lead.

"Let's do it," Thuan said. "Anything else?"

He saw the look on Iaris's face, and knew that it was only the beginning of all they needed to do.

15

The House, Dying

Thuan must have snatched sleep, at some point. He wasn't sure. The night passed in a blur, a confusion of meetings and decisions made about wounded, and supplies, and fires put out in various parts of the House; of corpses collected in the morgue, and lists of the wounded and the dead; of those trapped in debris that the Court of Strength was still trying to dig out. When he looked up, it was morning, and someone was shaking him awake.

"Berith," he said, his eyes gummed by sleep. Her dress had been vivid blue at one point, but now it was torn, and stained with blood and other fluids he couldn't identify. "I'm sorry, I said I'd come and see Ai Nhi—"

"Later, Thuan. Can't you feel it?" And, when he gaped at her, she merely pulled him up. "Asmodeus."

He felt the House, then, faint and struggling at the back of his mind. It had been screaming at him for a while, except that it was stuck behind a pane of glass and its voice was tinny, incoherent noises.

Berith's face was grim. "He's my Fall-brother. The link between us doesn't depend on the House."

"Where . . . ?" Thuan said. "Never mind. Tell me on the way."

He ran out of the overcrowded ward—so many people, such a press—past the mass of those still outside, looking at lists Iaris had had hammered on the hospital's front door, of the dead and the living. One of the neighboring rooms had had their ceiling cave in: dependents were still clearing away the debris.

Here.

Here they finally had space. He turned to see that Berith was still following him.

"The gardens," she said, her face grim.

"Hop on?"

He turned and stretched and changed, his body's coils pressed against the walls. She clambered over him, clinging to the spur at the nape of his neck.

He tossed his mane, stretched his long serpentine back until his antlers scraped the wreckage of chandeliers, and flew through the ruin of the House.

The gardens had never been pretty, exactly: they were still covered in the brackish waters of the Seine, and most of the pristine lawns had the slight elastic give of waterlogged land. Thuan had never been sure how plants grew at all—some of Lan's magic, as part of her work in the Court of Gardens.

Now there was no magic, just a churned mass of mud, debris, and exhausted *khi* elements. Trees had been ripped from the ground and flung into the river; some of them had burned where they stood, and pointed to the sky with skeletal branches.

"I can't see him," Berith said, with increasing frustration.

Thuan was flying close to the ground. He noted, with distant interest, the other plumes of smoke in the sky—the other Houses were burning, too. At least they were not alone in their misery. A thought for later. He turned, briefly—the House was a mess of smoking ruins and caved-in roofs. No sign of Asmodeus. Dependents, in the gardens. He'd have to tell Lan, if she didn't already know.

"He's here," Berith said. "He has to be."

Thuan tried to focus against the song of fear in his belly. He'd always thought of Asmodeus as a force to be managed or stopped, but his husband could die. He'd almost died, a year ago. He wasn't immune to damages. But where could he be? Trapped under a building?

They flew over a wing of the House Thuan had never seen, a small isolated building almost completely devastated by the blast, its door and a short fraction of wall remaining ludicrously open, papered over by ivy that seemed to have completely ignored the blast. There were no dependents nearby, or any sign anyone had been there in decades.

"This is pointless," Berith said.

Within Thuan, the House had sunk back—not because there was no danger, but because it felt exhausted and stretched. Which was another scary thought.

Hang on, he thought. *We're coming for you. If only we can find you.*

"He's not here," Thuan said. "Are you sure ...?"

And as he spoke, he saw, out of the corner of his eye, mist shrouding the thorn trees by the river's banks. He realized why they couldn't see Asmodeus: because there was one last hidden place of the House.

"Hang on."

He flew down to the ground in front of the mist. It receded as he approached, but he gathered the House to him in his mind, daring it to flee from him—and the mist rose again, sweeping even the ruins aside.

When he and Berith landed, they were in the midst of a grove of hawthorn trees. The mist hid almost everything—but not the long, desiccated bodies hanging in the trees, impaled on hawthorn branches. As Berith got up, brushing mud from her dress, the arms shifted, trying to grab her. She glared at them, and swept sideways with her hands. The arms stopped as if frozen.

Thuan stared at her. "Where did you learn that?"

Berith's smile was mysterious. And she turned serious again.

"Come on."

Thuan shifted to human again, because the dragon shape's bulk made it hard to avoid the trees. It wasn't that they could actually lift him into the trees, because he was too large and too heavy, but it was annoying, and tearing himself free of them was a waste of time.

"You're anchored in the House," Thuan said, as they walked. Berith was dying, and she'd needed some place to hold her power. "If it's weakening . . ."

A long, weighted gaze as they walked.

"You mean I shouldn't be upright? It doesn't work that way. Without an anchor, I can walk, at least until I can make another one. Just not very fast."

She didn't look weak, or in pain, but then that meant nothing. She'd always been good at hiding things. Thuan opened his mouth, closed it.

"Sorry."

Berith shrugged. "It's a good question, in the current circumstances."

The current circumstances. Hawthorn, weakened, perhaps dying. The thought that he'd lose it, that he'd lose the home he'd made and all it meant to him, was a stone in his stomach. He was feeling Asmodeus through the House now—not as a dependent in immediate danger, but something he couldn't quite place. He had a rising sense of dread, as if a candle were standing too near muslin or lace.

He all but ran through the last of the trees. The mist parted before him, and the ground underfoot was slightly springy, with bones crunching underneath. The air smelled of flowers and rot, with the faintest tinge of blood. Not the usual: the place was so saturated with magic its smell usually drowned everything else out. The *khi* elements weren't there, either: the water, which should have been strongest near the Seine, was hanging in wisps around him, limning his body and tapering off. Every other element—fire included—was so still Thuan could barely see them moving. Not normal. *Khi* currents were the fabric of the universe: they never lay still.

Ahead, a single silhouette limned in light.

Berith said, quietly, "Asmodeus."

He was sitting between two of the largest hawthorn trees. The one on his left held the corpse of his predecessor Uphir, a fair-haired, blue-eyed Fallen who looked almost as if he were alive, resting on the three hawthorn branches that had pierced his chest. Blood fell every time the wind shook the trees, spattering Asmodeus's jacket and face, but Uphir himself was still. Watching.

In front of Asmodeus, in the churned area where there should have been more hawthorn trees, there was only darkness: a huge, gaping hole in the earth that looked like nothing so much as a grave large enough to bury them all.

Within him, the House was silent—waiting, curling back on itself like a wounded animal.

"Asmodeus," Berith said again, gently.

He didn't move.

Thuan said, finally, "This one is mine."

"Thuan—"

"Too many cooks, remember?"

Thuan walked to sit by his husband's side. Up close, the hole was the entirety of the world—for the first few meters the sides were tightly packed branches, fragments of bones and gray-brown soil, and beyond darkness reigned absolute. It was like dropping into night—his gaze kept being drawn into it, and his body quivered with the effort of keeping away. It would be so easy, wouldn't it? Rest, at last. A final ending.

No. There was no rest: merely another life in a string of lives on the way to Nirvana. The House had his life already; why should it have his death, too?

"It's peaceful, isn't it?" Asmodeus said. "Everything, all our striving, all our struggling against the threads that bind us, leading us back to this single moment in the end."

Not what he wanted to hear. Thuan sucked in a deep, sharp breath, and thought fast.

"I'm with Berith," he said. "Come on, Asmodeus. We'll get you home and you can get some rest."

Asmodeus's eyes were still on the hole. There was no expression on his face.

"Home?"

"Your dependents need you."

"They don't." His voice was grave, utterly stripped of expression. No, not only that. It wasn't the distance he affected, but a lack of everything. Of hope. "The House is dead, Thuan."

"Not yet."

"It might as well be!" A trace of anger in Asmodeus's face. Bad. Thuan shifted halfway to dragon shape—because if he was going to have to catch Asmodeus, he didn't want to do it as a human. It had been much easier, and less frightening, when Asmodeus had been trying to kill people in retribution for the explosion. "There's nothing left. Look at it."

"I see a hole in the ground," Thuan said, trying to keep it deadpan, because the hole scared him, too. On the edges of the hole, he saw small, fast-moving shapes—the children of thorns, weaving in and out of focus. The House's eyes on them. "That'll close up, in time. And if it doesn't, I'll fill it up with enough *khi* water to make a pond. Things *heal*, Asmodeus. It's not all lost. Nothing ever is. Come on."

"Asmodeus."

It was Berith, kneeling on his other side. Uphir's corpse in the hawthorn tree moved when he saw her, its voice a hiss. "The errant brother come to rescue his brother? How touching."

"Sister," Berith said, her face hardening. "I know you're dead, but that's no excuse not to keep up with House business."

She held Asmodeus's shoulders, and simply rocked him from side to side, singing a wordless song—a slow rhythm slowly rising to a high, crystalline pitch. For a moment—a single, quivering moment—the ghost of something shimmered over the hole: a golden city of domes and spires, bathed in warm, sharp radiance, an even more alien place to Thuan than the House.

"Give, and it will be given to you. A good measure, pressed down, shaken together and running over, will be poured into your lap. For with the measure you use, it will be measured to you."

A low, bitter laugh from Asmodeus.

"I've always known my measure would be blood and pain. I have no regrets."

"Giving up," Berith said, "is a sin. Do you want that on your tally, Brother?"

A silence. Asmodeus's eyes were on the city—it was already vanishing, but something of its light remained in the air. Thuan slid his tail between him and the hole, coil by agonizing coil.

At length, Asmodeus laughed, and it was without a trace of amusement.

"I'm all sin, aren't I?"

He rose, shaking. Thuan was there to steady him, cushioning his body so he wouldn't fall, and then taking his full weight as Asmodeus all but collapsed in his embrace, cold and limp and still in a way that twisted at his heart. He'd have given anything for a quip; a wounding sentence; a shadow of the old sarcasm that had made him want to strangle Asmodeus so many times.

Berith's face was hard. "Let's go home."

They turned, leaving the gaping hole in the heart of the House behind them—back to the drowned gardens, the dependents in need of help, the slow tallying of the living and of the dead—the House that lay cracked open and vulnerable to its enemies, and that Thuan didn't know how to protect anymore.

It was an endless, nightmarish night—Frédérique, exhausted, could only remember snatches of it. The tall, elegant man with the predatory eyes, lifting Virginie's face while she beat on her daughter's wards, desperately trying to get through, desperately trying to understand what was happening. All sound was muffled and distorted beyond meaning, and all she saw was the man's face shift and become jewel-hard, like a Fallen in the instant before they lashed out and beat someone to death. Except that he'd released a weeping Virginie, and turned to face Morningstar—whose body was surrounded by dazzing light. A conversation she couldn't make out—then Morningstar lashing out, not at the retreating figure of the man, but at Aurore, whose face turned leached of all colors, as if she'd been afraid long before he'd turned on her. She crumpled like a puppet with strings cut.

The wards collapsed. Sound came rushing back, a painful rush in her ears that made her legs wobble. She pushed herself towards her daughter. Virginie was still on her knees, her eyes widened in shock.

"Mom. Dad ..."

"It's all right," Frédérique said, wrapping her arms around her and trying to believe it. "It's all right."

"What did he say?" Nicolas asked.

He'd moved Charles, the toddler, away from his shoulders, and was carrying him on his hips. He looked exhausted; wrung out. Frédérique ached to kiss him and lose herself in him—to forget everything that currently faced them.

Virginie closed her eyes. "He *saw* everything. He—"

"We have to go," Morningstar said.

He towered over them—bright and overwhelming, with the shadow of wings at his back—and all she wanted to do was fold herself so small that he wouldn't notice her. But it wasn't just her: it was her daughter, and her husband, and a toddler who'd never asked for anything beyond safety and love.

"I don't understand," Frédérique said. "Aurore …"

Morningstar's face was grim. "We don't need Aurore." He didn't spare her crumpled shape another glance. "She was just here to scavenge. She'd have turned on us eventually."

"But—"

"People are coming."

In the distance, booted feet.

"I don't think …" she started. "Virginie …"

Morningstar scooped Virginie up in his arms as if she weighed nothing. He must have done something, because instead of protesting her eyes rolled up, and her head lolled back as if she'd fallen asleep.

"Now!"

His light hardened around Frédérique, pushing her forward.

They ran.

Everything fractured, then. The great gates of the House, hanging askew. Threads of orange fire, slowly gathering under them until the streets were aglow with them, as if everything had been a thin mask hiding fire. They flared—walls of fire blocking their way, time and time again. Morningstar cursed under his breath, and changed directions. Nicolas was holding Charles, breathing with difficulty—but there was no time to take his load, because they were still running, and wherever they went the fire followed.

In Frédérique's mind, the link to House Harrier—once a weak and dying thing—flared, more and more painful as they got further and further.

"Morningstar," she tried to say, but he was striding ahead, and didn't hear her.

Run run run. Through streets filled with fire—wall after wall after wall of it. They were being herded, Frédérique realized, chilled. Or rather, kept away from wherever Morningstar really wanted to go—away from the Houses, away from safety. Every time Morningstar looped back to a street, the wall of fire would spring up again, inexorably cutting them off. Charles was screaming in Nicolas's arms, and then the screams sank down into frightened whimpers. In her husband's eyes Frédérique saw the same fear of being left behind—a whip, driving them ever onwards.

Once—only and exactly once—Morningstar stumbled. His face twisted in what might have been pain, and he turned back towards the House they had just left.

"Emmanuelle," he said, and it was almost pleading. "You were *supposed* to be safe."

He remained there for what felt like an eternity, while Frédérique struggled to breathe.

And then his face was expressionless again. Whatever he'd felt, it was over.

"Let's go," he said.

It was Nicolas—desperately rocking Charles in his arms—who said, "Your friend—"

"My friend has taken care of herself," Morningstar said, and started walking again.

Onwards. Again and again and again, back to the blur of featureless streets. In Morningstar's arms, Virginie's face was relaxed, utterly blissful in a way that was *wrong*. She'd wanted so much to protect her daughter—to shield her against the cruelty of the House. Only now the House was in her mind, and she could hear the beating of thousands of wings—the hawks, taking flight from buildings and doorways, making straight for her. Morningstar, she tried to say, but her voice was choked by the House, and they were still running, and she couldn't afford to stop because he would leave her behind without compunction, as he'd left Aurore behind. She didn't know why, but he could do that to Frédérique, too. In her mind, House Harrier was rising, a pain that obliterated everything, and she was running desperately, futilely trying to keep ahead of it.

When they finally stopped—when she saw, blurred and indistinct, Morningstar lay Virginie's still shape on the ground—her muscles gave up. She collapsed. If he decided to move again, she wouldn't be able to follow.

Footsteps. She tried to roll out of the way, but she couldn't. She was staring at the sky—and all of a sudden it lit up, and the ground under her shook, debris falling all around her.

The shape of birds, in the sky. Their screams—satisfied and triumphant, as they came for her. Morningstar was kneeling by her side, one hand on her forehead. He looked ... angry.

No. She tried to curl into a ball, to be as harmless as possible, but she was too tired to do more than make small, insignificant gestures.

"I should have known," Morningstar said.

His hand brushed her forehead. Something passed from him to her—pain flared up, the birds in her mind screaming and screaming, dragging her with them.

Then it was gone. All gone, and a curious sense of loss spread through her, as if a sound she'd heard all her life, like her own heartbeat, had finally stopped. Morningstar moved to Charles, and then to Nicolas.

Finished, he sat, thoughtfully staring at the sky. On the other side of him, Nicolas lay on the ground with his eyes glazed—until they finally closed, with a sigh, his breathing slow and utterly spent. Charles nestled against him: if she hadn't known any better she'd have thought they were sleeping. Frédérique crawled, centimeter by stubborn centimeter, to her daughter, wrapped herself around her still form. Fumbled, trying to breathe through the vise of fear in her chest—and found the faint heartbeat there.

"You can't move," Morningstar said—to her, to the sky? "And it's going to be ... difficult."

Frédérique curled around Virginie. Alive. That was all that mattered. How could she ever have believed he wished them well? He'd been so quiet and courteous, and she had forgotten that cruelty didn't have to be overt and brash, with knives and whips in belts and on tables in reception rooms, always at hand to punish the disobedient. Sometimes cruelty wore a mask of smiles and thoughtful kindness, which only broke down when things no longer went as desired.

Morningstar knelt by her side. His hand brushed her forehead, again—brushed Virginie's hair. She wanted to retch but no longer had energy left in her. Empty. She felt empty, as if he'd torn something primal and irreplaceable from her, a spring that had always been wound tight within her.

"What . . . ?" She swallowed, fighting to keep the taste of ashes from her mouth. "What did you do?"

"He's using the link to the House to track you down. I tore it out, but he knows where you are, now." Morningstar sounded . . . amused. Weary. Vulnerable, but she dared not voice the thought, because her legs were jelly and she could barely breathe through the hole he'd torn in her world. "He's always been a poor loser, and of course he's got nothing left now, poor soul." He didn't sound sorry about it, more amused by someone's misfortune. "His predecessor was no different. There's something about the House that attracts them, I think—some tendency to overreach until it all crashes down."

She was on the ground on some hard metal surface—rails, she realized, the bent shape of them going away in the darkness—and, looming over them, the larger shapes of devastated locomotives and wagons, headlights and chimneys glimmering in the darkness, with a smell of rust and congealed oil exhaled from broken wheels like a last breath.

"Guy," she said. "You're talking about Lord Guy."

"Of course. Who else?"

"The man . . ."

The one with the hard gaze, the one who'd looked into Virginie's eyes before turning away.

Morningstar's face was hard. "That one won't be bothering you. He can't come here. Not yet."

Hiding. They were hiding, and he was trying to gauge if he could run away once more—shedding more of them if necessary. Whom did he need, among them?

Virginie. Charles. The magicians. Of course he'd only bothered with the likes of them because they'd made things easier. But, if he could merely grab Virginie and go, why didn't he? She was between him and her daughter, but she wasn't arrogant or oblivious enough to believe she presented any kind of threat to him.

Exhausted. He was bright and terrible and possessed magic she'd never been allowed—and of which Virginie had only been allowed fleeting tastes—but he had his limits. Running from the man—whoever he was—and from Harrier had exhausted all his resources.

Limits.

He had limits.

Which meant her chance would come, if she rested enough. If she could find a way—any way—to outflank him.

Frédérique rested her head against her daughter's, and tightened her grip on her. There had to be a way.

She would be ready.

16

The Price of Power

The House was a wreck. Aurore had thought one of the explosions, the most westerly and southerly one, might be Hawthorn, and it had been. It ought to have brought her comfort, or some kind of vicious satisfaction. She was just exhausted, her breath clogged in her throat, her legs shaking under her. The hook that had brought her there had cared little about how it reeled her in, and she'd run the last hundred meters, pulled back to her feet every time she fell, dragged another few meters on rough cobblestones. Everything hurt, and her clothes were wet with sweat and perhaps blood. She wiped her eyes, shaking. Now that she was at the gates, the hook was fading, but she couldn't stay still. It would come back. It had always come back.

She tore her tunic open to reveal the shape of the disk on her chest, and walked between the ruined gates.

Everything after that was a blur. Pristine lawn covered in charred debris. Wounded dependents of the House limping or in shock, oblivious to her presence. Buildings that were charred ruins, the elegant staircases sharply cut off midway through their ascent. And inside—corridors with peeling wallpapers, rooms where the roof had collapsed, rooms without floors. A flood of people at gates she couldn't see, pressing against her. She elbowed her way through, ignoring their frowns.

She was in front of an orderly with no memory of how she'd got there, breathing through lungs that felt filled with dust and debris. The disk was no longer quiescent, but beating slowly and steadily on her chest—the hook gently dragging her to the right, back to its maker.

Asmodeus.

How dare he?

Another orderly was looming over her—had been for a while, but she hadn't seen him before. A whispered, worried conversation, and then they pushed and prodded her into an office, a hastily cleared space in what looked like the antechamber of the morgue.

The ageless, exhausted woman behind the desk took one look at Aurore and the disk on her chest, and snapped her fingers in annoyance.

"Head of House business. Get her there," she said with a vicious satisfaction.

The orderlies half-carried, half-dragged Aurore into a room, and threw her on the floor. The door closed with an audible snick, locked against all her attempts to escape. The disk against her chest was silent now, a gentle warmth spreading from its edges, a profoundly alien and disturbing feeling. A faint smell of bergamot and citrus hung in the air—for a moment Aurore was back in the cells, feeling the knife against her skin. Nothing had stopped him then, nothing would stop him now. She didn't have an ounce of the power she'd need to hold him at bay.

Bastard.

Aurore wasn't going to give him the satisfaction of humility, not even for her own survival. She pulled herself to her knees, and then shakily stood up, bracing herself with an anger she wasn't sure was wise, or sustainable.

"My lord," she said.

And was startled to meet the eyes of a child, who looked to be about five or six years old and fairly bouncing up and down on the floor, with discarded sheets of paper and coloring pencils behind her.

"Unka Thuan, Unka Thuan, there's a lady!"

Behind her, a young Annamite who'd been kneeling on the floor rose as well, eyes scrunched up in confusion and hands brushing the top of his topknot. There was a single bed in the room: the person in it was a sleeping Asmodeus, who still exuded grace and menace even when unconscious.

The Annamite's eyes narrowed when he focused on Aurore.

"You." And then, with a sharp look at the child, "Time for you to go, child."

The child pouted. Her face shifted between human and something else: a large muzzle and scales on her cheeks. Aurore caught her breath, held it. She'd known there were dragons in Hawthorn, but …

"Now," the Annamite said.

"You're going to be unpleasant again," the child said.

It was said with such glee Aurore almost took a step back.

"Perhaps." The Annamite's voice was gentle. "Sometimes you have to be unpleasant in the name of the House. Come on."

He walked to the door, and argued in a low voice with a guard, who came back and escorted the child over her protestations that she was tough enough to watch, and anyway it was going to be more fun than what she'd done so far.

The Annamite came back into the room, and stared at her. He wore the colors of Hawthorn, silver and gray perfectly cut against his slim form.

"You're a dragon too," she said. "The head of the House." Asmodeus's husband.

"Lord Thuan," he said. He walked to her—he smelled of nothing but distant brine, and the shadows of antlers hung in the air around him. He laid a hand, gently, on the disk on her chest. "House business." It pulsed, stretching towards Thuan's fingers as if they were all part of the same thing. "You're the one from the cells, aren't you? His pet project." He didn't sound impressed.

"I have a name."

"You do."

He waited, politely—as if he didn't have men at the door, ready to beat her up if she displeased him.

"Aurore," she snapped. And, out of nowhere, "Nguyen Thi Bach Diem."

"White Flame." His voice was thoughtful. "Interesting choice of name. Very … original." The way he said it, it was clearly a failure of her parents.

Her cheeks flamed. "Not everyone can claim centuries of tradition."

"Indeed."

He still had his hand on the disk, his fingers to it as if he was unsure if he was going to rip it out wholesale.

When he withdrew, it gave a little squeeze—a memory of the pain that had shot through her—and it took all she had not to fall to her knees, gasping.

"Take it out," she said. "Please. I've done my duty by him . . ." She gestured to the bed where Asmodeus lay.

Thuan's face revealed nothing of what he thought.

"I don't know what kind of duty he could impose on you."

How could he not know?

"A day and a night in Harrier," she said, spitting the words out. "He wanted a spy in the House, but there's nothing but ruins and fire and dead people!"

Thuan stared. Then he walked back to the disk, and tapped a finger against it. The same feeling Aurore had had in the streets spread to her chest—the one going up the soles of her feet when she'd tripped against the threads, except that this one was ice cold instead of warm. *Khi* water. Of course. She should have known. And the red shining threads had been fire, the element that Dân Chay seemed to wield with frightening ease. She could see the *khi* elements now. Had been able to ever since she'd seen Dân Chay.

She wasn't about to tell Thuan. Information was power, and he was going to share it with Asmodeus in any case.

At length, Thuan said, in a changed voice, "I'm sorry."

He tapped the disk again and it fell into his hand. Aurore stared. Had it been so simple all along? It seemed impossible that something that caused her so much pain could be so small.

"Pain every time you didn't follow directions. I ought to have known he wouldn't let go of anyone easily." He sounded like he was half talking to himself. Then he shook himself—droplets of shimmering water hung in the air for a second before vanishing. "Here," he said, handing her the token. "It's harmless now. Just wood. You can get the wounds checked out, though I'm really not sure how long it'll take before someone comes along. We're a bit overwhelmed." He sounded rueful. "And then we'll need help moving bodies, mostly."

Aurore stared at him. "I'm not House."

Thuan looked back. "I know. We could use some help, all the same."

"Because you've been nice?" She spat the words out. "Because you've been kind enough to remove what shouldn't have been there in the first place? You don't even know who I am or where I came from."

He didn't even know about her family. He didn't care. Why would he? He was the House's through and through, no better than his husband.

"Aurore—"

"Don't touch me."

She was up and running to the door before she could think it through. An abysmally pointless move: the guards would stop her before she got three paces away. How could she hope to get away?

The disk in her hand grew warm again—a net of cold magic settling around it, shining with a cold blue light. More spells she hadn't asked for, in that usual high-handed way of Immortals.

Thuan said, "Let her go. She's under my protection."

He wasn't her master. And she wasn't going to let him

put more chains on her, more ties to bind her to a House she didn't care one jot about.

Away. She had to get away.

No one else tried to stop Aurore. She wasn't sure if it was the disk—which had stopped shining by then, and was only slightly cool to the touch, like a memory of water—or if everyone was overwhelmed. She hadn't managed three hours in Hawthorn before being found out, but now the House was an utter shambles.

Good.

She was halfway out of the House before something caught her eye: a building that seemed to be standing alone in the midst of the ruins. When she got closer, she saw what had caught her attention: the door, which still stood whole, had a faded pattern of double stars. Odd, but not worth—

Wait.

She stared at the stars—reached out, and rubbed at the glass with the sleeves of her tunic. Yes. It was faint, but there'd been something else underneath. A raised network of sharp points.

The antlers of a deer.

She closed her eyes, trying to think back before all of this had happened—before the cells, before Harrier, before Dân Chay and Morningstar. She'd learned the map by heart—which directions to take through the gardens to get to the artifact's hiding place.

Left, *here*. Three meters at a hundred and twenty degrees, *here*. Another five at ninety degrees, past the fountain—there was no fountain anymore, just the rubble-choked ruin of one. Seven meters more, past the two cherub statues—not the babies with wings, but the six-winged, towering monstrosities that looked as though they'd reach out and grab her, no matter how devastated they were.

When, out of breath, she looked up, she was in the gardens again, staring at a building she hadn't seen before. It was isolated and small, like someone's home. A servant's house? The doors had been blasted open, and of its four walls only one remained. By its side was the ruin of another building: this one had no walls remaining at all, and just a deep, charred indentation on the earth from which sprouted a layer of ivy.

Something was wrong.

That wasn't ivy. It was thorns. Small, slender branches with hundreds of small, glistening thorns like a hedge or a rose bush.

Or a hawthorn.

There was no way the thorns could grow, not with the blast. Why were they not singed?

The disk in her hand flared to life again, and a feeling on the nape of her neck told her she was being observed. She turned, and saw them, watching her.

They were the size of children, but that was all they had of humanity. Their bodies were woven of thorns—their chests an elaborate impression of ribs and heart seen through cages of branches, their arms long, curving branches bending into a soft curve at the elbow, more like a tree in the wind than an articulation. Their faces were twigs and thorns, and there was deep darkness where their eyes should have been. Power roiled as they moved—magic reaching out, pinning her to the ground as surely as Asmodeus's magic had held her in place.

"I got lost—" she started, and a three-fingered hand rested on her lips, sharp enough to wound.

Don't lie.

"There's something hidden here. An artifact …"

Laughter, brittle and thunderous.

There is nothing here but us. The same hand lifted her face, tilting it left and right. *She'll do*, the child said.

Another one was prying open her hand, staring at the disk, lifting it to find the burn-marks underneath.

Is she not House?

No, the first child said. *She has nothing of the House in her.*

Magic again, foraging in her guts until she thought she'd puke—but she was held upright as surely as a fly in a spider's web.

A long, measured look between them, a conversation she wasn't privy to. Thorns. Children of thorns. She didn't know who they were, but she could guess.

"Did he send you?" Aurore asked.

A head, cocked her way like that of a bird.

Who?

"Asmodeus."

She ought to know he'd never let her go, even if Thuan had a moment of weakness where she was concerned.

A sound like branches shaken in the wind. She realized with a shock that it was laughter.

We send ourselves, child. The bindings holding her loosened a fraction: she tried to lift a foot, and still couldn't. *For the good of the House.*

"I don't understand," Aurore said. "What do you want with me?"

She already knew some of the answer—it was highly unlikely they were going to give her a kiss and a pat—but information was information.

Another sigh, halfway between the wind and the creak of parquet floors.

The House is weak.

Too weak.

The wards need blood to be replenished.

Blood and magic.

"I don't have any magic," Aurore said, trying to control her rising panic.

They wanted to take her apart to sustain the House. *Not this. Not this death.*

A gentle tracing of fingertips on her hand, beneath the disk.

Fire, the child whispered.

Khi fire. The tiger. The world, burning. The lines under her feet, springing to life as she ran.

"That's nothing," she said. "Not even a whisper of what you'd need."

Laughter, dry and amused. Asmodeus's laughter.

We're the judges of what we need, child.

And hands on her wrists and around her neck, tightening.

No. Aurore pushed with her right hand, trying to raise the disk she held in one hand.

"I'm under your lord's protection." It hurt to admit to that, but pride could come later. Survival first. "He said I shouldn't be touched!"

A pause. The child who had a hand around her neck didn't loosen it, but the other one—the first one who had spoken—looked at her as if puzzled.

You're hurting.

Aurore swallowed the angry retort that came to mind, and forced herself to be calm.

"You're holding me."

That's not what we meant, the first child said. Its hand rested on Aurore's chest, just below where the disk had been. *It hurts you, to admit you're beholden to the House. Why?*

Aurore debated lying, then gave up.

"It's not my House. It's not my home. Please. I just want to go home to see my family. To make sure they're not hurt."

I have a city to burn, Dân Chay had said.

Cassiopée. Marianne. She wasn't even sure they were alive. But if they weren't … then she'd track down Dân Chay and Morningstar and burn them to the ground.

That same creaking laughter.

I like her. Always looking to protect her own, and never bowing down to anyone or anything.

Like doesn't come into it. If we spare her, how will we replenish the House?

A pause, then. One of them turned to her with fluid inhumanity.

Tell me, mortal. Would you give your life, to protect what's yours?

Aurore, startled, said, "Of course."

The child nodded, with grim satisfaction. *Then they will, too.*

The dependents? another child asked.

A hiss. *We can't touch them. We've never taken from our own.*

Why shouldn't we?

He *said we couldn't.* A hiss. *That we aren't like the other Houses. That we* care.

He. Asmodeus. Caring. Aurore smothered a bitter laugh.

"He doesn't care." Her voice burned like acid. "He's never cared."

The empty place on her chest, where the disk had been, felt like an open wound.

Heads of wood and twigs turned in inhuman unison.

She doesn't know.

"Of course I do!" Aurore yelled. No House-bound had ever paid any attention to her or what she wanted—was it any wonder the House wouldn't either? "I was with him. He was the one who gave me the disk. He only ever thinks of himself, of how he can use and hurt people for his own pleasure." And, more viciously, without a shred of hesitation, "You're the same. You're all the same, all the Houses, all the House-bound. You take and take and grind it all into magic to feed yourselves. You're all the same! Why wouldn't you take your own?"

A silence. She realized, then, that they'd all turned to her, their faces frozen in that same mildly curious expression, as if watching a dog walking upright on two legs. They could crush her in a heartbeat. Her brain caught up, then, clamped her lips shut. But it was too late. The child closest to her wrapped its fingers around her neck—their tips, resting, lightly, on her larynx, a reminder it needed only to move to crush it. Fear choked her. To die, bound to Hawthorn …

A child said, *The House is dying. What matters is that some survive, does it not? That is our mission. The strong always walk on the bones of the weak.*

A hiss, from the child holding Aurore. *They rely on us.*

They have given their lives to the House before. How is this different?

Another silence. The hand on her throat tightened, fingers prickling her skin. Her entire heartbeat seemed to have moved upwards, to the point of contact.

At length, one of the children said, *It is agreed, then. They will replenish the wards of the House, as needed. Everything will be as it was before* he *came.*

And what of her?

The first child turned towards her. *Ancestors, if you'd ever felt like watching over me, this is the time.* Its eyes were two pits of night—holes into which she was drawn, to fall endlessly into darkness. There was nothing in them but hunger—endless and never sated, a burning need to sustain itself at the expense of everything else. They were going to take her too: an appetizer to their main meal, a pleasant distraction of unfamiliar magic injected into the House.

I have seen your like before. The child's mouth moved: a smile, though it revealed nothing but more branches, without teeth or tongue to sustain its speech. *For what you have given us, a reward, mortal.*

And, reaching out, it pushed her out of the other child's embrace—again and again, driving her towards the ruined building—until she stumbled on the wrecks of the steps and fell towards the charred, debris-covered ground. She expected to hit it flat, but instead it opened to receive her, and she fell into the earth like a grave, as rubble and gravel fell in a rain to cover her body.

Aurore pushed back, but it was holding her fast—branches and thorns climbing her arms and legs, weighing her down and tying her until any movement became painfully impossible. Over her, in the rapidly closing sliver of darkened sky, bent the child. Its fingers rested, lightly, over her eyes—and then, before she could even draw a breath to scream, it drove their points in.

Pain transfixed her, spreading from the arch of her eyebrows through her head, and then into her entire body, and for a moment she was forced from her body, her consciousness expanding to encompass the entire House—the earth and the buildings and all the broken things, the broken people it collected, the distant, cruel dreams of the sleeping Asmodeus, the worry of Thuan sorting out people in hospital—and then she was back, but her eyes felt gummed shut.

No, not gummed shut.

Sewn shut. There was no pain—just the feeling of hundreds of pinpricks in her eyelids. That made it worse. She'd have clawed at them, if her hands could move, but these were held, too.

The child withdrew its fingers from her eyes, and laid them onto her lips, briefly—and then on her forehead, as if anointing her with blood instead of holy water.

Breathe, it said, and her mouth moved of its own accord.

She inhaled only dirt and the taste of her own blood—

she was choking, struggling to find a way, any way, to breathe and not have her throat close up.

Marianne. Cassiopée.

Everything fuzzed and went still. And, in that moment when she hung at the doors of the Courts of Hell, something rose within her. It was warmth and power—something that filled her limbs and lungs with pure, sweet, liquid fire. It was embers in winter, water in summer: everything she'd ever thirsted for, a feeling that stretched in her chest until it became pure bliss.

The child withdrew its fingers from her face, and the thorns that held her eyes shut broke. She opened them, gummed with blood, saw it as if from a great distance, flicking its hand over the earth of the House. Something fell, watered the debris and muddy expanse underfoot. The thorns on her arms and legs withdrew, one by one—they left trails of fire on her limbs, but she didn't care. She pulled herself up with the fire coursing through her, feeling as though a wave of her hands would send the world reeling.

"What ... did ... you ... do?" Her voice came hoarse and painful, as if she'd been screaming her vocal cords raw.

Again, that expression that wasn't quite a smile, stretching across skeletal, hollow cheeks like a thicket of thorn-trees.

Gave you the power you craved.

"You ... You made me a House dependent."

Aurore's voice was shaking. But it didn't feel like Harrier, didn't feel like the link to the House. More like the one time she'd inhaled angel-breath, using it to carry Cassiopée—except ten times, a hundred times more powerful. This was a rising power that threatened to drown her. She lifted a hand, winced when an invisible wind ruffled the lawn in response.

Of course not, the child said. *That requires consent.*

And this did not.

You wanted the power to protect what was yours. Its voice was almost gentle. *It's in you now.*

The old legend. The artifact that gave someone the power of a Fallen. Only it wasn't an artifact. It was the House.

She stepped out of the ruined building, turned. In the debris was a deep, charred imprint of her body; and thorns, sprouting from it. The same thorns which had left their scars on her body. The House, driving itself deep into her.

Your life is that of the House now. Your power is vested in it.

Aurore took one, two faltering steps, and leaned against the building for support. It was warm and pliant like human skin; and she heard a panicked human heartbeat within it.

Her heartbeat.

She all but leaped away from it. All she'd ever wanted, and it was a poisoned, barbed gift.

"The House. You mean I'm one of you."

A casual shrug. *Not quite. Think of yourself as … a scout. A seed or spores cast on the wind. The questing filaments of a fungus.*

Another of the children said, *The House is dying and weak. Our salvation may lie in putting down roots elsewhere, to find the blood and magic we need to survive. This is where you come in.*

We may not leave the House, but you can.

"And you want me to help you?" Why should she?

We're not giving you a choice. As we said—your life is that of the House now. If we die, you die. But every time you sate your hunger—so will we.

"I'm not helping Hawthorn. I'm not helping Asmodeus."

A smile that was all thorns and teeth woven out of sickly white petals.

Asmodeus isn't us. And neither are we what you think of as Hawthorn. We are simply ... the power beneath it. Not the faction. The magic.

"I don't understand," Aurore said, chilled.

Another smile. *It means do what you want with the magic that we have given you. Because, no matter what you do, you remain tied to us. Your life is our life. Your hunger is ours, and what you take to survive will become ours.* A shrug. *Do what you want, with our gift.*

"Do what I want? Even if that involves going up against Asmodeus?"

Laughter. *That would be unwise. But likewise, we will make sure that he or his don't interfere with what you're doing.*

Aurore looked at the building with the imprint of her body, still feeling the heartbeat that coursed through the walls. Her heartbeat. She wasn't sure what she was anymore. They'd said their hunger was hers; which meant she'd need to feed them. Which meant blood and magic—but did the price matter, if she had the magic she wanted, and could use it for her own purposes?

"I want to go home." She hated herself for her weakness. "I want to help my people defend against a fire spirit. Are you really telling me you won't stop me, if I walk out of Hawthorn?"

The children moved to stare at her, the ground itself rumbling under her.

The House is dying. We *are dying. Of course we won't stop you, if you're going elsewhere to find sustenance.*

Aurore opened her mouth to say she wasn't going to find sustenance, but the sight of all the children staring at her with naked hunger stopped her.

We won't stop you. On the contrary. We'll come with you.

17
Survival

Philippe and Isabelle helped dig people out.

There seemed no end to the debris in the inn, or to those trapped inside. When they finally lined everyone up in the common room, Philippe took in a sharp, deep breath. He'd known most of these people—Sébastien from the docks, Aunt Vy from the bakery, Lucie from the butcher's. The waiters, the patrons—everyone was gone, as casually as if someone had snapped their fingers and snuffed them out. Javier was sitting very still in a corner of the devastated room: he'd helped dig in silence, and was now staring at nothing. Isabelle, at length, walked to him and started a whispered, low-key conversation whose tones were anger and grief and despair. Philippe clamped his lips on a sharp rejoinder about consorting with the Houses. That conversation would have to wait.

Overhead, the sky was still streaked with smoke. Tade came back with shrouds to lay over the dead, and with Frankie, who worked in the inn.

"Half the buildings are on fire. Scattered coals, I think. We'll need to organize some kind of firefighting force. And search parties for any survivors."

He stared at Philippe as if he was expecting input. The thought was terrifying. He was an ex-Immortal, an ex-enforcer who'd spent most of his life on tightly circumscribed missions before he was thrown out of the heavenly courts. Such a task would have been for Hoa Phong or Princess Liên, except that Liên was beleaguered, and Hoa Phong was a fighter, not a leader of people.

But then, neither was he.

He took a deep, shaking breath, opened his mouth to say he had to see Grandmother Olympe and the aunts—and then *something* bounced against the spells he'd drawn around la Goutte d'Or. Not fast, or in anger, more like a quiet raking of claws, a slow, determined digging. *No.*

"Wait here," he said to Tade, and ran out.

Outside the inn, it smelled of smoke and charred meat, and the air was a heavy mass of ashes and particles hanging in the air. He was breathing hard by the time he reached the southern border of the community.

Beyond the border—beyond the weave he'd drawn and its protection—the devastation was worse: pulverized cobblestones; people's corpses hanging from lampposts and windows; wrought-iron railings flattened as if by some enormous hand; the smoke so thick it hid the ruins of flattened buildings.

He hadn't meant the weave to keep people out—just the *khi* fire. But people were stopping nevertheless: and something had formed where he'd drawn the weave. A spreading pool of pure *khi* fire, a mass of swirling red and orange reminiscent of flames—and luminous orange threads ran to it, following the cracks between the cobblestones.

And he could feel, even from here, the protections he'd built struggling to contain it. A siege, of a sort. When his protections gave out—his fragmentary, hastily drawn protections, because there were so few people here who could wield the *khi* currents and he, Hoa Phong and Isabelle had had to cover such a large surface—they'd suffer the same fate as the Houses: a blast that would make everything so far look small and benign.

He knelt, gently weaving *khi* water and *khi* wood around himself as a protection. His fingers brushed, carefully, the surface of the pool—and darkness bloomed, hungering for shadows to devour. Within him, the shadows of Silverspires' curse stirred. He kept them contained—barely, because the Houses had started this, because they'd tortured a spirit into their perfect weapon, and never considered what would happen if he slipped their control.

The *khi* fire pulsed under his fingers. He wasn't sure what made him look up, but when he did, there was a man standing there, looking at him—or rather, half of one, because there were threads where his legs should have been, a mass of them rising from the ground and congealing together until the red-orange turned as dark as crusted blood. He was Annamite, in that uncertain ground between middle and old age, with gray hair tied in a topknot, and the robes of a scholar loosely hanging over his thin frame. Tanned skin, hands with long fingers stained with vermilion ink—no, not ink, but dripping blood. His blood—pinprick wounds on every finger, and further cuts on his face and neck, long and stretched. The marks of a whip.

"Immortal," the man said.

His shape shivered and wavered, and for a moment stripes covered his skin, as they did Aunt Ha's.

"Dân Chay." Philippe bowed his head, slowly and carefully—never taking his eyes off the man. Both because he didn't trust him, and because averting his gaze would have been a statement of respect he didn't feel. "My name is Philippe."

"Is it, now?" A wide, fanged smile. "It wasn't always so, was it?"

"It's what I go by now."

Philippe thought of Hoa Phong, and her questions—her offer of a home, when all was over, where people used his old name. It rang hollow to him now, a rusty thing that hadn't been used in decades. The name of a stranger.

"As you wish." Dân Chay smiled. "You're smart, but you can't hold out forever."

"And you suggest I yield?" Philippe spread his hands as the pressure of Dân Chay against his spells flared up sharp and unbearable. "You'll kill everyone if I do. That's not much inducement."

They stood in a widening circle of silence—Houseless self-preservation instincts held strong, and people were cautiously, casually moving away.

Dân Chay didn't appear interested in the other mortals, those outside the boundaries. Fire, Philippe thought, and watched the *khi* currents on the streets. Everything was spent and shriveled on Dân Chay's side: a hint of fire; there were the orange threads that formed his body and tied him to the ground. But all the other *khi* currents were gone, with only fragments remaining. *Khi* fire on its own could burn, but it required more fuel to create a large conflagration. To really set off a massive fire or an explosion, Dân Chay had to burn, not only the *khi* fire itself, but also all the other *khi* elements. Which meant he couldn't do that from his side, because there was nothing left. Not that Philippe would have gone over his own protections, because he guessed that even in the desert of *khi* currents he was standing in, Dân Chay could probably set off small fires—say, on a person—on *khi* fire alone.

Philippe could guess what kind of conflagration had so badly depleted the *khi* currents all over the city.

"You burned *all* the Houses," he said flatly.

He'd have said he was sad, but it would be a lie. The Houses had brought it on themselves. And yet … The Houses had always been there, to struggle against. The idea that they could be hurt—that they could be almost annihilated …

"Almost all the Houses," Dân Chay said.

Somehow Philippe didn't think he'd spared anyone out of the goodness of his heart. He might have done so, once—no, he wouldn't have, because he was the tiger, and all he did was devour those who strayed into the darkness.

"Didn't have the strength?" he asked.

An expansive shrug. Dân Chay was taking his measure, as if trying to see what he had before him.

"I struck … a bargain," he said. "For the time being. But bargains only last as long as the lives of those who've made them." He stopped, then, sniffed the air. "You have a friend here, don't you?"

Isabelle? No—why would Dân Chay care about Isabelle, an ordinary mortal with no particular House affiliations? He had to mean Hoa Phong.

"She's busy," Philippe said carefully. Undoing the damage Dân Chay had wrought.

The *khi* fire pulsed under his fingers, gently, carefully. Looking for a way past his spells of protection.

Dân Chay laughed. "You should run."

"Because I didn't protect you?"

"Because you stink of the Houses. You did their bidding once, didn't you?"

"You mean—when they captured and used me during the war?"

A low growl. The threads flashed darker—a shade of crimson closer to blood.

"I know your kind. The conscripts. You could have stopped it. You could have stood against it. Did you, Immortal?"

"Don't be absurd."

How could he? They'd all died, one by one—Ai Linh and Hoang and An Man, and all the other Annamites taken from their homeland. They'd only have died sooner—strung up as examples—if they had rebelled. He opened his mouth, and then stopped. Because he had been taken care of in an abstract way—as manpower, as cannon fodder—but he hadn't been in a cage. He closed his eyes, searching for the words. He'd always known that he and the others had been, in their own ways, complicit in the war. Following orders wasn't a defense, and nor was dying an absolution.

Dân Chay smiled. "All acts carry the seeds of their own burning, Immortal."

"And the people here? The Houseless? What crime did they commit?"

Dân Chay shook his head. "This isn't about guilt. This is about how it feels to dance on the ashes." He growled again. The elegant mask was slipping, showing, not the face of a tiger or a predator, but the same casual arrogance as the Houses. "Once, long ago, I listened to a human who talked me out of slaughter—who tricked me and burned me. Never again."

He stretched, and to Philippe's horror his spells of protections started to crack—*khi* fire pouring through a growing gap in the weave, and threads slowly, tentatively, spreading at his feet, blindly questing like snakes.

"Philippe!"

It was Isabelle, Father Javier and Frankie—and striding ahead of them, Tade, rolling up the sleeves of his shirt. His mnemonic tattoo was glowing with the same rippling light it had back in the tavern, except that it was now spreading to his entire arm.

"Get away from him," Tade said curtly.

"You don't understand—" Philippe said.

"I understand very well."

Tade said something at the back of his throat—Philippe didn't understand the word, but the insult was all too clear. Isabelle was kneeling a little further up the street, hurriedly tracing spells of protection to make another barrier before Dân Chay's *khi* fire could flow further inwards. But the spells were failing, and they were too close.

"Move back!" he screamed, and ran.

Things happened too fast, or too slow. The threads of fire hit his spell of protection, again and again, in a single place. It snapped. *Khi* wood and *khi* water flared, flailing wildly like the limbs of a decapitated animal—fire poured in, swallowing the other elements, the threads growing larger and fatter as it did, pulsing faster and faster. Philippe was already running, and so was Isabelle. She stopped, panting, in front of a bakery where the baker and her workers were attempting to pick glass from croissants and steamed buns; knelt, tracing hurried lines to block the flow of fire. It hit the first, shaking line, and broke against it. But the fire wasn't going to be held back for long. Not unless she could reinforce it, and she wouldn't be fast enough—she didn't have the experience.

He had to help her.

Philippe tried to follow her, but threads wrapped around his ankles, rooting him to the floor.

"I think not," Dân Chay said coldly.

Think think. He wasn't dead or burning, which meant Dân Chay couldn't strike at him yet. No, that wasn't it. Because Dân Chay wanted as large a fire as possible, and that meant waiting for enough *khi* currents to be absorbed. Waiting for enough fuel for his fire. What he'd claimed wasn't enough yet. Which meant they had time before that happened, but Philippe didn't know how much.

All right. If he couldn't help Isabelle directly, he could buy time for her. The explosion wasn't going to happen automatically: once he had gathered enough *khi* elements, Dân Chay would have to consciously trigger it. Which meant any distraction to Dân Chay gave Isabelle time to finish her barrier of protection, and make sure that Dân Chay's fire didn't go deeper into la Goutte d'Or.

If they could pull this off, Dân Chay was going to blow up the area between Philippe's broken protections and

Isabelle's new ones; but at least it wouldn't be the entire community.

Small comfort, but he'd take it with the desperation of a drowning man.

Dân Chay was walking towards Philippe, but Tade and Frankie interposed themselves. Frankie grabbed Dân Chay's arms, and Tade threw a punch—a low, fast jab aimed at the boundary between threads and torso. Light rippled; for a moment a larger, shadowy form congealed in the air. There was a sound like taut guitar strings thrumming—and threads snapped. Dân Chay shook his head. He lifted his hands, and a mass of fire grabbed Tade and Frankie and flung them aside, into a heap of debris. Tade rose, grimacing, with a hand on his chest. That odd rippling light covered him entirely, throwing the lines of his ribs into sharp focus. Even from where he was, Philippe could see that Frankie's skull had caved in, and that half her face was a bloodied mess.

Isabelle looked from Philippe to her incomplete spell.

"Don't," he said. "Wasted time." He hacked at the threads holding him with *khi* water, watching them shrivel and fall away, but when he tried to walk they grabbed him again. "Finish your protections."

He'd gone maybe three paces. Between the old spells and Isabelle's new ones, the *khi* currents were still being consumed. The threads pulsed faster and faster: the air was getting taut, as if they were moments from a monsoon.

Not good.

When he looked up again, Javier was standing in front of Dân Chay. The priest was shivering, his hair singed by the blast, his clerical collar askew, his red and silver uniform torn to shreds. He must have inhaled the contents of an artifact, because he swirled, faintly, with the light of Fallen magic.

"Javier!"

He was going to be slaughtered. Nothing in the Houses had stood against Dân Chay. They must have died in their hundreds, their spells and wards useless against the very weapon they'd forged.

Behind Javier, Isabelle was still kneeling, drawing the final parts of her spell. Philippe could see that she was forcing herself not to look up; not to worry about Javier. She finished, trembling, her weave. The *khi* currents she'd brought together shimmered and hardened, and Dân Chay's *khi* fire hissed away from them.

Philippe let out a breath he hadn't even been aware of holding. Safe. The community was safe, for the time being.

Dân Chay cocked his head at Javier.

"Silverspires," he said. His laughter was cruel. "Always on the wrong side of the divide. Were you even alive in the war, little man?"

Javier's face was set. "You know I wasn't."

"A child, then. Out of my way." Low laughter. "They're the Houseless, the insignificant. Why aren't you looking to your own House? That's what your kind always does."

Javier looked exhausted. "I'm a little tired of generalizations."

"Try being tortured and carved into pieces by two Houses in the name of power. You might mind them less, then. Oh, but I forget—you belong to one of these Houses. Morningstar's House." It was spat with such venom that Javier recoiled, and in that moment Dân Chay reached out, and seized him. Javier struggled to push off a grip like iron. "You're pathetic. There's nothing to you at all, is there? Just hollow masks."

Philippe managed to snap one thread holding him, as three more reformed. The *khi* fire was building, between the broken old protections and the new ones Isabelle had just finished. Everyone in that area—which included him and Tade and Javier and many of the onlookers—was going to die when the *khi* currents around them combusted. He tried to gesture to Tade and Javier, *move back*, and Tade nodded, ushering people back behind Isabelle.

Dân Chay was getting closer. Philippe pulled at the threads binding him with a growing sense of desperation, and they snapped. Before they could reform, he was running for Isabelle, making a last, desperate leap towards the meager shelter she'd made.

But Dân Chay's hands grabbed him, lifted him like a rag doll—a brief vision of the street upside down, of Javier running for Isabelle, grabbing Tade on the way. A swirl of fire beneath him, spinning and growing larger and larger.

But then the world spun and cracked, and he hit the ground. He pulled himself up, shaking. *Khi* fire was everywhere, a trembling wash that stung his skin: a prelude to a fire that would soon tear him apart. Dân Chay was fighting Javier—not with fire or with any kind of magic, but simply trying to beat him back. The light of Fallen magic limned Javier as he grappled, desperately, with the other man.

Javier shouted to Philippe, "Get behind the line, now!"

There was a noise. Distant thunder, he would have said, but it was exhausted and faint. The earth rumbled under them, and a flock of something rose into the sky. Not smoke, but a cloud of birds—of hawks, rising in the dark heavens and forlornly screeching with a sound that was almost heartbreaking.

Dân Chay stopped laughing, then, and it was the roar of flames.

"Finally," he said. "Even the great, powerful things enter their death throes."

Javier, exhausted, took his moment to grab Philippe and frogmarch him behind Isabelle's lines.

Dân Chay was still staring at the sky when the mass of *khi* fire ignited, and the entire world flashed orange and blinding white.

His voice came from the morass of light—an amused, angry growl directed at Philippe.

"Pathetic, Immortal. You do nothing but prolong your agony. But if that's the way you want to play, then by all means. I'll take your home street by street and building by building, and person by person."

When Philippe opened his eyes again, Dân Chay was gone. The threads remained, pushing at Isabelle's fragmentary weaves. Not a pool, because there was almost no *khi* fire left. In between, in the zone of fire, the cobblestones had been pulverized, and a cloud of dust still hung over the street. No people—they'd all run from the devastation. Twisted lampposts, broken windows and teetering buildings. Debris had been blasted out with the force of bullets. A few had struck Frankie and blood dripped lazily from her wounds—a reflex action, for it was utterly clear she was dead.

"What was that?" Tade asked.

Hawks, dying. Philippe said, slowly, carefully—because

he'd seen it only once before, a long time ago, and he'd painstakingly taught himself that it couldn't, wouldn't, ever be repeated rather than endlessly be disappointed.

"That was House Harrier. I think it's going to die really soon."

Dying. Scoured away by *khi* fire. If their own lives hadn't been on the line, he'd have been almost impressed. Almost tempted to cheer.

"Houses can't just *go*," Javier said, shivering.

He let go of Philippe, sat down heavily on the ground. He was breathing fast—faster and faster. Going into shock, and no wonder.

"Isabelle, can you take care of him?"

"I'm not the designated House person," Isabelle snapped. "Javier? Javier, come on."

Philippe stared at the zone beyond Isabelle's defenses. All the *khi* currents, gone, and even the fire was now a paler shadow of its former self. Nothing left outside their boundaries that could burn. But it wouldn't last. The *khi* currents in this area and in the rest of Paris would grow back. The threads would have something to feed on again. And Dân Chay would be back, with enough power to break Isabelle's weave.

And the truth of it—the naked truth—was that they couldn't hold him at bay.

He'd lost Aurore.

Thuan had been tired, running on too little sleep and accumulating worries like they were building blocks to something better. But it was no excuse for the words that had come out of his mouth. Or that his first thought had been to give orders as if she were a servant—he shouldn't even have done it to a House dependent. Was it better than what Asmodeus had done, tearing her from her life and sending her into Harrier like some kind of sacrificial lamb?

It was his House: he could order the guards to track her down, to bring her back and set her to work in their much-depleted hospital, or to imprison her again in the cells, as she'd been before Asmodeus sent her to Harrier. Asmodeus or Phyranthe would say she was a trespasser on Hawthorn grounds and deserved what she got. Thuan was sick of the discourse.

What harm could she do, anyway, being Houseless? Better to let her go. Asmodeus would have had plans for her—he could take those plans and stuff them. It was high time they stopped using people like pawns.

Ai Nhi had come back into the room visibly disappointed that she'd missed "all the fun", and was now fussing around Asmodeus—who, fortunately, was still unconscious. Thuan watched her for a while. It was almost restful compared to the growing list of his worries.

"Unka Thuan?"

"Yes?" Thuan said.

Ai Nhi watched Asmodeus. "What's wrong with him?"

"Oh. He's very tired, child. He had to help a lot of people in a very short time, and he needs to rest." If Thuan closed his eyes, he'd see the hole again, and the blood spattering on Asmodeus's face, from the trees shaken in the wind, and hear Asmodeus's voice, flat and utterly devoid of hope. "And he got very scared."

Ai Nhi coiled in the air in dragon shape, and nuzzled closer to Asmodeus.

"I thought Unka Asmodeus never got scared." Her eyes were thoughtful. "Even in the bad place."

Thuan jerked from his tea. "The bad place? The cells," he said, in a voice that he hoped was flat. "Child."

Ai Nhi scrunched her face. "He said he understood why I'd done it—the ice and Mélanie. That nothing more would happen to me, and he'd keep me safe." Her voice trailed off. "I said you and Auntie Ly were going to do that, and he got angry and said you'd been doing a terrible job of it."

A terrible job of it. Oh, Asmodeus. Typical.

A thoughtful, scrunched-up face. "He's scary, but he's okay. Mostly."

Ai Nhi laid her doll by Asmodeus's side. Thuan tried not to choke on his tea.

"I don't think he needs the doll," he said, finally.

Ai Nhi looked crestfallen.

"All right," Thuan said. It had been a long, bad day, and he really didn't feel like indulging Asmodeus's vanity. "Just don't let him see you laugh when he wakes up."

He went back, with a sigh, to the report about their depleted food reserves—which was like trying to balance a threadbare cupboard with a host of children lacking clothes. The only good news was that an emergency team sent into the armory had found nothing but crates of dusty weapons, and no hint of secondary fire.

There had also been a cursory investigation into the explosion, which had everyone from Fallen to dragons flummoxed. Something to do with *khi* fire, which no one thought would recur, if only because there was no *khi* fire left to burn. It wasn't very reassuring, and *that* was an understatement.

Thuan looked up. There was some kind of commotion beyond the doors of the room—which wasn't unusual—but the air was saturated with the smell of curdled brine.

He got up, threw open the door, and saw Phyranthe.

She was making her way through their improvised ward, carrying an exhausted, bloodied dragon on her shoulders like a scarf. Phyranthe didn't look much better herself: one arm hung loose, her face and arms were covered in myriad cuts, her steps were slow and faltering, and as Thuan watched a flare of *khi* water wrapped itself around her, coming from the dragon on her shoulder—not to heal her, but to give her the little strength she needed to go on.

Vinh Ly. Phyranthe was carrying Vinh Ly the same way Asmodeus had carried Aurore.

Thuan was out and walking through the crowd before he could think clearly, the dependents moving out of his way like drops of water from a fire. He thought it was because he was losing control of his dragon shape again, but his mind was icy cold, his body fully human, chafing against the constraints of the Hawthorn swallowtail jacket and aching to take flight.

"My lord," Phyranthe said. She'd stopped, trembling. They faced each other across a line of broken tiles. Her lips curled up: it would have been a smile, but there was too much blood and pain. "As I promised you—I won't kill her."

And she collapsed like a felled tree, with Vinh Ly on top of her.

*

Thuan leaned against the door jamb, watching Vinh Ly and Phyranthe. They'd put both of them in one of the smallest rooms: a glorified broom cupboard hastily emptied of its contents, one half filled with rubble, and the other crammed with two metal-frame beds.

They really shouldn't have been together, but of course Iaris was the one who made the decisions about hospital beds. She'd said something about how it would look to the dependents of the House, and Thuan had been too bone-weary to even react.

Mind you, in her current state, Phyranthe wasn't going to be harming anyone.

Vinh Ly was healing with the usual speed of dragons, though her wounds had looked nasty.

"Cuts and bruises, and two shattered ribs," Sang said, by Thuan's side. "And really nasty burns on her chest. Looks like flying masonry hit her when the House blew up," she added, in answer to Thuan's unspoken question. "There's some Fallen magic on her, but it was used to staunch blood flow. It looks to have been cast in a hurry."

They were walking through the House, trying to get away from rubble and debris, and wondering if they were going to make it at all. Healing each other.

I won't kill her.

Thuan watched Phyranthe. She was unconscious, her closed eyes dark against the extreme pallor of her face. Her chest barely moved, though from time to time she'd scream, a primal sound that seemed to remove all the air from the room and take root in her chest.

"And her?"

Sang sighed. "*Khi* fire."

"There isn't any on her."

"Aftermath," Sang said, curtly. "She's weak and quite close to death's door. It might kill her." She sounded grimly satisfied.

Thuan exhaled, slowly. He looked at Phyranthe again, and at the sleeping Vinh Ly.

"Can you heal her?" he asked.

"Your Majesty." Sang stared at him, shocked. "Surely . . ."

It wasn't like he had much of a choice. He could have let her suffer and die for Vinh Ly's sake, but what would that have made of him?

"Surely we're better than this? We are," Thuan said, more sharply than he'd intended.

"That's not what I meant." Sang's voice was sharp.

Thuan didn't budge. "I'm not abandoning Vinh Ly. I'll find another way. But this? This isn't it. Also, you forget—Vinh Ly had already started healing her."

"Because she knew it was the only way she'd get to safety."

Thuan said nothing, merely stared at her. At length, Sang nodded.

"As you wish," she said, with ill-grace.

Her healing was quick, and perfunctory: smoothing out threads of *khi* water and *khi* wood, and looping them around Phyranthe's body—the threads she wove sinking beneath the pale, bruised skin as if swallowed by it. When she was done, she bowed to Thuan, and left without a word. Her anger at him was palpable.

"An interesting strategy," Iaris said, from behind him.

Thuan didn't jump out of his skin, because he'd had plenty of practice at seeming impassive.

"Iaris," he said, wearily. "What is it this time?"

A shrug. "I wanted to admire your way of dealing with your problems," Iaris said, but she was so exhausted her usual venom didn't make it into her voice. "Madeleine was looking for you."

A few paces from Iaris, and looking decidedly ill at ease, was Madeleine d'Aubin, the House's alchemist. She had one arm in a sling, but the worry on her face seemed permanently etched there.

"My lord. There's something you should see. In the laboratory."

What Madeleine referred to as "the laboratory" turned out not to be the actual laboratory of the House—which was in a wing completely blocked off by rubble—but the annexe they'd opened to store those charged artifacts dependents had managed to rescue.

As they walked to it, Madeleine said, "Hm, my lord?"

"Yes? "

"Can … Can I ask how he is?"

Thuan stared at her. Iaris had disappeared: she'd clearly just been there long enough to make sure Madeleine found Thuan.

"Lord Asmodeus," Madeleine said.

There was something in her gaze he couldn't interpret, a mixture of fear of Asmodeus and genuine worry.

"He's fine," Thuan said, lying through his teeth. "He's been pushing himself too hard, that's all. He needs to sleep."

"Oh." Madeleine looked relieved. "I'm glad to hear that."

She and Asmodeus had some kind of rapport he wasn't privy to. When he asked why she'd been raised to the vacant post of alchemist, Asmodeus's only answer had been a curt, "She deserves it", that invited no further discussion.

Thuan hesitated. "You can go see him later."

Asmodeus would probably bite her head off for her concern, but she must have known that.

Madeleine nodded, and looked away from him.

The laboratory was a cavernous room that must have been one of the secondary pantries. On its sagging, rotting wooden shelves, bags of flour mingled with charged mirrors and knives, and a faint, electric smell of angel-breath saturated the air.

It was also full of roots.

Vegetation had climbed from the floor—slender branches bursting from between the cracked blue-and-white tiles, clinging to the faded wallpaper, questing until they'd stabbed through the shelves, and on upwards, pausing only to grab indiscriminately charged artifacts and cardboard boxes of eggs. The top of the shelves was festooned with white, sickly flowers, and the branches were so thick on the lower shelves Thuan could barely make out the items beneath. The flowers shone, faintly, with Fallen magic.

The *khi* currents in the room were going haywire: Thuan couldn't even pick them apart, and magic wasn't his strong suit. He had people to do that for him, though, nowadays.

And the strongest and most experienced of them was Vinh Ly.

"Explain," he said, curtly, to Madeleine. And, poking his head out of the door and gesturing to the first dependent he could find, "Get me Vinh Ly if she's conscious. Lan if she's not."

"I don't know." Madeleine took a deep, shaking breath. "I was working there." She pointed to the small table in the center of the room, on which crates of apples and pears had been pushed aside to make way for an opened mirror shimmering with Fallen breath. "There was a sound like … paper unfolding, and next thing I knew the branches were growing all over the shelves."

Thuan stared at the room. "They've stopped now. They didn't touch you?"

Madeleine shook her head. "I ran out."

Which was eminently sensible, and he couldn't fault her for it.

"Good."

Thuan walked into the room carefully. Behind him, Madeleine breathed in sharply, but didn't intend to stop him.

Nothing moved. He knelt by the lowest shelves, stared at the mass of thorns and branches and withered leaves—took a deep breath and reached out. Hundreds of tiny invisible spikes immediately pierced his hand. He withdrew it with a curse, staring at the blood beading on the palm of his hand. The wounds were already closing.

"Clearly I'm not allowed to touch," he said aloud, more for Madeleine's benefit than for his.

"My lord."

It was Vinh Ly, accompanied by Mia. She looked much as she always had, stern and unbending and unbowed.

Thuan fought the urge to hug her, which would have looked bad, but more importantly earned him an ear-splitting rebuke in full earshot of Madeleine.

"You wanted to see me."

Thuan said, "I'm glad you survived."

Vinh Ly snorted. "One advantage of being a prisoner is that I'm not allowed to escape by dying."

Mia bristled. Thuan said, "No quips. Can you take a look at the *khi* currents here? I want to know if it's dangerous."

Vinh Ly was already kneeling by Thuan's side. She looped, methodically, *khi* wood and *khi* water, cocking her head.

At last, Vinh Ly stood, thoughtfully. She shook her hands—droplets of *khi* currents clung to them for a moment before vanishing in the maelstrom underneath.

"Not dangerous, per se."

"But?"

Vinh Ly's face was grim. "You're not going to like it."

In their hospital-room-cum-office, Asmodeus was awake and sitting up, propped on pillows. Ai Nhi had pulled a chair over, stuffed it with enough cushions to sit at his height, and was currently watching, enraptured, as Asmodeus demonstrated how to peel an apple. Though, by the sounds of it, the conversation was about skinning, and not about apples at all.

"Blood is going to get in the way," Ai Nhi said, with a frown.

"That's why you have to be careful. And keep the blade sharp." Asmodeus angled the knife so that it caught the daylight. "Blunt instruments only lead to grief."

"Asmodeus," Thuan said, more sharply than he intended. And, to Ai Nhi, "This isn't appropriate."

Asmodeus raised an eyebrow. "Extremely appropriate, I would say. How else will she defend herself?"

Thuan closed his mouth on the most obvious answer.

"Well, you can resume your ... lessons later. With the permission of the child's aunt, obviously. Ai Nhi."

Ai Nhi gave an exasperated sigh. "Adults shouldn't have all the fun, Unka Thuan."

For various definitions of "fun", which most definitely didn't match Thuan's. Thuan waited until she was back with the bodyguards and the door was tightly shut before he pulled another chair to Asmodeus's bedside.

Asmodeus took off his glasses, and carefully wiped them clean on an embroidered handkerchief.

"You're upset."

His face was sharp again, but Thuan wasn't fooled. The way the cushions behind him were set, Ai Nhi had helped. Which meant he'd let her. Which also meant he was still exhausted and ragged, or he'd have sent her packing. He'd certainly never hesitated to before.

"We have a problem," Thuan said.

"Just one? At last count, there were several."

"The House is so weak it's eating our reserves of artifacts to replenish itself."

Asmodeus went very still. "Ah. *That* problem."

"I need to know two things," Thuan said.

And stopped, because his brain caught up with his mouth. He couldn't possibly ask Asmodeus how desperate the situation was—not when the previous assessment had driven Asmodeus to the brink.

Asmodeus's face didn't move. "You're not asking me questions." An exhaled breath. "Ah. You're trying to work out if I can take them."

Thuan watched Asmodeus, carefully. He seemed exhausted, run ragged; but nothing quite so bone-deep as he had in the grove. He finally exhaled.

"Do I pass the test?" A light, ironic voice that sounded almost normal. "You're quite free to take this up with Iaris if you'd rather."

Well, if nothing else, Asmodeus knew exactly where to apply pressure where it hurt.

"Iaris doesn't run the House," Thuan said, sharply.

Good-natured laughter, but with an edge beneath.

"True. Ask."

Thuan said, "How desperate are we, and how likely is it to escalate? Vinh Ly said that the artifacts were a piffle compared to what it took to maintain the House."

A grimace. "Not inaccurate." And, grudgingly, "She does have more uses than annoying Phyranthe."

"Thank you," Thuan said, more sharply than he'd intended. "I'm flattered. Can we come back to the matter at hand?"

Asmodeus leaned back against the pillow. Thuan found himself reaching out, squeezing Asmodeus's hand. No sarcastic comment whatsoever, just a weary sigh. Things were bad. Very bad.

Asmodeus said, finally, "You weren't there when I took the House."

"As I am frequently reminded."

"Behave." Asmodeus's voice was sharp. "This isn't about the old guard. The House needs blood and magic to sustain itself—and if it doesn't have them, it'll take them from outsiders." A smile that had barely any joy in it. "I taught the House what it meant to care for one's own, at all costs. That's what makes us different. The other Houses will eat themselves alive to survive."

To survive. Because they were going to die otherwise, like Harrier. Because Houses were vulnerable after all, and could be killed. Because Hawthorn itself could die, leaving them unprotected. The thought was a stone in his belly.

"And we won't."

"We're smarter than that."

"Smarter." Thuan stifled bitter laughter. "We don't look very smart, do we?"

"We will. At some point."

"If you say so." Thuan kept his voice light, but it cost him. "You forget the part where someone tried to kill us. And will try again."

"I'm not forgetting anything." Asmodeus's voice was sharp. "I've got magicians analyzing the ruins, and trying to raise wards against it happening again. Your dragons can help."

Thuan measured the depth of Asmodeus's fear, then. He'd never suggest this if he wasn't desperate.

"I'll tell them," he said. "But . . ."

But there was nothing they could do. But they were powerless and vulnerable against such an attack, and how could they tell if their would-be killer would strike again?

"I know," Asmodeus said.

"All right," Thuan said, fighting fear. "So that answers my question about how desperate we are. And the escalation—the next thing the House will do is attack outsiders.

We don't have any handy ones in the House." He stopped, then, with dawning horror. "We do, don't we?"

Aurore had left the grounds, but Emmanuelle most certainly hadn't.

"Emmanuelle?" A thoughtful look. Asmodeus didn't look despondent anymore—just chewing on a problem he could cow or stab into submission. "She's under the protection of another House, and not an easy target, even if that House is dying. They'd expend more trying to consume her than they'd get."

"It's nice to see you care," Thuan said, dryly.

"I do." Asmodeus looked annoyed. "I'll remind you we're wounded, with not enough manpower or supplies, and with a House that's certainly too weak to protect us against much of anyone or anything." Something that looked almost like a regretful smile. "My personal feelings about Emmanuelle don't rate above the survival of the House."

Nothing did, did it? Thuan exhaled.

"Well, I guess it's high time I went and checked in on Emmanuelle."

"You still think her responsible?"

Thuan said, cautiously. "I don't know. I don't think so."

He didn't voice the rest of his suspicions: that it was all linked to *khi* fire, which meant an Annamite, either mortal or Immortal or dragon, was the cause. It was all so precarious, without undermining the fragile understanding between him and Asmodeus.

"But I'd like to be sure. And"—he hated to say it—"the Houses are going to be at each other's throats again, aren't they? After this."

"Because we're all vulnerable and desperate?" Asmodeus smiled.

Thuan had to grant him this: he'd adapted remarkably quickly to a new order of things. Their world had utterly changed in one night: all the Houses under attack, weakened and perhaps dying; their own House frantically hoarding magic; their only advantage that it would not kill its own … And yet Asmodeus had never once attempted to argue they must have been mistaken. Whereas Iaris and most of the dragons were still in denial.

"You want a deterrent."

"I think it'd be good to know Silverspires won't attack us."

Thuan had the nagging suspicion they'd missed something. Something said quite recently that had stood out in the moment, but which he couldn't put his finger on now.

"So you're advocating keeping her? Indefinitely? You surprise me."

"You're the one who holds on to things," Thuan said. "I don't hoard, but I do hate to give up an advantage."

"Holding her indefinitely does have its merits."

"So you can toy with her?"

"You seem to expect me to act decently."

Thuan exhaled. "Well, you're definitely not putting her back into the cells. What's left of them."

"Mmm," Asmodeus said. A thoughtful snort. "Have it your way, then. But remember this isn't about being kind. It's about survival. Ours, and that of everything that belongs to and depends on us."

Being kind. Thuan sighed. He'd been hoping to avoid

the conversation for a while, but Phyranthe was going to wake up any time soon.

"We need to talk."

A raised eyebrow. "We're not?" But his gaze had turned sharp again.

Thuan exhaled, noisily. "Phyranthe."

"Ah."

A painful, charged silence. Well, there was nothing for it.

"We never did finish the conversation we were having, before the House exploded."

"The one where you kept expecting fairness from the world?"

"You're not going to blame me for trying to change things," Thuan said sharply.

He saw Asmodeus's face shift, and realized what he'd been doing. Answering insult to insult, and stoking tempers on both sides. What was it Asmodeus had said? It takes two for a fight. They were spouses, and joint heads of the House: they could do better than this.

He could do better than this.

"Wait. I'm sorry, that went wrong. I shouldn't have said this."

Another charged silence. At length, in a tone that was a touch softer, "You really need to stop apologizing for everyone and everything."

Asmodeus's own way of apologizing, Thuan guessed. As good as it was ever going to get.

Thuan sighed. And threw himself bodily into the abyss.

"I need your help. With Phyranthe."

Asmodeus said nothing. Thuan didn't dare to look him in the eye—because of what he'd see if he looked up.

Distant amusement? Contempt? The same regretful smile he'd had for Emmanuelle, before consigning her to the bottom of the priority list?

Thuan knew he wouldn't bear any of this.

He said slowly, "You said you wanted the House to change. To not be built on fear anymore. I ..." He spread his hands, frustrated. "You have to stand by these words. You can't just throw me into the pond and watch me struggle as I'm drowning." Ancestors, what an appalling metaphor, it wasn't as if drowning was ever going to be a problem for him. "Please. I really need the help."

A silence. The bed creaked. Then, unbearably close, the smell of bergamot and citrus, and the familiar warmth of a body next to his; a hand, lifting his chin so he'd look into Asmodeus's face.

Asmodeus had left the bed and was standing barely a handspan away from Thuan. His grip was iron; Thuan couldn't have looked away even if he'd wanted to.

Asmodeus's gray-green eyes were watching him, with an odd expression—not the fond amusement of watching someone thrash and fail, but faint exasperation.

"Oh, dragon prince. Pleading really doesn't suit you."

And his other hand, grabbing Thuan, locked them body against body, for the briefest of moments—Asmodeus's lips brushed his, a moment before he released Thuan. Thuan's breath came fast and ragged.

"Asmodeus ..."

A sharp, edged smile, but as with Phyranthe, Thuan saw that Asmodeus's anger was directed at himself: it was annoyance that things hadn't gone the way he'd wanted or foreseen.

"You could simply have asked," Asmodeus said, and it sounded almost plaintive.

The only words that came to Thuan were the truth. "You make that difficult."

"Why?"

"Don't tell me you don't know," Thuan said. "You despise weakness in everyone, and in yourself most of all. How …? How am I meant to keep your regard, if I abase myself before you?"

He didn't even see Asmodeus move. His lips were on Thuan's—the smell of citrus and bergamot in his mouth—and Asmodeus's hand was stroking, gently, slowly, the nape of his neck.

"We do run the House." Asmodeus's voice was a whisper on Thuan's lips, sending a warmth that spread to his entire face and made his breathing absurdly constricted. "Jointly. Of course you ask. You *always* ask. Otherwise I'll be … most disappointed." He bent down, and kissed Thuan again, running his fingers on the soft, quivering flesh at the base of Thuan's dragon antlers. "Now tell me what you need."

18

Extended Hands

Emmanuelle, lying in a heap at the foot of a ruined wall, heard the distant screams; the thud of masonry collapsing; the dependents calling for one another—the groaning sounds of the House reeling around her. Under her feet, magic flared like a hundred spikes—she had the feeling of a snake or some other massive animal, raising its head to sniff the air. But something turned it aside—another lure? Another thing of more interest, or easier to get at?

When she managed to get up on shaking legs, pushing away plaster and debris, she tottered to the door and tried to open it. The wards pushed her back, gently but firmly. Asmodeus's friendly, courteous magic: sweetness around a core of steel.

She managed to find her way to what remained of the bed, and sat down, exhausted and wishing the world would stop spinning around her. The link to House Silverspires was calm again—she clung to it, to the calm, steady presence of Selene like the only lifeline she had left. The link was there. She could still feel it; could still feel Selene's distant presence. They were alive. The House wasn't wounded or dying.

It had to be.

What had happened? The same thing as Harrier, but why? Was Guy still hunting Darrias? But how could he reach into another House? And he hadn't seemed to know how the explosion had happened when she'd been his prisoner, merely scrambling to preserve himself and his grip on the House.

When the nurses came—two frazzled women in the colors of Hawthorn, with burn marks on their hands and dozens of scabs on their faces—the tremor had subsided. Emmanuelle was sitting on the bed, endlessly reciting Our Fathers and Hail Marys in the vain hope of keeping herself from worrying.

"What happened?" she asked.

Neither of them answered. The examination was perfunctory. They spoke in monosyllables, and then left, leaving dried food, a flask of water and a package of pills on the table.

"Wait," Emmanuelle said.

One of them turned, on the threshold.

"We've got other emergencies to deal with. Consider yourself lucky we came at all." A snort, to her colleague. "Freaking Silverspires, think they own the world."

And then she was gone.

Emmanuelle ate, because it would be a shame to let the food go to waste. She wasn't sure about the pills, but if Asmodeus had meant to kill her he would hardly go about it in such a roundabout way. Even drugging her to keep her docile was unnecessary—he could easily cast a spell for that, or force sedatives on her. So she took them, and didn't feel they made much of a difference at all.

Selene, damn it. I want to be home.

She was going to cry again, and sentiment had never got anyone anywhere.

When the door opened again, she wasn't sure how much time had passed. She'd dozed or slept, she couldn't be sure, but she snapped out of the fuzzed darkness with panic clenching her guts. They were coming for her.

The person at the door stared at her, expressionless. An Annamite, his long hair tied in an impeccable topknot, his gray and silver suit incongruously pressed. He must have used magic to do it—highly unlikely anyone had managed to get a steam iron going in this much devastation.

"Thuan."

Emmanuelle rose and tried to bow, but her legs wobbled too much, and she fell flat on the floor. *Great. How pathetic.* She scrabbled to get up, and heard him come into the room, calm and measured steps towards her.

Thuan knelt. One hand brushed the short curls of her hair—the other rested on her forehead. Coolness spread from his fingers, gently penetrating her mind. Her thoughts seemed to fuzz and freeze again.

He inhaled, a slow sharp breath that resonated in the room.

"Nasty injury."

"So I've been told."

Emmanuelle's tongue felt stuck to her palate, every word a struggle.

"Hang on …"

Thuan's fingers tightened and ice spread, cold enough to burn—she bit her lip not to cry out—and then it passed and there was nothing but a fuzzed, pleasant coolness, all the way down to the sharp, clean taste of melted water on her tongue.

"There. Better?"

Not ... not what she'd expected. She couldn't seem to focus on anything. It felt like a roiling storm in her brain, stirring up old memories, old wounds. Rejecting the name Morningstar had given her; meeting Selene, flirting and kissing in the shadow of Notre-Dame; racing along a corridor on Ash Wednesday to find a mildly annoyed Javier and his congregation waiting for her in the chapel of House Silverspires.

"Somewhat," she said.

He offered her his hand to pull her up, and sit on the bed.

"Your husband would have enjoyed watching me struggle to my feet," she said, and then clamped her lips shut. "Sorry."

Thuan laughed. He sat in a chair by her side, watching her with curious eyes.

"I'm not him. As you should know. Give it time. It's a bit of a hodge-podge healing; all I can do right now, I'm afraid."

She oughtn't to have spoken up, but she was tired of fencing with people who wished her harm.

"My memories feel shot to hell."

"Yes." Thuan grimaced. "Closed-head injury, right? Iaris told me that might happen. Your memories should sort themselves out at some point."

"Including ..." She hesitated. "Including the parts I don't remember?"

Thuan was silent for a while.

"Memory is tricky. Maybe. Maybe not. Maybe there'll be a gaping hole where those should be, forever."

"Or a lie," Emmanuelle said.

"Only if you want to tell yourself that lie. I can only return what's here, not make things up for you."

Great; though whether or not she'd meddled in House Harrier affairs seemed such a small worry, compared to what had happened. What she'd felt through the distant link to Silverspires—there had been an explosion there, too. Which wasn't good news.

"You'll want something, I expect," Emmanuelle said. "In return for the healing."

Assuming it was a real healing, and not some barbed thing. She didn't have much experience with Thuan—he seemed honest, but honesty wouldn't get you anywhere in the Houses.

Thuan looked at her for a while.

"Some truths." His face didn't move.

"I already told Asmodeus everything I know about House Harrier." Emmanuelle leaned against the bedpost, frustrated. "I don't see what I could add to it."

"Answer me this, then. Did you cause it? The explosion?"

The question was absurd.

"Of course not," Emmanuelle said.

"Hmm." Thuan pondered that.

Emmanuelle said, "Your House blew up. I'm sure you've got better things to do than worry about a lone hostage. Such as whether or not it's going to happen again." She exhaled sharply. Time to get unpleasant. It was much easier with Thuan—because she had no history with him, because his presence was comforting and steadying, very different from his husband. "We both know the moment you harm me, you lose your leverage. Selene won't negotiate if you touch me."

Thuan said, "There are different kinds of harm."

"I think you'll find Selene doesn't quibble over points of semantics."

"Mmm," Thuan said. "Asmodeus seems to think she'd offer concessions to get you back."

Asmodeus, which meant not Thuan.

"Oh, she would." Emmanuelle kept her voice light. "And then she'd come after you with everything she's got until you were dead."

"Huh. She'd have to join the queue," Thuan said.

A hint of laughter in his voice. She didn't know what to make of him.

Emmanuelle decided to take a stab in the dark.

"I think it's a time for all Houses to stand together, isn't it?"

"An alliance? I'm not sure what you have that we don't."

"Food. Medical supplies. Water," Emmanuelle said.

That got his interest, but barely.

"You'd help us? You're as devastated as we are."

"But it's unlikely we're all missing the same things you are, isn't it? We could … share. Help you find whoever caused the explosion before they strike again."

She was making wild promises in Selene's name, not even sure she could hold them. But wasn't that the game, in the end?

Thuan steepled his fingers in front of him. He wore gloves—elegant cotton ones in a vivid red, like two splashes of blood.

"Mmm," he said. "The blind leading the blind." A pause; a sigh. "Asmodeus won't stand for it, you know. He hates losing his playthings."

Emmanuelle shrugged. He wanted to scare her, but he'd already half decided. She was a bother rather than an asset. If he could get rid of her and get something of actual value in exchange . . .

"Selene will stand by my promises." Which was for little enough, after all; they were unlikely to have much to share. "Or we can play the game of who's going to harm whom most. Your choice."

She lay back down on the bed, winded. It was out of her hands now, and all she could do was pray. If she had any prayers left in her. A moment of silence. Thuan's slow, even breath. The sound of running feet outside the room, and dependents gently coaxing someone into walking.

At length, "I'll take that alliance. You'd better honor it, though." Another pause.

"I'll sign for it."

Another amused laugh. "I love words and their bindings, but right now paper is worth less than ashes. I had something else in mind."

What Thuan had in mind became obvious when Emmanuelle—escorted by two bodyguards—reached the wrecked wrought-iron gates of Hawthorn, and saw Darrias waiting for her.

No.

She had a brief movement of recoil.

"I don't think—"

Thuan's face was unreadable. "Darrias knows the streets

by heart. She'll see you home safe. And make sure Selene knows what you've promised us."

"Was this your idea?"

A blank, but not puzzled face. Not his, then. Asmodeus's. Or Darrias's. She wasn't sure which was worse.

It wasn't going to be a long walk. A couple of hours? She could bear it. She could get home. She breathed out slowly, evenly. Only a few hours to home.

"Let's go."

Aurore wandered back to la Goutte d'Or in a daze.

Everything hurt her, and everything delighted her. The air was a hundred, a thousand, prickles on exposed skin, as if the thorns had left a thousand bleeding wounds on her body, and all of them hurt at the same time, except that it was a hurt that reminded her how *alive* she was—a giddy rush of power that flowed within her, a sense that she could do anything, go anywhere.

One of the children had come with her: the one who'd pierced her brow and tied her to the House, a dark shadow in her wake no one else seemed to see. It didn't speak, or wasn't in the mood to speak anymore, but she could feel it, nevertheless, a trailing heaviness behind her. A link to a distant House where her heart was now the heart of a building.

It didn't matter. She'd made her choices; claimed her power.

In the ruined streets, people crept away from her—staring at her and finally *seeing* her, that she could be as frightening as any House-bound. More so, because there were no Houses left—just Silverspires, just the dying remnants of Morningstar's House, awaiting its final fading away.

Just us, the child whispered in her mind.

She couldn't feel Dân Chay's threads under her feet anymore; just the weight of her own footsteps, making the earth tremble with pent-up magic. But, when she reached the boundary of the community, the threads of *khi* fire became more and more numerous, running under the cracks of the cobblestones, forming a low, ankle-level pool of shimmering light at an invisible boundary. More threads, on the other side of that wall, except that these were *khi* water and *khi* wood—and they were holding it back.

Philippe? But he didn't have that kind of magic.

Did he?

Whatever it was, it wasn't enough. It kept Dân Chay at bay, but it wouldn't kill him.

Not enough.

She didn't want to announce her arrival by striking against him, though. She needed, desperately needed, like a person dying of thirst, to know that Cassiopée and Marianne were fine. That they were alive. What was the point, otherwise?

She stepped over the small pool, bracing herself for . . . something, anything, but there was just the distant sense of exhilaration from the magic in her blood. The pool was nothing but colored light.

Their small flat was empty: neither Marianne nor Cassiopée there, but the acrid, diluted tea was still warm on the table. Where . . .?

The child shifted, next to her. Her mind flew,

abruptly—blood to blood and flesh to flesh, because her family was *hers*, because they were the ones she'd sworn to hold close and protect. And, like a hook sunk into her ribs—like the disk, all over again, except that it barely hurt this time—she knew exactly where she had to go.

Philippe had wanted to hold the meeting in Grandmother Olympe's flat, but Olympe had demurred. Too many people. Her tone suggested she didn't want Philippe to upstage her, either, so they took over one of the tea houses just next door to her flat, with her and the other aunts taking pride of place in the center of the floor.

If he closed his eyes he could feel the relentless press of the flames, Dân Chay's never-ending attack on them—the fragility of the wards he and Isabelle had drawn. He'd had Hoa Phong take a look at them. She'd said nothing: mostly because she didn't know, anymore, what they were facing, what mixture of predatory spirit and twisted weapon the Houses had unleashed on them.

Hoa Phong and Isabelle arrived, carrying Aunt Ha's limp shape. She'd said—quite rightly—that she wanted to know what was happening; and of course they couldn't leave her alone.

"She's getting worse," Isabelle said, flatly. "Isn't she?"

Aunt Ha's entire skin was tawny now, and in the intervals between two convulsions, black, charred stripes would briefly appear. Even her voice, when she whimpered, was lower pitched and more raucous.

"You should get her out of here," Isabelle said. "Can't have enemy agents here—"

"She's ours," Grandmother Olympe said, giving Isabelle

a long, hard look. "If we sacrifice even one person for the good of many, we're no better than the Houses."

Some Houses are like that, Philippe thought. Not all of them, and the thought was alien and frightening, a dance on the edge of the precipice. He watched elderly Annamites file in: the men and women of the docks, of the factories, the ones with filmed eyes, with fingers worn down to the bones, with broken bones and the careful gait of those with misaligned hips and spine. Mothers holding babies in their arms and sliding on to benches with the grim look of fighters who'd defended their home and seen off invaders as if it was all in a day's work.

Olympe said, sharply and loudly enough to be heard, "Refugees from other Houses aren't enemy agents, either. Anyone who wants to shelter here and will help us help others is welcome. In all fairness—everyone should know we're also the next target of Dân Chay, which makes us a dangerous shelter."

Tade's face was thoughtful. Surprised. Pleased. Philippe remembered what he'd said about refugees.

Not everyone in the audience looked happy.

Aunt Thuy said, "Regardless, we don't have enough food. Or water."

Olympe's gaze was withering. "We have a duty. The sense of compassion is the beginning of benevolence, is it not?"

A silence, and slow, grudging assent.

Cassiopée was at a table, calming a weeping toddler—Cassiopée's sister, he suddenly remembered, had gone to Harrier, been caught in the games of Houses, and not come back. Another loss in the sea of their losses, but that was too facile. For that child, it was the end of her world.

He wished he could really offer blessings, and miracles; but he wasn't that sort of Immortal. Instead, he walked to her, smiling with a confidence he really didn't feel.

"Can I?" he asked.

She nodded, exhausted.

The toddler—Marianne, he abruptly remembered, the Republic's first name—stared at Philippe, hard, when he shuffled on to the bench.

He called *khi* wood—not *khi* fire, too dangerous—let it burn on the palm of his hand, a fire the green of fresh leaves, of grass after the rain.

"Look," he said. "Magic."

"My mummy knows magic," Marianne said scornfully.

"Don't mind her," Cassiopée started, but Philippe was already weaving colored figures: a singing fisherman, a boat, a palace with a trembling light in its window.

Marianne watched, entranced, while the little figure in the boat floated closer, and the shape of a woman with an elaborate crown appeared at the window—the fisherman stretching into the shape of a dragon, flying to meet his love.

"More! More!"

"The man is exhausted, little fish," Cassiopée said.

Philippe laid his hand on the table, and the *khi* wood clung to it, still illuminated—still showing a dragon embracing a princess.

"Here," he said. And, to Cassiopée, "It'll be gone in half an hour or so."

"An eternity for a toddler." Cassiopée smiled. "Thank you."

"Your sister …"

Her face set, a careful, fragile mask over despair.

"I'm sorry," he said.

"Don't be."

She stared at the figures of light as Philippe left, feeling obscurely like he'd failed them. Party tricks. Children's stories against the fire.

Javier was sitting alone on a bench, staring at nothing. He'd not spoken a word since facing down Dân Chay, and Grandmother Olympe had found excuses to keep Isabelle busy. Philippe wasn't sure what to think, anymore. Javier had walked into fire for him, twice, when he could have let them die—the priest's fondness for Isabelle didn't extend to Philippe.

There were decent, brave people in the Houses. He'd always known that. It didn't change a thing. He couldn't let it matter. It was House Silverspires that had hurt Dân Chay in the first place, had made him a monster.

But wasn't that a facile excuse, too? If all the hurt and tortured had turned into monsters, the community would be replete with these, the easy-smile, smooth-tongued killers. In the end, wasn't it about what you chose, with the hand that you were given—rather than what you were made into?

He didn't know, not anymore.

"Philippe." Hoa Phong had left Isabelle minding Aunt Ha. Her face was grim. "You asked how we face a tiger. There's something they do, in Annam."

Her voice was low and intense. Of course, she was a fighter and wouldn't have liked sitting by like this, powerless and watching her patient's body fail.

"Something?"

"Raj merchants brought it to Annam. Mustard oil and latex," Hoa Phong said. "They spread it near the tiger's watering hole, and when he comes out to drink or to take his prey, his paws become sticky. When he tries to rub it off, he becomes blind from dirt, oil and dead leaves he's picked up."

Philippe raised an eyebrow.

Hoa Phong snorted. "I'm not suggesting we try mustard oil. But if we could spread something sticky on the ground . . ." She raised one hand, stared until the faint outline of petals became visible on her skin. "Then I could blind him. And maybe contaminate him with Fallen magic from my wounds." A low, bitter laugh. "They might as well be useful."

Philippe said finally, "I'll think about it."

In truth, he had other ideas.

Ahead of them, a circle was forming: Grandmother Olympe and the aunts were going to speak.

"We'll talk later," Hoa Phong said, slipping back to join Isabelle.

"You all know we are under siege."

Grandmother Olympe was sitting in the center of the floor, with the aunts spread around her, a queen in her own court. She looked at Philippe. He didn't want to join her, didn't want to be the face of the community, but this was no longer about his personal preferences so he went to stand with them. Stared at faces he'd laughed with, eaten with—healed, taken food from.

"We face a fire spirit. A weapon from the Great War. And he won't rest until he's destroyed the city."

A silence.

Aunt Thuy asked, "The city, or us?"

"The community. You can leave, but he may follow."

Some of them would leave, he knew. Olympe had made it clear she wouldn't stop anyone, but she didn't expect a flood of people to go—mostly because she and the aunts had gone to most of the community's dwellings, making it clear what their wishes were. Typical. He'd have found it amusing, in better times.

"Isabelle and I have drawn walls. They're holding, for now."

He could feel them flex: the patient, relentless digging of claws. *I'm coming, Immortal.* Something else had caught Dân Chay's interest for now, but he would be back. And they had nothing, in the end—nothing but goodwill, which had never stopped fires.

"We'll fight him." Isabelle's face was grim. "To the end."

Philippe looked at Javier again. He said, slowly, carefully, "There might be another way."

The door opened, slamming on its hinges.

"There is another way."

A Fallen stood in the doorway. No, not a Fallen—for a moment he thought it was Françoise, but she would not come back for a community which had ostracized her. No, it was someone he didn't recognize—not until she stepped out of the darkness. Aurore, Cassiopée's sister—except that Aurore had been small, and diminutive, with a sense of coiled intensity. The person in the doorway was ... taller, larger, the planes of her face all smooth, translucent skin taut over fine cheekbones. When she walked, light clung to her—and a sense of a deep, abiding presence that was somehow more than her, a link to something deeper and larger than herself. He'd felt such a thing once, and only once—in the bright and terrible presence of Morningstar in a crypt below Notre-Dame.

Cassiopée rose, staring at her sister. On the bench beside her, Aurore's daughter had fallen asleep, clutching a tattered blanket.

"You did it," she whispered. Her voice was full of an almost religious awe.

"I found a way."

When Aurore spoke, something else spoke with her—an echo of branches bending in the wind, of distant, familiar screams. She scared Philippe stiff.

"Magical artifacts won't save us," Grandmother Olympe said, scornfully. "When the magic runs out …"

She gave a disturbing, alien smile. He'd seen it somewhere already—where?

"I *am* the magic. It will never run out."

There was … There was something in the room with them, a shadow that moved when she did, stretching long, insectile fingers with every gesture of her hands.

She crossed the room to Aunt Ha. Hoa Phong rose, grimacing, her face shivering, on the edge of turning into flowers again. A large, oily stain had spread across her tunic.

"Fallen magic can't heal." Her voice was level, utterly matter-of-fact. "If you want to fight Dân Chay, go ahead. But you won't touch her."

Aurore stared at her, for a while. "She healed me when I walked here. Did they tell you that? I carried my sister all the way from Harrier, and she sat with us both all night because it was the right thing to do. I don't mean her harm."

Hoa Phong's face didn't move. "You don't have to intend harm to do harm."

"It's not a healing," Aurore said. "More . . . an exorcism."

She reached out, and the light around her intensified. Where it touched Aunt Ha's face her skin turned lighter, and fuzzy—no, not fuzzy. Furry, and the lines beneath it were the same orange threads as in the streets.

"See? Some part of him is trapped in her. Like a flame away from the body of the fire. It's burning her because that's all it's got."

Hoa Phong, entranced, turned her gaze away for a fraction of a second. It was all it took. Aurore's hand snaked below her guard, touched Aunt Ha's face.

No.

Philippe moved—too slow, too late, he was too far away.

For a moment—a moment only—Aurore was surrounded by dazzling light, and in that light Philippe saw the shadow clearly. Something small; a child, only no child had exposed ribs on their chest, and stretched, skeletal hands which ended in three fingers as sharp as claws. It stood behind her, face stretched in an emaciated face, as her skin touched Aunt Ha. Light spun between them, passed into Aunt Ha—sharply underlining her skin until every color seemed washed out. The black, charred tiger's stripes appeared again, as Aunt Ha started screaming.

Her body arched, convulsing. Aurore had withdrawn by then, watching her with a growing horror on her face—gradually replaced by a hard, expressionless mask. Hoa Phong was frantically weaving threads of *khi* currents together. She reached, cursing under her breath, for *khi* fire, stopped, and scattered into a thousand *hoang mai* flowers, a wind that wrapped itself around Aunt Ha like a cloth, tightening until the convulsions seemed to take both of them together, sending flowers flying through the air in an explosion of diseased colors.

Something cracked. A bone, then another. Philippe grabbed Aurore, threw her out of the way—or tried to, because the moment he touched her something arced through him, a power that sent him sprawling to the floor, struggling to breathe. Bones continued to crack, one by one. A faint music was rising in the air—the distant sound of a flute playing an Annamite scale, even as petals fell in a shower that had no end.

Silence, spreading slow and dreadful over the inn. Philippe pulled himself, shaking, to his knees. Aunt Ha had stopped moving. As he watched, she rose, a disarticulated, boneless doll slowly putting itself back together, limbs flopping, her pose gradually hardening into a distorted version of a human being—as if some huge being had been molding clay with only a perfunctory idea of how bodies worked. Orange threads flowed from her body, as if squeezed out—and shriveled and died when they met the swirling petals. Whatever was holding Aunt Ha let go, then, and she flopped to the bench again.

The petals flowed, reformed into a shaking, shivering Hoa Phong—who bent to the nearest window and retched and retched, a process that seemed to have no end. Others looked from her to Philippe, and then back again, with a familiar dawning awe and fear on their faces. She'd be lucky if she didn't end up with her own cult in some hastily repurposed flat—not to mention the blistering earful Philippe would get from Grandmother Olympe for failing to tell her who Hoa Phong really was.

Philippe walked to Aunt Ha. He reached her at the same time as Aurore. They stared at each other over the limp body. Her eyes swirled with Fallen light. He'd thought he'd been scared when she'd come in, but it was nothing compared to facing her. She was Fallen, and not. Wrong in a way that he'd seldom seen. He could understand Dân Chay—the rage and anger and everything the Houses had twisted and set afire—but Aurore was … not herself anymore. Something walked in her skin and talked like her, mimicking humanity or Fallenness with very little idea of what either concept meant. When their hands met, her skin was brittle, as if he could push through and touch bone.

Aunt Ha's pulse was … thready, and weak. He felt the knots of healed bone protruding under his touch—in her fingers, at the meeting point between collarbone and sternum, at every rib. The bones felt wrong, too—too thin, too brittle. Fallen bones, only they were wrong for that, too: too large and too rough.

He'd have been out there with Hoa Phong, vomiting, but if he did that, everyone would give in to their fear. There would be a stampede to reach the exit. Instead, he turned, and stared at the mass of people—at Grandmother Olympe, who gazed steadily back at him. They nodded to each other: each of them choking on fear, but hiding it.

"It's strong magic," Grandmother Olympe said slowly, steadily. She didn't even blink. Her voice picked up as she did so. "But it won't be enough."

Aurore shook her head. "I'm more powerful than any Fallen."

"But Dân Chay isn't Fallen," Philippe said.

A lingering silence.

"You have Fallen magic. House magic. The Houses lost against him."

"They're not dead." Aurore's voice was level.

And wasn't that the scariest thought of all?

Grandmother Olympe said, with a nod towards Aunt Ha, "We've seen your … exorcism." She said the word like *curse*, or *wounding*. "Will Ha get up in the morning, do you think?"

Would she get up at all? Philippe closed his eyes for a moment against a vision of something rising—boneless and shambling, held upright by magic like a puppet without strings.

A level gaze. "Everything has a price."

And everyone had a price they weren't willing to pay. This was his, he guessed. The other line he'd said he wouldn't cross—the vow he'd made never to bow down to Houses again, to power, to cruelty … He'd break that vow, if that meant not beholding himself to her, or whatever she was. At least the Houses were a thing known and weighed.

In the name of survival …

Philippe said, "You can hold him at bay. For a time. But it won't be enough."

He looked from Aurore to Javier. Javier's eyes were half-lidded. Of course. Not his fight. But he had gone into fire for them before, when he didn't have to.

"Father," he said.

A word like ashes on his tongue. Respect. Humility. Abasement. All he'd sworn never to do before Houses or their dependents.

Javier opened his eyes, looked at him.

"Will you help us?" Philippe asked.

Silence. Light streamed from Aurore's still shape. He could have sworn he heard whispers—a hint of a voice that was the wind in the streets, the patient push of roots within the earth, the popping sound of leaves unfolding from a bud.

"Two Houses made Dân Chay what he is," Philippe said. "A weapon for the war. Silverspires was one of them. And you'd never have a weapon without some means of control."

A short, bitter laugh from Javier. "Does it look like we have any control over him?"

Tade said, from his table, "I have it on good authority that Silverspires still stands."

"And you think we did this?" Javier's face was closed, angry. "That we would countenance any of this? That Selene would ever think this was acceptable?"

"No," Isabelle said.

"I don't know," Philippe said.

"You want our help, and first you accuse us?"

"Be fair." Grandmother Olympe's voice was cold. "Houses have done much worse in the name of power."

Javier's face didn't move. "Only a monster would think devastating the city was any way to get power."

A silence, as he chewed on his own words.

Aurore said flatly, "You are the monsters. You freed him. The House did. Morningstar did." The words were pure venom. "He bargained immunity for the House, in exchange for the deaths of all the others."

What?

Morningstar. Philippe stared at her, trying to process the enormity of what she'd just said. He wasn't the only one: Javier looked as if someone had punched him in the gut and stabbed him afterwards, for good measure.

"He what?"

"I saw him."

You're lying. But why would she? She'd been in House Harrier. And she didn't want them to involve Javier or any House, but why such a precise, elaborate lie?

Grandmother Olympe said, "We're going to need more than your word."

Aurore snorted. "More than my word against *his*?" She shook her head. Her long, black hair streamed in the darkness, glimmering with sparkles of Fallen magic. "What more do you need? His House still stands, unscathed. And he's still here."

"I don't understand."

"He's *immune*." She spat the word. "Morningstar bargained for safe passage for his dependents and his House, in exchange for freeing Dân Chay."

Philippe thought back to Tade, nursing shattered ribs. To Frankie, thrown aside, with her head caved in. And to Javier, who'd gone to face Dân Chay twice, and had nothing more than the wounds he'd suffered when the inn collapsed around him.

It was ...

Too much. Too big. Too monstrous, in a city of monsters.

Javier opened his mouth again, closed it. He didn't know. He hadn't known. But Philippe saw the moment his mask slipped on again; the moment his face became smooth and distant and expressionless.

"Morningstar is no longer the head of House Silverspires. I'm Selene's right hand. I can tell you she'd never approve of this. Of any of this."

"Then help us," Philippe said. "Make it right. Please." Another word as bitter as ashes.

A long, weighing look from Javier. That was when he was meant to offer something, he guessed. Some riches from devastated streets, from impoverished, blind and broken-fingered people. Some inducement to goodness. As if decency needed to be induced.

"Please," Isabelle said.

"We don't need him." Aurore's voice was low and angry. "You know what he brings already. What his kind always brings."

He forced himself to be calm. Thought of Diamaras and her empty museum, and of the lines of exhausted, traumatized refugees from Harrier.

"We're all part of the same city. But it will never be the same." Most of the Houses wouldn't recover. Silverspires? He didn't know, because it had been the weakest, because it had withdrawn from the intrigues of other Houses. "You may need us, one day."

He thought Javier would laugh. Would snap that they were Houseless, that they had nothing to offer—and he didn't know what he'd have done, then. But the other man didn't move. He ran a hand through his singed, blackened hair.

"We are the only other place untouched by the fire. We could simply watch you burn."

"And then he'd come for you," Philippe said. "The House that imprisoned and tortured him. Did you really think you'd be spared? *Bargains only last as long as the lives of those who've made them.* You have safety for now, but it'll be short-lived."

Another long, hard look from Javier.

"It's not much," Grandmother Olympe said, with that deceptive softness of hers—the one that suggested sharpened steel wasn't far away. "What we're asking. Hardly something we can ever turn against you."

They were *begging*. Making themselves harmless and small, asking for charity. Philippe swallowed back bile.

"No," he said. "Not much. We're asking for an alliance. To deal with him. If we get rid of him, then you're not going to be the next target. That's worth something to you, surely."

"What do you want?" Javier asked.

Philippe said, stiffly, "Respect."

He could have threatened them—could have told them he still had Silverspires' curse within him, that he could find a way to harm the House. He didn't know if it was true, but Javier—who remembered—would have believed him. The time for alliances of fear between unequal partners had passed.

"Respect," Javier said. "That's a very abstract notion."

"Don't plunder from us. Don't harm us. Don't treat us as servants or victims. That's not abstract to us."

He knew how it would go: they would take what they wanted, what they needed, as they always had.

Isabelle said, "Javier. You know what he means."

"What I don't know," Javier said, with a touch of annoyance, "is what side you're on anymore."

Sides. Divides. Philippe wanted to say something, but he was exhausted. Dân Chay was battering, again and again, at the defenses in his mind. Aurore was glowering, but clearly Grandmother Olympe's authority was still enough to hold her back.

"We're on the same side. That's the point."

"Only for now," Javier said, stiffly and not at all amused.

19

How Far to Go

Outside, it was chaos. The area around the House had been leveled, the various buildings turned to shreds of wood and stone debris. As they walked on, away from Hawthorn, it got better—marginally. Buildings were still standing, except that they were hollow, their windows blown out, parts of their walls missing, their insides blown to smithereens. Bodies lying in the streets; smoldering fires from inside deserted communal flats. The Seine ran black and oily, but every bridge was a gaping wound, with pieces broken off, and only fragments of arches remaining on the water. Instead of a line of buildings and streets, it was toppled ruins as far as the eye could see, a vast sea of devastation with the occasional wasted skeleton of a tree or lamppost standing alone, stripped of leaves, twisted out of shape, cobblestones torn from the streets, leaving only bloodied indentations on the ground—turned into deadly projectiles, striking walls and people with equal force.

People were trying to pull others from the rubble, calling desperately for them. Emmanuelle stopped at the first such place, but the bodyguard with Darrias—a man with spiky hair and glasses called Victor—stopped her.

"We have a mission, my lady."

"I'm not a lady." She wasn't the head of the House, just her partner. "Someone—"

"Someone else will help them," Darrias said, inexorably steering Emmanuelle back to the path they'd been picking through the rubble. "We have to see you safely to Silverspires."

After kidnapping her and holding her prisoner.

"Tell me why I can't stop and help."

"Because," Victor said, gently, as if to a child, "if you stop, they'll realize you're Fallen, and that they outnumber you. Can you imagine how much they're hungering for magic right now? You're worth more to them dead than alive."

Emmanuelle opened her mouth. She stared at the grimy, shocked people with barely healed wounds, trying to dig through rubble to find someone who might well be dead by now. Something, long held, finally snapped.

"Take me back."

"I'm sorry?"

"We're not that far from Hawthorn, are we?"

"No—"

"Take me back."

Emmanuelle stopped, and crossed her arms. She felt light-headed, and if she thought about it for a moment she would back down.

Darrias sighed. "It's on your head."

Some un-Fallen angel must have been watching over her: they hadn't been gone that long, and Thuan was still at the wrought-iron gates of Hawthorn, talking to a dragon dependent who was nervously running a hand over her antlers.

"Emmanuelle? Are you so much in love with the place?"

Emmanuelle planted herself firmly in the earth, looking at him and desperately scrabbling for arguments she didn't have.

"You've been outside."

A raised eyebrow.

"It's chaos. The Houseless areas are devastated. People have died. The living are digging through the rubble to find, most likely, corpses, and it's going slowly because they have neither magic nor manpower."

The raised eyebrow didn't move.

"The Houses should be out there, helping them," Emmanuelle said.

She'd tried to help, before. She'd gone out on the streets, talking to people, asking what they needed. She'd tried to share. But that had been too little, and always inadequate. She'd gone back to the House; and only her and a few people like Aragon had ever tried to help.

Thuan laughed. "And you come to me for this? I'm not Selene."

"You're closest," Emmanuelle said. She could convince Selene, given enough time—her partner was a reluctant ruler of the House, derived no pleasure from crushing others and doing what was needed—and it wasn't as though any other House was going to argue with them if Silverspires chose to waste its time. She'd also follow Hawthorn's lead, if they were allied. "And we help each other."

Thuan didn't move. "A bleeding heart on two legs," he said, but the tone was the same as Darrias's, low and almost affectionate. "And to think I believed you had something to do with the explosions."

"The rules have changed. The city has changed, and you're going to need friends, if you want to survive. And you'll need them to help you, too."

A short, amused laugh. "No. If we help them, it's not on condition that they dance to our tune," Thuan said. "That's not reaching out. That's just self-interest. They won't stand for it, and neither should we."

He was half-turning away: the conversation was over, and she'd lost.

She could have gone on, found better arguments. Further threats, but she held no hand that mattered to him.

"Please," she said. And, slowly, carefully, "The House welcomed you in, once. Wouldn't you want to do that for someone else?"

His face didn't change. "What I have, I took. It wasn't given to me."

"Do you think that's the way it should be? That we must always take things by force to be acknowledged by the Houses? That fear and strength is the only currency?"

"The Houses. You're House. You were *born* House."

"That doesn't mean I'm wrong," Emmanuelle said stubbornly. "Tell me I am."

Thuan exhaled. He didn't seem annoyed, just weary. "You can't change everything at once. Believe me, I tried."

"I'm not asking for everything. Just for something that moves us forward. That reaches out. Everything has to start somewhere."

A silence. He stared at her, head cocked, with the shadow of antlers above his topknot. Then he laughed, finally.

"You never let go, do you? And when you get to

Silverspires you're just going to mercilessly nag your partner until she gives in, too. I can see why Asmodeus likes you." His face relaxed, a fraction. "Fine. We'll see what we can do."

After they left Hawthorn for the second time, they walked in silence until they reached the ruins of the Trocadéro. Darrias crossed, not through the gardens, but through a network of small streets behind them, barely looking up to orient herself—as if the debris and people digging through it didn't matter to her. People stared at their House uniforms, barely noticing the colors or the crests. There should have been envy, or fear. Something—anything. Not that dull, hopeless shock.

They were taking a side street back towards the Seine, in tense silence, the sky overhead dark with smoke. Emmanuelle was trying to steel herself for the Alexandre III bridge, and her first view of Silverspires—how much of a wreck was the House? Were the spires of Notre-Dame still standing?

Selene ...

The earth under them rumbled, and then that rumble faded as if utterly spent, replaced by a noise that twisted in Emmanuelle's chest, a slow rhythmic sound that grew clearer and clearer as they got closer to the Seine, squeezing her ribs so hard she thought she'd choke.

And, as they reached the river and its bridges—the only intact things on a sea of ruins—she saw the Alexandre III bridge covered in orange, ethereal light. For a moment she caught a glimpse of a distinguished Annamite in old-fashioned clothes, leaning against the plinth of one of the ruined statues. He was looking intently at something, his smile sharp, hungry, disquieting. As she followed his gaze she saw that along the edge of the Seine almost every building had toppled into shredded debris—the empty Champ de Mars, House Fontenoy, House Mansart and Les Invalides, House Solférino. And, along that line of uninterrupted sight, she saw what the man was staring at.

"Darrias," she said.

Over House Harrier, the plume of smoke was gone: what was rising from the heart of the House was a dark flock of birds, slowly fragmenting into a thousand burning embers above the city. The buildings had been shimmering with a faint, incandescent light. That was going away, as if some huge cloud, driven by the wind, were passing across their facades and bringing only darkness in its wake. The rhythmic beating of the birds' wings—the same noise twisting in her chest—was the only sound in the silence: a hundred, a thousand of them stretching towards the Champ de Mars, and ten thousand more sloughing away from the flock and fragmenting into nothingness.

A last, exhausted and drawn-out rumble underfoot, and the buildings went dark. A distant sound of falling masonry and breaking glass, and then the flock of birds faded away, leaving only the smaller heart of it on the Champ de Mars.

"It's dead," Emmanuelle said, trying to breathe. "House Harrier. It's dead."

At the center of the remaining flock of birds was the shape of a man—and behind him, the handful of soldiers that had to be still following him.

Guy. The hawks. A darkness of talons and claws and raucous screams, headed straight for them.

Darrias's hand on her wrist, tight enough to bruise.

"I told you. He'll have nowhere to go. He's not here yet, Emmanuelle. We have to go." She pulled, but Emmanuelle was still staring at the birds. They were dark now, the color of ashes, of smoke—too far away for her to see the patterns of faded stonework and wallpaper on their wings. "There's still time to escape this, but we have to move now."

The knot of continuous, tense fear in her, tightened too far, finally broke. A wave of coolness on her brow; a memory of ice on her skull and on her tongue, and Thuan's amused voice. Darkness, rising around her: not the flames still smoldering in every House, not even the fire in Harrier, but the trembling one of House Harrier's corridors. The doors, opening; Guy, smiling at her with the crazed smile of one under siege.

"Darrias is coming for her family. I've always known she would, from the moment she slipped my grasp. I've been waiting a long, long time, Emmanuelle."

And, when she didn't answer, "Tonight. And you'll watch. Everyone will watch. Silverspires and Hawthorn and all your masters …"

He laughed, and it would have been almost more bearable if it had been high-pitched and uncontrolled, but it was simply the good-natured laugh of someone looking forward to an evening with friends.

Morningstar, standing at the door of her room in House Harrier. His large, pale hands were empty: no weapon, except the translucent radiance of his magic, briefly lighting up his cornflower-blue eyes.

"Emmanuelle, what's wrong?" And, abruptly, crossing the space that was separating them, his hand resting briefly on her cheek. "You've been crying."

It should have fuzzed. It should have become distant and unattainable, on the edge of that chasm she couldn't hope to bridge. Instead, merciless and clear, it went on.

"I can't stop her," she'd said. She'd sat, shivering, on the bed, hands crossed in her lap. "She's going to go up against Guy, and she's going to die."

Morningstar looked puzzled, and then his gaze turned sharp.

"Your friend Darrias? The defector. Then tell her to stop."

"It's too late."

It had been too late since Guy had taken her; and he'd known it. Preparations were already made. She'd tried to find Darrias, and found only the House, barring her way at every step. Dependents directing her elsewhere. Cowering servants telling her Darrias wasn't there. Smiling Fallen suggesting something else she might want a look at. A barely subtle, barely pleasant steering away from her friend.

A show, for Harrier's sake. For Hawthorn's sake. For Silverspires' sake.

"There's nothing I can do." She shivered, remembering Benedict's corpse in the Great Interior, and Andrea sitting by her son's side, her face set in that careful mask—on the edge of irremediably cracking. "It'll just go on and on, won't it? What they do to people. What they do to parents. What they do to children." He was sitting next to her, his warmth and radiance driving out the dark—a promise of power and comfort. "Please," she whispered. "Isn't there anything you can do?"

A silence.

"There are hundreds of people like Darrias, Emmanuelle."

"And that's a reason to stand by?" She knew all the reasons this was a bad idea—the risk of setting off a civil war in a House while they were still trapped in it. The affairs of Hawthorn, which weren't their own. "That's how you justify it, so you can sleep at night? I couldn't help everyone, therefore I helped no one?"

A sharp, weighing look. "You're really upset. We're talking about friendship, are we not?"

"Please."

Morningstar said nothing, for a while. At length, he rose.

"Friendship." His voice was almost tender. Light trembled on his broad hands, on the yellow fairness of his hair. For a moment, it was at his back too, as if he were still carrying the wings that had been his weapon of predilection. "I can't promise anything. But every place has its buried shadows, and Harrier has been sitting on these for a long, long time." He turned back at the door. "You have to leave."

Emmanuelle stared at him. "I don't understand."

A silence.

He said finally, "It will … not be safe anywhere in Harrier, soon. Go. Get to the gates. And remember, whatever happens—it's not your fault. They brought this on themselves."

It will not be safe anywhere in Harrier, soon.

Morningstar had known something. He'd left her and

gone somewhere, and the House had exploded. He'd done it.

But only because she'd asked. Because she'd been desperate and crying, and she'd begged him to do something, anything. And when he'd stood at the door—when he'd spoken of buried secrets, of hidden darkness, when she'd known in her heart of hearts that what she'd just agreed to wasn't just him nicely asking Guy, that it was going to involve widespread death and destruction in the House—she hadn't stopped him. She'd known, and she hadn't stopped him.

How far would you have gone for friendship, Emmanuelle?

All the way.

"Emmanuelle!" It was Darrias, shaking her, in the present. In the time when House Harrier was already ashes and dust—when Hawthorn and every House in Paris had blown up. "We have to move!"

She'd done it.

I don't know what you're failing to remember, but it's not going to be more than a book you failed to read or an overpolite, unpleasant conversation you had with someone.

If only.

"Emmanuelle!"

With a strength she didn't know she had, she threw off Darrias's hands.

"I can't," she said. "It was me, Darrias."

"Emmanuelle—"

"Harrier blew up because I asked Morningstar for help. Because I told him to save you, and he destroyed the House to stop Guy from killing you."

And, in that instant when Darrias, shocked and

horrified, looked at her, Emmanuelle pushed her to the cobblestones, and ran. Away. Away from Darrias and Victor and Hawthorn—away from the Seine and the flock of birds, and away from Guy coming for his revenge.

Thuan and Asmodeus found Phyranthe sitting in her bed, her head against the frame of the metal bedhead, a thin blanket covering the lower half of her body. She was in animated conversation with one of her interrogators, a mortal named Denise. She smiled when she saw Asmodeus; that smile remained frozen in place when Thuan joined him. Denise bowed and made her excuses, leaving the three of them in the room.

"My lords," Phyranthe said.

Asmodeus unfolded from the door jamb, graceful and smooth.

"It's good to see you recovered."

Phyranthe's face was a careful study in neutrality.

"I can't claim all the credit for that."

She kept her eyes on Thuan, unwaveringly. He shrugged, with an ease he didn't feel.

Asmodeus withdrew a flask from his inner jacket pocket, uncapped it. The smell of whiskey saturated the room—not just whiskey, but the one he kept in the decanter in his office, the good stuff of which there was so little left in Paris (and even less now, with the city in ruins). He handed it, wordlessly, to Phyranthe, who looked at it as though it was a snake that might bite.

"It's not poisoned. You know I don't resort to such cheap tricks. And you could use a drink, considering."

Phyranthe said, carefully, "You know my loyalty has

never been in question. I've always done what you tasked me to do." She was shaking. "The dragon is my subordinate, and my responsibility, and she's shown no such loyalty or respect to me."

"I know." Asmodeus's voice was curt. "If you ask me, she deserves all of what's happened to her." An expansive shrug. "Your loyalty has been exemplary." He paused, staring at the knife he'd just pulled from his sleeves. "I don't have anything to fault. Even at a time like this, when it's important to make strong examples lest we descend into chaos. I do need …" He paused, the knife spinning in his hands. "A favor."

"My lord." Phyranthe looked aghast.

Asmodeus laughed. "I'm not asking you to spare the dragon. Merely to have a word with Thuan on the matter."

Phyranthe's face closed. "We've already had words."

"Oh, I'm certain of it. Happy and conducive, in the best of all worlds. Nevertheless …"

He let the word hang in the air, like a blade in the moment just before it broke skin and blood pearled out.

"A word. That's all?"

"Well, obviously a sincere chat," Asmodeus said. "It would be a shame if someone storms out of this room screaming within the next five minutes." A quick, amused smile, and a glance at Thuan. "That includes you."

Thuan shrugged. *I can give you the introduction*, Asmodeus had said. *The rest of it—the way you want to do it—that's on you.* He'd sounded thoughtful, chewing on something unexpected.

I know, Thuan had said. *You wouldn't have done it that way.*

Oh, as I said—I do trust you, Asmodeus had said, and his smile had been incandescent and wounding, and Thuan had stopped fighting the thing in his chest and simply kissed him.

You can thank me later. Assuming it does work. A finger on his lips, and magic stilling his tongue in his mouth. *I will expect ... a demonstration of gratitude, never fear. An extensive one.*

That had been then. Now it was him and Phyranthe, and it was going to be awkward if he was lucky, excruciatingly painful if he wasn't. If he failed at convincing her, Vinh Ly would pay the price, and his own authority in the House would be broken, probably past salvaging.

Asmodeus left, waiting theatrically outside the door, though he had the decency to draw it closed—not only that, but Thuan heard the snick of the lock engaged.

Great. At least they were not going to be disturbed.

Phyranthe set the flask on the bedside table, looked at him levelly. Her blue gaze was impassive; her wounds all closed. She looked exhausted; and if she was anything like Asmodeus, that would make her sarcastic, her words biting. She said nothing, merely waited for him to open the conversation. Obviously she was never going to make this simple.

"Thank you for saving Vinh Ly," Thuan said.

"As I said—I do keep my promises. Don't make the mistake of thinking it changes anything."

"I'm well aware it doesn't." Thuan sighed. Well, nothing for it. At least it was private. "I think we got off on the wrong foot."

A raised eyebrow that was pure Asmodeus.

"I should never have interfered in the business of your court," Thuan said. "Not just once, but twice. Asmodeus is right—you've been unfailingly loyal. We ... We trust you to do your job."

"Flattering me? That's interesting."

"You don't understand." Thuan swallowed. He'd gotten used to being the one responsible; the one who cared for his dragons, from Ai Nhi to Sang to Vinh Ly. This one was going to hurt. "I'm saying I won't interfere again. In the matter of Vinh Ly, or any other. Not without going through you first."

A silence. "So you leave your dragon to me? As a ... sacrifice for my goodwill?"

"Don't think it doesn't cost me." Thuan couldn't help the slight acidity in his voice. "But I trust you to treat her fairly."

"Are you relying on my decency? Because she helped me carry her to safety? That's novel."

Thuan thought—of all people—of Emmanuelle. Everything has to start somewhere.

"Tell me something. Did you like the House under Uphir?"

"You know I didn't." Her voice was level again, but her hands had tightened in her lap. "Be thankful you didn't live through that. Uphir cared about no one and nothing. He harmed as he wished."

"As he wished." Thuan kept his voice as emotionless as hers. "And have we changed, really, since Uphir? Or have we just found new ways to harm each other?"

A silence.

"That's not the same."

"Really? You said you didn't take advantage. You said you wanted justice." Thuan kept his voice quiet. "You said Vinh Ly was yours to deal with. Then tell me this—given everything that happened, what would be fair?"

Phyranthe watched him, her eyes burning. "You really believe it, don't you?" Her laughter was bitter. "That people are decent and kind. That we won't give in to our wildest urges and do everything that is allowed of us. That we will be fair."

Thuan shook his head. "That people are fair? No. I don't. But I believe *you* are."

"I know exactly what I am."

Thuan walked to her, then; knelt, so that he was looking her in the eye.

"I know what you are," he said. And, after all, it was no more and no less than Asmodeus. "And I also know that we're not defined by the things we're capable of, but the ones that we choose to do. And I know who I am, and all the things I'm not happy or proud of."

A snort. "You?"

"Quick to anger, trying to solve all the problems on my own, and riding roughshod over people? You tell me," Thuan said.

Short, bitter laughter again. "Idealist." But it wasn't angry like the last time, but quietly resigned. And taut with something else, too, that hadn't been there before.

"I'll take it."

Thuan moved away from her, leaning against the wall and trying to disguise the tremor of exhaustion running through him.

Phyranthe watched him, unmoving. He said nothing;

merely waited—because whatever happened next was out of his control.

At length she said, and her voice was flat, her hands utterly steady, "Fairness."

Thuan forced himself to shrug. "Yes."

Phyranthe shifted against the bedhead, winced.

"I can't abandon discipline altogether, you understand. There will still be consequences." She reached for the flask Asmodeus had given her on the bedside table, unstoppered it, and stared at its contents, thoughtfully. "But, all in all, perhaps I can see that Vinh Ly has already paid most of the price for her … lapse." She smiled, her teeth as sharp as a cat's. "Preventively, for some of it."

"Perhaps." Thuan kept his voice flat, hardly daring to hope.

A shrug. "As you said—things can and will change." She held out the flask to Thuan. "We might as well drink to that."

"So?" Asmodeus asked when Thuan came out of the room. "I didn't hear any screaming or knives being drawn, and you seem to have survived with all your limbs intact."

"It'll do," Thuan said curtly.

Asmodeus detached himself from the wall he was leaning against. He took the flask of whiskey Thuan was proffering to him, and tucked it back in his jacket.

"Good for you. I must say, appealing to her principles wasn't on my list of means to persuade her."

Thuan suppressed a weary smile. He was barely keeping himself upright and from shaking: he'd gambled too much on too little energy, and the confrontation had left him wiped out.

"You prefer more explicit pressure?"

"You malign me. I've found whiskey and a heart to heart talk are usually enough, with her," Asmodeus said. "It wouldn't have worked for you, though."

"Because I hate whiskey," Thuan said, deadpan. He tried to lean against the wall; and found Asmodeus's arms holding him. "Is this really the time?"

"To prevent you from totally collapsing? Yes."

Asmodeus bore him against the wall and held him there, lips on his, for a moment that seemed to stretch into eternity. Fallen magic washed over Thuan, a warmth spreading over his aching muscles until everything felt afire—and Asmodeus's head resting against his, one hand running in his hair. He made a wordless sound at the back of his throat.

Asmodeus released him. "There," he said. "Better?"

"In a … manner of speaking," Thuan said in a strangled voice.

And stopped, because the link to the House flared, abruptly, in his mind—Lan, the dragon who was in the Court of Gardens. She was in mortal danger.

"Asmodeus."

Asmodeus's face had hardened. "I feel it."

Thuan moved away from the wall, heading towards the distant source of the danger, but before he could even move two paces, her light … went out. Not snuffed out, just removed from him. As if she'd been torn from the House.

And she wasn't the only one. There was another

light—not gone, but hovering on the edge between life and death, except in a different place. Lan had been in the Court of Gardens; this one was a Fallen called Aerneth, who worked in the Court of Hearth, and she was somewhere near the bedroom where he and Asmodeus had made their headquarters.

Near where they'd put Ai Nhi and Camille.

His blood went cold. He couldn't possibly cover them both.

"That's two dependents in two very different places."

"Yes," Asmodeus said. "Which one do you want to check out?"

He wanted Ai Nhi to be safe, desperately, but the danger to her was only uncertain, whereas the one to Lan was real.

"I'll take Lan," he said curtly. "Can you check in on the children at the same time as Aerneth?"

"Of course."

"And send me Mia and Vinh Ly? You know where I'll be."

"All too well," Asmodeus said. "Let's find out what's going on."

A last, regretful look between the two of them—a last brush of hands—and then they parted ways, and Thuan started running.

Vinh Ly and Mia caught up with him as he ran out of the ruins of the House, and into the gardens—to that last presence he'd felt from Lan, before the link had been taken from him.

She was on her back in the mud, eyes vacantly staring at him.

"My lord," she whispered, though her voice was a liquid gurgle.

She was half in dragon shape, but her scales had been torn off, scattered like withered petals on the ground—their faint iridescence quenched. They'd left a trail on her body, an imprint like a dragon's scale drawn in blood.

No.

No.

Dragons didn't die. Not like this. Not this easily.

"Lan," he said. "Come on."

He knelt by her, putting together a spell of healing.

"My lord," Vinh Ly said, gently taking his hands from Lan's body. "Let me."

Her spell of healing was swift, and sure. And it was like pouring water into a gaping, never-ending hole. Not a wound on Lan's skin closed; not a drop of blood coagulated, not a single scale regrew, or found its luster.

She was staring at him with that vacant, utterly frightening smile on her face.

"It's all right," she whispered, except he couldn't believe that's what she wanted to say. "There is a time for everything, and a season for every activity . . ."

A Bible quote. How apt. He bit back on an angry answer.

"Child. Stay with me. Please."

But her breathing only grew more and more erratic, and as he watched she sank into a torpor that was a prelude to death. At length, Vinh Ly withdrew her hands from the body, and sank down on her haunches next to it.

"I'm sorry, my lord."

He didn't deserve that title, if all he did was fail his people.

"Stop calling me 'my lord', please!"

A hard look from Vinh Ly. "That's who you are."

"Fine," Thuan said. "Then you can start taking my orders, and mend your behavior with Phyranthe."

Vinh Ly stared at him. Thuan sighed.

"I sorted out the situation with her. Just don't make it bad again."

Another hard look. "Is that an order?"

"Or a commonsense thing. Take your pick."

Vinh Ly opened her mouth to say something, but Thuan didn't hear the words. Because, in his mind, Aerneth blinked out, and then another light, the same as Lan, then another and another. *No. No.* Was the House dying? The damage wasn't that bad. They were weak, yes, but they would rebuild. He'd have a home again. A place where he'd have a purpose. Where he'd have Asmodeus with him, and the fragile understanding they had, which might not be love, but was still enough.

Stop.

Stop.

Mercifully, it did. Seven dependents: six in the gardens, and Aerneth. Was something prowling the edges of the House? But there had been one in the buildings, too.

"Mia," he said.

Mia had already half-left, in a wave of glitter, as he and Vinh Ly looked at Lan's body. When they tried to move it, something broke: a bone in her arm, followed by the skin wrinkling and tearing itself off.

"There's nothing left of her," Vinh Ly said. "It's … It's

as if she used up all her magic to defend herself."

Except that she shouldn't have been able to do that, because her body should have stopped her long before that. Dragons didn't routinely commit suicide through over-exertion.

"I lost her," he said. "Did you feel it?"

Vinh Ly grimaced. "She was in danger, and then she was gone. As if she was very far away."

"No," Thuan said. Even far away, he would have felt her, because he was the head of the House and he always had a sense of his dependents. "She was torn from the House."

And it shouldn't have been possible, unless they were talking about something *seriously* nasty.

An old, unpleasant memory at the back of his mind: a thought he didn't dare to utter. No tracks, no traces, just magic taken.

Mia came back, out of breath, but completely unharmed.

"There's no one," she said. "Just dead dependents. You can come and see."

They'd been trying to dig someone out from a ruined pavilion deep in the gardens: whatever had struck them hadn't left tracks, whether physical or magical. They had no wounds he could see. One of them, a middle-aged man, had been carrying a charged artifact: it was now empty, and brittle, as if he'd used it all in a single rush of magic. But there was no trace of any spells he might have cast.

"I don't understand," Mia said.

Five of them. And the sixth was Aerneth. Thuan knelt, to stare at the dead dependents. Their skin didn't show the wounds that had killed Lan, but a hundred, thousand, ten thousand pinpricks like the bites of an insect. Most of them were so fine they hadn't drawn blood.

Not an insect. Not a creature.

Thorns. The marks of thorns. And the children, when they walked, left no imprint upon the earth.

What was it Asmodeus had said, when they'd talked about the thorns in their pantry? *The House needs blood and magic to sustain itself—and if it doesn't have them, it'll take them from outsiders. That's what makes us different.*

That was what Asmodeus had taught the House. But lessons could be forgotten. Could be set aside, if the stakes were high enough.

"It's not a thing," he said, slowly, carefully. "It's the House. It's taking dependents apart for their magic."

It … It was dying. The thought was a stone in his mind. All the dependents, unprotected and naked against everything else, the dangers of the streets of Paris, the other Houses' depredations.

How could he justify letting that happen on his watch?

Mia stared at him, with dawning horror in her gaze.

"I … I don't understand. It'll stop, surely, when it's replenished itself?"

Thuan stared at the ruins all around them, breathing in the distant smell of smoke from the places where fires were still burning.

"I'm not sure where it's going to stop," he said. Or even if it was ever going to.

20

Those Dying of Thirst

Emmanuelle ran. In her mind, the memory of Harrier's destruction played, over and over, a never-ending stream of words and sounds—the trembling, overpowering light of Morningstar's body, the dim shadow of wings at his back. The way he'd said "friendship" in that fond and exasperated tone, before breaking the city apart for her sake.

How far would you have gone?

You'd have thrown away Selene's instructions and entangled yourself in a heartbeat.

Street after street after street—once, her path was blocked by a low wall and a few barricades, and a concerned Annamite with a rifle staring at her. Behind him were others with swords.

"Elder aunt?"

They were young, barely out of their teens—their eyes limned with gray, their bodies sagging with fatigue. They stood in the ruin of their streets, on split cobblestones crunching underfoot with debris, and they had nothing but worried solicitude in their eyes.

"Elder aunt? Are you all right? Come inside ..."

No. She was so not all right that she was choking on it.

"Stay away from me," she said. And, when they still didn't move, "Now!"

She called magic and pushed them away from her, and ran, stepping over the low wall and weaving her way through the barricades. They'd be after her. They'd know. They would never let her into their homes. Of course they wouldn't. Her arms tingled. Magic was painful, burning her from the inside—her muscles, her skin, her veins.

In the distance, birds screamed. A beating of wings—not in the darkened corridors of Harrier, but here, in the streets.

"Emmanuelle!"

Hands grabbed her—and when she tried to wriggle free, to push them away, magic rose, binding her to the ground and locking her arms into place.

"Emmanuelle!"

It was Darrias, out of breath and looking angry. Behind her came two of her escort, with more guarded faces—the older man, Victor, was taking his rifle down, scanning the street for threats.

"Go away," Emmanuelle said.

The bindings on her loosened, but Darrias had her in an iron grip.

"No," Darrias said.

"I destroyed the House. I—"

Darrias's face was angry. "You're deluding yourself. We've had this conversation before."

"You don't understand. I *remember*."

"You told me—"

"Thuan healed me." Emmanuelle's breath came fast and difficult. Every time she inhaled it felt as though a vise was constricting her chest. "I remember. I truly do." She paused. That corridor, with the smiling Fallen. Guy, waiting for her. "He *knew*, Darrias. Guy knew why you'd come into House Harrier. He knew you weren't just there for the presentation, but to snatch your family away from him."

Darrias opened her mouth, closed it.

You'll watch. Everyone will watch. You and Silverspires and all your masters.

"He was going to arrest you and execute you at the banquet. He …"

She breathed in. The buildings on either side of the ruined street seemed alive with shadows—and every time one of them shifted she heard the silky sound of wings opening. Every time she moved, and light glinted on oiled windows and polished door panels, she saw the yellow, unblinking stare of hawks. She was trapped in the House that she'd never managed to leave in time, listening to the way the future was going to pan out and utterly powerless to change it.

"He told me. He said there was nothing I could do, that the die was already cast. That I'd have to watch. To pretend not to care."

Darrias's face was unreadable. Shock. It was shock, but Emmanuelle had never seen it on Darrias's face.

"That's impossible."

"I tried to warn you, but the dependents of Harrier prevented me," Emmanuelle said, and it was more plaintive than she'd have liked. "They kept me apart from you until it was too late."

A silence.

Darrias said, finally, "There were many dependents tailing me in the House. I assumed they didn't trust me because I was Hawthorn. Not ..." She wasn't the kind to flinch at near-death, but even so she looked taken aback. "He told you. And—"

"I asked Morningstar for help." To do something. Anything.

A silence. Darrias's face didn't move.

"And he destroyed the House. Fine. Let's say it's true. Let's say it all happened, exactly like that. It's still not your fault."

"You don't understand," Emmanuelle said, frustrated.

She'd known. She'd known when she'd asked that he wouldn't have a quiet chat with Guy. And when he'd told her to flee the House ... She'd known it wouldn't be small, or innocuous. No, she hadn't known the specifics, but she'd unsheathed a sword. She couldn't claim innocence when it killed.

In the silence, a sound, rising. A slow, ponderous beating of wings. Another memory—but no, Darrias was rising too, keeping her eyes on the skies.

"Darrias—"

"Run," Darrias said.

But she'd barely managed three paces before the sky filled with them: a heaving flock that seemed to color the sky with shades of bricks and chimney mantels and wallpaper, all the colors and textures of Harrier. Emmanuelle forced herself to run through the fear gripping her– and found herself ringed by hawks, a never-ending weave of birds circling her, weighing her down as surely as chains, passing close enough that she could feel them, could feel the magic tight in the air, hungering for her end.

More birds: a slow, languorous flock like an arrow, descending towards the ground. They pooled like shadows—and behind them was the large-shouldered shape of a Fallen.

"Well, well, what an unexpected surprise. I should have known you wouldn't be far from your family."

No. Not him. Please, God, no.

The birds parted, replaced by people in the colors of Harrier—marching Emmanuelle and Darrias along to face Guy. There were far fewer of them than there had been on the bridge, and they were haggard and covered in blood. They must have fought their way across the Annamite barricades to get there, and it had cost them dearly.

She couldn't see Victor or the others anymore. Craning her neck, she saw slumped bodies on the ground, and birds tearing at them, lifting gobfuls of flesh like carrion-eaters. She hadn't even heard them die; but they had to be dead, because they weren't moving or screaming, and no one could have borne being torn apart in this stoical way.

Dead.

No no no. But it was too late, and she could change nothing.

Guy had changed. When she'd last seen him, it was only the House that had been beleaguered. Now his face was a faint gray, with marks on his cheeks like bruises, and gray circles under his eyes. He'd been portly before, and still was, but something in the way he moved wasn't smooth or arrogant anymore.

He'll realize he's standing in a field of ruins with nothing worth crowing about.

But it went deeper, didn't it?

"Where is Andrea?" Emmanuelle said, before she could think.

The woman holding her twisted her arm, forcing her to bend. Guy made a gesture, and the pain abated.

"Andrea is … indisposed. As you well know."

Dead, Emmanuelle thought, with the clarity of her own impending death.

At her side, Darrias said, "You'll pay for this."

"Will I?" Guy shook his head. "Your master is busy, Darrias. And, in this new order, who will claim or enforce reparations?"

One of the hawks landed on Darrias's shoulder. Its talons *sank* into her skin—not because they were sharp, but because they went through her skin as if there was nothing there. Darrias's face twisted in pain. The bird continued to dance on her—every time its talons went down, Darrias shuddered, closing her mouth on a scream. A second bird joined it, on the other shoulder.

"Stop," Emmanuelle said.

A third bird joined the others, and this time Darrias's voice came out in ragged, drawn-out whimpers—not even screams, as if she didn't even have those left in her anymore. Her hands opened and closed—and *something* dripped from her skin, not blood or sweat but something faintly luminous, caged light become liquid drops.

Guy smiled. "I warned you before. You'll watch, Emmanuelle. And there's nothing you can do."

Someone on either side of her, forcing her down; magic like chains, binding her to the cobblestones. She tried to look away but the magic held her; held her eyes open. More birds, flocking to Darrias, and Darrias was sinking to her own knees, legs limp, the radiance of Fallen magic flowing from her with every passing moment. Her breath came fast and ragged, and every sound she made tore at Emmanuelle's gut. Guy stood in front of her; and for a moment Emmanuelle saw, when he moved, that his clothes were feathers, and a bird flowing out of them to join the flock around Darrias, its feathers the pale marbled tone of skin and fat. The marks on his face—they weren't bruises. They were the ghostly imprint of feathers. Of birds, held within his skin.

It wasn't possible.

"Guy," she whispered.

The magic holding her felt like tar on her tongue, but it didn't prevent her from speaking.

He turned, briefly, to her. Wings beat under the flesh of his arms, and in his eyes a distant flock veered and turned, growing larger and larger, briefly darkening the whites of his eyes to the russet color of plumage. He didn't control the birds anymore. They were in him. Had subsumed him. The House made manifest.

"Watch."

He turned away again, as Darrias continued to whimper and wither away. One hand hung completely limp and boneless—as if everything had been sucked away or broken.

No time left. And, when Darrias's agony finally ended, hers would start, because she had no doubt that Guy would get as much pleasure from her pain as from her powerlessness. Emmanuelle struggled to free herself from the bindings, but they held firm.

There was a hawk on Darrias's face now, tearing at her eyes. What came out wasn't flesh but that same liquid light. Its beak stabbed, again and again, and her eyes darkened, torn fragment by torn fragment.

Emmanuelle gathered the magic within her, and started pushing at her bonds. No yield. Except ... Guy was watching Darrias die, entranced. When she collapsed to the ground, the magic that held Emmanuelle flickered. Emmanuelle pushed, hard—and felt something shatter, even as Darrias curled into a ball, her body covered with hawks pecking at her flesh.

She rose, shaking—took one, two tottering steps, trying to. She didn't know what she was going to try, other than to reach into the morass of birds and pull out Darrias, one way or another. She was going to die anyway, so what did it matter if it happened faster?

Guy turned, eyes shining yellow. His hands shook. All that came from his mouth was a harsh shriek, jumbling any words into meaninglessness.

Two birds flowed from his outstretched fingers, making straight for Emmanuelle. She tried to move, but she was too slow, and the birds grabbed her shoulders. Pain flared, unbearable, except that when she tried to scream she found that beating wings were in her chest, choking her lungs.

Time slowed down, froze into treacle. As she sank to her knees, struggling—with none of Darrias's endurance of pain—the link to the distant, beleaguered House of Silverspires blazed. Selene's presence came into her mind, acrid and sharp, a jolt that sent Emmanuelle's legs sprawling, desperately struggling to pull her body up.

Run, Emmanuelle.

Run.

But it was too late.

Aurore walked home with Cassiopée and Marianne. In their small, cramped flat, Cassiopée brewed some fresh tea, while Marianne clung to Aurore for dear life, whispering "Mummy mummy mummy you came back", over and over again.

The child of thorns moved like smoke through the room, its fingers resting, lightly, on the table, between two broken bowls. Its face was an inscrutable, perpetually amused smile—an inhuman, alien version of Asmodeus's own amusement at the pain of others. It was invisible to Marianne and Cassiopée, who simply swerved to avoid it without noticing they'd altered their path. Aurore could see nothing but it. It shone, in the gloom of that unbearably dingy flat: a rippling light that threw into sharp relief every crack in the parquet, every sewn patch on the chair.

Marianne wouldn't leave Aurore's lap during the meal. It was past her bedtime, but neither of them had the heart to tell her to leave.

"Where were you?" Marianne asked.

Aurore took a deep, shaking breath. Something sharp and stinging moved within her chest, like branches and sharp twigs.

"I was in a bad place," she said. "But I'm fine now."

Marianne slid down from her lap, stared at her quizzically.

"You look better," she pronounced, with the unfazed assurance of a three-year-old. "Did you hit the bad guys?"

Aurore thought of Morningstar and Dân Chay—of Harrier and Guy, alone in a House under siege.

"No," she said.

She wanted to say she'd made sure they wouldn't hurt them anymore, but they were under siege in a ruined city.

For a time, the child said. *But you'll make sure that siege is broken.*

Grandmother Olympe had been adamant she didn't have the power. Philippe, she could have dismissed. Grandmother Olympe was harder to ignore. In four years, she'd spoken little, and when she did it was either true or about to become so.

"I'll make it better," she said finally, and Marianne made a face, because she didn't know what Aurore was talking about. "Come on. I'll tell you the story of the rice ball."

A story of how the very first rice came to houses in balls that found their own way into jars, and how a disrespectful, lazy woman failed to sweep the floor properly—and the rice ball burst into ten thousand fragments, setting humanity up to forever pick rice from the paddies. Marianne always laughed when the rice ball burst, and Aurore made all the proper faces of people's shock. But this time, when she laughed, it felt like a knife slowly twisting in her gut—like a reminder of how fragile, how utterly defenseless they all were in the face of what the world threw at them.

That's what you do for them, the child whispered. *Defend those who cannot defend themselves. Fight to the death for them. As Hawthorn does.*

She didn't want to be reminded of Hawthorn. She wasn't Asmodeus, or soft-spoken, ruthless Thuan—who was slow and dependable and stabbed people when the House required it. She'd never be like them.

As you wish.

The child settled on the windowsill, framed against the hole in the oiled paper. At least she could fix that. Aurore got up, gently disengaging a sleeping Marianne from her lap, and laid her hands on the window frame. Power surged, electric, exhilarating. The paper started to warm, and then melted, flowing, slowly and carefully, like panes of water.

When she withdrew her hands, the window was a translucent, shimmering surface—not dancing in the wind anymore, but thick and firmly anchored in place. She breathed out, slowly, evenly. She kept expecting something to hurt or burn or some other side effect, but nothing happened. She didn't even feel exhausted.

Of course not. This is yours, now and forever. Part of you.

Everything she'd ever wanted. She looked at Marianne again, gently bending to kiss her.

"Goodnight, little fish."

In the other room, Cassiopée was sitting in a chair with a book in her lap, precariously balancing a notebook and battered fountain pen in the other.

"I don't even know how you manage to take notes," Aurore said.

"Practice." Cassiopée laughed. She stopped writing, stared at Aurore. "Tell me."

The child was leaning against the table again, watching her.

Aurore said, "It's not an artifact. It's ..."

A deep, shaking breath. Nothing hurt when she spoke,

or chose not to. It was … like stepping into a thicket of thorns and seeing them part underfoot.

We told you. This is freely given. What you do with the knowledge is your own.

"It's the House," she said. "It's the power of the House."

"You're a dependent now?"

Cassiopée rose, putting down the notebooks and grabbing her cane. Her gaze was sharp as she moved closer to Aurore.

"No," Aurore said. "The House lends me its magic." She wanted to talk about the gardens, about the grave, about being under the earth and feeling thorns burrow into her mouth and eyes, but just the thought of that made her sick. "I … It wasn't simple."

"I can guess." Cassiopée's voice was soft. "Prices to pay. But this is yours? The magic?"

"Yes."

Because it was not only a thing that belonged to her, but what sustained her. What she *was*.

Cassiopée's eyes were wide, almost tearful. "I can't believe it was real. That it worked. Old books and old texts aren't supposed to …"

Aurore stifled a bitter laugh, thinking of Dân Chay; of the tiger and of fire.

"Of course it worked." She squeezed Cassiopée's hand. "And it's all thanks to you."

"Both of us," Cassiopée said, still sounding star-struck. "It's real. And you can defend us now."

We could leave. The thought came, unbidden, to Aurore's mind. They could run …

As they'd run from Harrier? Her stomach

clenched—wobbling legs, the baby moving within her, the weight of Cassiopée on her arms, digging into her skin. The pain everywhere—the one thought running through her as she stumbled onwards—*please be alive, please be well, please please.*

Never again. Enough pleading. Enough running away.

"How long since he came here?" she asked.

"Not long. A day and a half," Cassiopée said. "Sébastien died. And Nene. And Frankie."

And so many others she'd known, in a litany of losses. It had happened often enough—to lose people to the predation of Houses—but not on such a scale. Not with such suddenness. She fought her anger.

"I didn't know." It felt like yesterday since Sébastien had helped her upstairs. "I'm sorry."

"We're lucky. Most of us couldn't afford glass, so when the shock wave hit the windows just burst open instead of sending lethal shards everywhere." Cassiopée's laugh was bitter.

"It's all right." Aurore held Cassiopée's hand, squeezed. "Go to bed. Tomorrow I'll see how I can help."

"Until Father Javier comes back?"

"He won't come back. Houses never do."

A sharp, amused smile from the child. She wasn't sure what it meant.

Cassiopée said, "Philippe—"

"Philippe doesn't know everything." Aurore forced herself to smile. It hurt. "Sorry. I'm tired."

"You're the one who should go to bed," Cassiopée said, laughing.

But she was still the first one to retire, slowly making

her way to the bed where she lay down and fell asleep in moments.

Aurore remained alone with the child. Fortunately, it didn't attempt small talk, because she didn't have any. She sipped her tea—the familiar, acrid taste in her mouth, a luxury that hadn't been allowed to servants in the House. She was back. She had everything she wanted. The only thing on her mind ought to have been Dân Chay, and how she was going to face him—but instead she found herself unable to focus. She felt . . . stretched. Hollow.

You're unused to power, the child whispered. *It will pass.*

It didn't, and tea didn't make it better. She rose, and left the flat, walking towards the edges of the community.

There were people in the streets, the way there always were in late summer: playing encirclement chess on battered tables, selling food, talking over a meal. The atmosphere was more nervous than usual, though: conversations muted, and those snatches she caught usually about the tiger, and the fire—and what it meant for them.

This was her home—the only one she'd known for three years—the one that had healed her, asked no questions, and welcomed her as if she'd been born in it. And yet, seen with the child in tow, it seemed wrong. Not grimier than she remembered, but simply not what she'd expected—buildings slightly smaller than she remembered, the cobblestones under her feet sharper, the angles at which the streets met unfamiliar and out of kilter—as if her memories said one thing, and her eyes and body another. As if . . .

As if she was an adult, coming back into the rooms she'd left as a child, and finding everything diminished and packed closer together than it should be. Except that all that had changed was her. The child, grown up. The adult, breathing in magic, and becoming ... different. Larger.

It will pass, the child said.

Would it? Did she want it to?

She reached, at last, the border. Philippe's walls, and the ever-patient threads of fire, gnawing at them. Some of Philippe's threads were now all but chewed through. In the distance, a flare of light, as Isabelle and Hoa Phong renewed their spells of protection.

She could do the same. The knowledge to draw her own wards was within her, suddenly as familiar as stretching an arm or a leg. Or she could reach for Dân Chay's threads and burn them at the root, squeeze them out as she'd squeezed them out of Aunt Ha's body.

A flash of memory: Aunt Ha, hanging limp and unresponsive, with fire flowing out of her, and Aurore tightening her grip, pressing down with magic as if with unfamiliar muscles until Aunt Ha's face stretched into a scream that never reached her mouth.

Aurore closed her eyes. Something was twisting in her gut, awkward and painful and unbearable.

She knelt, and slowly, stubbornly, started to draw wards behind Philippe's: a complex pattern that seemed etched in her mind, her hands leaving traceries of light like unfamiliar letters on the cobblestones. By her side, the child was kneeling. As she finished each pattern, it would touch it, lightly, with one long, sharp finger, until the light turned a murky green, and the ground tightened under her.

She didn't know how long she'd been working when a noise tore her concentration to shreds. She looked up—and realized she was shaking with fatigue. The wards she'd traced stretched along an entire length of street: a good ten meters of intricate, shimmering light.

The sound came again. A harsh, raucous cry, like a challenge, coming from above her. A familiar cry.

A hawk.

It was impossible.

The House was at the other end of Paris, and it was dead.

She looked up, and it was there, shimmering with magic: a bird with spread wings, riding an invisible thermal. Looking at her, as the birds in Harrier looked at their victims, moments before they dived and bodies crumpled like wet, wrung-out clothes.

Her muscles clenched, then, to flee. Back to the flat—grab Cassiopée and Marianne and go, flee to a place where it couldn't touch her or hers.

Beside her, the child rose, slowly and deliberately, staring at the sky with head cocked—as if considering the value or the threat of the hawk.

It screamed again. Aurore's heart beat, madly, against the confines of her chest. How could the child remain so calm? How . . .?

Because it had power.

Because it wasn't defenseless. Because she wasn't, either—not anymore.

Magic swirled within her, pure and unadulterated, a warmth that spread to her entire being, taking all her fear and quenching it like a spent flame. She forced her heart to slow down, and looked at the hawk. It folded its wings, and dived, screaming.

Not her. It had never been looking at her, but at something else.

Aurore ran, keeping her eyes on it, jostling people out of the way for street after street until the people ebbed away, and she was on the other side of the wall—the side where the buildings were twisted and collapsed and hollowed out, and bodies littered the streets. Broken cobblestones crunched underfoot. The bird was diving into an alleyway that was little more than debris packed on top of other debris, and …

She stopped, then.

There were *dozens* of them in the alleyway, perched in hollow window frames, on twisted lampposts—on the corpses that hung draped over broken walls and splintered furniture. More were perched on a corpse and tearing away, again and again, at its flesh as if it were the most delectable meal. The thing that spattered when they raised their beaks wasn't flesh or blood, but it was glistening in an utterly familiar way—and it was *wrong*.

It was magic. Fallen magic, except that what should have been shimmering light was brown, muddy, devoid of any substance—and instead of that familiar sweet, sickening tang in the air, there was nothing. A profound, far-reaching emptiness.

The birds turned to Aurore, all heads moving at the same time. The two on the corpse had bodies of smoke and flower wallpaper; the ones in the windows were fragments of clocks and mantelpieces; and the others the patterned, burned stones of Harrier's buildings.

As one, they flew at her.

She had to run. Now.

Aurore closed her eyes for one timeless moment—opened them again, overriding her muscles' desire to run, trembling with the effort.

No running. Not anymore.

The child of thorns, who had been trailing Aurore, stepped in front of her, hands outstretched, just as Aurore wove her own wards. The light streaming from her merged with that from the child's hands. The birds struck it, and bounced off as if they'd hit a physical barrier. One of them—the last and smallest one—scattered into a thousand shimmering pieces, carried away by the wind. The others regrouped, staring balefully at Aurore.

One of them spoke. "You will regret this."

It was Lord Guy's voice.

She'd heard it too often to mistake it for anything else. Not her own sentence of death in Harrier, obviously—she had been too small and too insignificant for that—but he'd passed enough sentences on everyone else. He'd sat, watching, while mortals were slowly taken apart for his own pleasure—and forced the servants to watch, too.

She . . . She was out of the House and Harrier was dead, and it couldn't touch her or harm her anymore.

"Go away!" she screamed, and power streamed out of her, shaking the cobblestones.

The birds watched her. They were going to attack again. She braced herself, shaking, for that to happen. She could do it. She could face them, no matter that her legs felt turned to jelly.

But instead they lifted off, one by one, flying away. The last one, perched on the body of a woman in a broken doorway, remained. The child of thorns made a stabbing gesture with one hand, and the ground under the bird heaved. It lifted into the air. Its body was that familiar flower wallpaper, the green and yellow one in the rooms of the Master of the Warded Quarters. She remembered the way her heart would clench whenever she entered the room, her eyes downcast, her body hunched small, knowing that making herself small was no protection.

It said, in Lord Guy's voice, "We will find you, once we are done with the others. And it won't be so easy, next time."

And then it left, and it was just her and corpses in an alleyway, and that odd feeling of desolation underfoot, the utter absence of threads on the ground, everything burned and charred. And an immense, overwhelming sensation of fatigue, as if she'd drained a well dry. She needed magic, she needed it *right now* or she would collapse and never rise.

She walked to the corpse the birds had been tearing at. It shone in her field of vision like a beacon, its magic an unbearably sweet promise. She needed sustenance urgently—the child was by her side, trembling with that same hunger—she needed it so badly . . .

Her hand connected with warm flesh. A shock, muted and clammy, swept through her entire body, and then magic flowed up her arm even as flesh shriveled under her touch, flesh wrinkling and shrinking even as bones collapsed. She breathed in—she hadn't realized air could taste this sweet, this exhilarating—breathed out, reveling in how tremblingly delightful it felt. She thought she'd weep with joy.

"Aurore . . ."

The corpse stared at her—no, it wasn't a corpse, it was alive, barely—and she knew the face.

Niraphanes.

Her House uniform had crumpled, and the two birds against the burning tower were charred silhouettes. The gaping hole in her chest glistened like an empty maw. She was little more than translucent, wrinkled flesh over brittle bones—because Aurore had taken her magic. She tried to breathe, but it came out as a wet, wrung-out gasp that should never have been.

A word, which might have been her name.

"Help."

"I can't help you."

Aurore hadn't expected the words to be so bitter on her tongue. Niraphanes had been kind to her once, but it had been out of self-interest—she was Fallen and Harrier and couldn't be trusted. It served her right, to end like this.

Niraphanes' head moved. Shaking. She was trying to shake it. A word, then another Aurore couldn't understand. And then it was over, the light rushing out of her body—and into Aurore, through the hand she still had on Niraphanes' chest, a rush of sweet magic that made Aurore feel warm and safe and …

Sated. Content. The words felt alien on her tongue.

She stared at Niraphanes for a while. The child withdrew its own hands from the body, and grinned at her with a mouth of branches, and twigs glistening in its maw.

Don't be sad. She was dying and you couldn't have helped her, even if you wanted to.

She wouldn't have wanted to.

Would she?

"She said something, at the end," Aurore said.

The child grinned. *Yes.*

More lies. Useless pleadings. She ought to have felt some vicious satisfaction, but instead she was queasy, struggling to find words. Niraphanes had helped her, and in return Aurore had drained her of everything and let her die in agony.

"What was it?"

A silence. That was unexpected.

"You don't know? I thought you could do anything."

More silence.

Finally: *She said, "Not me. Them. Guy. Morningstar. You have to . . ."*

It took a minute or so to sink in, but then her heart felt squeezed in a fist of ice. "Them" wasn't, of course, referring to Guy or Morningstar, but to Niraphanes' family. Frédérique. Virginie. Charles.

Once we are done with the others.

The others. Of course.

That was why Guy was here—because somewhere nearby was Morningstar, and the children he'd been using as a shield against Dân Chay. Of course. She didn't know how they'd come to be here, but it didn't matter.

"Them," she said, aloud. "Her family. Guy has them."

Or Morningstar did—she wasn't sure which was worse.

A puzzled look. *They're not yours. Why should you care?*

"I . . ." The sickness was still roiling in her stomach. Why was she feeling so queasy? "*Children*," she said. "Morningstar is using children as shields. And Guy wants to use them as weapons."

"So the lives of children are worth more than those of others?"

"No," she said. A life was a life no matter how young or innocent it was. She stared at Niraphanes, and remembered the dizzying, sickening rush of power as she'd drained the Fallen. She wanted to articulate something, but it wouldn't come. "It's just that I have a child, and I wouldn't ever want her used this way."

Decency. How much would that matter to the child of thorns?

It stared at her. She might as well have been speaking the language of Heaven, alien and incomprehensible to everyone but Immortals. In many ways, it was like the Fallen she'd dealt with all her life. It didn't care about Aurore's anxieties, who she loved, who she cared about. All it understood was ownership, and selfishness—and the desperate need to replenish magic. How much of being a Fallen was about being never sated?

"They are mine." Aurore put just the right inflections on the words to make it sound true—the same ones she'd heard Asmodeus use, once. "Not Morningstar's."

Laughter, like a hundred thorn prickles in the air.

You want to take what's his from him?

"For their sake. For mine."

Greed, too, they could understand, and the hunger for power. She thought of the flight of birds across the sky. Powers on the move—the House of Harrier, Morningstar. Whatever they did wouldn't be small, or discreet.

"Where are they?"

21

Held at Bay

Asmodeus wasn't back in their room: the only one there was Madeleine, the alchemist of House Silverspires, who looked downright apologetic.

"He's not here," Madeleine said.

"I can see that." Thuan bit back a curse.

That meant Asmodeus was still with Aerneth, or whatever had harmed Aerneth. Which was … on balance, probably not good.

Madeleine was waiting for him, nervously wringing her hands. So afraid of the House; but then it occurred to him that she hadn't been that way when Asmodeus was in the room. Just afraid of Thuan. He must have looked like he was about to bite her head off.

"Sorry," he said. "It's urgent."

The last thing Thuan had felt from Aerneth came from a room just next to theirs: one of the small rooms where they'd stored bandages and medical supplies. He threw open the door to it, bracing himself for whatever was within.

The room was empty, with only thorns and flowers clinging to tables and disinfectant bottles.

"Asmodeus . . ."

No, not quite. It contained a corpse. Aerneth, the dependent Asmodeus had been checking on, the one who hadn't been in the gardens with the other corpses. She was Fallen; and like Lan she seemed to have shrunk and shriveled on herself, her skin punctured by hundreds of thorn pinpricks.

The House. The same House that was now hollowing out and killing its own dependents to survive, using creatures no one saw coming and no one could defend against. Thuan took a deep, shaking breath. Breathe. Don't panic. He could still feel Asmodeus's presence through the link—anything so momentous as the death of the House's head would have sent devastating panic coursing through every dependent of Hawthorn.

The death of the House's head. That sounded so absurdly abstract—it was his *husband* he was talking about—his sarcastic, heartbreakingly infuriating husband.

Breathe.

Panic would be of no use.

"My lord?" It was Vinh Ly, standing in the door frame with Mia a step behind her.

"Find Berith," Thuan said. "And Iaris." He paused, for a moment. "And Françoise, Camille and Ai Nhi."

"My lord, this is no place for children."

"This is the safest place in the House now." Thuan bit back on the anger that rose through him. "Get them."

He crouched on his haunches in the meantime, staring hard at the corpse. Not much there. A husk sucked dry of magic. The House retaking what was its own; a huge, ponderous creature finally biting the hands that fed it. But no, it wasn't a dog or a cat, but something far older and far more dangerous, a hunger for safety and comfort that would never ever be sated.

He had nothing.

Think.

Asmodeus was alive, or he'd have felt his death. And he wasn't in immediate or mortal danger. Which meant the House had taken him, but not drained him. So it wanted something from him. It *needed* something from him.

"Thuan?"

It was Berith, and by her side an exhausted Françoise, with the bandages still covering her face. Françoise was clinging to a sleeping Camille; she sat down after she'd entered, rocking the toddler to sleep. Behind them were Vinh Ly and Ai Nhi, and Phyranthe and a similarly exhausted Iaris, though she was struggling not to show it.

Thuan had no patience for Iaris's pride anymore.

"The House has turned on us," he said. "I need you to . . ." He stopped. What did he have, to defend against it? He was its head. He'd always relied on it—but no. Once, he had been a prince of the dragon kingdom, infiltrating Hawthorn. "Vinh Ly? Is there something that will keep the House at bay?"

They were all looking at him as if he'd suggested that the Seine was flowing backwards.

"The House needs blood and magic," he said. "It took it from outsiders, once. But that's no longer enough. It's taking us now. Its dependents."

In other circumstances, he'd have treasured the look of utter shock on Iaris's face.

"Lord Asmodeus—"

"The House has Lord Asmodeus."

Thuan kept his face light, expressionless. Nothing of the gut-wrenching panic he felt. Once the House got whatever it wanted from Asmodeus, it would kill him. It had never had any use for the weak, even those belonging to it; any care taken for them had been Asmodeus's ideals imposed on it.

"Thuan." It was Berith's hand, lying on his shoulder and squeezing. "What do you need?"

He reached up, squeezed her own hand.

"I want the children safe. Vinh Ly, we have shields against Fallen magic." He ignored Iaris's disapproving face. "The other dragons can start protecting the dependents. Iaris, get it organized."

"My lord . . ."

Thuan's face didn't move, but he allowed the human shape to slip, so she faced the maw and streaming mane of the dragon.

"Now," he said.

Iaris opened her mouth to protest, but Phyranthe got there first.

"I'll do it, my lord."

Iaris glared at Phyranthe, whose gaze didn't waver. At length—grudgingly—Iaris bowed to Thuan.

"My lord."

She'd be looking for a way to make him pay, but her authority had been dented. And it didn't matter, because there was something more urgent.

Françoise spoke up. "Thuan? What now?"

He came to kneel by her side. Ai Nhi had left Vinh

Ly, and was now clinging to him, making small contented noises.

"Unka Thuan Unka Thuan . . ."

His heart felt like it was going to burst.

"Now I'm going to go get Asmodeus back."

There was, after all, only one place he could be.

Frédérique didn't know how much time had passed when Morningstar moved. It felt like barely a heartbeat; but she must have blinked and lost count of time, because when she heard him move, she came awake with a start, her arms wrapping around her daughter again.

There was a sound in the distance—an awfully familiar one—and after one more heartbeat she realized it was the sound she'd been listening for all her life: the shrieks and wingbeats of Harrier's hawks. Coming for her.

She rose. Or tried to. Because magic grabbed both her ankles and forced her down. Morningstar was bending over her. No, not over her—over Virginie.

"Leave her alone," Frédérique whispered, but his grip was like iron as he held her at bay.

His hand placed something against Virginie's chest: a large wooden disk that clung to her flesh as if it had been sewn there. Virginie convulsed and screamed as the disk's light faded into her skin.

No.

Frédérique tried to rise again, but the magic held her firm.

Morningstar moved away, barely looking at her.

"I'll be back," he said, matter-of-factly. "I would advise

you not to free yourself. I won't be happy if I have to track you down."

And they would pay for it in pain. The threat wasn't even implicit. Why had she ever thought she could trust him?

Enough. She couldn't afford to waste what little time they had on self-recrimination.

And then he was gone, without so much as a backward glance. Nicolas moved by Frédérique's side. He looked at her, his handsome face gray with fatigue.

"I can't move," he said. "I don't think the children—"

"No," Frédérique said.

Not that it mattered since they were both unconscious, and Virginie too heavy to be carried, but when she tried to shift her daughter's hand she found it held by an invisible manacle. Frédérique's own bonds held her legs, and rooted her to the ground as surely as chains.

Nicolas grimaced. He reached into his shirt pocket, rooting for something.

"We had her teaching artifacts," he said. "But . . ."

But they were not magicians, and as likely as not they'd waste the magic in trying to use it.

A harsh cry. No other sound that she could hear, but there was a dark shape, gliding over the broken trains and the twisted rails, headed straight for them.

"Nicolas!"

And then another and another, until a dozen hawks were overhead, circling them as if hesitant to go for the kill.

Nicolas's face was grim. He held something to his mouth, inhaled. His lips shone, briefly, with light—which spread beneath his skin but didn't illuminate much. Because it had been empty, or because he didn't have enough mastery of Fallen magic for it to matter?

Frédérique turned her gaze away from him—because it didn't help, because it didn't take them one step closer to being free. She turned to her daughter, gently shaking her—and then more and more frantically, trying to bring some life into a body that was as limp as a broken doll.

"Virginie. Little fish. Come on. Please." *Please please please.*

Overhead, the birds circled lazily.

"Wake up, little fish."

Footsteps, on the rails. Frédérique tensed to flee—a futile, nonsense gesture when her feet felt fused to the ground—and then stopped, when she saw who it was.

"Aurore?"

Philippe found Isabelle on the southern edges of the community, dangling her feet on a broken fragment of wall. Ahead of her, Dân Chay's threads built up, slowly and inexorably—no longer a concentrated pool of *khi* fire, now reaching into the cracks of their weaves, slowly pushing inwards.

It wasn't going to hold. They'd built a second weave of protections behind it: a thinner, flimsier thing because there had been no time for more, and they were running ragged. Grandmother Olympe had insisted they pile all the furniture they could find into the streets to form illusory barricades—as if anything could protect them against the fire—but sooner or later it was all going to burst.

He was out of ideas, which was why he'd let Hoa Phong

smear something sticky and eye-wateringly sharp over the back of the barricades. He couldn't see how it could possibly work, how Dân Chay wouldn't laugh and sidestep it, but they didn't have many better options.

"Are you all right?"

"No," Isabelle said.

She stared at the weave again. Beyond it was Silverspires, and—somewhere he couldn't see—Javier, trudging home. Dân Chay would see nothing more than one of the Housebound abandoning a fight he had no part of; he'd sworn not to harm him in any case, but who knew what he'd do, if he learned what Javier was looking for in Silverspires?

"I wanted to go with him," Isabelle said. "So badly." She raised a hand. "Don't tell me what they'd do to me there. Is it really worse than the fire?"

At least the fire was clean. Philippe clamped his lips on that remark.

"You didn't. Go, I mean."

A short, bitter laugh. "I'm not completely irresponsible. Hoa Phong, you and I are the only ones who can draw the wards. And maybe Tade. I want to, but I can't afford to."

"It's good of you."

"No. It would be monstrous of me to put my own interests first, right now." Another bitter laugh. She scared him. The easy-going smiles, the delight in life she'd shown before—all of it seemed to have snapped, and he didn't even know when. "I saw you watch me like a hawk. Ready to grab me if I bolted."

"You're not a prisoner here."

Her gaze was distant. "If you're preventing me from

doing something I want, even if it's for my own good, what else does that make me?"

A child, Philippe wanted to say, but again he clamped the thought down. More and more threads were gathering in front of their protection spells: the entire weave seemed to glow orange. The pressure he felt in his mind, the ever-present threat of his spells collapsing, rose to an unbearable high. A low-pitched, buzzing sound was ringing through the ground—a distant growl in a distant jungle, enough to make Philippe's legs tense in preparation for a desperate dash to safety.

Except there was no safety. Not for people like him. And especially not for people like her.

"When this is over ..." He stopped, then, because he didn't know. "Hoa Phong asked if I would return. To Annam."

It felt unreal. A thing he'd wanted for decades turning suddenly true.

Isabelle said nothing, for a while.

"You could come."

"As a foreigner in a foreign land?" Her voice was biting. Then she stopped. "I'm sorry. I forget ..."

That he was the foreigner in a foreign land? And then he realized with a chill that he'd been in Paris for far longer than she'd been alive.

"Come on," he said. "Let's get—"

Something burst, far away. Heat filled his thoughts—fire dancing, shriveling. And someone was running towards him, calling his name.

It was Tade and a couple of other dock workers, Mélanie

and Hugo. He was out of breath, the mnemonic tattoo glowing like a small sun.

"He's through."

"I know," Philippe said.

He ran in Tade's wake, struggling to find words for a prayer to some unknown deity—and worried that the only one around who even remotely fitted the definition was him.

Please. Just a little time. Just let us hold until Javier . . .

But would Javier really bother to come back, now that he'd returned to his House? Or would he leave them to fend for themselves, as his kind had always done?

Deep, deep down, he knew the answer. He'd always known. But he couldn't bring himself to voice it; to acknowledge that he had no hope left.

In the street where Frankie had died, Hoa Phong knelt on the pavement. The dress she'd worn was spread on the floor in a wide circle of cloth, and her arms were spread out, too, her skin turning into rot-flecked petals and flattening itself until she seemed to be at the center of three large, overlapping circles: the one of her dress, and the other two of petals drawn from her own body. In front of her, Philippe's spell of protection was riven through, threads racing through a hole the width of a person. Except that, instead of spreading through the cracks of the street, as they had done before, these were spreading through the flowers, veins of darker orange leaving shriveling petals in their wake. Hoa Phong's face was set—not in pain, but in acute concentration, as if she was trying to solve a difficult problem. Petals peeled off, carried by the wind. They were black and charred, and smelled sharp and acrid, like smoke.

Another crack rent the weave. More threads converged on Hoa Phong. Philippe looked behind her: at the buildings, bakeries, cafés where people were starting to mill, their eyes widening in horror. These absurd, useless barricades, with old people sitting behind them, their eyes narrow, their gaze sharp. Hoa Phong's useless concoction, because the threads didn't really seem to care about glue or whatever she'd spread on the barricades.

"Get them out," he said. "Isabelle—"

Her face was grim, resigned. "I know. Stay back."

The buildings were protected, which meant they could redraw a line just behind Hoa Phong, just behind the protections that had caved in—at the other end of the café and block of flats that had been the edges of their first line of defense on that street. Isabelle was already kneeling in the center of the street, drawing another jagged line on the cobblestones.

"It's not going to hold!" she said, her eyes on the threads.

The threads were fast. Too fast. They'd been complacent; holding their council of war, wasting time they didn't have while Dân Chay contemplated the best way to get past their defenses. Philippe ran to join her; knelt, frantically gathering *khi* currents in his hands. They moved away from each other: Isabelle towards the shuttered windows of the café, and him towards the block of flats. His fingers were leaden, clumsy things—no matter how much he gathered or how many meters of weave he laid on the ground, the other end of the street remained impossibly far away. Isabelle was working in grim silence, and meanwhile more and more petals were peeling off Hoa Phong's still body. Tade was herding people away. You'd think it would have been enough to see the mess on the streets, but there was a bottleneck of confused bystanders who thought the rules didn't apply to them.

They had to hold. They just had to hold until Javier …

Javier wasn't coming. The thought coalesced in the silent, exhausted part of him, the darkest corner of his mind where the curse of House Silverspires still lurked—as cold and as lucid as the ringing of a bell and drum at a distant pagoda, acknowledging the inevitability of death. He wasn't coming.

Even if he'd wanted to, even if he'd convinced Selene, there was no time. There was no way they could hold for that long. Ahead of him, Hoa Phong's body was almost all blackened petals—he couldn't even guess what strength of will kept her upright.

They had the second weave. Of course they did, but if the first one had been breached, what chance did a thinner one stand?

Each of them was perhaps twenty centimeters from their end of the street when Hoa Phong collapsed. It was slow and gradual and almost obscenely graceful—her arms spreading out, long sleeves flaring out, merging into petals, her entire tunic billowing in the wind, now a mixture of orange and black, and the smell of charred flesh in the air. For a moment, as she crumpled, her eyes shone orange as if she'd swallowed the fire's light.

The threads raced past her, grabbing and fusing Tade with the ground. Fire flickered around him, absorbed by the mnemonic tattoo. They took Isabelle, binding her to the ground as surely as ropes. *No time.* Philippe reached out, stretching towards the wall of the block of flats—his hand brushed a glass window, the weave of *khi* currents stretching from the street to rest on the building. He just had to …

The threads reached him, tore the weave from his hand like paper—grabbed his hand and twisted. Pain shot up his wrist as bone cracked, and he bit his tongue, tasting blood. Then they were past him, butting at the second weave, at their last, shivering line of defense while he still struggled to stand. They reared up, and the ghostly shape of a man wearing the old-fashioned, billowing clothes of an earlier dynasty formed just in front of the weave.

Dân Chay.

"Immortal."

He had legs this time: his body was changing into threads only at the very hem of his robes, though he still moved in a flowing, disturbing way that didn't actually involve walking. He stared at Philippe, while the rest of the threads continued to push against the weave, insinuating themselves in every crack, every flaw in their hasty pattern. Tade and Isabelle were on the ground, struggling to escape their own traps.

The threads that held Philippe tightened, the pain in his wrist becoming unbearable.

"Where is your vaunted composure now?" Dân Chay asked.

He once fasted in a cave to achieve it, his thoughts only on Heaven—except it all seemed so far away now, an unattainable fantasy.

"Dân Chay …"

The eyes in that face were luminous—amber held to light, to fire, and in the background only the roar of flames.

Dân Chay moved away, with a shrug. He was staring at the weave again, with that overwhelming hunger on his face—the urge to see everything dance in the firelight. He didn't really care about Philippe or Hoa Phong—or even the people involved. The Houses had made him their means to an end, or was that too facile an explanation?

Philippe pulled, futilely, at the threads holding him to the ground.

They had nothing, nothing that could hold Dân Chay back. It had never been possible. He'd race along the currents of *khi* fire to the center of the community—until Grandmother Olympe and the aunts, the bakers and the dockers and the seamstresses, all that he'd become part of, would vanish in a maw of fiery, unquenchable thirst, another explosion that would destroy buildings and incinerate people with casual ease.

There was nothing.

22

Against Darkness

The child of thorns led Aurore through the ruins of a rail yard: the massive grouping of rails and stabling spaces that had once held the trains behind Gare du Nord. Broken locomotives and wagons littered what was left of the rails: the metal was twisted and rusted, as if a giant had reached down and pulled again and again until nothing was left but a disordered jumble. Metal creaked as she walked through the yard: the wagons shifting positions. Had to be. This was a bad place for ghosts.

Harsh cries, overhead—and she didn't need the child after all, because a dozen hawks were circling as if over prey. She ran then—over the uneven ground, the power of the thorn children rising through her like sap in trees, so charged it was almost unbearable.

Frédérique was on the rails, stretched out over her daughter. She was trying to shake her awake, while her husband Nicolas—Aurore had to struggle to remember his name—was standing with the faint light of magic beneath his skin, hesitantly staring at the birds. Aurore knew that expression all too well.

"If you don't know a spell, it won't help you."

He wasn't Fallen, or a magician. Raw power might have helped them, but clearly he'd inhaled so little it wouldn't make a difference. Aurore threw a glance at the birds. One of them saw her; or changed its mind, and dived. She raised a hand, wincing as the power flowed through her. The bird struck the invisible barrier she'd erected, and bounced off it, shrieking.

Neither Frédérique nor Nicolas had moved. Aurore peered at them, saw the invisible bands of magic pinning them to the ground—a warm heat like a sun, even at this distance.

"Morningstar?" she asked.

"He's gone. He said we shouldn't move." Frédérique laughed, and it was bitter. "I guess he still has a use for us. Or for her."

Aurore followed her gaze, and saw the disk on Virginie's chest. Her blood ran cold.

No. How dare he.

"What does he want?"

The birds dived, again and again, their small bodies striking her barrier. Every impact was a jolt in her body, but the child stood with its hands pressed against the barrier, whispering indistinct words as they fell—no, not indistinct, but a song like a nursery rhyme, counting sticks as they were laid down.

"What do *you* want?"

"To help you."

"No one does." Frédérique's voice was sharp. "Tell me. Why did Morningstar strike you down? He said you'd have betrayed us eventually—and I see that you have bought yourself some Fallen magic. The power you so craved, at last. I wonder what currency you used."

Nothing but herself. She'd have laughed, but it would have sounded desperate. The birds kept diving, launching themselves at the barrier until it shook with their weight.

What could she tell Frédérique? That Niraphanes had asked the same—moments before Aurore drained her dry because she'd needed magic like a dying person needed water?

"Let's get you out of here," she said.

She stared at the birds again. There didn't seem to be more of them, but that was no guarantee. And if they were there, it meant a warded Harrier magician wasn't far away. And she didn't want to face *them.*

"Come on!" Aurore said. The barrier was shaking, and she now felt each impact as a jolt up her entire arms. "We can argue about what happens later."

"No," Frédérique said."That's exactly what I did with Morningstar. Not again."

Nicolas said, "Frédérique …"

He'd stopped looking at the birds and was using the magic to slowly saw at his own bonds. Aurore couldn't be sure how long he'd need to free himself.

"Shut up," Frédérique said, not even looking at him. "We've run for enough, Aurore. If this will simply trade one master for another, I want to know now." She pulled herself up, tugging at Virginie, who still didn't move—Aurore saw her face twist with worry and fear, but she hid it well. "I want to know the price."

What could she tell Frédérique that wouldn't make her run away screaming?

Aurore said, finally, "When the House threw me out, I was pregnant."

Frédérique's face had gone still.

"I didn't lose the baby," Aurore said.

Marianne, clinging to her legs; Cassiopée, ensconced in her chair reading a book as Aurore went to bed, her hair and face limned in lantern light.

"I made a life away from Harrier. A *family*." She used the French word *foyer*, the one that meant both family unit and hearth. "My daughter, Marianne. My sister Cassiopée. Only I couldn't protect them."

She felt it twist in her gut, again—could feel the pain of the disk against her chest, the perpetual tug back to Hawthorn, like a fish hook—could remember what it had felt like, to walk away from Marianne and Cassiopée.

"That's what I want. That's all I ever wanted. I just . . ." She spread her hands, carefully—seeing, from the corner of her eye, the child of thorns rise and spread its hands in a similar gesture. "I just want you to be safe, like Marianne. That's all."

Safe, the child of thorns whispered in her mind. *They're so much yours it hurts, doesn't it? Feeling that, if something happens to them, you're the one who failed to protect them?*

Yours now and forever . . .

At length, Frédérique's face relaxed a fraction.

"Fine," she said. "For now."

Her voice clearly said it wasn't over; but that she at least trusted Aurore not to be Morningstar.

Aurore hadn't thought it would feel like such a twist in the gut.

"Come on," she said.

She knelt and, slowly, methodically, started sawing through their bonds, while behind her the world shook and trembled with the weight of the hawks' dives. The child of thorns came, and stood by Nicolas's side for a while. She couldn't read the expression on its face, but at length it moved away from him, and came to kneel by Aurore's side, its fingers lingering on the disk on Virginie's chest.

Not now, Aurore said. The child's hands danced on the disk, wisps of magic clinging to its fingers. *Not now!*

In her mind, something large and immeasurable shifted, like a whale in the depths or the mass of a fungus's roots dormant underneath. The children, she thought—and then she realized with a chill that it wasn't. It was her. It was a sharp, vast hunger—like the hunger for power she'd felt once, but magnified until it seemed alien.

Her. It was hers. The hunger was hers, the power was hers, and so was the price and the consequences.

She clamped down on it, struggling to breathe. Not now. The last of Frédérique's bonds parted under her hands. Something spiked, then—like a beacon or a signaling fire. She held it within her, feeling its warmth burn her. The child of thorns moved, resting its hands on her shoulders. They tightened, piercing skin, and the feeling died away as abruptly as a quenched candle flame. Aurore breathed out, slowly.

Morningstar, the child said, sounded annoyed. *A signal to him, to let him know that they are slipping his control.*

Of course. Morningstar wouldn't have wanted to let go of his precious children. The shields against Dân Chay's wrath, the Harrier weapons he could sharpen to his own needs. The thought of facing him was … not frightening or blood-curdling, as it once would have been, but merely exhausting. The smiling, bad-faith excuses about how important he was, how important the House was. All of it masking his desire for survival, cloaked in the hollow language of morality.

Aurore laid her hands on Virginie's bonds—they were thicker, more deeply rooted into the cobblestones.

Nicolas was free now, profusely bleeding from ankles and wrists. Deep, blotchy bruises spread across his lower arms and calves, but his whole attention was on the sleeping Charles: he was slowly and methodically hacking at the boy's bonds. Aurore could hear his slow, labored breathing—his voice chanting a litany of fear and hope. She fumbled at Virginie's bonds, feeling the power within her slosh, like a brim full glass—any false movement and it would incinerate the child. The air was trembling now with the birds' cries, and the beating of their wings. She was ten years old again, watching them gather, watching the poor mortal that Guy had singled out—birds, peeling away from walls and doorways, made of bricks and glass and iron railing … Her own barriers were buckling and she wasn't strong enough to hold them at bay.

No.

Again, that vast and almost unbearable thing. It was hers, it was sheer stubbornness and refusal to lie down, the same coiled spring that had kept her walking in the dark, carrying Cassiopée's body, thinking only of getting away from the House. It was … hunger for power and refusal to lie down and pride and all the things in between.

The last of Virginie's bonds broke under her hands, and then Frédérique was lifting the child away from her, while

Nicolas continued slowly, stubbornly, to worry at Charles's own bonds. He had three already loose, and the fourth crumbled as Aurore reached him. She laid a hand on his shoulder, feeling power slosh and burn, a jolt in his entire body.

"Run," she said.

The barrier above them broke.

A haze of shrieking birds dived towards the tracks, their wings outstretched, the walls and streets of Harrier's buildings descending upon them all, a darkness hiding the gray skies and the broken locomotives and the twisted rails at their feet.

Aurore met it, her arms outstretched.

There was a jolt through her entire body; a burning fire—the touch of wings on her hands, her wrists, climbing up within her skin, bulges that sought to tear their way out of her. The House; the flat cages; the birds; Lord Guy and the other Fallen, thoughtlessly, needlessly cruel.

You will pay for it all.

She said nothing, because she didn't need to. She took them all in—all their hatred and their contempt and their need to crush others for their own happiness—and she crushed them all like paper lanterns, feeling brittle bones snap like charred kindling, and with every bird that died, the House shriveled, grew weaker and more distant, and Guy reeled from the blow she had given him. She took the birds from him and tore them apart with lashes of thorns, stripping him of everything until his mastery of the House meant nothing, because it was all but dead, and its only power now would be used to keep the carrion-eaters at bay.

And then it was over, and she was standing in a circle of charred cobblestones, breathing hard. The birds were gone. Harrier was gone. The House was gone. It would never again come for her or the ones she loved again.

She'd won.

"Aurore ..." Frédérique's hesitant voice.

She and Nicolas were looking at her with something very much like wary awe in their eyes.

"It's all right," she said, slowly exhaling. The child of thorns moved; she looked at it, startled, because she'd almost forgotten it was here—like her own arm or her own leg. "But we have to go before Morningstar comes back."

Nicolas said, slowly, hesitantly, "You could fight him."

Could she? Power still coursed within her with the same inexorable push as sap in spring. She'd held a House at bay until it had to reel back to lick its own wounds. She ...

But there was a child to protect.

"Perhaps," Aurore said. "But we should get her to safety first."

The word burned on her tongue. Where could she possibly take them? Anywhere that wasn't the ruined train yard; anywhere that wasn't ashes and ruins, except that the entire city was ashes and ruins, and the community was under siege. Still ... Still, it was the only place that would shelter them.

"Philippe," she said, and then stopped. "There's a few of us—Houseless—that have got together. I can't promise much, but it'll be better than the Houses."

Better than Silverspires, or Morningstar.

Frédérique started, "Niraphanes—"

"She's dead," Aurore said. "I'm sorry. The birds ..."

The lie tasted acrid and sharp in her mouth.

A long, weighing look, and then Frédérique looked away. Aurore's guts twisted, but it was brief and fleeting, a shame she was getting used to. She thought the child would speak up, would tell her again how justified she had been, but it was silent.

"It's your best chance," Aurore said. "We can stand together."

She knelt by Virginie's still shape, her fingers millimeters from the disk—she could feel its heat, its power, a faint memory of Morningstar's own radiant power. It wasn't frightening—compelling, yes, but not that murky attraction she'd once felt, a moth drawn to the light that would burn it. It drew her because like called to like.

"But we need to get that away from her first."

Frédérique's face was drawn. She looked at Nicolas, and then back at her daughter. She looked broken and exhausted, and Aurore wanted to wring Guy's and Morningstar's necks for inflicting that on her.

"Do what you must," she said.

Aurore grabbed the disk. Magic flowed upwards, into her fingers and her hands—not like Niraphanes' or the House's, but a slowly growing warmth under her skin, as if she'd been holding her hands to a fire. Then she realized, trembling, how exhausted she was; how much it had cost her, to defend Frédérique and the others; how much she needed magic, a thirst in her like a dying person's. She had to take this, to take all of it in, now, a sweetness like that at the heart of a translucent dumpling, the sustenance she so desperately needed, just as she'd needed Niraphanes' own magic to replenish her own ...

No.

No.

She'd drain Virginie dry. She couldn't …

Of course she could. Of course she deserved it. All of it, and why should she ever think of stopping? Hunger had driven her all her life, and it was only right that it be sated.

No. Please no.

But the part of her that was saying this was small and insignificant, and held fast within her with bonds of thorns, as surely as Frédérique and the others had been held in Morningstar's coils.

The hunger was hers. The power was hers. And it was her due.

Javier was in the library at Silverspires, and it was not going well.

Selene had been decidedly unhappy that he would strike an agreement without her—and even more unhappy and uncomfortable that Morningstar might have something to do with the explosions. It wasn't just his testimony: a lone survivor of Harrier, Lorcid, had turned up demanding an explanation for the kidnapping of their dependents by Morningstar. Fortunately she didn't come with the authority of the head of the House, and Selene had forestalled her so far, but the situation was nothing short of disastrous.

House Silverspires was the leader of a ruined, devastated city; and they were in no state to do much of anything, either. The House hadn't exploded, but the shock wave had torn it apart. The buildings had held, the wards had held—but dependents had not. The hospital was full of people with torn faces and punctured eyes, and those were the lucky ones. The unluckier ones had broken bones ranging from ribs to collarbones to limbs, and burst organs when the shock wave had picked them up and shaken them like limp rags.

Javier hadn't fought in the war, but he'd been born in its wake, and he could recognize sea changes when he saw one.

He'd left Selene chewing on the consequences for the House, and had gone to the library.

Emmanuelle wasn't there—another reason Selene wasn't, either. She wouldn't break: she'd always done what had to be done, and she certainly wasn't about to start because her partner was missing. But she was annoyed and short-tempered, and given half a chance she'd level Harrier all over again. Or Hawthorn, just as a precaution.

None of the harried archivists knew where he could find information on the House's war research. He'd ended, finally, in the older stacks, amidst the smell of mold, and the sharper, more acrid stink of magic gone slightly stale. He was unstacking book after book, not feeling sanguine about his chances.

It had been bad for the Annamites. He didn't have much time—if he had it at all. And he still needed to get back there, which was going to be laborious enough.

With a sigh, Javier turned back to his books. He offered a brief, desultory prayer to the God he was sure had stopped listening a long time ago, and turned pages, desperately looking for something of use.

"Here," a voice said.

Javier, startled, looked up. It was Selene. The head of

House Silverspires wore her usual suit, the swallowtail jacket impeccably cut. Her hair, cut short, framed a face awash with the light of Fallen magic. She was holding out a book.

"It's in the restricted section."

"The restricted section?"

"The one for the head of the House." Selene's voice was bleak.

"You're unhappy about this," Javier said.

Selene laid the book on top of his pile. "Of course I am."

"There won't be reparations to pay. Even if Morningstar did … do something rash."

"I know the lay of the land," Selene said sharply. "No House is in a position to demand reparations from us now. The world has changed, hasn't it?"

Javier thought of the sky, burning above them. Of devastated Houses with broken buildings and a sea of dead, struggling to recover.

"The city has. But yes."

"And you think we should acknowledge this."

Javier was silent for a while. He looked at her. He couldn't be sure that she'd like his opinion, but he'd never let that stop him before.

"Is it the alliance with Houseless you don't like? Do you think we should just take what's offered? The leadership of the city?"

Selene sighed. "Of course not. We can barely take care of our own. Would we crow over a field of ruins? How very Asmodeus-like."

Or Morningstar, Javier thought, but didn't say. He opened the book, scanned the first paragraph.

"Then you agree we have no choice."

"I agree. I didn't say I liked it." She looked thoughtful again.

Javier said finally, "I didn't see Emmanuelle."

Her face froze. She said finally, "She's alive, and not in immediate danger anymore."

Which meant she had been.

"She'll come back," Javier said.

A long, piercing look. "Is that the advisor or the friend speaking?"

Javier said, because she scared him, "Please don't lose hope."

Selene didn't move. "I don't want to."

He'd never thought she'd break his heart with four words.

"It'll be all right," he said gently. "I swear it will be."

A gentle snort. "Of course." She rose, graceful, elegant. "I'll have a car readied for you, when you're done. See me in my office."

And then she was gone, and it was just him and the book, and the weight of dusty years, and all the sins of the war.

When he was done. *If* he was done. If there was still time.

Thuan stood in the grove of hawthorn trees, beneath the tree on which Uphir's desiccated corpse hung. The rising wind shook the branches, and blood splattered on the scales of his dragon form. A few centimeters away the wet, churned earth became a gaping hole, the ground falling away into endless darkness, like a grave.

Darkness. Birthplace and grave. What lay under the earth?

Berith, crouching by his side, said, "I could—"

"No," Thuan said. "Your family needs you."

A raised eyebrow in an expression that was achingly familiar.

"I take it Asmodeus isn't my family?"

"You're right. He is. I'm sorry."

Thuan looked again at the hole. Around its edges were hazy silhouettes, slowly converging on them: the children, light glimmering on the woven branches that made them, on the drops of waters caught on the thorns of their bodies. They stopped, well away from Berith and him. Waiting.

"It's for the head of the House."

"That's what you said the last time." Berith sounded amused. "I can't say it worked out very well."

Thuan thought, for a while. He *knew*, in a way that he couldn't quite articulate, that the children would let him pass unharmed, but that they would tear Berith to shreds if she dared the same. The House didn't like Berith, as evidenced by the fact that Uphir—who now belonged to it in death—had misgendered her.

"Let's compromise," he said. "Wait here, and only go down if I haven't come back up in a couple of hours?"

Berith looked unconvinced.

"Trust me," Thuan said, with a confidence he didn't feel—and, slowly, ponderously, launched himself into the air, and down into the darkness at the heart of the House.

It engulfed him, not slowly and gradually, but rising up to meet him like tar. The small halo of light with Berith's waiting silhouette vanished, and he was flying through darkness—except that nothing held him up, and that it was like a never-ending fall. He thrashed, trying to control something, anything—tail and body and arms, pushing back against the air that held him, but nothing made a difference. He was still falling—faster and faster, with nothing to slow him down. He'd been so conceited—thinking that the House wouldn't hurt *him*, because of course he mattered, of course he was its head and no mere dependent, of course they wouldn't dare—except none of that meant anything, down here.

Something loomed out of the darkness—a branch, extended along the width of the hole with the inexorability of a trap. Thuan, unable to move, hit it at full speed. The thorns embedded themselves into his body, settling in the hollows between his scales. They burned like branding irons, except he had no time to think about it, because there was another branch—and another and another until the world was dislocated, fiery pain—and the weight of thorny offshoots wrapped around his body, trussing him up like a pig for the slaughter. He thrashed again, trying to escape them; but he was weakening, and it felt like struggling against an unmovable wall. Still falling, and heavier and heavier now. He couldn't move, and he wasn't flying, merely falling, loaded with heavy chains, into a pressing darkness, eager to swallow him whole …

He hit the ground. It flattened him, sent him flying again—and a third time before he realized it wasn't earth, but a pool of water. The branches were dragging him down: unfolding in the darkness and questing for the bottom of the pool he'd landed in. Everything was fiery pain. At least one arm had been broken, and it was slowly struggling to heal itself, pulling on exhausted currents of *khi* water. It was … almost peaceful. Nothing to struggle against, just the familiar coldness of water, and his sinking further and further into the mire, the House, growing more and more distant from him …

No.

The House.

Asmodeus.

Thuan moved, again and again, struggling to grasp *khi* water that wasn't his. He couldn't seem to grab the currents, but the branches unraveled. One last one clung to his right leg: Thuan kicked it off, and arced upwards, towards the surface.

He'd expected it to be dark—and really, it wouldn't have made any difference if it was, because he had excellent night vision—but it wasn't. The Gothic novels Asmodeus so liked to read would have had mysterious glowing mushrooms, but it wasn't that kind of light, either. More like the one in the dragon kingdom: of sunlight refracted through water, except that it was the sun of before the war, yellow and blinding, untainted by magic and unmasked by any pollution. He'd almost forgotten what it looked like.

And in the light … huge masses of hanging threads. No, not threads—roots, inverted pyramids, a seemingly endless succession of them rising in his path as he flew. None of them quite the same, but all a tangle of thin, aerial roots narrowing to one or two thin ones trailing in the water. And where they touched the water, a single widening ring, as if water were continuously dripping from the tree roots into the underground lake. The *khi* currents were … weird. Not exhausted, as in the rest of the House, but bent in odd shapes, curving away from the trees in all directions.

Asmodeus?

The link wasn't clear, of course, but he had a sense of his husband's presence—amused, sarcastic, unchanged, a comfort so strong he thought his heart would burst from his chest. Not the best time to be sentimental, as Asmodeus himself would say.

There was a tightening in the air, all the roots lifting away to point in a particular direction. A clear sign. The House was testing him, not trying to kill him.

Well, it wasn't as though he had much choice.

He looked down at the water, considering swimming rather than flying. It was his first instinct, except that the water seethed with frenzied branches, slithering above and below the surface, the large thorns glistening in the light. When he flew lower to have a closer look, the branches extended, whiplash-quick, trying to grab him. He withdrew, shaking, though not before one of them scratched his scales, leaving an imprint that burned like fire.

Make that no choice at all.

Thuan flew onwards. There was never an end to the masses of roots, but at length something rose on the horizon: a distant, gray mass. As he flew nearer, he saw it was the foundation of some immense edifice—and that it kept receding as he flew. His wounded leg was beginning to shake with effort. The fall had taken its toll on him. The House, on the other end … His sense of it, diminished after the explosion, grew and grew until it became a constant pressure in his thoughts—the desperate hunger, the need to protect the dependents arrayed like candles in his mind. He couldn't see the children, but he was getting closer to the heart of it. Not the grove; not the trees, but what lay underneath it. Its origin.

More tangles of roots, straining to catch him—he gave these a wide berth. More widening circles in the dark water. An endless landscape that didn't seem to change. There was no sound here, only a growing silence, and the faraway drip of water droplets; and something else that made the water shake, a slow immense beat like that of a giant heart. The House.

He was flying lower and lower, swerving to avoid the branches that lashed out of the water. He couldn't keep this up much longer. They were going to catch him again, and he would be dragged back down into darkness …

Just as he thought he couldn't take it any more—that he was going to falter and fail—the edifice resolved itself, became a wall of packed earth with a thin, small sliver of land in front of it. The invitation couldn't have been more obvious. Thuan flew to it, shaking; and made a shabby, catastrophic landing belly down in the sand, scraping his lower half raw. For a while, he could focus on nothing but his own breathing, his muscles spasming and relaxing, still locked in that desperate effort to fly to land.

Finally, he rose, shedding the dragon shape and becoming once more the dapper, elegant human the dependents were more used to seeing: the head of the House who was Asmodeus's consort and equal. The House's presence was engulfing everything—almost everything—and what remained in his mind was his slow, irrevocable anger.

By the time Thuan found Asmodeus, he was running out of patience.

Asmodeus lay unconscious at the foot of the wall—which

wasn't a wall, but a mass of thorny branches pressed together until the individual branches were almost invisible.

"Asmodeus!"

Thuan shook him. He had a pulse, and nothing seemed wrong—no wound that Thuan could see, and the familiar light of Fallen magic was streaming from his face and through the thin cotton of his gloves, the pristine white now soiled with mud and earth.

"Asmodeus!"

He gave up, and sent a jolt of cold water through his husband's chest. The body under him arched—and Thuan bent with all the weight of his dragon shape, holding him down as he struggled and coughed, spitting out water as dark as blood. His arm ached: with an effort, Thuan prevented it from healing itself. He wasn't going to claim any magic here, not in the heart of the House.

Come on.

His hands were shaking; he didn't have much left in him, but demons take him if he was going to lie down and surrender.

Come on, come on.

Asmodeus's eyes opened. For a moment, they were as lambent as the rest of his skin—unfocused and relaxed in a way that was profoundly *wrong*, and then they focused on Thuan.

"Thuan?"

A fraction of a second only, and then they were jewel-hard again, but Thuan had seen the utter exhaustion in his husband's eyes.

"We don't have time," Thuan said coldly. "How bad are you?"

"On a scale of one to ten?" Asmodeus slowly pulled himself up, fell again to one knee, slow and graceful. He was shaking; a tremor he disguised with an effort. "Eleven, I'd say. If not more." A pause, then he said, "How bad is it?"

Too many things welled up within him.

Thuan said, "Pretty bad. The House has been killing dependents for its sustenance."

Asmodeus's eyes narrowed. "So not only Lan and Aerneth."

"Seven so far. What happened to you?"

"The children," Asmodeus said. "They came into the room when I was examining Aerneth. They made … an invitation that was hard to refuse."

The House kidnapping its own head. How bad was it? Eleven, indeed.

Dragon-born.

He looked up. On the beach, in front of the frothing water, stood four children of thorns, staring at them. Light glistened on their bodies: they must have walked out of the lake. Their eyes were holes in the vastness of their faces, and everything about them was … hollow. Humanity drawn by someone who hadn't quite known the blueprint, a shape assumed for their convenience. They walked towards them—and even their movements were not quite human, their hips dislocating too much with each step. Thuan's hands tightened on Asmodeus's shoulders: with a great effort, he took them off.

"Sorry."

Asmodeus didn't speak. His attention was on the children.

"Why are we here?" he asked.

One of the children stopped, its hand millimeters from Asmodeus's face—as if to deliver a blessing, or to puncture his eyes.

You are our guests.

"What for?" Thuan asked.

A silence. The sound of the wind in branches; that slow, steady heartbeat of the House, making the ground under them thrum. Thuan forced himself to be calm. Panic would serve no one, but any moment now his self-control was going to slip, and it wasn't going to be pretty. They were in a place of alien rules, at the mercy of beings who thought nothing of draining the magic from people to save themselves.

We are weak, one of the other children said. *The dependents are not enough.*

Thuan hadn't thought his blood could go colder.

"What do you want?"

The child standing in front of Asmodeus tilted Asmodeus's head upwards, stared into his eyes as though trying to see the answer to a puzzle. Drops of blood congregated on the tip of its fingers—Asmodeus's blood. Asmodeus didn't flinch. Obviously. The day Asmodeus flinched, things were very very bad indeed.

Mind you, they were bad enough already.

We mean that we require more. The odd dependent killed—

"They were ours." Asmodeus's voice was cold. Thuan couldn't see his expression. "Don't dismiss them so easily."

The House is yours. It is your protection and your sustenance, against the barbarity of the city outside. But we cannot provide that protection anymore.

Thuan said, "What do you want?" but he already knew.

A third of them should do, the child in front of Asmodeus said. There was no expression in its voice: predators didn't feel for the prey they consumed. It was wasteful and unnatural. *Enough blood and magic to draw the wards again.*

A third of them. A third of the dependents.

When Asmodeus spoke again, his voice was level, but it obviously cost him.

"Why are we here?"

Because you have a choice.

Because you would hinder us.

Because they are yours.

Their voices rose and mingled with each other until Thuan couldn't tell which one belonged to whom. Finally—at last, at long last—they fell blissfully silent, and the child in front of Asmodeus released his face, and spoke again.

A House needs its heads. You are here for your protection.

Thuan wanted, so badly, to ask whether they had started taking the dependents, but that would have been pointless. He'd asked Vinh Ly for protections—surely they'd have something, by now. Enough to slow the children down, if need be.

You may choose the ones you need, or the ones you favor, another of the children said, cocking its head like a bird of prey, its neck bending at an almost forty-five-degree angle from its body. It was uncanny. *They will be spared.*

Thuan said, finally, "You can't do that."

Choose, the child said. *Or we will choose for you.*

Choose life.

Choose death.

Which meant they hadn't started yet.

"Can we discuss this between us?" Thuan kept his voice from shaking. He was quite proud.

There is nothing to discuss.

"You asked us to choose. Or was that just for show?"

A silence. Thuan watched the water—watched the *khi* currents swirl in the background, arching away from the mounds of trees. Watched the wall of packed thorns, the currents over it disturbed and wild, as though over a huge, ponderous living thing, whose heartbeat was the creak of parquet floors and whose blood was the swirl of dust in abandoned buildings.

Very well. Discuss.

They withdrew, walking backwards in exactly the same way they'd walked forward, standing with their feet in the water. Thorns crawled over them—thickened them, crawled away again, remaking them with every passing moment.

As if he needed more creepiness in his life.

He turned to face Asmodeus. His husband was still on one knee, his face gray, the light of his magic almost extinguished.

"Well?" he asked.

"You know the answer." Asmodeus shook his head. Thuan had never thought he'd see extreme anguish on his face—the kind that twisted his entire body out of shape. "But I can't help you. Too … weak."

He sounded disgusted, and exhausted. He'd always hated weakness.

"But you agree," Thuan said. "There is no other way."

Asmodeus's eyes were haunted. "It could change. The House could change. We could ask …"

Thuan shook his head, gently. "It's too old, Asmodeus." He gestured to the roots trailing in the water, the gentle drip of liquid like blood. "And it can't change, not this. This is entwined in its very foundations." A bright, intense hunger—a desperate need to go on at any costs. Blood and magic and the eating of its own. "You taught it otherwise, but it forgot. It will always forget, when things get bad enough."

"It's . . . It's not a choice. The House . . . I don't remember a time when I wasn't part of it. We can't . . ." Asmodeus paused, then, stared at the wall behind them, the foundations of that alien edifice towering over them, built and mortared with blood and thorns and living beings. "They'll bury us in there, if we lose. For an eternity of pain."

Thuan laughed. He was surprised it came out as amused and carefree.

"When has pain ever prevented you from doing the right thing?"

A low, amused chuckle. "You seem to believe I've ever done the right thing in my life."

Thuan shrugged. "There's a time for everything."

He bent, gently, kissed his husband's lips—drinking in all of him, that faint trace of bergamot and citrus, the sharper tang of blood, the roiling warmth of Fallen magic, the lips tightening under his, breathing him in. He wanted this to last forever; and knew it couldn't.

"I've got this," he said, gently brushing Asmodeus's cheeks with the index and middle finger of his hands, feeling the pleasant sharpness of cheekbones under his fingertips. "A spouse's role is sometimes to do the things you can't bear to."

He rose, walking away—shifting to dragon shape as he did so, wincing as his raw belly scraped the sand.

Heads of the House. Of the place that—warts and court intrigue and all—had become his home, in the short time he'd been there. The people that were his, that he had sworn to protect. Be their rampart against the attacks of the other Houses and the devastation in the city.

It was too large and too old, and couldn't be changed or shifted aside or sustained another way.

Behind him, he heard Asmodeus move—felt the warmth of his unleashed magic, to stop the children as they flowed towards him. But he was flying already, not towards the beach or the roots, but towards that living wall—and as he flew, he pulled on the *khi* water in the House. It was not his. It had never been his. It was claimed. It belonged to the House.

But he *was* the House.

And, in that instant of confusion when the children were still fighting Asmodeus, he called on old, old pacts, and *pulled*—and felt, ponderously, the *khi* water shift to him in an atavistic reflex. Power flowed into him, not the heady rush he was used to, but a slow and tentative cold seizing him as he struggled to stay in the air. Old, old things. They were slow on the uptake.

The House had almost died, once, because of *khi* ice; because of a rebel dragon and her spells.

Thuan wasn't a rebel, but he did know how to fashion ice into killing spells.

His maw connected with the thorns of the wall, which writhed under him like a tangle of limbs. He threw all the *khi* water he had, like a questing spear or arrow—fashioning it into killing ice, the same ice that had almost killed the House, once before.

The wall itself screamed. A high-pitched sound which tore at the air. Thuan grimly continued fashioning ice, turning all the *khi* currents into coldness—into a deep and profound thing that seized the branches and the roots and dotted the length of the wall with shining crystals.

The House convulsed. The entire beach went sideways, sending Thuan flying away from the wall. Something caught him—an unbreakable vise of Fallen magic. He thrashed, trying to free himself, and felt the characteristic sharp and wounding touch of Asmodeus's magic.

"Don't struggle."

The vise threw him back, arcing towards the wall. It was falling away, disintegrating into chunks of iced-over thorns—and in Thuan's mind the House, wounded, reeled back. He pressed on, relentless. A wave of Fallen magic from Asmodeus, who was all but overwhelmed by the four children of thorns. Thuan had expected the wall to collapse, but it was the water that frothed away, opening itself up beneath each of the masses of roots to reveal graven circles on the muddy floor—written in a language that seemed hazily familiar, as if enough time spent studying it would reveal its secrets.

How dare you?

Thuan hung on, grimly. The ice traveled on, into the crevices of the letters on the lake floor—upwards, into the tangles of roots, into that dizzying, infinite wall that kept falling apart. Something within him *tore*—like a huge, nebulous organ he couldn't place, leaving him dizzy and weak and in so much pain he couldn't help but scream, his own heartbeat becoming impossibly, agonizingly loud in his chest. All the lights in his mind—all the dependents he had sworn to protect—snuffed out, each of them burning as they vanished, a sense of arching overwhelming pain. He had failed them, he had failed them all, he'd always known that he wasn't suitable, not ruthless enough. He had to stop—he had to do something, or be forever unable to breathe.

But, if he stopped, the House would recover. And then his people would die.

At last, at long last, it ebbed away. Darkness fell across his field of vision. He lay curled on the beach, his entire body scraped raw as if he'd been scaled and filleted, and the screams of the House had been replaced by the endless sound of falling masonry splashing into the water.

There was a gaping hole in the world, in his mind. The pain had sunk to low embers, but had been replaced by a rising, absolute certainty that nothing would ever make sense again.

The House was his, and he had killed it.

Someone was sitting by his side. Asmodeus. His husband looked as raw as Thuan felt, his skin bleeding from ten thousand thorn-punctures. Behind him were the splayed-out bodies of the children of thorns, unraveling under the weight of ice. Asmodeus's lips curled into the ghost of his old sarcastic smile.

"It's almost beautiful, isn't it? A death unlike any other . . ."

Thuan heard his raw despair—the scream that had been the House's and that was now lodged as deep and as sharp as a shard of metal in their bodies. He curled around Asmodeus's body, watching that impossible light falter and fade above the frozen root masses.

"Ssh," he said, hugging his husband's stiff, bleeding body. "Sshhh. It's going to be all right."

23
Everything Feared

Philippe was sitting on the ground, pulling on threads of *khi* water. In front of him, Dân Chay was in a similar position: cross-legged on the cobblestones with *khi* fire spread all around him, staring at the weave. It was almost all fire now, all of Philippe's spells undone, a heat he could feel, physically, even from where he was sitting.

They weren't going to last.

In the distance came a roar he couldn't quite make out. The ground, shaking. A distant cry, like a bird of prey—an odd sound, because all the birds in Paris were in cages now, the war having purged them from the sky. Dân Chay still didn't move. Why would he? After all, he only had to wait.

When Philippe looked up again, the shuttered door of the café was open, and Javier was kneeling on the threshold, trying to free Isabelle.

How . . .?

He must have gone through the back door, instead of through the street. How had he come back so fast? The cars. Silverspires' fleet of cars, magically powered. Even navigating streets clogged by debris wouldn't have delayed them for long.

Javier was holding some kind of knife and was hacking, one by one, at the threads that held her. When he touched them, they turned ... an odd, faded color, a maroon red with a silver sheen, and became brittle. Isabelle was pulling them off her like spun glass, her own hands a different red: that of opened wounds on her skin.

Javier looked up, and saw Philippe. He nodded, grimly, made a gesture with his hands.

Soon.

He was getting Isabelle out of harm's way first. Philippe opened his mouth to tell him to hurry, that the community was more important, but the words shriveled on his tongue. He didn't want Isabelle to die again. He wanted her to be safe.

Dân Chay hadn't moved. But the moment he did—the moment he looked in that direction—he was going to see them. Philippe gave up on trying to free himself, and gathered threads of *khi* water, *khi* earth and *khi* wood. He flung them, like lifelines, at the weaves of the second line—in front of Dân Chay, on his side. They connected with a jolt that resonated in his entire body—and moved towards the other threads, the ones of the weave. Like called to like; except that as they moved through Dân Chay's own threads, they ate at them like acid.

Dân Chay turned, too fluid and fast. He stared at Philippe. His face flickered; became covered with fur again, his fingers stretching into sharp, glistening things that were *definitely* not nails. Another heartbeat, and he was standing next to Philippe, grabbing him by his tunic.

"Do you think you do anything but prolong your agony?"

He was hanging in the air, struggling to breathe—to

find again the serenity that had suffused him when he had ascended into Heaven—but all he could see was Dân Chay's eyes, and the fire that burned within them. Not the fire that lurked in the jungles and would take them all, but the one the Houses had lit, the weapon they had forged, the one that had forgotten how to howl in pain and only knew how to kill and kill to sate its hunger, just like the Houses themselves.

Dân Chay hauled him up. Philippe, struggling, managed to touch the ground again—but it was only the points of his feet, and he couldn't push against them or find any strength at all. As Dân Chay lifted him once again, he saw Javier moving away from Isabelle, something passing between them. No, no, no, that wasn't what was supposed to happen.

Isabelle rose, graceful, impossibly lithe. Her face was roiling with the light of Fallen magic. In her hand was the knife Javier had used, except it wasn't a knife, but a slender cane that stretched as she did, like the rattan ones used for beatings in Annam. *No no no.* She struck the ground with it, once, twice—and where it touched, threads became dark and dull. The ground shook—and Dân Chay let go of Philippe, snarling, took one, two steps backwards, towards the second weave.

The ground shook again. The threads holding Philippe grew still—and before he knew it Isabelle was kneeling by his side, pulling them off him.

"Isabelle ..."

Ahead of them, Dân Chay was on his haunches on burst cobblestones. The orange threads were flowing from the second weave to him, a light that filled him from inside, his entire skin translucent amber, streaked with darker stripes. Philippe expected him to become the tiger again, but instead his face was sharper and more angular, and aside from the skin he'd never looked as human as he did now—except that he was growing tall and bright and terrible, and the fingernail guards on both his hands were as wickedly sharp as needles. The air was taut, a dry, oppressive heat pressing against them until breath was a struggle. Gathering himself for a fight.

Against Isabelle.

"It doesn't have to be you," Philippe said, desperately. "Javier could ..."

Her voice was gentle. "It's our mess. Javier was very clear about the conditions."

"Isabelle ..."

He'd wanted her to be safe. To be ... anything but this, flush with the light of Fallen magic and headed into the kind of battle that had killed her in House Silverspires.

She smiled. "You don't approve." She reached out, touched his hand. "I know, Philippe. I've known for a while."

"I don't understand."

"It wasn't the ritual of resurrection that failed, was it? You made me mortal."

His stomach clenched. But she didn't seem angry. Just sad. In a way, it was worse.

She said, "You can't keep making choices for me, Philippe."

"I ..." The words were bitter on his tongue. "I can't keep you safe."

"No." She rose, holding the cane much as she would a

sword. "But you don't have to." And, more gently as she withdrew from him, "We all grow up. You learn to let go."

He got up, struggling to breathe. "Isabelle!"

If I'm not a prisoner, what does that make me?

A child.

We all grow up.

He knew that, but he didn't want to.

"Isabelle!"

But she was already gone, and his hand grabbed only air.

She said something to Dân Chay as she caught up with him. His smile was sharp, gleeful, as he rose from his crouch and she switched the cane from one hand to another.

"House-bound."

Isabelle moved, lashing out. Dân Chay wasn't there when she struck. She made a small, frustrated noise at the back of her throat, and the light around her intensified.

She was everything he'd feared. Every nightmare he'd had about her—the memories in which she stood, hard-faced with Fallen magic streaming from her, coldly and casually saying that only the House mattered, that all others could die in agony for its sake. She was again the Fallen he'd run from, because he couldn't bear what she'd become. As she danced with Dân Chay, she was once more bright and terrible, with the shadow of dark wings at her back—Morningstar's heir in all the ways that mattered.

Someone was pulling at him. Javier.

"You can't help her."

Philippe turned, trying to keep his voice level—and failing.

"You gave her magic."

Javier's face didn't move. "It's a Fallen artifact. Of course I gave her magic to use it. Or it'd have burned her to cinders."

Philippe tried to speak—but fear choked the words in his mouth. He'd wanted her to be safe. To be away from House Silverspires and the death that had found her, once—back when he had failed her. But . . . But he'd wanted so many other things for her. For it to be different.

You made me mortal.

Isabelle was trying to reach Dân Chay with the cane; but he danced out of her way gracefully, time and time again. His smile was grim.

"Is that all you have, House-bound? Do you think it's going to be enough to hold me?"

Isabelle lunged. Once, twice, but she was too slow. Too weak, and would it even have made a difference if she'd been Fallen?

They'd lost.

A wind rose behind him, carrying, not the smell of smoke or rot, but a distant, heartbreaking one of flowers. Petals fluttered past him, the golden color of New Year's Eve flowers.

Hoa Phong.

She'd risen, trembling, from the circle where she'd fallen. She was all petals now, with only the faintest suggestion of a woman at the center of them all—only the flaring sleeves of her dress, and the unbearably sharp golden color. The wind rose, became stronger. As Isabelle danced, futilely, with Dân Chây, desperately trying to reach him, Hoa Phong's petals came to the barricades, touched the back of them, lightly—and plunged towards Dân Chay, glistening with the substance she'd smeared across the furniture.

In the circle, Hoa Phong's shape barely held constant. Philippe held his breath. Dân Chay snarled as the petals swirled closer to him. He moved, fluid, inhuman; but he couldn't avoid both her and Isabelle. Petals stuck to his hands. He grinned, moved away—making no move to brush them away. Hoa Phong was almost spent: he probably felt her presence like insect bites, if at all.

Isabelle lunged again. Dân Chay moved beyond her, towards the last of the walls, their last line of defense against the fire's reach. In her circle, Hoa Phong screamed, long and shuddering—and completely disintegrated, a whirlwind of petals going straight for Dân Chay's face.

He sidestepped, or tried to. His claws batted petals away, and where he struck them blood fell on the ground, and the storm of petals shuddered and almost came apart—but it didn't. It held—and, in that single moment when he failed to avoid them, Hoa Phong managed to cling to his face.

His mouth opened. Hoa Phong's petals thronged to fill it, swallowing up his scream. He raised his hands to claw her away, and the petals still clinging to the backs of them—shining with blood and charred ashes and the faint bluish tinge of Hoa Phong's wounds—flowed away to join the others in a loose patchwork on his face and neck. The petals clenched, tightening around his neck like a vise. Dân Chay shivered, hands clenching, once, twice—stopped, immobile for a bare moment.

Isabelle's cane connected with him. A sickening crunch, and welts of blood opening on Dân Chay's chest and shoulders. Hoa Phong's petals still clung to his face and his neck—it had to hurt, as the cane struck at her again and again, but she didn't move.

Once, twice, and Dân Chay was falling back, snarling, his clothes in bloodied, shredded tatters. Isabelle came at him again. As the tip of the cane trailed on the cobblestones, they split asunder, the threads in the cracks growing dull and cold. Dân Chay's breath came fast and heavy and ragged—they could hear it from where they stood, choked and on the verge of faltering. Hoa Phong's petals finally scattered away from his face and mouth, reforming into the prone, burned shape of a woman on the ground, at the foot of the remaining wall. Where she'd touched him, his skin was mottled with the rot of Fallen magic. His eyes were swollen shut, their contours bluish and rotted, the exact same color of Hoa Phong's wounds.

Isabelle's next strike sent Dân Chay sprawling to the ground—stretching, lithe and fluid, struggling to escape her. The ground under him was now red—a luminous, shifting thing that could only be blood. In the silence, they heard his ragged breath. His smile was terrifying.

"House-bound," he whispered.

When the cane fell again it smashed through the hands he'd lifted to protect himself. A crunch like bones breaking—he screamed then, an inarticulate half-pitched thing, but Isabelle was already raising the cane, again and again and again. The sound it made was liquid now, sinking into pulped flesh—and still she beat at him. The air was tight with the smell of blood and charred flesh.

A hard knot was growing in Philippe's chest.

"She's not going to stop, is she?"

Javier said, "He wasn't going to stop, either. He leveled half of Paris, and she's only doing what needs to be done. What did you think was going to happen, when you asked us for a weapon?"

Not this, and again words, too many and too jumbled together, failed him.

House-bound.

Philippe had wanted her to be mortal, not because he wanted her to die or to be weak, but because what he'd feared most was her cruelty. Because what he'd tried to teach her, this time around, were the things the Houses never stopped to consider. He'd wanted her to be whole and balanced and . . . He groped for words, and only found an antique, almost desperately old-fashioned word in Viet. *Nhan.* Humane. Compassionate.

You have to let go.

She'd wanted to make her own choices—and in that he had failed her. But it didn't mean he had no advice or reminders to offer her. He remained, after all, her teacher. Her guide.

Her friend.

"Isabelle!"

She didn't even turn—too wrapped up in beating a spirit to death. So he caught the *khi* currents around her, and conjured out of *khi* wood and *khi* water a memory from an earlier, quieter time: the ghostly pages of the papers they'd found in Diamaras's museum, with their detailed diagrams on how to make a living weapon. How to make a monster, he would have said, except that the monsters were also the ones holding the cages' keys.

He wanted to run to her, to catch the hand holding

the cane; to push her away from Dân Chay. He forced himself, instead, to walk. To go towards her slowly and deliberately across the wasteland of the street, his eyes on her all the while. Hers were on the images he'd conjured, one hand going to her mouth in that familiar, surprised gesture. The other still held the cane—used it, effortlessly, to hold Dân Chay. The quivering mass under the cane, bleeding and heaving, was barely human or tiger anymore. Even the light was draining from it, from translucent amber to dark, rotten blood.

"Isabelle."

He stood, waiting, stilling his urge to move. It cost him.

She didn't move. At length she said, without looking at him, "He would kill us all, and not bat an eyelid. You know this. As long as he lives, he'll try again and again."

"Yes." Philippe weighed words in his mind. Finally he said, "This isn't about him."

She turned, to face him. Her eyes were bottomless holes in the paleness of her face.

"I'm not like the people in those papers." And, in a lower, slower voice, "Am I?"

House-bound.

A silence. The clatter of the cane as it left her hands, falling to the pavement. He'd thought she would collapse, but she remained rigidly upright, staring at him with that brittle look that meant she'd snap at any time.

"What now?"

He walked to her, hugging her, as the cane glimmered in the light, begging to be picked up. To be used, always hungering for blood and magic and destruction. In his mind, the darkness of Silverspires' curse stirred, stretched ghostly hands for it.

No.

He supposed he was meant to be tempted, but he was too old, too tired, to want more than to destroy it just as Dân Chay had destroyed all the other Houses.

Instead, he knelt by Dân Chay's side. Light, sickly and dark red, was pooling in the hollows of the cobblestone.

"I know you can hear me," he said.

Silence. At length, a low, wheezing sound that felt like Dân Chay was coughing his lungs out.

"You ... have ... my ... attention."

"You talked about a bargain, earlier. You said you kept your word."

He'd spared Javier, even though he didn't have to, earlier.

Another amused wheeze. "What ... did ... you have ... in mind?"

"Go home," Philippe said. The irony of saying that to an Immortal who'd been there longer than him wasn't wasted on him. "The Court of the Jade Emperor needs you."

Philippe looked back, for a brief moment, at Hoa Phong's body, scattered petals and cloth. He couldn't even be sure if she'd survived—but then he saw that the petals were quivering in the breeze, slowly flowing back together. Still alive; though what would they get, when she was in human shape again?

If she was in no shape to travel, the duty would fall to him.

Out of the ruin of Dân Chay's face, two eyes, tawny and slitted, stared back at him.

"Do they?" A low, amused laugh. "This is … justice, isn't it?"

No. It could never be. The Houses had made Dân Chay into what he was, but that was no excuse for what he'd done—for what he'd tried to do. Justice was death, but the only way to kill him was to beat him, as Isabelle had tried. Atonement? But Philippe didn't believe in that, either.

"This is … mercy." He'd thought the word would be hollow and bitter, but it wasn't. "Kindness." Not a Confucian word this time, but *tu*, the Buddhist one. "Do we have a bargain?"

That wheeze again. Flesh was knitting itself back together. Watching wounds that should have killed him slowly narrowing to thin slivers of scabbed blood—Dân Chay's breath caught as they closed. It was neither painless nor easy. Philippe wanted to say Dân Chay had deserved it, but what would that make him?

"Done." Dân Chay laughed, and it rattled amidst broken bones. "Kindness."

Behind them, Isabelle still stood, staring at the cane, holding herself very still, the light glinting on the tears in her eyes—and, behind her, the devastation Dân Chay had left in his wake, the city that was now ruins and blown-open buildings, with one single tottering House still standing.

Kindness. Compassion. Humaneness.

Not what Philippe or Dân Chay wanted—not what Dân Chay deserved—but perhaps, in the end, all they could hope for.

*

Under Aurore's fingers, the disk was growing paler and paler; but so was Virginie, skin stretched over high cheekbones, bones protruding through the atrophied muscles. It was what she wanted. What she deserved. The cost of power she'd accepted.

No.

No.

Power was a *thing*, and she was its master.

She withdrew her hands. It took everything she had, and they continued to shake. She'd never wanted to reach out again so badly; to touch the disk and feel the magic sliding down into her chest again, the sweetness of it, like air to choked-out lungs.

"I can't do it," she said. "Let's get back."

"You said you would." Frédérique's voice was a mixture of anger and fear. "He'll find us, if you don't take it off."

"You …" Aurore tried to speak, felt again the power welling through her.

Her hands moved of their own accord, stretched towards Virginie again. She put them behind her back. The child of thorns had its own hands hovering over Virginie's face.

"No," Aurore said sharply to it.

The child didn't move. It gazed back at her, unperturbed.

You know the price.

"You have to take it off," Frédérique said.

"You don't understand," Aurore said. Every word felt uttered through tar. Power flowed through her and choked her. "I'll kill her, if I do it."

She found her hands in front of her again.

No.

She moved away from Virginie, stood on the tracks,

pacing up and down and listening to her own footsteps ringing on the metal.

"So you can't control it." Frédérique's voice was flat. "Power, always changing things to match its shape."

She—she was the magic. She was everything she'd ever wanted to be. In her mind, she could still feel the thorns, piercing her—could remember how it had felt, to open eyes gummed with blood onto a world that felt hers for the taking. She could feel the power coursing through her—the sheer satisfaction of destroying one bird after another until she knew with absolute certainty the House would never come back.

And yet … And yet, she'd drained Niraphanes before she could think. And it was only because Virginie was a child—because some gut reflexes had kicked in—that she'd stopped. Even now … Even now, her steps were taking her back towards Virginie.

She opened her mouth to argue with Frédérique, but a sudden, piercing pain stabbed through her entire body, and sent her to her knees, gasping to breathe.

"Aurore?" Frédérique, from a wary distance. "Aurore!"

The pain stabbed her again—knives, driven again and again into her. No, not knives but something thinner and colder—ten thousand needles infusing into her flesh and muscles a cold so deep it burned. She managed, struggling, to lift a hand: saw red, inflamed skin, in the instant before the pain struck again, and fatigue fell on her like a shroud. She hit the ground: her limbs flopped, out of control, on the tracks. She couldn't breathe, couldn't think, couldn't focus on anything except the enormity of the pain consuming her.

Someone was shaking her—the child of thorns—and the pain within her was so great she couldn't even feel the prickles from its sharp hands.

You have to help.

"I don't ... understand," Aurore said. The words tasted like blood on her tongue.

He's killing us.

Cold was stealing over her, stealing all feeling from her limbs. Somewhere—somewhere distant and hazy, the House was freezing. The House was dying, and she couldn't bring herself to care.

Help us. It's your life, too.

She'd done it once. She'd stood up, shaking, in the alleyway behind the House with bruises and cuts and every part of her body feeling broken. She'd carried Cassiopée to la Goutte d'Or. She could do it again.

But she was so exhausted—warmth leaching out of her with every passing moment, and the fatigue from killing the birds, and it would be so much easier to lie down, to sleep. Marianne and Cassiopée were faraway thoughts, ghosts she couldn't keep fixated on. And even if she had—what could she possibly do?

The child was gone, and it was just her, sinking into a cold deeper than the winter nights without fuel. Falling asleep ...

And then, with a shock like a jolt in her bones, she saw that the child wasn't gone, but that it was staggering towards Virginie with three-fingered hands outstretched, a white trail of ice filling the ground under it.

No.

Not that.

She pulled herself up, shaking, caught a glimpse of Frédérique's face, frozen in a horrified and heartbreakingly familiar expression, something that tugged at her but barely made its way through the pain. Beneath her feet, ice bloomed, festooning the edges of the tracks in killing flowers.

"Stop," she said. Her voice was rough, scraped from within a tomb of cold. "Stop!"

The child of thorns didn't waver.

Aurore ran. She was moving through treacle—staggering, her feet skidding on the iced ballast and rail sleepers. She fell, once, twice, picked herself up again, and every time it was like pushing against a heavier descending weight. It was colder and colder. She couldn't feel her hands or her feet, and even her heart felt sluggish—a rising silence in her ears. Her thoughts slowed, scattered. She had to run. She didn't remember why, but she had to run.

She ...

Virginie.

She kept running. A heartbeat—an eternity—later, she stood, trembling, between the child of thorns and Virginie.

"No," she said.

Stand aside.

It was coming apart—its branches unraveling, brittle and thin, under the weight of the ice, its face gleaming with the crystals lodged in every cavity.

"She's not yours," Aurore said, coldly.

A pause. She could have sworn the expression on its face was surprise.

But she is ours. She is yours. Is she not your sustenance?

She remembered the trembling joy she'd felt when

draining Niraphanes—the desperate hunger sweeping through her, vast and unbearable, and her shocked realization that it had always been there. Frédérique had said that power changed things to its shape, but the truth was that this power also took the shape of those who wielded it. It sharpened their flaws into weapons to crush the weak. It was anger and hunger and resentment and cruelty. It was the desperate desire to protect people at all costs; the arrogant, innate belief in the superiority of the Fallen. It was her own anger and resentment and her desire to hurt others as they had hurt her. And always—always, in the end—it was the inability to renounce power once you had it, to become smaller and weaker once again; that impossible, terrible desire to keep things the way they'd always been, forever.

"No," she said, again—and, with the last of her strength, grabbed the child and held it to her chest, locking it in an unbreakable embrace. She fell to one knee, shaking—ice seized up her heart, choked her chest with its crystals like a hundred pinprick wounds.

You will die, the child said, its voice vicious and angry.

Aurore—trembling with the effort to keep it against her—didn't speak. Her thoughts ran sluggish and slow. She felt Marianne held in her hands again, wet with birthing fluids—heard the familiar sound of Cassiopée leafing through books as she fell asleep in their small flat—smelled the distant odor of steamed buns, the juice of mushrooms flooding her mouth.

You will die.

But she'd looked at death already, and had found no fear left in her.

The cold spread. Under her, the tracks turned a silvery gray. The child slowly fell apart, branches crackling as they broke, thorns glistening with ice as they fell away—its face contorting as water pushed it out of shape, its limbs bursting apart, a shower of wood shards clattering over the ground of the yard and the metal shells of trains.

Aurore sat down, feeling the barrier slowly disintegrate behind her—and within her, something large and essential fall to pieces, leaving her reeling and struggling to breathe. The ice felt permanently lodged in her; all she wanted was to sleep.

Hands on her shoulder; a hesitant touch that felt unlike Frédérique's or Nicolas's. Virginie. The child's small face was creased in thought; and the faint light of magic still played beneath the planes of her skin.

"Are you all right?"

No, Aurore wanted to say, but she didn't have energy for words.

They could leave her here. It would only be fair.

"She's not." Frédérique paused, for a while. "Come on. We have to get away from here."

Virginie rubbed the disk on her chest. "This—"

"I know what it is." Frédérique's voice was hard. "But I don't think anyone here can take it from you."

"It's almost loose." Virginie frowned, and pulled at the disk. Her hands moved; Aurore couldn't see what she did. "There."

She started peeling it off, and then paused—inhaling a sharp, shocked breath.

"It's hurting you," Frédérique said. "Leave it."

Virginie's face set. "I can take pain. I've done it before."

She tore it from her chest, leaving a bloodied circle of skin on her chest. Her voice, when she spoke again, was shaking. "I'll be fine. Let's go."

Someone lifted Aurore—Nicolas, throwing her over one shoulder.

No, she thought, but everything blurred into unconsciousness.

Emmanuelle was sinking to the ground, struggling to breathe under the weight of the birds on her shoulders. The link to House Silverspires was growing sharp and panicked in her mind, begging her to run with energy she didn't have anymore.

Warmth flooded the cobblestones under her: a sharp, radiant, *familiar* light flowed over her, and the birds' talons digging into her flesh abruptly vanished, leaving only a faint taste of ashes in the air.

"Let her go."

He stood at the entrance of the small street, limned in light, the shadow at his back like huge, spread wings, his fair hair shining like a beacon. His eyes were hard.

"Morningstar?" Her voice was only a croak. The storm of wings within her chest remained; as if she would at any moment disintegrate into birds. "What are you doing here?"

Guy turned, then. As he did his body fuzzed at the edges, became the outline of hundreds of wings.

"Such a busy place." His voice was sarcastic. "Rescuing your dependents?"

"You forget." Morningstar's voice was grave. "I'm no longer the head of the House."

"I didn't forget," Guy said, and his voice was sharp. "Running after her, are you?"

Morningstar's only answer was a blast of power that sent Guy reeling back, birds detaching from his body with raucous cries.

Emmanuelle, shaking, trying not to choke on the storm within her, made her slow way to Darrias. Guy's liveried people were moving towards Morningstar—who didn't even spare a glance for them.

Darrias was on the cobblestones, sprawled out. Her face was pale, drawn. Emmanuelle laid her hand on her wrist—felt her pulse, which was the slow, lazy beating of raptors' wings. *No no no.*

She had magic. It could not heal—it could never heal—but perhaps it could cleanse. Shaking, she started to say the first words of a spell: a variant of the one Darrias had used, a lifetime ago, to boil water in Harrier. A thin sheet of fire danced on her fingers, passed beneath Darrias's skin. Emmanuelle's hands shook: she didn't have much left within her. Selene …

She wanted, so badly, to go home.

Come on come on.

Darrias convulsed under her hands. The ghostly shapes of birds flashed beneath her skin. A distant shriek, and then they were fading. Darrias coughed, spluttered—what came up was only gray balls like bunched up feathers, and fragments of pinions.

Come on come on.

Darrias's eyes opened—unfocused and filled only with confused panic. Her mouth shaped a word—Emmanuelle's name? She couldn't be sure. Then her eyes closed again, her head lolling back, utterly relaxed. She seemed to be sleeping. Her pulse was slow; but at least it was a Fallen's pulse again, and the light of magic streamed, once more, from beneath her skin—trembling and weak, an unbearably faint radiance.

She was alive.

A hand on Emmanuelle's shoulder.

"You should think of yourself as well, you know." Morningstar's voice was low and amused.

His magic ran through her—a faint fire coursing in her veins, a tingling that seemed to expand into flames in her chest. The world suddenly became fire and smoke and she couldn't breathe. She gasped, desperately inhaling and hearing only pointless wheezing in her nostrils—and then it passed, and she was on her knees, coughing up fragments of bricks and cobblestones and feathers herself.

Morningstar held her, gently, until it passed. Warmth and magic, trembling on her skin—all the comfort of the familiar, the memories of how it had been, before Harrier, before Hawthorn. A taste of the home she so desperately craved.

"Sssshh. Breathe. Slowly. Breathe. You're all right."

"Guy . . ." she said, looking up through tears.

His face was hard. "Dealt with."

A body lay on the cobblestones behind him, turning into shrieking birds; and those of Harrier's people, sprawled broken and bloodied. So much waste. So much destruction.

"He was weak. Too many pieces of him lost. A House needs a head to be strong."

He winced as he moved. He made it sound simple, but

she could see he was shaking; that his skin was not the familiar milky paleness but an unhealthy gray, his light sunk to the level of warm embers instead of the blinding radiance that usually surrounded him.

"What . . .?" Emmanuelle found her voice. "What are you doing here?"

"I had a few mishaps." Morningstar shrugged; winced as he did so. "I ran away from an angry magician. It looks like he's gone now." An amused, disbelieving snort. "Annamites. Full of unexpected surprises. Come on. Let's go home."

"Home."

The word sounded alien and distant to her, an impossibility.

"The Houses are ruins. Only Silverspires remains. There'll be no one to stop us." A thoughtful pause. "There are some people I need to get first, though."

He . . . He'd destroyed Harrier, and the others. And she had let him.

"Morningstar—"

"Ssh." His hand squeezed her shoulder. "It'll be all right, Emmanuelle. No one can harm you anymore. I promise." He glanced at the unconscious Darrias. "We'll take her with us. Give her refuge. Hawthorn isn't in a position to protect her. Silverspires is now the only House left, and has mastery over Paris."

Emmanuelle finally found her voice. "Is it why you did it?"

"Did what?" His voice was mild.

"Destroyed Harrier. Destroyed the Houses."

A silence. She found herself braced against the answer.

"You *asked*," Morningstar said. "You'd never pleaded for help. I'd never seen you look so desperate."

"I didn't ask you to—"

"You don't choose the terms under which help is given. Nor could I choose what could or could not be done." A silence, then, "I'm sorry I didn't come earlier, when you almost died in Harrier. I thought you'd got out of the House."

"I didn't," Emmanuelle said.

There seemed to be no words that would cover the nightmare of walking the ruins; of meeting Guy; of the birds' wingbeats rising behind her, the utter certainty they would catch her.

Gone.

They were gone, and she was left with the consequences of what she'd done.

There will be no one to stop us.

That was all he saw among the destruction; among the deaths; among the utter overturning of the order of Paris.

"Come on." Morningstar rose—disguising the shaking of his hands—offered her his. "Let's go home."

She could take that hand. She could remain silent. She could follow his lead—as she'd once done in House Harrier.

"No," she said. The word caught in her throat.

A pause. Light flickered on the planes of his skin.

"No?"

"It can't be that way," Emmanuelle said slowly. "There . . ." Her voice caught again. She kept it under control. "There are consequences."

"Are there?" His voice was amused, puzzled.

He didn't see. He never had. Asmodeus had once told her Morningstar couldn't tell the difference between removing a splinter and setting fire to the hand. She'd reflexively denied it, but now—much too late—she saw it for herself.

"We're not setting ourselves up as the ruling power of Paris. We're going to help them."

To atone, though really, how could she atone for any of it?

Another raised eyebrow. "You're not the master of the House."

No, but she was Selene's lover, and she knew that Selene had never wanted to rule.

"Neither are you," Emmanuelle said. "Morningstar . . ." She pulled herself up, shaking.

Morningstar's voice was flat. "I did all of this for you. Made tenuous bargains with a being who could have burned me alive, been hunted by Harrier like an animal, left my safe haven to come to your rescue even, whatever it meant facing, under whatever terms. And now you have the gall to say you're unhappy with it?"

He'd died, and been reborn. He wasn't the Fallen who'd once ruled his House with a fist of iron, and sacrificed dependents as casually as pawns on a chessboard. Not the one who saw dissent as rebellion. Except that for a moment the mask he wore wavered, and she saw his old self laid bare. The cost of defying him was annihilation, or worse.

And in her mind was his voice, from long, long ago.

Emmanuelle—you and Selene always do what's needed.

"No," she said, again. "I am grateful for it. But asking for your help doesn't mean you're above criticism. It doesn't mean we're above judgment or regret."

"Judgment? You think yourself better than me? You, who are always prim and proper and unwilling to pay the price for what you want? Your friend would have *died*, Emmanuelle."

"I knew," she said, quietly. She rose, shaking. She ought to have felt powerful and decisive, but she was small and scared. "I knew the price when you left the room. When you told me to run. I could have stopped you. I didn't. And the worst . . ."

The worst was that, if it happened again—even knowing all she did, knowing how it all turned out, the price they all paid—she'd still be *tempted.*

"I'd still want it to happen. I'd still want Guy to pay." She'd always thought of herself as kind, as caring—but she could hate so much, so deeply. She'd hated Guy and his delighted cruelty. It was like a jolt of acid in her veins: self-knowledge acquired too late, at too great a cost. "But it'd still be *wrong*."

Beneath her, Darrias's eyes fluttered open again: watching, shocked.

"Please, Morningstar. You have to stop."

"You . . .?" He stared at her. "*You're* telling me to stop?"

"Someone has to."

What friends were for, she thought, soberly, bitterly.

"And what are you going to do if I don't?"

"You don't understand," Emmanuelle said. "If all that stops you is threats and fear . . ." She held herself straight, ignoring the shaking that had seized her entire body. "Then how much of a person are you, really?"

A silence.

Then Morningstar said, slowly, carefully—as if putting together the pieces of something infinitely fragile, "I would have died for you."

"I know. I'm not asking you to." And then, softly, "You asked me if I thought myself better than you. I don't. I know that I'm not. I know we all Fell. I know we're all sinners. What matters is what we do with that knowledge."

A low, despairing laugh. "Redemption?"

"No one ever said it was impossible," Emmanuelle said. "No one ever said it was wrong to strive."

A long, weighing look from him. She thought, for a moment, that he would gainsay her—that he would say he remembered Heaven and its City, and what the Fall she couldn't remember had truly meant.

But instead, he said, with a bitter laugh, "I wish it were that simple. But who knows, really?" A pause. He looked at her gravely. "I've gone too far, haven't I."

It wasn't a question. Emmanuelle didn't make the mistake of giving him an answer.

"You're wrong," Morningstar said finally. "Some things can't be atoned for." He shrugged, and for a moment the shadow of great, shining wings seemed to move with him. "Go home, Emmanuelle. There's one last thing I have to do."

"Morningstar …"

He was already walking away from her. Emmanuelle threw a glance at Darrias—who'd pulled herself to her feet but still looked groggy—and cursed.

"Morningstar!"

Footsteps, getting near. Annamites?

No.

A disheveled, pale group: a woman carrying a toddler, with olive skin and hair as short as a man's, who reminded Emmanuelle of a more brittle Selene; a man with dark hair, carrying an unconscious woman over his shoulder; and a girl wearing the colors of a warded magician of Harrier, who couldn't have been more than seven or eight years old. They stared at Morningstar with an expression of such abject fear that Emmanuelle's heart constricted in her chest. The girl's legs clenched as if she'd flee, but then she turned, defiant, to face him.

Some things can't be atoned for. What else had he done?

Morningstar had spread his arms, not looking at them. "I mean you no harm. I'm sorry—"

The girl threw something at him, which bounced off his chest. It was a wooden disk Emmanuelle couldn't see clearly, but she was close enough to see the circular, bloody imprint on the girl's chest—three layers of torn cloth through the uniform, all the way to the skin it had fused to. The girl's mouth opened, shaping on words that choked her.

"Yours." Her voice was cold, but she was shaking. "Take it back, and don't ever bother us. Ever again."

Her skin was alight with magic—the strongest of all of them, though she was seven years old and looked heartbreakingly small compared to Morningstar. His hand tensed—he could easily backhand her to the cobblestones. Emmanuelle found herself, futilely, reaching out—knowing she'd be too late.

A cold, sliding sound. Morningstar's mouth opened—made no sound, only gushed blood. He had a shocked expression as he collapsed to the cobblestones. Darrias, breathing hard, withdrew the dagger she'd stabbed him with—and knelt, drawing it in one smooth, easy movement across his throat, even as her other hand sent burning fire into his chest.

It shouldn't have worked. One couldn't kill a Fallen so smoothly, so easily. One couldn't kill Lucifer Morningstar, first and foremost of all Fallen, founder of House Silverspires, like that. Emmanuelle found herself biting back a scream—but of course he was weak, his magic spent fighting Guy. Fighting for her sake.

It shouldn't have worked. But blood tinged with light fountained out from his throat, eagerly lapped up by the cobblestones. Darrias held him with practiced ease as he writhed and flopped and finally fell still, and the light fled in a rush from his gray skin, like the sun overtaken by clouds.

The woman said, slowly, carefully, "Darrias?"

"It's all right," Darrias said. She sat holding Morningstar's corpse, her face graven in shock. "We're safe now, Frédérique. We're all safe."

They all looked as though they didn't believe her, didn't believe that their ordeal had ended. What had Morningstar done to them? What atrocities had he committed, in the name of his survival, in the name of House Silverspires' survival?

Some things can't be atoned for.

Emmanuelle found herself staring upwards, at the sky slowly blurring into unfocused insignificance—at the distant light that might have been the City, that might have been a glint of glory on angels' wings.

24

Coming Home

Aurore woke up, disoriented. For a brief, panicked moment she thought she was back in House Hawthorn's hospital, but then she saw that she lay on Marianne's bed in the flat.

"Big sis." It was Cassiopée's voice, thick with relief.

"Mamma mamma!" Marianne came barreling from the other room, struggling to climb on the bed. "Mamma awake."

She'd thought everything would hurt, but she just felt … exhausted. Alive when she had no right to be so.

"How …?" she asked.

"You were healed."

A man detached himself from the wall of the room. She'd seen him before, but couldn't place him—and then it hit her like a blow to the gut. Dân Chay. Behind him was a glowering woman in an old-fashioned, elaborate *ao dai*. The cloth was so new and so finely embroidered it was almost incongruous.

"You …" She tried to speak, but it came out as a croak. "You tried to burn us."

Low, amused laughter. "I've had … a change of heart. Don't worry. Your community is safe."

The woman behind him glowered even harder.

Aurore was too tired to even attempt to be diplomatic. "I don't understand."

Dân Chay came to sit by the foot of the bed, ignoring Marianne's attempts to bounce up and down on it. When he moved, she could see the shadow of fire, clinging to the cloth of his tunic.

"I mean you no harm, child. But I know what you did. And why Philippe couldn't heal you."

Aurore looked up. The room was suddenly very conspicuously empty of adults, Cassiopée and the woman having withdrawn to the kitchen to talk in low voices.

"I'm not ashamed," she snapped.

While *that* was debatable, she certainly wasn't going to be lectured by him, change of heart or not.

An amused snort. "I understand hunger, believe me. And the thirst for revenge."

"Not revenge," Aurore said. Marianne was now attempting to burrow into her chest. Aurore held her, ignoring the winces of pain from her ribs. "Safety."

Dân Chay's face didn't move.

"I don't understand why I'm alive," Aurore said. "The House died."

"The House was killed," Dân Chay said. "The other Houses are still tearing themselves apart, preying on their own dependents to survive." A pause. "They won't survive, either."

"Good." Aurore didn't even attempt to hide the viciousness from her voice. Why should she? "And you—?"

"Oh, I'm leaving," Dân Chay said. Another smile, revealing teeth too sharp and yellow to be human. "You gave everything you had to House Hawthorn, didn't you? Hollowed yourself out in the name of power."

Aurore thought, again, of the rush of joy when she'd drained Niraphanes. Of Aunt Ha's horrified face after her healing. Of standing up to the child of thorns, shaking and struggling to hold her own spell.

"I have no regrets." And then, in a lower voice, because he was there, because he was a stranger and wouldn't judge her the way the community did, "Tools that cannot be controlled have to be set aside. Or destroyed."

A head cocked, considering. "Don't blame yourself. The Houses have always been hungry, and always turned on their own to ensure their own survival. It would have happened, to someone else, if not to you. Not all power is doomed to be uncontrollable." Dân Chay smiled again. "And you can't heal a hollow thing, but you can fill it with new power. And, as I said, I've always had a soft spot for hunger."

He extended a hand. A flame of *khi* fire danced, trembling and stubborn, on the darkness of his palm—except that it was the color of his skin. And Aurore felt something move within her in answer, sluggish and tentative, a warmth like breathed-on embers.

"I . . . I don't know what it means," she said.

Dân Chay smiled. "Everyone can learn to manipulate the *khi* elements, given enough time and study. I've just given you a head start, when it comes to using *khi* fire. Enough knowledge to make it answer to you more easily."

"Why?"

"Consider it . . . a parting gift," Dân Chay said. "And a thank you, for trying to protect me against Morningstar, back in House Harrier."

Back in Harrier's ruined armory, when they'd found the box. When she'd told Morningstar to leave Dân Chay alone, that he'd hurt Dân Chay enough and that he needed to stop. It felt like a lifetime ago. Her cheeks burned. It had been the height of foolhardiness.

"I didn't do much of anything," she said, looking away from him.

"And I'm not giving you much in return," Dân Chay said. "I'm leaving. Back to Annam. I don't imagine you'd want to go there."

"I've got nothing to do with Annam," Aurore said stiffly.

Another amused snort. "Not quite true, is it? But I understand the sentiment."

He rose, started to walk away. At the door, he stopped, watching her with no expression on his face. His eyes shone golden, and for a moment only she saw the vertical slits of a tiger's gaze instead of a human one.

"It wouldn't have been fair to leave this as a surprise. That way you know. What it all means ..." He shrugged. "Many things are up to you, child."

And then he was gone.

"What did he want?" Cassiopée asked.

"I don't know," Aurore said.

She extended a hand, the way he had; felt the slight tug of fire within her. Hollow, he had said. She didn't feel hollow. Just exhausted and wrung out and unsure of what anything was going to be like, anymore.

"You have visitors," Cassiopée said.

Aurore, startled, looked up from her bed. Marianne

was sleeping in her lap, contentedly wrapped up around her mother's legs. Aurore felt all she did was sleep, and watch the world pass her by. She'd offered to help with the reconstruction effort—she could have cooked for people, or sewn clothes—but Cassiopée had been adamant she needed not to fall over when she got up first.

"Visitors?"

They were already crowding behind Cassiopée: a Fallen she didn't recognize, wearing the colors of Hawthorn. For a panicked heartbeat Aurore thought they'd come for her again, but then she saw Frédérique and Nicolas by the Fallen's side.

"This is Darrias," Frédérique said.

The Fallen had a shaved head, and an elaborate set of henna markings on her skin that looked like words.

Her wife. Aurore looked at her. Darrias looked back, levelly.

"I came to thank you," she said, inclining her head. "For saving my family."

For almost killing them. Aurore's mouth clamped on the words. Darrias was still speaking.

"I think Frédérique wanted a longer word with you."

She inclined her head again as she left. Nicolas nodded at Aurore, and left with Darrias.

It was just her and Frédérique. They stared at each other, for a while, awkwardly.

"How are you?" Frédérique asked. She looked thin and gaunt, and the Hawthorn uniform sat awkwardly on her frame.

Aurore tried to shrug. "I've been better. You?"

Frédérique's lips tightened. "Healed, mostly."

"Virginie—?"

"She'll be fine," Frédérique said. "And we have Darrias."

But they had lost Niraphanes.

"I'm sorry," Aurore said, finally.

Dân Chay's face swam in front of her. Something warm and alien shifted within her, the same fire that had been steadily growing in her.

Don't blame yourself.

As if he really understood what contrition was.

Frédérique shook her head. "Don't be. If you hadn't been there—if you hadn't killed the birds—we wouldn't have survived."

"You know what happened."

"Of course," Frédérique said. "I won't forget it. But I can still acknowledge the good. You should, too."

"You didn't have to carry me back," Aurore said. "When I collapsed."

"Don't be absurd." Frédérique looked at Marianne's sleeping face. The child moved. Aurore stroked her head, gently, rhythmically. A sigh. "I wanted to protect my family. I let them take Virginie. I let them *teach* her. I did worse than you."

"You couldn't have known."

"Sharing blame?" Frédérique shrugged, again. "I didn't come here for that. I just wanted to let you know how we were."

"And to tell me we probably shouldn't see each other again," Aurore said, shrewdly.

Frédérique was silent, for a while.

"I should, shouldn't I? That's what Darrias would say, but Darrias's hands aren't exactly clean either."

She fished into her pocket and laid a paper on the bed. It was a white cardboard piece with elaborate gilded patterns of flowers: the old invitations sent for parties or weddings, with Hawthorn's crest at the bottom.

Aurore stared at it for a while: it represented a world she'd never moved in, and never would. She opened her mouth, but Frédérique got there first.

"I thought it looked pretty, and we have so few of these left. But you don't need it per se if you want to visit." She rose, graceful and fluid.

Asmodeus's House. The children's House. Aurore's hand strayed to her chest, where the disk had once been.

"Thank you. I'll think on it."

Frédérique's smile was brief, but for that moment it changed her entire face, smoothing away the gauntness and making her stand taller.

"Until we meet again."

Cassiopée showed them out in silence, and then came back into the room.

"What was that about?" she asked.

"I'm not sure yet."

Aurore picked up the piece of cardboard, held it to the light. It gleamed, like liquid gold.

She set it down, and picked up the cup by her bedside table. Then, as carefully as if she were flexing an unfamiliar muscle, she called on the fire within her. It took three tries before it would even answer; but when she did, light danced within the water, washes of reds and oranges sparkling against the glass, glinting like a thin layer of crystal.

Power. Magic. She looked at the cardboard again—saw

herself at the gates of Hawthorn, walking into the House with that fire within her held like her lifeline.

"Until we meet again," she said, aloud.

And now she knew they would.

"You're fidgeting," Selene said.

"Not at all," Emmanuelle said.

She'd put on a somber scarf to cover her hair, and a simple and sober dark dress to match. Black didn't suit her, but she was the partner of the head of the House, and it was all but required at funerals.

Selene came to stand in front of her, frowning—and then bent down, arms wrapped around her, for a kiss. It was so good it was startling. Emmanuelle let desire arch up her spine, send quivering warmth in her entire body.

When she came up for air, she said, "This isn't—"

"Appropriate?" Selene arched an eyebrow. "You'll forgive me. I have some catching up I'm desperate for." She kissed Emmanuelle again, this time a shorter, almost playful embrace.

The clock on the mantelpiece struck a quarter to one. Selene straightened up.

"Time." She cast a critical eye at Emmanuelle. "I'm not even sure you should be there."

"Try and stop me," Emmanuelle said.

Aragon had been more reluctant than Selene to let her out of hospital, but even he had had to admit that her presence was necessary.

They walked out of their quarters, and into the corridors of the House.

It was a ruin now, a jumbled mass of banyan roots and

collapsed corridors. Entire wings were open to the wind and rain, the faded wallpaper peeling off. But they'd stretched tarpaulins over broken roofs, and erected tents in the courtyard—and all the ruined buildings were full of Houseless refugees. Emmanuelle had never seen so many children in the House.

Inside the ruin of Notre-Dame, Morningstar's throne still stood empty. But, where the burned pews had been, a crowd was waiting for them, facing the pyre where Morningstar's body lay.

They had buried most of the bodies, or left them on ice in the common morgue so people could find their family. But Selene had been adamant on this one. Emmanuelle understood: it was a symbol, and it sent a simple, devastating statement. No one would scavenge Morningstar's magic. He had once belonged to House Silverspires, but the order of things had changed.

"For you are dust, and to dust you shall return …" Father Javier's reedy voice, rising in the broken church, speaking the words he no longer believed.

In front of him, the crowd—the dependents, the Houseless, the Annamites and the other natives. An old Annamite woman standing next to Philippe with the bearing of a queen, and a black man wearing a kaftan and ample yellow *agbada* with elaborate embroidery around the sleeves and neck; the exhausted Hawthorn delegation, with Asmodeus and Thuan, grave and composed, and a little further Darrias and her family; and Lazarus, Solférino, Stormgate, Minimes, remnants of the other Houses, which had died before they could stop their own wards turning on them. And here and there, a few Harrier uniforms worn like funeral shrouds, or badges of pride. A prim envoy from the dragon kingdom, ramrod straight and keeping a wary distance from everyone else: the devastated kingdom had taken no part in this, and didn't look likely to involve itself in the city's affairs again.

"To every thing there is a season, and a time to every purpose under the heaven. A time to be born, and a time to die ..."

There was a speech. A eulogy; a quiet, careful dance around what Morningstar had done and failed to do. Overweening ambition, arrogance, cruelty. Drive, vision.

He'd helped her, or tried to. Had risked his life; had come back to save her from Guy. And he'd been a monster, and none of her own experiences would change any of that. They'd paid off the people he'd harmed—Virginie and Darrias's family, and the Fallen Lorcid, and the Harrier refugees—but there was no proper way of offering restitution, given the magnitude of what he'd done and their own ruin. Too little, too late.

Selene walked to the pyre, and laid her hands on the kindling. Fire spread, slowly, lazily as Fallen magic flared up. The smell of smoke filled the cathedral. Emmanuelle watched, dry-eyed, as it consumed Morningstar's corpse until he was nothing more than ashes dancing in the air.

And then it was over, and she and Selene were on the parvis, accepting the mourners' well-wishes. Selene's face was expressionless. Emmanuelle felt exhausted again.

"My condolences." Asmodeus's face was stretched in his customary smile—except that, looking at him, Emmanuelle saw the sharpness was tinged with pain. "I believe we shall not see his like again."

Selene raised an eyebrow. "Is that a personal assurance, Asmodeus?"

A shrug. "It would be in everyone's best interest, wouldn't it? Even if I were in a position to bring him back."

"He's not," Thuan said, bluntly. He put a hand on Asmodeus's own, as if to keep him and Selene apart. "We've had our differences in the past, but they no longer apply. We cannot afford them."

"I'm glad," Emmanuelle said.

Selene said, with a touch of unpleasantness—she still hadn't forgiven either of them for imprisoning Emmanuelle, "I wasn't aware House Hawthorn still existed as an entity."

"Oh, Hawthorn is more than a collection of wards," Asmodeus said, sweetly. "I can assure you Thuan and I have things well in hand."

Thuan inclined his head, not missing a beat. They both wandered off to talk to others.

Another person came up, and another and another, an endless flow of people and platitudes. Emmanuelle's face ached with the effort of keeping up the smile.

Someone grabbed her, and pulled her away from the press of people.

"What are you doing?"

Darrias smiled at her. "You look like you need a break."

"But Selene ..."

The Annamite woman she'd seen earlier with Philippe was bearing down on Selene with the determined air of someone who'd spotted prey.

"I'm sure she'll cope," Darrias said. "Come on."

She dragged and cajoled Emmanuelle all the way to the back of the cathedral, to a small garden overlooking the devastated Seine. They sat on a broken stone bench, looking at the skies. Out of nowhere, she produced a metal flask full of liquor, which she handed to Emmanuelle.

"Here. Drinks always help."

"Getting drunk at a funeral." Emmanuelle snorted.

She sipped at the liquor—it was some kind of sweet herbal one she couldn't place. It was weird, to be waiting for him in her office in the archive—to expect, at any moment, the light of his magic. To remember his voice, grave and reassuring. *I'll stand by you no matter what happens.*

But she'd been the one, in the end, who couldn't stand by him.

"There are worse things than being drunk." Darrias's face was deadpan. "How are things?"

A shrug. "Too many people, and not enough time." She was on a cross-faction committee, organizing food supplies—her own, inadequate way of making amends. "You?"

Darrias shrugged. "More people than I'd thought," she said. "We're going from flat to flat looking for survivors. I thought it'd be mostly corpses, but life has a way of holding on."

Didn't it just.

"How is your family?"

Darrias shrugged. "All right. They'll get better." Her face was set. "Virginie still gets that look on her face, sometimes. I'm sure she wakes up at night, but she doesn't want to bother me."

Emmanuelle opened her mouth, closed it. "I'm sorry."

"Platitudes." Darrias emptied the flask in her mouth. "I'm not."

"Not sorry that you killed him?"

They were alone now. She hadn't told Selene, though who knew how much her partner might have guessed on her own. Selene had been dealing with many who were unhappy with Morningstar and what he'd set in motion.

"He'd had it coming for a while," Darrias said. "After what he did—"

"What I did, too," Emmanuelle said sharply.

She'd told Selene *that*, and got a look that could have shriveled stone, followed by a stern rejoinder never to mention it again.

"You *know* I'm not talking about this." Darrias had the same look as Selene on her face. "Will you forgive me, for what I've done?"

She didn't mean killing the Fallen who'd stolen her family, but taking a friend from Emmanuelle.

A friend who'd harmed, again and again—for her sake, for the sake of the House, caring little for decency or consequences. She'd never known him well, had she?

"I could have stopped him," Emmanuelle said.

Darrias handed her the flask. "You did."

"Only when it was too late."

A silence.

"You know what I learned, when Guy cast me out on the streets? 'Could' and 'might' are stones around your neck. The present is all that matters."

"I ..." Emmanuelle took a deep, shaking breath. At any moment she still expected the sound of wings to fill the cathedral's gardens. "I don't understand how you can forgive yourself."

Darrias's voice was grave. "You don't. You try to make things better." A bitter laugh. "Not that I'm a good example, mind you."

Emmanuelle looked at the ruined stones, at the melted stained glass windows. The air was crisp, sharp with a faint taste of ashes.

How do you forgive yourself?

You don't.

Try to make things better.

"I can do that." The words tasted almost alien on her tongue.

"Firebrand," Darrias said, fondly.

She rose, tucking the flask in the folds of her vest.

A knock at the door. Philippe, startled, looked up. He'd expected Grandmother Olympe or Aunt Thuy, with more papers about the hospitals, and which buildings they could hastily convert into more bed space for patients.

But it was Hoa Phong, followed by Dân Chay. They both wore court clothes: the colors were sharp and crisp, the embroidery on their five-paneled tunics intricately detailed in a way he'd almost forgotten—a reminder of what it had been like to be part of that world, several lifetimes ago.

"We came to say goodbye," Hoa Phong said.

Behind her, Dân Chay was silent. It was hard to reconcile the courtly, elegant man with the lined, kind face of a scholar official, with his other face—fanged and limned with fire, laughing as they died.

Kindness.

Humaneness.

Forgiveness.

He still couldn't be sure it was the right choice; but they hadn't had much of one. Short of imprisoning Dân Chay again, and the only jail they could draw around him would have been Silverspires' and Harrier's, which had broken him before.

"You don't always get what you want," Dân Chay said, as if he'd guessed Philippe's thoughts. His voice was sharp.

Philippe said nothing.

"You can still change your mind," Hoa Phong said.

It would be a long trip back to Annam. He couldn't even be sure the boats were still running, and that they wouldn't end up going overland, making their slow way home.

But that wasn't what stopped him.

"I'm not going." He gestured to the battered table, the sheet of oiled paper over the window, the steaming baskets holding Isabelle's latest attempts at buns. "This is home."

Hoa Phong was silent, for a while. How can you bear it? she'd asked, once. But she was young, and freshly arrived, and she couldn't understand, not yet.

"As you wish," she said. She used the pronoun for a high-ranking official.

Philippe laughed. "Not that one." He bent, and rubbed his nose against her cheek, as if he were an older relative of hers. Dân Chay, leaning against the wall, made no move to come forward. "Safe travels, child."

After they'd left, he stared, for a while, at the table. He wasn't aware of time passing until footsteps on the cracked stairs brought him out of his reverie. It was Isabelle and Tade, laden with the empty baskets they used to carry supplies to the refugees. Petals still clung to Isabelle's: she must have insisted on taking people flowers again, to fill their homes with something bright and colorful.

Philippe's eyes focused on Tade, on the tattoo on his arm. It had gone dark again. He'd noticed it at the funeral but hadn't had time to ask.

"Your tattoo …"

Tade shrugged. "You remember it's the mnemonic of the creation myth? I think it could sense primal energy from the creation building up, and it responded to that. Protecting me with energy of its own, so I could defend my own home."

Philippe's face burned. Home. Such a loaded word: never just the land of your birth, but the place you settled in and built so many hopes and connections into.

"I see."

Tade smiled, to smooth over the blank in the conversation.

"Who knows, it might come in handy again one day. You look idle, Philippe. Daydreaming?"

Isabelle was more observant. "They left, didn't they?"

"Yes."

Philippe felt … strangely empty, a stretched hollowness that was almost familiar. An edge to the world. And then it came to him: it was that same feeling he'd had when he'd been fasting, before he'd ascended.

"And you're still here," Isabelle said.

"So are you," Philippe said, though she'd become their

unofficial liaison to House Silverspires—the patch of the House's crest on her arm was proof of that.

Isabelle said nothing for a while. She withdrew the baskets from the stove, and opened them up to reveal lopsided dumplings.

"Ah well. I thought these would come out better."

"Not the way you shaped them," Philippe said, before he could think.

She laughed. She handed a basket of dumplings to Tade, who sat down with a sigh.

Finally she said, and her voice was grave, "They offered to make me a dependent again."

Philippe was silent for a while.

"It's your choice."

The words would once have burned him—now they came easily, like an exhalation of air after a breath held too long.

Isabelle looked at him, weighing words. "Yes, it is. You were talking about home, and I don't think mine is in Silverspires. It was once, but I died." Her face was grave. "Things have changed. *Everything* has changed."

So home was here. Something squeezed Philippe's heart in his chest, made breathing painful and burning.

"You'll get used to it."

"We always do, don't we?" Isabelle rubbed the patch on her arm again, thoughtfully. "I don't think I'm ready for this just yet. One day … who knows?"

We. She'd used *we*, deliberately.

Philippe picked up a dumpling, bit into it, letting the sweet, earthy taste of carrots and mold fill his mouth. It didn't taste like anything he'd ever eaten in Annam; but that didn't mean it was wrong. It was just the way things were—the way they were made, with what they had.

"So you're here," he said. "With me." There. He'd said it out loud.

Isabelle looked away. "I can ask someone else in the community to offer me a room, if you'd rather not. But . . ." She spread her hands. "But I'd still like to learn from you, if I can." A heavy silence. "There's so much I don't know, isn't there?"

Philippe stared at her, measuring exactly what was being offered. Everything he could think of was too heavy—would so easily break a moment that was as fragile and trembling as a spider's web across a river.

"Here."

He grabbed the *khi* water and *khi* fire around the room, laid it on the table in an intricate weave—exaggerating his movements so they'd be slow and deliberate, his intention unmistakable.

"It's like your buns," he said finally. "Bound to get better if you practice."

Isabelle sat down, staring intently at the *khi* currents—and slowly started weaving her own pattern in answer to his.

"Home," Philippe said, almost to himself.

The word felt large and fraught and almost unfamiliar; but slowly melting on his tongue like the sweetest rice.

Thuan had walked to the grove.

It was churned earth now, with frozen hawthorn trees slowly shriveling under the weight of the ice, the older bodies crumbling into shards when the wind caught them.

The hole had been fenced off as best as they could. Amidst the myriad things they were dealing with, the last one they needed was a Silverspires or Houseless envoy falling down a black mysterious hole in the center of their gardens.

Not, mind you, that the other Houses were faring any better.

He crouched, for a while, by the fence; watching the darkness. A faint smell of rot, and the clean, sharp feel of ice in his throat. No children, or that sense he was being watched. The House was a large, silent emptiness in the center of his mind, a hole in his world as large as the one in front of him. Somehow, he kept expecting it to spring up again—it had survived so many things, so why not this?

But he knew the answer already.

His day had been meetings, and committees: who needed food, who needed shelter; the Hawthorn delegation to the common hospitals complaining of a lack of respect; Phyranthe running, grimly, through those (thankfully few) dependents who'd harmed others to steal their possessions; Iaris trying, again, to run circles around him over medicines she thought would serve Hawthorn best. And all the while he'd felt as though he was trying to function with a hole in his heart where the House had been. He'd look up, half-expecting to see the children or feel a dependent in need, and hear only final, unbroken silence.

With a sigh, he rose and walked back to the ruins of the House. Silence there too. The wards were dead, and they'd only redrawn hasty, less powerful ones. Asmodeus had said something about making things better, but they'd both known that was as protected as they'd ever be.

He felt raw and pummeled and defenseless.

"Unka Thuan, Unka Thuan!"

Two young children barreled towards him on the ruin-covered lawn—Camille babbling her usual collection of incomprehensible syllables, and Ai Nhi changing, at the last minute, into a dragon and wrapping herself around his legs. He stroked her mane, gently.

"Where is your auntie?"

"She's admitted defeat, I think," Asmodeus said. He came up behind the children carrying a bottle of wine and two glasses.

Thuan looked at him, hard, but saw neither Berith nor Françoise. "They left you in charge of the children?" He grabbed Camille as she tottered forward, and put her on his shoulders—to squeals of delight.

An amused snort. "Françoise and Berith are having a meeting of the Parental Relief Committee. The children are a change from former Houses. At least I only have to deal with stolen toys."

The other Houses had come out worse off than Hawthorn had—cannibalizing their own Fallen, magicians and dependents before finally dying of magical starvation. But the weaker they were, the more aggressive they got. Asmodeus had thrown himself into the role of enforcer of the new, fragile peace with such glee Thuan half-suspected him of making up half the quarrels he ruthlessly solved.

Asmodeus held out the glasses. Thuan was about to ask if it was the best time for a drink, and then stopped. It was never going to be a good time.

They sat on the lawn, sipping the wine. Thuan watched, warily, the two children racing each other, sidestepping the debris with almost supernatural agility. Ai Nhi had gone dragon again, and she was attempting to lift Camille off the ground.

Thuan said, "You do miss it."

"The House?" Asmodeus was silent, for a while. He drained his glass, and set it on the lawn, then pulled a knife out of his jacket pocket and played with it, eyes carefully away from Thuan. "It's a hard thing to give up."

But Thuan had seen, before Asmodeus looked away: a shadow of that unbearable anguish he'd had in the roots of the House, the grief he carried with him and didn't know how to deal with. And it wasn't the first time, either: he'd watch Asmodeus talk to a dependent while walking in the gardens, and see the way his gait was a fraction less assured, a fraction less cat-like, how from time to time his husband's face would smooth and become a brittle, hollow thing. He didn't know how to deal with it. His own grief was one thing, but seeing his husband weak was unsettling.

He realized Asmodeus was speaking to him.

"I'm sorry?"

"I asked if you missed it." Asmodeus's voice was sharp.

Like a yawning gap in the world.

Thuan said, finally, "I'd been part of it for a few months."

"A year and a half." A sharp, amused smile, a mask taut over pain and grief. "I counted. Some things will fill the world, given half a chance. Grief isn't a function of time."

Thuan reached out, squeezed Asmodeus's hand. He half-expected Asmodeus to stab him, but Asmodeus merely squeezed back, gaze distant.

"Are you giving me permission to weep?"

A shrug. "In a manner of speaking. You know what I mean."

Thuan did. He was silent for a while, his whole self straining again for something that wasn't there; because he'd killed it.

"It was the right thing to do, though."

"Are you looking for reassurance? I wasn't aware you were so sentimental." The glib mask was back on.

Thuan couldn't help himself. He snorted. "You realize," he said, finally, "that we didn't have to do any of this."

"Helping the Houseless?"

"We came out ahead. Not as much as Silverspires, but . . ."

Asmodeus put the knife in his pocket.

"Are you trying to understand why we're being kind?" He said the word as he would *weak*. "You're the decent one in this relationship."

Thuan almost choked on his wine.

Asmodeus said, finally, "We could have ruled. But the situation would have been untenable. Too many people and not enough of us. There is such a thing as overreaching."

"You don't know what that word means."

"I'm a fast learner. Besides, influence is a handy substitute for direct power. And you have to admit—fields of ruins lack attractiveness, as a dominion."

"Such as our own field of ruins, you mean?"

"*That*," Asmodeus said, "will be sorted out." He put the knife back in his pocket jacket, and strode towards the now fighting children, sharply separating them. When he came back up the lawn, followed by two chastened little ones, he said, "I do wonder how it will all turn out, though."

Thuan stared at the river spread below them; and back, for a moment, at the buildings with broken roofs and stone-choked corridors. The air was no longer dark with smoke, but the smell of ashes and dust clung to the city. In his mind was only desolate emptiness where the House had been.

He said, slowly, carefully, trying each word on as if it were new clothes, "What will it all become? Something, I think, that none of us have seen before."

Something as fragile and as new as seeds blooming in the ruins.

A note on French and Vietnamese transcriptions

This book includes significant portions of both French and Vietnamese, both languages that use the Latin alphabet, but with diacritics that are by and large seldom used in English. I figured that French would pose few problems, so it's rendered exactly as it would be written, though I translated part of the names to make the story flow more easily: hence La Villette Basin rather than Bassin de la Villette.

Vietnamese was always a trickier proposition, as it has higher diacritics complexity: it doesn't just use letters like é, ă, ô, đ, etc. but it also combines them with tonal accents on words, which means that words like thế giới are commonplace. I made the choice to continue stripping the diacritics from all Vietnamese words to preserve the continuity with the rest of the series, as in both *The House of Shattered Wings* and *The House of Binding Thorns.* This prevented characters like Thuan suddenly becoming Thuận, but obviously has drawbacks in that it obscures somewhat the original meaning of the words.

The exceptions I made were for legibility: Dần Cháy became Dân Chay to prevent an immediate association with the English first name Dan, and the same with the imperial city of Huế, which became Huê to prevent confusion with the English word hue, and Princess Liên, who kept her circumflex for similar reasons.

For the curious, the names of the main characters are as follows in unstripped Vietnamese

Philippe:	Phạm Văn Minh Kiết (prior name)
Thuan:	Rồng Minh Thanh Thuận
Françoise:	Lê Thị Ánh Tuyết (full Vietnamese name)
Aurore:	Nguyễn Thị Bạch Diễm (full Vietnamese name)
Cassiopée:	Nguyễn Thị Bạch Tinh (full Vietnamese name)
Dan Chay:	Dần Cháy
Ai Nhi:	Ái Nhi
Hoa Phong:	Hoa Phong

Names in Vietnamese start with the family name and end with the personal name, so Rồng (=dragon) is Thuan's family name, Minh his middle name, and Thanh Thuận his personal name, frequently abbreviated to Thuận.

Where I grew up, aunts and uncles are not referred to by name but rather by number in the family, so the eldest daughter is "Second Aunt," the second eldest "Third Aunt", etc. (Southern Vietnamese starts counting at two rather than one, and "aunt" really encompasses a variety of words depending on whether the aunt in question is a sister of the father, mother or married into the family . . .). To prevent confusion between Second Aunt (Ngoc Bich, Thuan's aunt who rules the dragon kingdom) and Vinh

Ly's character, as referred to by her niece Ai Nhi, I made the choice to have Vinh Ly referred to as "Auntie Ly" rather than have another "Second Aunt" in the narration.

I won't go here into detail on the complexity of the Vietnamese pronoun system, but the choice of I/you pronoun depends on the relative age, gender and status of the speakers: different levels of formalities use different kinship terms. So, for instance, "grandmother" is used towards a person much older than oneself, and the corresponding "I" pronoun would be "child". I've rendered both the pronouns con and cháu as "child": technically con means child or descendant, and cháu can mean child, grandchild or nephew depending on context, but I thought we didn't need that added complexity in the narration!

Acknowledgments

Writing a book with two young children in the house is always a challenge, and I would like to thank everyone who supported me during that process. To my beta-readers for speedy and sometimes multiple reads: Tade Thompson, Vida Cruz, Alis Rasmussen, Rochita Loenen-Ruiz, Fran Wilde, and Likhain. To my friends who agreed to cameos in the book: Tade, Vida, Victor Fernand R. Ocampo, Nene Ormes, Fran (as Frankie), Alis, and Rochita. To Zen Cho, Jeannette Ng, Gillian Polack and everyone else who weighed in on what to call a colonized person in the metropole (an unexpectedly complicated question!). To Nadjah M. Oumid, for helping me with Muslim practice. Any mistakes that remain in the book are my own responsibility!

To my friends for support: Zen Cho, Alessa Hinlo, Elizabeth Bear and Scott Lynch, Inksea, Laura J. Mixon, Ghislaine Lai, D. Franklin, Zoe Johnson, Michelle Sagara, Juliet Kemp, Ken Liu, Cindy Pon, Rachel Monte, Stephanie Burgis, Kari Sperring, Genevieve Cogman, Samit Basu, Charles Tan, Vic James, Adrian Tchaikovsky, Liz Bourke, Paul Weimer, Cheryl Morgan.

To Peter Kenny for his audiobook reads, but most of all for nailing the Asmodeus segments!

To everyone who helped with turning this manuscript into a book: my awesome editor Gillian Redfearn, my agent John Berlyne, my publicist Stevie Finegan, Jen McMenemy in marketing and the rest of the Gollancz team.

And to everyone who spread the word about *The House of Shattered Wings* and *The House of Binding Thorns*, for keeping this series and this author going.

To my sister, for being always there.

And to my two sons, the snakelet and the Librarian, and my husband, for bearing with me while I hammered this into shape.